THE
ROAD
RANGER

THE
ROAD
RANGER

KARL MILDE

Cover illustration by

Bob Berry

iUniverse LLC
Bloomington

THE ROAD RANGER

This is a work of fiction. All of the characters, names, incidents, organizations, and dialogue in this novel are either the products of the author's imagination or are used fictitiously.

iUniverse books may be ordered through booksellers or by contacting:

iUniverse LLC
1663 Liberty Drive
Bloomington, IN 47403
www.iuniverse.com
1-800-Authors (1-800-288-4677)

ISBN: 978-1-4917-1775-2 (sc)
ISBN: 978-1-4917-1774-5 (hc)
ISBN: 978-1-4917-1773-8 (e)

Library of Congress Control Number: 2013922491

Printed in the United States of America.

iUniverse rev. date: 12/06/2013

This novel is dedicated to my wife, Cheryl Milde, for her love and encouragement over the three years it took to write. Along the way it was read and refined by my friend Vin Dacquino and the many literary voices in his Mahopac Writers Group and by Tom Kersting and the wordsmiths of his Lake Writers Group in Carmel. And finally, it was beta tested and critiqued by my friend and the brilliant financier Andy Szabo, who read the final manuscript and provided his insightful commentary.

PROLOGUE

The building was an anomaly. It stood alone in an open area in a run-down residential neighborhood of the city, a windowless two-story monolith of concrete. It had been vacant and abandoned for as long as the young boy could recall, but it had just recently come to life with internal activity.

The boy, Richie, was just barely into his teens, and, partly from malnutrition, he looked younger than his years. His ragged jeans and oversized T-shirt, purchased for a few dollars from the Salvation Army, contributed to his waiflike appearance. He was indeed an orphan in the strict sense—both his parents had died when he was too small to remember—but at least he had a home with someone who cared. He lived with his grandmother in her rented apartment on a third floor walk-up.

Natural curiosity got Richie started. He paid little heed to the building at first, but he grew more and more curious as he gathered intelligence about the strange goings-on. He eventually spent hours and days watching from a safe distance as the heavy garage door on the front of the building rose up to allow a small car to either enter or leave and then lowered and closed itself again. It was as if the building swallowed the car whole and then, at some later time, spit the car out. Usually the car that came out had a different color than the one that went in, but it was always the same type of car: a Mini Cooper. At first Richie thought the cars were painted inside, and he began writing down their license plate numbers in an attempt to keep track. From this he made a startling discovery. No two plate numbers were ever the same.

As he watched the building, Richie could detect patterns of activity. The workers were there every day except Sunday, and they always left at about the same time, between nine and ten in the evening. On Sunday the place appeared vacant, but because it had no windows Richie could not be sure no one stayed inside to stop intruders. One Sunday Richie got up the courage to try the side door but found it locked.

A Mini Cooper arrived about every other weekday, and another one left the building about a day later. By watching carefully Richie noticed something odd. The Mini Coopers that came out appeared to ride lower on their wheels than the ones that went in, as if they were carrying a heavy load.

Over time Richie grew an urge to look inside the building to see what was going on. Initially, the urge was just an idea that he rejected as being impossible to carry out. But the urge grew stronger with each passing week and month until eventually it was not whether he would attempt to break in, but how.

Frequently a black limousine drove up and stopped in front of the garage door. The driver, a very large man, would get out and open the rear car door for his passenger in the backseat. The passenger was a woman who would sometimes take her time in stepping out, barking orders into a cell phone held up to her ear. One of the workers would come out to meet them and they would talk for a few minutes. The driver and the woman would enter the building through the side door, leaving the worker to guard the limousine outside. Richie could see he had a weapon, something that looked like a large, heavy rifle. About an hour later the man and woman would emerge from the building, climb back into the limousine, and drive away. The worker with the gun would return to the building through the side door.

Richie finally built up the courage to talk to this woman, who was clearly in charge. The next time he saw the limousine arrive he came out of hiding and walked up as she got out of the car. The driver who held the car door glared at him fiercely. Richie sensed a hostility in this man but couldn't understand why this was so. He stifled an urge to turn and run but instead took a deep breath and pressed forward to speak to the woman.

"Go away," the limousine driver ordered with a gravelly voice. The woman turned to look at Richie and then held up her hand to signal silence.

"What do you want?" she demanded. Richie looked up at her and had to avert his eyes. Her pupils burned into him with an intensity he had never seen before. Before shielding his own eyes he caught a glimpse of what seemed like the red laser eyes of the devil.

He managed to say, "I . . . I'd just want to know what you're doing inside the building."

"Why?"

"I . . . I don't know. The building's been empty, and . . ."

"What is your name, boy?"

"Richie. Richie James."

"Where do you live?"

"I . . . I live up that street over there . . ." Richie pointed in the direction of his grandmother's apartment house.

"Well, go home. You're trespassing. Do *not* come here again. I am warning you."

"Uh, okay, I'll go. But can't you just tell me what's going on? What's the big secret?"

At this point the limousine driver interrupted the exchange and commanded, *"Go now!"*

Richie turned on his heels and complied. Not to appear afraid, although he was, he did not run, but he walked as quickly as he could toward the street where he lived with his grandmother.

Richie should have heeded the warning, but it was too late for that. He just *had* to look in the building to see what was there. He decided to go the very next Sunday. He would knock loudly, first on the garage door and then on the side door, to make sure no one was inside. If the coast was clear, he would break open the side door with a crowbar. The next morning the workers would discover someone had broken into the building, but even though they might suspect he was the one, they could not prove it. They would look around to see what was taken, and, finding nothing was stolen, they would not call the police.

On Sunday, Richie awoke early, excited to carry out his plan. He grabbed the crowbar he had scrounged for the day and crept quietly out of the apartment without waking his grandmother. He took a circuitous route to the building to avoid any chance of detection.

Breaking in was no problem. The door gave way and snapped open on his first try with the crowbar. Richie quickly stepped in, pulling the door closed behind him. With no windows, the inside of the building was dark. Richie stood on the threshold for a moment, waiting for his eyes to adjust. The first thing he noticed was an orange glow emanating from the center of the large, open space. The second thing he noticed was the heat. The inside air felt uncomfortably hot, reminding Richie of a warm oven.

Richie looked around and noticed a light switch on the wall. He flicked the switch, heard a thunk from an electrical box somewhere nearby, and banks of kliegs above him suddenly bathed the entire space in artificial light.

What immediately caught Richie's eye was a large cupola furnace with a ladder leading up to its open top. It stood alone, ominous and silent, the source of the heat and the orange glow that escaped through small cracks near the bottom. Occupying nearly the rest of the space in the building was a number of Mini Cooper cars in various stages of disassembly and repair. They lay on the floor like carcasses, their insides open and exposed.

Richie walked toward the furnace, and as he came close, he shuddered. The open top of the cupola was nearly big enough to swallow a whole car. He looked about and noticed several groups of rectangular molds. He walked over to examine them but stopped short to listen. He thought he heard a noise, the sound of a car driving up outside. He froze.

There was no place for him to hide, but if there were he could not have made use of it. Panic had set in and immobilized him. His brain went blank.

Suddenly a man burst in through the side door behind him and shouted hoarsely, *"Don't move!"*—as if Richie was capable of running away. Richie managed to lift up his hands while standing with his back to this man at the door. Richie slowly turned around with his hands held high until he could see who was there. He instantly recognized the limousine driver. The man stood holding a pistol pointed straight at his face.

"You again!" was all the man said and fired once. Richie felt a jolt and a stab of pain in his left shoulder. The man continued to train his gun on him and walked toward him, glaring at him in anger. "Turn around!" he shouted with a gravelly voice. "Climb that ladder!"

In front of Richie was the ladder that led to the top of the cupola. He walked up to it and grabbed hold, but instead of climbing, he turned back to face the hostile man. "Wha—what are you going to do?" His hands were trembling. He tried his best to hold back tears.

The man with the gun shot again, this time hitting Richie in the leg. The young boy screamed in pain and fell over. "Go up that ladder!" the man barked. *"Now!"*

"D—do—don't shoot!" He grabbed hold of the bottom rung with his right hand. His left shoulder and leg were shattered and bleeding badly. The gunman came forward and lifted him off the ground so he could start climbing with his free arm and leg. Almost fainting from the pain and shock, Richie did as he was told, grabbing one rung after another with his right hand while holding on with his left, slowly pulling himself up. Every movement multiplied the pain. He finally reached a point where he could look into the furnace from the opening above. He saw orange-hot metal bubbling at the bottom. It was like looking down into the fires of hell.

The man with the gun suddenly charged up the ladder behind him. He grabbed hold of Richie's legs and lifted him up past the top of the ladder. Having nothing to grasp on to, Richie teetered in space in unspeakable horror and then plunged over the edge of the furnace into the fires inside.

CHAPTER 1

Bonnie came running out of the RoadWheels office when she saw Tom pull into the Clarence Travel Plaza with his all-white tractor-trailer and ease to a stop, air brakes hissing. Bonnie reached Tom just as his tall, lanky frame swung down from the tractor and his cowboy boots touched the tarmac. Without so much as a "Hello! How are you?" she let him have it with both barrels: "Houston," she said urgently, "we have a problem."

"Let's talk" was all Tom said to her as he motioned to Bonnie to follow him and pressed a hidden button on the underside of his trailer. A powered doorway on the side flipped outward and down, forming a staircase. Tom climbed up the few steps into the building on wheels and, when inside, took another narrow stairway to a second floor deck. Bonnie gave her blonde locks a quick shake, kicked the stairs to knock the dust off her UGG boots, and dashed lightly up, two steps at a time, following the tall man up to his spacious office.

Bonnie sank into one of the comfortable seats at a conference table. Tom took a seat facing her and nodded. "Okay, talk to me," he said. "What's going on?"

"For some months now I have . . . noticed things," Bonnie began, slowly and deliberately. "I think we have become a link in a chain of smuggling into Canada."

"Smuggling? What, drugs?" Tom stared at her, startled, his square jaw tensing.

"I don't know. Maybe."

"Why would anyone use our system?"

"I think . . . to avoid detection. Possibly getting stopped on the highway by the police."

"Stopped for what?"

"For anything. Speeding, changing lanes, broken taillight. DWFB, whatever. The police have their quota."

"DWFB?"

"Driving while female blonde," she said sarcastically, giving her shoulder-length blonde tresses a toss for emphasis.

"Yeah." Tom smiled, conveying he liked the joke. "So how do you know there's a problem?"

"Their cars are—uh—different. They've been modified."

"Modified?"

"They're Mini Coopers—very heavy, like they're carrying lead. But they're powerful. Been souped up."

"How do you know this?" Tom asked.

"We drive them on and off the trailers, remember? The guys have even weighed these cars."

"Weighed them?"

"We became suspicious, so we got some road scales. Like the ones they use at the truck weigh stations." Bonnie's voice inflected upward as if she had asked a question. "Placed them at the end of the ramp and weighed the cars as we backed them out. Nobody could guess what we were doing."

"What'd you find out?"

"We knew the standard weight of that model Mini Cooper. We knew the weight of the driver. We just subtracted them from the weight we measured."

"There was a difference?" Whatever the difference was, Tom knew, was probably contraband.

"It varied a bit from car to car. But the average load on those Mini Coopers was about one hundred pounds."

"What about luggage? That could explain it," Tom probed.

"I suppose. Pretty heavy luggage, though. And you could see into the trunks of those cars through their back windows. The luggage compartments were empty."

"So the cars were extra heavy. That's it?"

"No. There's more," Bonnie continued.

"Oh? What's that?"

"The cars would never travel south with us to New York City. But we noticed these same cars kept coming back *from* New York. It was always one way."

"Same cars? How did you know?" Tom looked at her skeptically.

"Good question. The license plate numbers were always different, but we checked the VIN numbers on these Minis. Our guys became familiar with these cars. It got so we could easily identify them."

"Did you check out the license plate numbers?"

"Yes, we did. Those plate numbers were issued to real people, all right, but when we checked on these people, it was clear they weren't the ones who owned those cars. The plates on the Minis were fake. Made with forged numbers."

Tom paused for a moment to reflect. "Did you alert the police?"

"No. I wanted to speak with you first. We don't want this to affect our business. It might scare customers off."

"Don't worry about that," Tom said assuredly. "I want RoadWheels to do the right thing. But the police might spook these guys. Once they're onto the police, they'll just stop doing what they're doing and the police won't have enough evidence to get a conviction. Maybe I should check into it first."

"I wouldn't do that if I were you," Bonnie warned.

"Oh? Why not?"

"These cars trickle in on a steady basis. When they arrive, there's this kind of entourage of forces that meets them here at this RoadWheels station and follows them north toward Canada."

"Entourage?"

"Nothing too obvious. It's just that if you were here, operating this station as long as I have, you would start to notice things. Whatever's in those cars must be very valuable and worth protecting. Those guys have guns. I've seen them."

"How do you know they're heading for Canada?"

"My boyfriend's a customs officer at the border. He tells me things."

"Things? Like what?"

"Like the Mini Coopers that leave here always cross into Canada."

"If your—uh—boyfriend suspects them, why doesn't he check out the cars at the border?"

"No probable cause. They can't just tear a person's car apart with no good reason. The drivers have passports; the plates appear legal."

"What about that entourage? Doesn't that raise enough suspicion?"

"That's just it. Those guys with guns never cross the border. My boyfriend's never seen them."

"Do you think another group meets the car on the other side?"

"I don't know, but I would think so. They're going to a lot of trouble to make sure the cars get to wherever they're supposed to go."

"Well, it should be easy to find out just where those cars are going. Just tail one of them," Tom said definitively. "I can do that."

"Don't let them know you're following," Bonnie cautioned.

"Don't worry, I can stay well back—provided you do one thing for me."

"What's that?"

"I want you to attach this device to the next suspicious Mini that comes in." Tom stood up and, reaching over to his workbench, picked up a black object that looked like a small hockey puck. "It has a magnet on the bottom, so it will stick to the car wherever you put it."

"It's a bug?" Bonnie asked.

"A locator. I'll be able to trace the car with my computer."

"Wow, that's great! You just sit here in your office and watch where it goes."

"Unfortunately, it only transmits a couple of miles. And if you put it out of sight under a car, it can't transmit to a cell tower or a satellite. I'll have to follow with my van on ground level to pick up the signal."

"Got it. No problem. I'll take care of it," Bonnie replied, getting up from her chair and starting to leave. She wore a form-fitting sweater and tight jeans that showed off her contours.

"Thanks," Tom said. "So how long do you think it will be until the next Mini comes in?"

"Well, as a matter of fact, my men are unloading one as we speak."

CHAPTER 2

"Don't call the police just yet," Tom said. "As soon as I come back, we'll talk and make a plan."

Bonnie stood and faced Tom squarely as he also rose to leave. "Please be careful," she admonished with real concern in her voice. "These men are dangerous. There's no telling what they'll do if they find out you're on to them."

Tom nodded as if to give Bonnie his promise and led the way out and down to the tarmac. As Bonnie was about to go, he held out his hand. "Thank you, Bonnie, for watching out for the company. There is so much more to running a business than running a business."

Ignoring his hand, Bonnie embraced him with a big bear hug. "Don't mention it. Just come back safely—and *soon*."

When Bonnie left, Tom sprang into action. He climbed the few steps and entered his trailer again, but this time he turned to the right on the main deck to face a large control panel on the wall. Throwing one switch he closed the door behind him and, activating two others, he raised the rear door of the trailer and ejected a ramp down to the ground. He then walked back through the garage space in the interior of the trailer, past a low-slung red sports car, to a white panel truck in the rear.

Tom climbed into the driver's seat of his van and backed it out. Pressing buttons on a small device clipped to the visor, he reversed the commands and watched as the ramp retracted into the trailer bed and the rear door lowered itself, leaving the trailer enclosed and secure.

Tom then headed over to the restaurant and restroom facilities of the huge travel plaza and parked the van inconspicuously in plain sight, as if he were one of the hundreds of visitors that stopped there each day to take a break from a long drive on the New York State Thruway. While he waited for a call from Bonnie telling him the Mini was on the move, he set up the van's telecommunications system to receive and process the locator signal and to display the Mini's position on a dashboard-mounted computer screen.

Within a few minutes, Tom got the call.

"Tom, you there? It's me, Bonnie."

"I'm over near the restaurant, parked and ready to go."

"The Mini's heading out. I don't see any others following."

"Maybe they're getting cocky . . . no, wait. There's a black Mercedes that's just backing out of a parking space here. Maybe—oh, and there's another! They are both queuing up to leave and appear to be waiting for something . . ." Tom paused for a moment. "Yes! Here comes the Mini, and one of the Mercedes cars pulled right out in front of it. The other one is . . . following the Mini now. I'll wait until they're out of sight and follow them."

"Do you have the locator signal?"

Tom glanced over at the map on the dashboard screen. There it was, a little red dot moving slowly upward on the road that represented the thruway.

"Got it! We're set. I'm on my way."

"Be *very* careful" was the last thing Bonnie said. Tom heard her voice tighten with concern.

"Don't worry. I'll check in frequently."

Tom backed out of his parking spot and headed for the superhighway. As expected, the Mini and its entourage stayed on the thruway past Exit 49 and took Exit 50 for Niagara Falls. Following the three cars as they traveled the interstate I-290 northwest to I-190, and then heading northwest again on I-190, the main route to Niagara Falls, Tom stayed back a good mile to avoid any chance of detection. The red dot on the screen kept moving steadily forward on I-190 as it traversed the Grand Island and finally crossed over the Niagara River into Canada.

The customs station was on the Canadian side of the river, just over the Peace Bridge. Tom noticed the little red dot had stopped at that point on the map, and although he slowed while still traversing Grand Island to give the Mini time to pass through customs, he nevertheless caught up and caught sight of it as he approached the booths. The driver had stopped at one of the booths and was apparently being interviewed by a customs official.

However, the Mercedes were nowhere in sight. *Where did they go?* Tom wondered, looking around to see if they had stopped at other booths or were turning around to head back to Grand Island. They had vanished into thin air.

Tom picked the shortest line and pulled up behind another car waiting to pass through another of the booths. He watched out of the corner of his eye as the Mini was cleared to enter the country and took off again on the Queen Elizabeth Way toward Toronto. Still thinking about the two black Mercedes, he edged forward toward the customs booth as the car ahead of him was cleared and sped away.

"Hello, officer. Here's my license." Tom held out his driver's license for the official to review.

"Sorry, we need your passport."

"Damn! I completely forgot. I don't have it with me."

"You people always think of Canada as just another state. Well, hello! We're another *country*, eh?"

"That's very funny. I'm sure you get a lot of laughs with that one." Tom looked at the young man and took a wild flyer on the off chance that the customs official happened to know Bonnie by way of her boyfriend. "By the way," he added, "have you heard of a Bonnie Salerno?"

"Why do you ask?"

"I'm her employer. She works for RoadWheels."

"You're . . . Tom Smith! Well, *duh*. Sorry I didn't recognize you. Welcome to Canada, my friend."

"You mean I can go in?"

"Well, no. No passport, no entry. That's the rule nowadays."

"You still didn't answer my question."

"Can you come in? The answer is no."

"I mean my other question. Have you heard of Bonnie?"

"Yeah, of course! Everyone here knows Bonnie. She's our best customer."

"Best customer?"

"On a good day she sends us almost a thousand people."

"That's a good thing?"

"Good for the economy, eh?"

"She told me her boyfriend works here."

"*Boyfriend?* She called me that? I'm flattered."

"*You're* her boyfriend?"

"The one and only. At least I think so."

"She said you've been nice enough to provide her with certain . . . uh . . . *information*."

"Issat so? Now what kind of information is that?"

"About some Mini Coopers that keep going back and forth between our country and yours."

"She told you that?"

"Yes," Tom acknowledged.

"Okay, yeah. We're looking into that, it's true."

"Small Mini's without a mini weight."

"Aye. We're trying to find out where they are going. They keep giving us the slip."

"So you're on to them?"

"Bonnie thinks they may be smuggling something in."

"Why don't you just tail them?"

"Can't. No probable cause."

"Well, I can. And I was tailing one of them until you stopped me."

"You were?"

"Yes. And if you let me pass I'll catch up with the guy and maybe find out what's going down."

"Nope. Nice try. Can't let you in. No passport, remember?"

"You'll make me turn around and go back?"

"You can't go forward, that's for sure. You see any other way except back?"

"You're very funny," Tom said, looking in the rearview mirror and seeing a car directly behind him. "So how do I do that?"

"Head over there and turn around." The customs officer pointed to a marked-off area to the left. "I'll bet that next time you'll bring your passport!" he shouted as Tom sped away.

Neither Tom nor the customs officer noticed a black Mercedes with tinted windows parked way over on the side of the large expanse of roadway.

CHAPTER 3

Tom was allowed to drive forward through the customs booth area to turn his car around. Returning in the way he came on I-190, he chided himself for forgetting his passport.

As he crossed over the bridge onto Grand Island, he glanced in his rearview mirror and noticed a black Mercedes tailgating closely. The car could have easily passed him on this near-empty stretch of superhighway but it continued to follow. Before he had time to think about what to do, he noticed a second black Mercedes dropping back on the highway in front of him. The timing was too perfect. The Mercedes behind must have called the Mercedes in front. Obviously, they were working together, but what did they want?

It didn't take long for Tom to find out. No sooner did Tom realize that he was locked in tight, between these two black cars, than his cell phone rang. He answered using his cell's Bluetooth connection by saying aloud, "Accept the call." Instantly, background highway noises came over the speaker and, after a beat, a gravelly male voice announced, "Pull off at the next exit."

"That's not where I'm going, fella," Tom replied, with as much conviction as he could muster under the circumstances.

"Yes, you are. You can't see them, but we have guns trained on your vehicle."

Tom was in the right-hand lane. He tried to move left into the passing lane, but the car behind him sped up while the car in front slowed down slightly, adjusting their speeds until they both made contact with Tom's car, front and back. Tom's car was suddenly squeezed between them like a hamburger patty between two buns. He considered briefly turning the steering wheel sharply to the left to force his way out of the box but thought better of it, realizing that his car would become unstable and start tumbling, involving the Mercedes in a major tangle that could cost him his life. Instead he eased off the gas, and he and the two Mercedes, behind and in front, began to slow down.

"You're doing just fine so far. Now we'll get off at the next exit," came the gravelly voice.

As if Tom had a choice. He passed a sign that announced Whitehaven Road and knew he had only a few brief seconds to take some action before he reached the exit ramp. He grabbed his cell phone and dialed 911.

"Don't do that," came the voice over his speakers.

"Do what?" Tom said aloud. He couldn't believe what he was hearing.

"You're calling 911. Put down the phone, *now!*"

Tom dropped the phone. The Mercedes in front of him started moving to the right to leave the highway, and Tom had no choice but to follow.

"At the end of the ramp take a right on Whitehaven."

When Tom was halfway down the ramp, the car behind braked abruptly, giving Tom's car space to maneuver. Tom stopped at the bottom of the ramp and turned onto Whitehaven, with the other Mercedes leading the way.

The Niagara River between Lake Erie and Lake Ontario splits into two, the East River and West River, with Grand Island between them. Whitehaven is a ruler-straight, east-west highway that bisects Grand Island at its widest part. The western half of Whitehaven passes through marshland, devoid of development, in a long, lonely stretch where the Mercedes in front pulled off the road and stopped. Two men got out of the car and flagged Tom to a stop behind them. The other Mercedes pulled up behind Tom.

Tom sat in his car and thought, desperately trying to formulate a plan. He could make a run for it, now that the other cars had stopped and their drivers were standing there outside, but he felt sure that the men were carrying guns and would blast away at his car, blowing out his tires at the very least but more likely putting a bullet through his head. He felt his safest option was to play along with them at this point, talking with them and trying to learn their game. This was a Hobson's choice, to be sure, but it was better than stopping a stray bullet.

"Get out of the car." The driver of the rear car turned out to be the one with the gravelly voice. This man stepped up and stopped behind Tom's side window, like a police officer walking the walk, and assumed command. Tom complied. He didn't know whether or not he should put up his hands, so he kept them down at his side, ready to use them in self-defense. He wouldn't have much of a chance anyway. The four men, each presumably with a gun, eased into position at the four corners of a square with him at the center.

"You were following us." The gravelly voiced man stated the obvious.

"I wasn't. You were following *me*."

"I'll tell you this just once: Don't piss me off. You won't like what happens. Just answer the question. Why were you following us?"

"I wanted to find out where you were going."

"So you saw we were going to Canada. So what?"

"So nothing. You didn't go to Canada after all. Here we are in the United States."

"I hate wise guys. You're pissing me off now."

"What do you want from me?"

"I don't want nothin'. I want you to cease to exist."

"Just because I followed you?"

"That's it. You're dead." The man nodded and his men moved in. Tom attempted to spring away but one man immediately grabbed him from behind. There was no way he could escape. While the man behind held him tight around the neck, another one stepped up and slammed him in the face with his fist. A terrible pain exploded through Tom's entire body.

The third man reached down and quietly pulled a bowie knife out of his tall boot as if he were a golfer pulling out one of his clubs. "Stand out of the way," he told the man who was now repeatedly slamming Tom in the head and stomach. The beater stepped aside and allowed the other full access to their victim, who by now was almost unconscious and slumping in the grasp of the man holding him tight by the neck. The man with the knife drove the blade home in the center of Tom's chest, and Tom went limp. The man behind released his grasp and let him collapse on the ground.

"All right. Let's go," said the gravelly voiced man. The four men climbed into the Mercedes cars and, without so much as a sideways glance at the bloody body, turned their cars around and headed back toward I-190.

Streaking past the two black cars unnoticed, coming in the opposite direction, was a brown and white vintage motorcycle, its rider having the appearance of a ground-based astronaut in natural leather and a spherical helmet, bent all the way forward over the handlebars as he raced down the straight road at breakneck speed. The two Mercedes were no longer in sight when the cycle rider braked sharply to a stop and dismounted to inspect the body lying in the ditch.

CHAPTER 4

Tom's consciousness sputtered on and off several times like a broken lamp and finally flicked to a steady on, allowing him to hear quiet voices in the background. He lay there trying to make out what people were saying, but the sound was soft and muted. He felt it would take enormous effort to open his eyes, but after a while they just popped open by themselves.

Everything was blinding white: the ceiling, the walls, the bedding—everything in view. He lay there, silently hoping his head would clear, but it didn't. He finally summoned the energy to utter a weak sound.

"Hello? Where am I?"

Three people came instantly to his bedside and stared down at him: a woman dressed all in white and two other people he thought he could recognize. One was Bonnie Salerno, one of the managers of his company, and the other a man he thought he had seen before.

"Hello to you!" said Bonnie, staring him in the face and smiling. "Welcome back, boss . . . er, Tom. You've been through hell and back. How does it feel?"

"Uh, not so good." Tom winced. "Must admit."

"The doctor says you'll make a full recovery. You dodged a bullet back there."

"I, uh, don't remember. Wha—what happened? Where am I? Who are these people?" Tom looked at the other two who were smiling down at him.

"This is your nurse. Peggy's her name. And this is my boyfriend, Alonzo. He saved your life and brought you here."

"'Lanzo? I . . .'" Tom closed his eyes again.

"Alonzo," Bonnie repeated. "And you're safe now. You're in a hospital in Toronto."

"Toronto?" Tom was having difficulty making sense of so much information.

"Stop right there. Let him rest now," the nurse commanded sternly, adding reassuringly, "He'll be fine."

"Thank God," Tom heard Bonnie say in parting as the three people quietly left the room and he lost consciousness again.

When Tom awoke the room was nearly dark. He felt a bit better and made an attempt to sit up. When he did so, excruciating pain ricocheted in his chest and radiated outward to every cell in his body. He lay back and waited for it to subside, closing his eyes and pressing his teeth together tightly to block the sensations. No sooner had he relaxed somewhat than the lights in the room came on again and Nurse Peggy walked in with another man dressed in a white coat. They came right to his bedside and looked at him intently. The man took hold of his hand and felt his pulse.

"His pulse is stronger," the man said. "I can examine him."

"Do you need me, Doctor?"

"No, you can go. But please call that Good Samaritan guy, Alonzo, and let him know he and—what was her name?—can see him again."

The nurse left, and the doctor pulled back the covers to check his patient.

"Name's Bonnie," said Tom weakly.

"What? Who?" the doctor asked, startled.

"Bonnie. Bonnie Salerno. The woman with Toronto."

"You mean Alonzo, not Toronto."

"Where are we again? They told me, but . . ."

"We're in Toronto."

"That's it! Toronto."

"No, Alonzo."

"I'll call him Toronto," said Tom, smiling fancifully to himself as he closed his eyes again and drifted off.

The doctor simply shook his head and checked Tom's vital signs once more while he lay there dreaming.

As he was finishing his examination, Alonzo rushed into the room, followed closely by Bonnie. "Hello, Doctor," Alonzo said. "Peggy called and said he came to?" Alonzo turned this statement into a question as he looked down and saw that Tom was apparently sleeping again.

"Yes. He awoke for a moment, but he's facing quite a long convalescence, I'm afraid."

"Really? How long?" Bonnie wanted to know. "I thought he was going to be okay."

"Oh, eventually he will, but he was pretty badly beaten. The knife punctured a lung, and there's a lot of internal bleeding. He's lucky to be alive."

"How long will he have to stay here in the hospital?"

"About a week, I imagine. But then he'll need to rest a month or two at home. Where does he live?"

Bonnie thought for a moment. "I really don't know. I think he lives in a tractor-trailer."

"A tractor-trailer? That can't be. You said he owned this huge company, RoadWheels. He must have a home somewhere."

"That's just it. He has a bedroom in the same trailer where he has his office. He's on the road all the time."

"I thought I'd heard about everything," said the doctor. "Sorry to say he'll have to stay put. And he'll need a nurse or a companion with him practically around the clock to help him with physical therapy, prepare his meals, that sort of thing. Right now, though, all he should be doing is lying flat to give his insides a chance to heal."

"Whatever it takes, Doctor," Bonnie replied. "We'll figure it out, even if he has to crash in my apartment."

"Well, for now we'll give him painkillers and monitor him closely. He's not out of the woods yet. I'll check in periodically and keep you informed of his progress." The doctor turned to go. "You two have any questions?"

"Can we talk to him now? I mean, when he wakes up?" Bonnie asked.

"Sure, but keep it brief. He needs a lot of rest. I'll give the nurse the instructions for his medicine."

"Are there any special things he might need? Oxygen tank or whatever?" Alonzo looked around and saw a lot of equipment in the hospital room, making him wonder what the convalescing would entail.

"Yes, there will be things you will need. That's why I don't think he'll be going back to that trailer anytime soon."

Alonzo looked at Bonnie, and she nodded, indicating she had no further questions either. "Well, I guess that's it, then. Thank you, Doctor. We'll just stay here and keep Tom company, even if he is fast asleep."

Just as soon as the doctor left and the door clicked closed behind him, Tom opened his eyes again and haltingly told his startled visitors, "I've been awake . . . the whole time . . . and heard everything . . . that guy . . . just said. I want to . . . tell you something . . . now . . . that you have to keep . . . absolutely secret. I do have . . . a place . . . where I can . . . go."

CHAPTER 5

Tom's tractor-trailer pulled up in front of the Smith homestead and came to a smooth stop, its air brakes hissing. Alonzo switched off the big diesel engine and climbed down out of the cab. Tom's sister, Amy, who had been informed by phone of their imminent arrival, stood waiting to greet them. Amy's husband, Henry, stood by her side with anticipation, ready and able to assist. The two came forward to meet and thank the man who had saved Tom's life.

"Hi, I'm Alonzo," he said cheerfully, walking up to them. "Your brother Tom calls me Toronto and you can too." He held out his hand, and Amy and Henry, in turn, shook it warmly. "Come on," he said, beckoning them to come with him. "Let's go see him." With that, Alonzo, a.k.a. Toronto, turned on his heels and walked back to the huge trailer.

Pressing a hidden button underneath the trailer bed, Alonzo caused a side door with steps to swing down, providing access to the interior. He stood aside and motioned for Amy and Henry to climb up. Bonnie appeared in the open doorway at the top of the stairs and invited them in.

"Hello. You must be Amy and Henry. Welcome to Tom's trailer—his home, really. Tom can't wait to see you. I'm one of his employees, by the way. Bonnie Salerno. I run his outfit in Buffalo." She said these sentences in the rapid-fire manner that was her trademark way of speaking. "Tom's on this floor, not upstairs. He needs to lay prone a bit longer. Couldn't chance bringing him up those stairs." Bonnie waved her hand in the direction of the narrow stairs to the upper floor of the trailer. "Follow me."

Amy and Henry climbed the few steps from the outside, followed by Alonzo, and were guided by Bonnie to the back of the trailer. There, in a hospital bed affixed to the floor behind his white van, lay Tom, looking pale but otherwise quite normal, propped up slightly so he could read and use his laptop computer. "Hello, everybody!" Tom beamed from ear to ear. "I've been grounded for a while but there's no place I'd rather be than where I grew up."

Amy rushed up and gave her brother a gentle, loving hug. "I've been so worried about you. They told me not to fly out to see you in Toronto because you'd be coming to see *us*!"

"Here I am, still kicking—thanks to those two." He nodded toward Alonzo and Bonnie. "Hope it's all right to barge in like this."

"You're our honored guest as long as you'd like to stay. Henry and I have prepared a room for you on the first floor next to the kitchen and the downstairs bath. Your friends Bonnie and Alonzo can sleep in Tom's and my old bedrooms upstairs."

"Toronto," Tom corrected.

"What's that?"

"Toronto. I call him Toronto."

"Oh, Toronto. Should we call him that too?"

"He's family now whether he likes it or not. And in our family, we'll call him Toronto."

"Did anybody ask *him*?" Amy wanted to know, giving Alonzo a wink.

"I kind of like the name," admitted Alonzo, who stood in the back. "That's where I'm from, and everyone's heard of it, at least."

Tom adjusted his position slightly and winced. "How are you feeling?" asked Amy, suddenly concerned and realizing her brother was still gravely ill.

"Not good. This trailer ride's been a bit rough. Not at all like those TV commercials we run for our business, with people riding in our eighteen-wheeler lounges and sitting comfortably, enjoying the trip," Tom said, giving a self-deprecating look. "With my tender insides I could feel every bump in the road."

Always the organizer, Bonnie broke in. "We'll get you out of here right away and into your room, where you can rest." Pressing a button, she raised the large rear door of the trailer, and she and Toronto quickly unhooked the gurney bed from the floor. Henry stepped up to assist, and he and Toronto lowered the bed carefully onto the road, keeping it level as best they could. Once it was down, everyone surrounded the gurney and helped roll it over the front lawn to the house.

Once in the house, Tom felt relieved, because the jiggling was over. Every little jounce of the bed had produced stabbing pains in his chest. Toronto and Henry rolled him into his room and helped him into bed, where he could rest at last. After thanking them with drooping eyelids, he quickly fell fast asleep.

Amy poured coffee in the kitchen. She and Bonnie sat at the round kitchen table, followed by Toronto and Henry, and they all discussed their plans for the coming month.

"I've got to fly back to Buffalo right away," Bonnie began. "My people there need constant direction, I'm afraid, and I also need to find out if the smuggling's still going on."

"Smuggling?" Amy was taken aback by the remark.

"We weren't sure, but we are now. Tom was following a car we suspected of smuggling something—what we don't know—into Canada. That's what got him almost killed."

"Oh my God!" Amy was shocked. "Following smugglers? Why didn't you call the police? The FBI?"

"We weren't at all sure. They wouldn't do anything, couldn't do anything, with what evidence we had. We also thought the police presence would tip them off."

"Well, you've called the police by now, I assume," Amy said with a tone of relief.

"Actually not. They are using us to transport their cars with the drugs or whatever. We're in the best position to find out what they're up to."

"Let's see if I understand this correctly," Henry broke in. "Tom was following some smugglers, and they attacked him, left him for dead, and he would have died except for Toronto here coming to the rescue, and you're not calling the police?"

"I know it sounds crazy, but—"

Toronto interrupted. "We didn't know how dangerous they were. Now we do. Tom's the one who suffered the consequences. We'd like to give him the chance to make the call if he chooses to bring in the police when he's well enough to think this through. It might be bad for business if his customers found out they were riding along with some dangerous killers."

"Toronto will take me to the Hartford airport to catch the first flight out," Bonnie continued, now that that little detail was put to rest, "and will then come back and stay here, if it's all right with you. We know you have work to do, and Tom needs someone by his side day and night while he convalesces. Doctor's orders."

"What about Toronto? Doesn't he have a job to get back to?"

"I quit," Toronto said flatly.

"Quit your job?"

"It was a dead-end job, and, to tell the truth, I was looking for a way out. Being a Canadian border guard is *really* boring. I'd much rather be with Tom."

"Well, you're certainly welcome here. And it would be a great help to us if you would stay and help out. I'm sure Tom would greatly appreciate it," Amy said finally, satisfied and glad that it was all settled.

"I'll drive Bonnie to the airport and come right back. It should take two hours at most."

"You plan on taking that big tractor-trailer to the airport and back?" Henry asked. "You can use our car."

"No, sir. Bonnie and I have a much quicker way to go."

"How's that?"

"I have my Indian motorcycle in the trailer."

CHAPTER 6

Tom convalesced and got stronger every day. About one week into his prescribed one-month stay at the family farm, Toronto insisted he commence a regimen of physical therapy. The therapy began benignly enough, but it escalated in intensity day by day until eventually Tom protested about the pain. "No pain, no gain," Toronto would always say, ignoring his patient's complaints.

In fact, Toronto was right. Tom healed rapidly and soon surpassed the level of fitness he had before the vicious attack. By the end of the month he was doing more push-ups and pull-ups and running faster and for longer distances than he ever had in his life. Toronto turned out to be a natural personal trainer, and Tom finally felt better and more physically fit than ever before.

With two days to go before his scheduled departure, Tom sat with his sister at the kitchen table to reminisce and to talk about what the future might bring. Toronto was out riding his motorcycle, and Henry was at the mine, excavating rocks containing those precious small slivers of silver.

"Do you need money?" Tom asked with brotherly concern for his sister. "I have plenty, you know."

"I know. I read everything there is to read about your company. It is just amazing what you have accomplished. But no, Henry and I are doing just fine. My silver business isn't big, but it's steady, and we make enough to get by."

"How is the mine holding out?"

"It will support us for a long time. And we also get some rent, you know, from our tenant farmer. We're fine, Tom, thank you. It has been a treat to have you with us. We'll treasure this past month in our memory, but now, sadly, your visit is almost over. You and Toronto will be greatly missed."

"I'll be back, sis. I'd forgotten how nice it was here when we grew up, and it still is the same. Just like old times. Remember when you cried that time when Dad accidentally tossed out that silver pebble?" Tom glanced at his sister with deep affection, almost afraid to look her square in the face.

"Yes, I do," Amy replied. "Almost like it was yesterday. And you were so sweet to me. You got me through that, you know." She paused for a moment, and so did Tom.

"Before you go, there is something I'd like to give you," she said finally. "I didn't know what to provide to the brother who has everything, so I made this little thing." Amy reached into her shirt pocket, pulled out what appeared to be a coin, and handed it to Tom. "I created a mold so I can make more of these. I can make as many as you like."

Tom took it and turned it over in his hand. It was a small silver disk, identical on both sides, in the shape of a tiny tractor-trailer wheel. His eyes twinkled and his mouth spread into a wide grin as he realized what it was. "I love it!" he said, gazing first at the coin and then at his sister. "It's perfect."

Tom's nonverbal reaction told Amy more than any words could conceivably convey. It was indeed the perfect gift, and she felt her heart leap with the knowledge she had made a difference in her brother's complicated life.

The roar of Toronto's motorcycle engine, just outside, broke the spell. Tom and Amy both rose involuntarily from the table as if the magical moment was too vivid to bear. A few moments later, Toronto entered the kitchen with his helmet under his arm and stood at the door, staring back. No one said a word for a moment until Toronto broke the silence with a puzzled "What?"

"Nothing," Tom said awkwardly. "We were just talking. Brother and sister stuff."

"Oh. Well, I hope you were giving some thought to the dangers of going back."

"What do you mean?"

"Those guys that tried to kill you. They think you're dead. When they find out you're not, and that you're on to them . . . it could get dangerous."

Amy looked at her brother, alarmed. "I never thought—"

"And another thing," Toronto continued. "You've been getting really famous because of your business. That makes you a target for any crazy guy out there who thinks you have something he wants."

"Your point is? Round-the-clock bodyguards? No, I can't have that."

"There's another way," Toronto suggested.

"Oh? What's that?"

"You can disappear."

"Disappear? How? You don't think people will wonder where I went? Everyone will want to know, and I'll be on the front page of every newspaper."

"What if we let it be known you are actually dead?"

Tom stood there calmly, looking first at Toronto and then at Amy and allowing Toronto's suggestion to sink in. He had been thinking for some time about a strategy for catching the smugglers, and each time he considered what to do, his mind kept coming back to the same idea. It would be best if he could catch the smugglers off guard, thinking they had succeeded in killing him.

Amy was the first to respond to Toronto's remark. "Toronto saved your life by bringing you to the hospital. The people at the hospital know what really happened. The word is out."

"No, it's not," Toronto replied, defending the idea. "First of all, the hospital is very careful about holding medical information about its patients in confidence. We have laws in Canada about that, just like you do. And second, only a small number of doctors, nurses, and administration staff know about Tom. We can speak to them and ask them not to let anyone know."

Amy was still unconvinced. "What about the people in Tom's business? News of the attack on Tom must have spread throughout the company by now."

"The only person in the company who knows is Bonnie. And she's not telling."

"Are you absolutely sure?" Amy was beginning to warm up to the idea.

"As a matter of fact, I called her today," Toronto explained. "She agrees with me. We ought to hold a funeral for Tom."

Amy looked first at Tom and then back at Toronto. After a moment she nodded and said, "I'm in."

She knew her brother was fearless, a characteristic that often led him to take risks that got him into trouble. Amy therefore also knew her brother would be safer dead than alive.

CHAPTER 7

The memorial service took place in Tom's hometown in Connecticut and incited a media storm. The village green across the road from the classic, colonial-style Congregational Church, which several New England guide books called "the most photographed church in America," was ground zero for an assemblage of print, radio and television journalists from Hartford, New York City, and beyond. They came from as far away as Los Angeles to inquire, learn, and report about the extraordinary life of this entrepreneur who had grown up poor on a farm nearby and had proven that the American dream was still available to all of us in this modern age.

At the outset it was decided not to reveal that Tom had been attacked near the Canadian border. This would have launched an investigation about the attack and prompted questions that both Tom and Toronto wished to avoid. According to Tom's obituary, posted by the immediate family on www.roadwheels.org, the official website of RoadWheels, Tom died of unknown causes, but the reporters would not be satisfied unless and until they received an explanation. Finally, it was offered that Tom had suffered a motorcycle accident while trail biking on the family farm and that the death certificate had been signed by a physician who, upon request of the family, would remain anonymous. The family, they said, wished to avoid all publicity surrounding Tom's death and in this way shielded the physician from prying questions of reporters.

Of course, no death certificate was ever issued, but no one bothered to check with the Bureau of Vital Records in Hartford. Because the announcement came from his sister, it was accepted that Tom was indeed dead.

Friends, business associates, and politicians at every level came from far and wide to pay their respects. Tom's sister, Amy, and her husband, Henry, worked day and night for a week in advance of the event, first making a to-do checklist and preparing Tom's obituary and then announcing Tom's passing and attending to all the arrangements a family must make when a loved one dies. To start the process, Amy notified all of Tom's friends and business associates by e-mail blast and sent the obituary to the newspapers and television stations. She and Henry then contacted the Congregational minister and, with his advice and counsel, they planned the church memorial service. Once that was done, they turned their attention to arranging for a huge catered reception following the service. They called a local supplier to erect a big white tent in an open hayfield on the farm and to fill the tent with chairs, tables, and lavender tablecloths. To maintain order as the cars streamed in, they notified the police about the event and asked a local automobile dealer to have a mechanic with a wrecker on hand and to provide valet service for parking in the field surrounding the tent. The final step was to discuss the food and drink with a caterer and plan the timing and agenda for both the service and the reception. Everyone they invited to speak and deliver a eulogy about Tom's life was honored and accepted with great humility.

The funeral director who had previously made the arrangements for laying Tom's parents to rest was brought into the circle of confidentiality and informed about the family's plan to fake Tom's death. He recommended burying an empty casket at the local cemetery next to the resting place of Mary and Frank Smith and planting a simple stone, with only Tom's name, flush with the ground at the foot of the grave. This was done quietly on the day that Tom's death was announced. When members of the public called the funeral home, they were informed that Tom had been buried in a private, family ceremony but told they were welcome to visit the grave and pay their respects at any time.

No detail was too small or insignificant to be left unattended. An answering service was hired to answer questions about the event, and both vocal and written condolences were accepted through a toll-free telephone number, the company website, a Facebook page, and Twitter messages.

Information about Tom's extraordinary life was made available online and saturated the media. Tom's passing was the big news of the week. One journalist put it this way:

> Litchfield, Conn.—It was a simple idea that launched his business and made him a fortune. It came to him while leading a convoy in the service of the US Navy on Interstate Route 95, a

superhighway that traverses the East Coast of the United States from Portland, Maine, in the north down to Miami, Florida, in the south, a distance of about two thousand miles.

During this particular trip from North Carolina to Washington, DC, Tom Smith looked ahead at the stream of cars in front of him, all moving quietly, in unison, on the ribbon of highway extending out to the horizon. From his perch high up in the cab of his three-quarter ton truck, he had a commanding view of the road ahead. All these people were wasting gas and wasting the miles on their cars, Tom thought. There ought to be a better way.

That "better way" was what made Tom rich, just like Fred Smith, who founded Federal Express, before him. Tom's idea was to transport truckloads of cars and their passengers together from one city to the next along I-95. He would set up a tractor-trailer station in the parking lot of a rest stop, close to each big city along the line, to pick up cars for transport, each hour on the hour, to other cities up the line. The cars would be loaded into specially built trailers, as many as could fit one behind the other, while their passengers climbed a circular staircase to a comfortable café lounge above the "garage deck" to relax and enjoy the trip. As Tom envisioned it, the trailer rooftop lounge would be outfitted with huge windows for watching the passing scenery, built-in tables with recessed lighting for reading and writing, Wi-Fi, and video screens for personal entertainment.

The real genius of this business concept was the way it generated money. In working out his business plan, Tom foresaw the advent of the ultrashort "citi-car," like the Smart Car, the Fiat 500, the Honda Fit, and the Mini Cooper. These cars ran inexpensively and were easy to park in the city, but they were less than comfortable to drive on long trips. Tom's idea was to charge a fee to his customers, based on not only the mileage to their destination but also on the length of the car. His economic model favored small cars, and small cars he got—in ever-greater numbers. Paying customers lined up with their citi-cars at their nearest loading station on I-95. If the cars filled a trailer, as they often did, there was always another tractor-trailer ready and waiting to be loaded. As soon as a trailer was filled it was sent on its way. And at the top of the hour, filled or not, the tractor-trailer took to the highway so that customers never had more than sixty minutes to wait.

And that was not all. Tom let everyone who worked for the business work for themselves as independent contractors. This invoked the magic of the entrepreneurial spirit.

The eighteen-wheeler drivers who loaded and hauled the trailers owned their own rigs and bid on their routes. They would cut their charges to the bone because it was steady work and made money for them mile after mile. And when they made money, so did Tom.

Each of the trailer rooftop lounges was also a separate profit center, as a café with its captive traveling customers. The "restaurant owners," as they were called, ran their own entrepreneurial businesses, some operating in just one lounge as a mom-and-pop establishment, while others bid on and received contracts to operate fleets of lounges, much like fast-food franchises. The restaurant owners were free to offer their own cuisine and to experiment, within limits, of course, to find out what their customers wanted and what made them the most money. And again, when they made money, so did Tom.

This business, which Tom called RoadWheels, attracted such media attention when it was launched that he scarcely had to advertise. Every car owner from Maine to Florida learned about it over and over again and was eager to try it. By far the majority of those who tried the service enjoyed the ride and told others about it until eventually RoadWheels became part of the fabric of life on the entire East Coast. People loved traveling in the comfortable lounges and having their own cars with them when they arrived at their destinations. Tom worked hard at making the traveling experience better and better, and his business boomed.

It was Tom's vision to extend his East Coast network across the entire United States and then eventually to Canada. Whether this happens or not will now depend upon the new owner or owners of RoadWheels, whoever he or she may be.

Throughout his life Tom was a very private person and kept quietly to himself. He never married, although he was rich and very handsome—an unbeatable combination that led to more than just a few broken hearts of the opposite sex. Only the managers of his RoadWheels stations can really say they knew this self-made billionaire who roamed the superhighways with his specially built, all-white eighteen-wheeler and appeared like a phantom out of nowhere, dropping in unexpectedly at one of the forty-eight RoadWheels stations. His managers loved him and looked forward to these surprise visits by their legendary boss. He was their hero, and he will always hold a special place in their hearts.

CHAPTER 8

A week before Tom's "death" was announced, Amy had made a personal call to each of Tom's forty-eight trusted managers, one at each node of RoadWheels, and asked them all to come to the farm for a private meeting. Receiving the call from Tom's sister confirmed the managers' worst fears. Tom had been unavailable by phone or e-mail for over a month and had not returned their messages. Each and every one had been chosen by Tom to serve in his business, and each had his or her own special relationship with this man. Their collective grief was all too real.

They arrived from all over the country by planes, trains, automobiles, and even RoadWheels tractor-trailer trucks. Amy had reserved rooms for them at the local Litchfield Inn, and upon their arrival they were instructed to meet at 6:00 p.m. in the Grand Hall. Dress, they were told, was business casual. Fifty chairs were set up in the room, theater-style. Coffee and pastries were available on the sideboard.

At the appointed time all forty-eight were assembled and seated in the hall, all talking to the people seated next to them, in part to be polite but in part to mask their unsettling nervousness at what the future would hold. When Tom walked in at precisely 6:01 p.m., followed by Amy, Henry, and Toronto, they instantly stopped speaking, gasped in amazement and relief, and jumped to their feet in spontaneous applause.

Tom strode to the front of the room, stood there smiling for a moment, and motioned for them to be quiet and listen. He had an important message to convey. They complied, and the room became suddenly silent and still. One by one, they gingerly took their seats again and sat erect, ears alert, in anticipation of what was to come.

"In two days," Tom began, "my sister, Amy, will announce that I have died."

The audience stared at him blankly, trying to comprehend what he had just said. Tom continued after only a brief pause.

"What I say to you today you must hold in the strictest confidence. You are not to tell anyone, not even your spouses or your closest friends. Do you understand? Can you agree to this?"

They all looked at one another at first, not knowing what to say or do, and then tentatively nodded their heads in affirmation.

"Does anyone have any problem with this?"

No one responded. One could've heard a pin drop.

"All right, then. I'm counting on each and every one of you to keep this promise." Having thus bound his managers to secrecy, Tom went on to tell them about his forthcoming funeral and his plans for the future.

"I have chosen each and every one of you to run an operation of this company we call our RoadWheels. As our top managers, you are exceedingly important to the company, and there is nothing I will not do to help you in this endeavor.

"In two days you will receive a formal announcement of my demise. I have called you all here to assure you that this report of my death will be somewhat premature. We are all going to pass on to the great beyond someday, and none of us can know when that day will arrive, but I hope and pray that I'll live on for a few more years at least and be here to help you grow this company and take advantage of its potential.

"I'm sure you are wondering what this is all about. Why would I want to fake my own death? If I'm not really dead, where will I be? Who will be running the company?

"I called you here today to explain all that, and to reassure you that I will remain available to you at all times even though I have supposedly left you, never to return."

For the next hour Tom explained the history leading up to his decision to drop out and disappear, a decision he knew would be a shock to his friends and business associates alike. He also explained that for his managers, he would *not* disappear, provided that they took great pains to keep secret his continued existence as the leader of their company. He would continue to roam the highways with his specially built tractor-trailer, dropping in on each manager from time to time, and he would continue to be available to them at all times by all the different modes of electronic communication. They each had a personal password to enter the computer system, and each was responsible for the profit and loss of their own station. It was as if the company was made up of forty-eight distinct companies, each competing with all the others.

"I'm going to be there for you, holding your hand when you stumble and cheering you on when you succeed. All I can ask is that you do your best and cooperate with each other to make our company run like fine clockwork."

Tom shot a look at Amy, Henry, and Toronto, who had been sitting in the back row, and they rose on cue and came forward. Tom introduced the assembled managers to his sister and her husband, and they both took a small bow. Tom continued, motioning for Toronto to come forward, saying, "And this is my faithful companion Toronto. He came to my rescue when I was lying on the side of the road, unconscious and close to death, and I'll always be indebted to him. Toronto has agreed to ride shotgun with me to investigate the band of smugglers who are using the services of our company and who tried to kill me.

"Now, as a token of my commitment of continued support, I have a little gift for each of you that Amy designed and Henry made for me." Tom took a small leather bag from Amy and reached inside with one hand. Everyone stared, intensely interested and wondering what it was that Tom was about to reveal. He felt around inside the bag and, after a beat, took out and held up one of the silver wheels. Turning it in his fingers to show everyone, he addressed the group: "Keep this silver wheel in your pocket as a remembrance of me and also as a reminder that we must continue to work together to keep our RoadWheels turning."

The room exploded in applause. Everyone stood up as one and roared their approval. They felt honored to work as Tom's cadre in this very special company that Tom called RoadWheels and felt doubly honored that he had shared this special moment with them.

Tom stood in front of them as their source of inspiration and acknowledged the applause by blinking back his tears.

"And one more thing." Tom executed a quick about-face, turning away from the group, and reached into his breast pocket. A second later he turned around again and stood facing the leaders of his company with silver aviator sunglasses covering his visage like a mask. "From now on," he announced, "whenever you see me, I'll be wearing these."

CHAPTER 9

Unlike Tom Sawyer, Tom Smith did not stay to attend his own funeral. He and Toronto left the next morning, and the two were on the road with Tom's eighteen-wheeler at the crack of dawn with Toronto's Indian Scout motorcycle stowed in the back. Before taking to the road, they had the white tractor-trailer repainted black from stem to stern to avoid being recognized on the highway. Tom also started wearing a pair of aviator glasses that covered his eyes with dark mirrored surfaces. From this moment on he was incognito.

The forty-eight managers also returned to their home bases that day to await the notification of Tom's death, only to return again a few days later to express their deepest condolences to Amy and Henry at Tom's funeral. It was purely a charade, to be sure, but they understood the necessity and did their best to shed their tears over Tom's passing. Some even got into the act and were able to sob openly during the many moving eulogies that extolled the life of the great man.

Tom and Alonzo, a.k.a. Toronto, headed west along the New York State Thruway, crossing the Canadian border at Niagara Falls and, late in the evening, pulled up and stopped outside a two-story frame house in the Little Spain section of Toronto. It was the home of Alonzo's parents, Lisa and Tony Sierra, the home where Alonzo was born and grew up, and the home where he still lived in a renovated basement apartment for which he now paid his parents a token rent.

The arrival of the huge tractor-trailer did not go unnoticed in the tight-knit Spanish neighborhood. Alonzo had alerted his parents, Tony and Lisa Sierra, by telephone, and Lisa had prepared his favorite meal, her special *jamón serrano*. When Tom finally air-braked to a stop and switched off the big diesel engine, not only Tony and Lisa but also a host of friends from the neighborhood emerged on the street. They all gathered around the eighteen-wheeler to welcome Alonzo and his unknown companion to their friendly corner of the world. Whoever was a friend of Alonzo Sierra was certainly a friend of theirs too.

Tom's face was partially hidden behind his aviator glasses as he climbed down from the cab, as his new incognito life now required. He was no longer Tom Smith, the famous entrepreneur. He was, well, just Alonzo's friend who had stopped by for an overnight. Little did Alonzo know at the moment that this would be his last trip home—and, more importantly, his last visit with his mother and father—for quite some time.

At the evening meal with Alonzo's parents the red wine flowed and the Spanish ham was so good that Alonzo and Tom asked repeatedly for extra slices until the large dish was empty. When complimented on her cooking, Lisa explained proudly that the recipe had been handed down and improved upon in her family from one generation to the next until eventually it had attained its present state of perfection. Alonzo was relieved to see that Tom knew better than to ask his mother to reveal this precious family secret.

Alonzo hoped his parents would not ask why their guest, whom he had introduced to them as John Reid, kept his aviator glasses on, even during their candlelit dinner. Whether or not they found it strange, they were too polite to ask why.

After dinner was over and the compliments on the meal had been enthusiastically offered to Lisa and graciously accepted, Tony raised his glass and spoke from the heart.

"To family and friends! You are what make life worthwhile." Tony took a sip and put down his glass. "I'm just an old carpenter, but I know what I know. Nothing makes me happier than when you come home, Alonzo, and especially when you bring a dear friend. And it is clear to your mother and me that John Reid here is your *compadre.*"

"All I can say, Dad, is that we have a special chain that binds us together. It's a long story how this came about, but now's not the time. We're tired from a long drive and need to turn in. Tomorrow early I'm going to pack some of my things in the trailer and we'll have to go."

Alonzo's father frowned. He gently pressed him, trying to learn about his future plans.

"Leaving so soon? For how long?"

"I can't say. It's kind of a . . . secret mission."

"You can tell your mother and father, no?"

"If I did, it wouldn't be secret, now would it? By tomorrow night the whole neighborhood would know."

Tony paused and thought about this a moment and then looked squarely at Tom. "This mission, it isn't dangerous, is it?"

"We don't really know," Tom answered for Alonzo. "But dangerous or not, I'll watch out for your son. I promise to protect him from harm and bring him safely back home, no matter what dangers there may be out there on the road."

Tony's face turned dark, reflecting his concern. He turned to Alonzo. "What? Where are you going? What about your job with the government? What about Bonnie, your girl? Does she know about this?"

"As a matter of fact, she does, Dad. She knows all about it and wants me to go. But don't bother to ask her. She's sworn to secrecy."

"Oh my goodness! What is going on?" Lisa finally spoke, suddenly alarmed by what was being said.

"This is not a dangerous mission!" Alonzo replied, as convincingly as he could muster to his own parents who loved him and had only his best interests at heart. "We are just going undercover for a while. If anyone comes to you and asks what happened to me, to John, or to the tractor-trailer that is parked outside, you tell them the truth: *you don't know.*"

Lisa and Tony sat there silently, staring at him with worried looks. Alonzo knew that in their minds they blamed this new friend "John" for enticing him away. If this "mission" was not dangerous, why couldn't he tell them about it? They were his parents after all. They were clearly unhappy with this new relationship that was taking him away.

CHAPTER 10

Gunther Sachs lay sleeping, flat on his back, in the center of the enormous, soft, circular bed that, with its silvery sheets and pillowcases, was not unlike a white billowy cloud. Sunlight filtered in through the sheer drapes and coaxed him awake.

Sachs's awareness switched on, setting his mind in motion, but he continued to lay still on the bed with his eyelids comfortably closed and his thoughts running free. Sachs relished these moments in the morning when these fleeting thoughts and ideas bubbled up in his unfettered brain like spurts from a geyser.

Sachs had the greatest respect for his brain because it had found new pathways through the jumble of thorny brambles in the complex world of finance. His brain had thought its way up through the ranks to make Sachs a master of the universe and enabled him to enjoy those pleasurable perks that only enormous wealth can bring: a trophy wife, a sailing yacht, a private jet, and, of course, a mansion on the north shore of Lake Ontario.

This morning Sachs directed his mind to think about a piece of news that had come his way just yesterday: Tom Smith had passed away. What did this mean? What would happen to his company, RoadWheels? Who would own it? Would they want to cash out? Should he reveal himself as a buyer? Should he use a straw man? Work through a broker? What price would they ask? How could he negotiate that down? What if there were other buyers?

What had caused Tom's death? He couldn't have been older than forty. Was he killed? If so, by whom? Who would benefit? Was it about transporting cars? From where to where? For what reason? Did Tom's company interfere with the transport? How important was control of the company? Who were these people, anyway? How could he find out?

Sachs was not normally in the business of making money the hard way, which was by producing a product or providing a service that others wanted to buy. He made money off other people's blood, sweat, and tears as a financial middleman. He expanded the money supply through his GS Investment Bank, a private bank that attracted deposits from wealthy investors. It held 10 percent of the deposits in cash available for withdrawals and prudently invested the other 90 percent. But the law allowed the bank to loan out ten times this 90 percent of its asset reserves, and presto, money was magically created. To be sure, the money was often used by other people to grow their businesses, giving a lift to the economy, but Sachs could care less about the social benefit of what he did. He was in the game for one reason only: to make as much money as he possibly could.

His bank took an obscenely large fee for handling OPM—other people's money. As Willy Sutton once famously replied when asked why he robbed banks, "That's where the money is." Gunther Sachs *owned* a bank for the very same reason: that was where the money was.

Sachs had started his career in finance by writing a computer stock-trading program, based on a mathematical algorithm he developed for his doctoral thesis at MIT. Even today, thirty years later, his program continuously siphoned money out of TMX, the Toronto Stock Exchange. When the stock ticked up, the program sold, and when the stock ticked down, the program bought, all in femtosecond after the uptick or downtick and before the electronic signals reporting the TMX trades had time to reach the public. This was because Sachs's program ran on a computer that stood *right next* to the stock exchange computer and received the signals first. Sachs never questioned why they let him make money this way, draining profits from stock trades at the public's expense, since the word *fair* was not in his vocabulary. He paid attention to what was *legal* because it kept him out of jail, but morality and fairness had nothing to do with it. The goal was to suck as much money out of the financial system as he possibly could with a minimum of effort. He didn't give a damn or even a thought to where, or from whom, the money came from.

At first Sachs made all the important investment decisions himself, but as the GSIB developed a following and grew, other traders were brought in and began to influence the culture of the firm. The GSIB became known to operate on the edge, using all the leverage that its money advantage could muster and eventually pushing what some considered to be the envelope of legality. After all, what business activity could be said to be "inside information," unavailable to use for investment decisions, if one's investigators could easily obtain it through corporate spying? And if one were to devise a derivative security so complex that no one understood it and could then unload it on a buyer that was all right too. If the buyer didn't read or couldn't understand the fine print, and if the value of the derivative sank to zero, it was caveat emptor—buyer beware" The result may not have been fair, but it too was on the fuzzy edge of legality.

Yes, Gunther Sachs was a master of the universe, and this was just the beginning. There would be no stopping him now. As his wealth grew and grew, he could take more and more risks, and he was always on the lookout for opportunities.

CHAPTER 11

As Sachs well knew, it took money to make money, and the more money one had at one's disposal, the greater the risks one could take without taking a risk. He had learned this lesson the hard way early in his career.

Upon receiving his doctorate in finance from MIT some twenty-five years ago, Sachs took a much-needed summer break in the French Riviera, enjoying the sun and the warm, festive atmosphere on the topless beaches before reporting to work at his first real job. Prior to leaving, he studied a well-known Martingale system for playing roulette at the casinos in Cannes and Monte Carlo. The system was simple enough: play both red and black at the same time, starting with a minimum one-euro bet and then doubling and adding one to the bet each time the color lost. When one color lost, the other color would win and return the total amount of money he had bet on that color, with a bonus of as many euros as the number of spins of the wheel that it took to win. If he won on the first spin, he would get his euro back with one winning euro. If it took two spins to win, he would have spent four euros (costing him one euro on the first spin and two plus one on the second), and he would win six, leaving him a gain of two. Unlike the greedy casinos in Las Vegas, the French casinos left the money on the table when the ball happened to land in a green slot.

What was of concern to Sachs was the small but real chance that he would run out of money when doubling and adding one, should the ball land repeatedly on the same color, red or black. If Sachs were unable to keep doubling his bet, the system would break down. Before leaving MIT, he had calculated the mathematical odds and knew this risk was not insignificant. Even if he kept all his winnings from the time he started playing, and even though he won money on the other color at each turn of the wheel, these winnings, all added together, were not sufficient to cover the money he needed to guard against the chance of a streak of one color.

Knowing the mathematical probabilities, however, was different from *understanding* them, in the sense of understanding his own rationale for playing the game. Young Sachs walked into the Cannes casino knowing full well the limitations of his system of play, and, as a consequence, he had established ground rules for himself to protect against this real possibility of losing all his money. What happened next was a lesson he would never forget.

It was late in the afternoon on a Friday, and the casino was starting to fill up with gamblers—suckers, really, for it was known to all that the odds favored the house. Most of the blackjack tables were in play, although a few were still available and waiting for people to arrive. Sachs viewed the blackjack gamblers with disdain because he knew that unless they could remember all the cards that were played, which only a handful of people in the world could actually do, there was no possibility of beating the dealer in the long run.

Sachs passed by the bar, strategically placed at the center of the facility to make it easy for customers to grab a drink on their way to the tables, and entered the roulette arena. He felt, at that moment, like a master of this universe, because he had done his homework. To avoid its possible theft from his hotel room, he carried with him all the cash he had brought from the United States—ten thousand dollars worth of euros—but notwithstanding the strength of this wealth, his ground rules were simple. First, he would always place only the minimum one-euro bet to start, and second, as he doubled his bet and added one, he would never place more than one thousand euros at risk. That allowed him to double and add one to his bet nine times in a row. The probability of having to do this was exceedingly low: one chance in 1,024. He would assume that risk and, by following his rules, guard against it. Although it was indeed a lot of money, he could afford to lose a thousand euros.

Sachs went to a cashier's window and exchanged his entire ten thousand dollars worth of euros for casino chips. He knew he wouldn't use the chips, but it was fun to play the part of a high roller just for once. Later he would sell the chips back to the casino at the price he paid. As he made the exchange he imagined he saw the lady teller at the window look at him with due respect. It felt good.

Stashing his mother lode of chips of various denominations in a cloth moneybag, Sachs headed toward one of the four active roulette tables to play the game. He sat down on an empty stool and eyed the board.

Six other players sat on both sides of the layout, and several more stood around and watched. The croupier was just paying out a lucky winner of a number that paid thirty-five to one. He had played a ten-euro chip and so received a stack of chips worth three hundred and fifty euros—a lot of money in those days. Without even a trace of a smile, he gave the croupier a fifty-euro tip and left the remainder of his winnings on the board, spreading them among five different numbers. The other players dropped their chips on various numbers and combinations like odd and even or high and low. The croupier spun the wheel, snapped the ball to race around the slot in the rim in the opposite direction, and called for the betting to stop.

All eyes followed the little brass ball as it hugged the rim for a while and eventually slowed and spiraled down smoothly and then bounced about on the ridges that divided the wheel into colored segments: alternating red and black as well as a green segment with the number zero. With the wheel still turning, the ball bounced one last time and got caught in a red segment with an even high number. The croupier dropped the dolly on the number twenty-two.

Feeling comfortable with the game, Sachs began to play by placing a minimum one-euro chip on the board, for both red and for black. Most of the people at the table didn't notice this, but one well-dressed lady on the opposite side of the board stared at the layout and then looked at him strangely. "You're betting against yourself?" she asked, rhetorically.

Sachs eyed her and winked. "Safer that way."

The croupier spun and the ball landed on the green. No one had bet the zero, so no one was a winner. The croupier collected all the chips on the numbered bets but left the rest and spun again. The ball landed on black eleven. Sachs lost on red but won on black. He took his winnings, two euros, and replaced his bets, one euro on black and three on red. The lady on the other side seemed impressed.

The wheel spun and black won again. No problem. Sachs bet one euro on black and seven on red. This was repeated five more times, with Sachs playing his system running the betting up to 127 on red. He began to sweat, but the chance of red coming up eight times in a row was only one in 256. As the wheel turned for this eighth time, Sachs tried not to show nervousness, especially for the lady across the table from him, but he could feel his blood pressure rising. He stared at the wheel and the ball landed in black again. He counted out chips worth 255 euros, placed them on red, and held his breath. Again the ball chose black. The chances of this happening again were a miniscule one in 512! But happen it did, and Sachs was over his limit of one thousand euros, having lost 1,013 on red and won nine on black. He had already reached the limit of his ground rule number two; he should cut his losses and walk away.

CHAPTER 12

Sachs well knew, at least intellectually, that the chance of the roulette ball landing on black again was fifty-fifty. But the ball had landed on black nine times in a row, so, he rationalized, the chance of it landing again on black was statistically extremely low: one chance in 1,024. On average this should happen only once in a thousand turns of the wheel. His nerves were warning him against making a false move, but he decided to go for it. He had plenty of chips left, so he doubled his bet once again and added one.

He counted out 511 euros worth of chips and pushed them onto the layout, forming a small pile in the area marked "red."

Gunther Sachs could feel his mind go numb and his eyes glaze over as he watched the brass ball move around several times in the groove that surrounded the rotating roulette wheel. The ball seemed to run free at a constant speed, and that would have been just fine with Sachs if it stayed that way, but he could finally see it was slowing down. He resisted closing his eyes and watched helplessly as the ball bounced around and then got caught in a slot and moved with the wheel. It was on . . . black, again!

The attractive lady across the table stared at Sachs curiously. "Bad luck" was all she said. Sachs could not tell if she was sad or glad for his misfortune. He felt his face turn red with embarrassment. So much for an MIT education!

Now was clearly the time to retreat. But Sachs had invested so much money in the game at this point—1,523 euros, to be exact—if he walked away he would forfeit it all. Surely black would not, could not, continue to win. He would try just one more time, and if he lost again, well, he knew better than to stay in the game. He counted out 1,023 euros worth of chips and placed them on red.

This time Sachs was really scared, and he didn't care if he showed it. He suddenly realized he had lost his self-control. The entire situation would right itself, he knew, if that little ball would just land on red. He would then recoup all of the money he lost to this point and then some—one euro for each spin of the wheel. If only . . .

The lady facing him shook her head from side to side, slowly and almost imperceptibly, warning him against continuing on. No one else seemed to notice, but Sachs got the message. He hesitated. The croupier was calling for the bets. All the others at the table finished placing their chips on the layout, and the croupier briefly cast an expectant glance at Sachs. Sachs was undecided, but he had no time to think this through. He had enough money to play two more times. That was a comfortable margin. He was already deeply in the hole—2,033 euros, an amount that was real money—so it was a no-brainer. He would play just one more time and then fold.

In the meantime, Sachs's mood had darkened, and he felt suddenly depressed. He moved his chips into place compulsively but did not expect to win. And he didn't. The croupier called out another black and took his money off the table. Sachs was sure he saw the hint of a smile on his face as he did so.

Okay, now he was angry. He couldn't let the house beat him down. He had plenty of money left. He doubled down again and added one for good measure. 4,095 euros were riding on red and, if he lost, he would be pretty much wiped out. He had enough chips to play one more time, but if he did, he would be totally out of money and could not even buy food, let alone pay for his hotel.

The croupier again spun the wheel and snapped the ball in opposite directions. Sachs had the feeling that if he could, the croupier would have made the ball land on black again, but that was impossible, wasn't it? The croupier did not have that kind of control. It certainly seemed that way to Sachs when, all too quickly, the ball slowed down and dropped into a slot. Sachs was afraid to look, and anyway, he could feel that the eyes of everyone at the table were on him. They were watching him closely. He pretended not to care where the ball landed and merely listened to the croupier. *"Impair et . . . noir."* *Black* again. He had had a premonition that would be the outcome. It was the *next* turn of the wheel that would be his redress. He would show them all how to play the game. He had nerves of steel. He knew he would finally win on the very next turn.

Deep down inside Sachs was sorely afraid of the outcome, but he was way beyond that now. He had masked all feeling and was operating without logic or guidance as to what to do. He counted out chips worth 8,197 euros and placed them on red. This time he didn't place any chip on black. It didn't matter anymore. The chances were still fifty-fifty of losing, but he wouldn't lose this time. His would win and walk away whole. It was his time to shine. He had only a few euros left to his name, so he *had* to win. There was no turning away.

Sachs's heart sank when, just moments later, he thought he heard the croupier say the word *noir*. His mind went blank. There was no turning back or turning away.

CHAPTER 13

Sachs stared remorsefully as the croupier used the rake to drag his entire pile of chips off the table. What should he do now? He had only about twenty-five euros worth of chips left to his name. If he cashed these in, he would have barely enough money to get to the airport to fly back home. His parents were divorced and had started anew, so neither his mother nor his father cared or even thought about him at this stage in their lives.

Even if his parents were not totally without feelings for him, Sachs was much too proud to turn to them for help. He was on his own and he knew it.

The situation couldn't be much worse. Sachs had never been destitute before and was unprepared to face the world without money. This couldn't be the end of his life—or could it? In a desperate attempt to claw his way back to solvency, he took out five of his remaining chips and placed them on a number: the number twenty-two. Everyone stared at him, whether out of *schadenfreude* or pity he couldn't tell, but what little embarrassment he might normally have felt at that moment was completely washed out by his financial plight. The pretty lady across from him, the only one at the table who showed any kind of emotion, scrunched her lips together as if to say, "I feel your pain, and I'm so sorry."

The croupier turned the wheel again and called an end to the bets as he sped the ball on its way in the opposite direction. The ball rolled, seemingly endlessly, but finally dropped into a slot on the opposite side of the wheel from the number twenty-two. Sachs had lost even this precious five euros. At least the color was black again. That was a small consolation.

Sachs had essentially no money left. He no longer could pay for the necessities of life. He was almost totally broke and in a foreign land, far away from home. He couldn't imagine how he could live or what he could possibly do now. He might find work as a day laborer, but he didn't even know enough French to apply for a job—assuming he knew where to apply, which he didn't. Sachs reached into his pocket and jangled the few chips that were left. About twenty, he assumed, since he had already risked five and had lost them to the casino.

Sachs took out all of these chips and placed them on the table. He counted out ten, reached over and dropped them on the green number zero. Two hours ago he had money in his pocket and a future to look forward to. His plan was to play the game logically and, if he lost a thousand euros, he could easily recover and go on with his life. But now he had lost everything, and he had only himself to blame. He tried to remember how he had allowed this to happen. What was he thinking? His disjointed thoughts cast desperately about for a cause of his plight. He vaguely recalled learning about the St. Petersburg paradox while studying the irrational exuberance of those who played the stock market. The paradox was based on a game of chance not unlike the game he had just played—and lost.

The game was simple enough. You repeatedly toss a coin until heads appears and you win the pot. The pot starts at one dollar and doubles whenever tails appears, so that if heads appears on the first toss, you win one dollar; if it appears on the second toss, you win two; if it appears on the third toss you win four—and so forth. If you were lucky enough to see a string of ten tails before heads appeared, you receive five hundred and twelve dollars for the price you paid to play the game.

Sachs recalled calculating that the sum of the probabilities was infinite, so that a player would surely come out ahead in the long run, no matter how much he had paid to play and no matter how many times he had to play to beat the system. There would eventually come a time when the payoff would be greater than whatever total sum the player had paid to play the many games.

The paradox was that most people would pay no more than five dollars to play. Risk takers would go to twenty-five, but not much more. A rational person would realize that, no matter how much money one paid to play each game, you could always get all of your money back and then some if you played long enough. But people weren't rational. Why?

The answer was found deep in human nature. Simply put, losing and winning weren't equal. People hated to lose money more than they liked to win it.

Sachs had just learned the hard way why this was so. After millions of years of feeling the consequences of losing, risk aversion was indelibly written in the genes.

Sachs would never take a chance like this again. If only . . .

The little ball dropped down from its groove on the side of the roulette wheel. It bounced twice in the slots and landed on the green number zero. Sachs stared in disbelief as the wheel kept turning, carrying with it the ball around and around as it hung on in the green. He had won, finally!

Sachs looked up and saw the lady smiling at him, beaming, really, feeling his elation. No one else showed any emotion except one person: the arrogant croupier. Normally aloof and robot-like, he could not conceal a frown as he counted out three hundred and fifty euros worth of chips and pushed them forward toward Sachs.

Sachs tried not to reveal the enormous relief he felt as he took his chips and quickly left the table. It was protocol to tip the croupier at this point, but Sachs was not about to part with any of his winnings. He felt completely drained, but he had come away with enough money to survive another day. He had learned a lesson the hard way—a lesson that would stay with him the rest of his life. He would never play a game of pure chance again.

CHAPTER 14

Sachs pressed the speed dial for Dakota Berk and waited impatiently for his call to go through. Glancing at the caller ID, she picked up on the first ring. "Hello, Gunther. What's going on over there?"

"Have you heard about Tom Smith?"

"Yeah. He's dead. So what?" Berk replied flatly.

"So, what's going to happen to his company? Who owns it now?"

"I'm way ahead of you. He's got a sister, Amy. She lives on their old man's farm and scratches out a living."

"I'm thinking of buying RoadWheels," Tom announced.

"Oh, really? Why?"

"It's a good opportunity. I'll have to act fast, though. Don't want a bidding war."

"Well, back off," Berk snapped. "For reasons you'll never know and I'm not going to tell you, you interfere in this and I'll break your legs."

"What?" Sachs remarked, taken aback. "Who the hell are you to tell me what I can and can't do?"

"I don't fuck around, Gunther. My turf."

"Your turf? *You* back off. It's a business opportunity, and I'm going for it."

"Well, I'm telling you you can't have it. It's mine."

"I'm quite amused, Berk. We'll see about that." Sachs was about to end the call but thought better of it and waited for a response. When it didn't come, he added, "Hope you don't mind a bidding war" and pressed *end*. A second later, his phone rang and he pressed *answer*.

"Don't you ever, *ever* hang up on me again." Berk's tone of voice made Sachs's blood run cold. *She really is a bitch,* he thought.

"Sorry, Dakota. You wanted to say something?"

"I don't think you got the message. Butt out, you SOB. My turf. Got it?"

"And if I don't?"

"*Don't try me,* Gunther."

"You are really something, you know? It's a free country here in Canada. More so even than your stinking US."

"It's not so free as you may think. I know where you live, remember."

"Is that a threat?"

"No, it's a warning. Butt out and you can live a long, prosperous life."

Sachs was incredulous. "And if I don't *butt out,* as you say?"

"I wouldn't want to be you." Berk's menacing tone said even more than her words.

"Okay, I guess we got off on the wrong foot. Let's start again. Maybe this will help: tell me, why are you so interested in Smith's business?"

"Let's just say my business depends on Smith's business."

"Okay. That's a start. So what's the connection?"

"Don't even go there, Gunther. I'm telling you one last time—that company's *mine.* You get it?"

"You're in the gold business. So what do you want with RoadWheels?"

Dakota Berk rang off, leaving Sachs dumbly holding the phone to his ear. He sat there in stunned silence for a moment and then angrily slammed the phone down. Extremely annoyed by Berk's attitude, he asked his assistant to find the number for an Amy, nee Smith, who lived on a farm in Connecticut where Tom's memorial service took place. Five minutes later she came back with the phone number.

Gunther placed a call but got no answer. Still annoyed, he figured she would not return his cold call, so he left no message. The best and maybe the only way to reach her, he thought, would be to show up on her doorstep. Was it worth it, or should he let it go? Ordinarily he wouldn't make such an effort to make contact with a stranger on the off chance that it could lead to a business opportunity, but Berk's interest in this very same company had forced his hand. He told his assistant to arrange for his private jet to take him to Hartford. If there were an opportunity here at all, he would at least have a chance to beat that bitch.

During the short flight to Hartford, Sachs took a crash course in Tom's business, RoadWheels. His assistant had stuffed his briefcase with both historical data and business reports, and he skimmed through all of these materials while sitting in the comfortable cabin, his steward filling and refilling his cup with strong coffee. By the time he stepped off the plane and climbed into a limo to drive to the farm, he had the background he needed to make an intelligent play for the company. The business was worth a lot, he had learned—a lot more than he had ever imagined—although the figures were sketchy.

When approaching the farm, Sachs asked his driver to first drive by it so that he could assess the lay of the land. What he saw as he did so was a working dairy farm, with the usual run-down buildings in need of both repair and about three coats of paint. No showplace here, but it appeared operational. Amy was not scratching out a living below the poverty line, but she was also clearly not well-to-do. This seemed odd for a person who just had inherited a going business worth millions of dollars.

After passing by the farm, Sachs asked his driver to turn around and stop at the farmhouse. When the limo finally came to a halt he stepped out and walked up to the door. Taking a deep breath to clear his mind, he knocked three times. There was no doorbell. The door swung open and there stood an attractive woman of indeterminate age with an inquiring look on her face. "Hello. You are?"

"Gunther Sachs. I'm from Toronto. I was in the neighborhood and just dropped by to pay my respects."

Assuming that Sachs was a friend of Alonzo, who she knew also came from Toronto, Amy invited him in.

"Did you know Tom?" she asked politely after she offered and Tom accepted another cup of coffee. He thought, at least, that the caffeine sharpened his wits, so to maintain his mind at a consistently high level each day, he progressed from cup to cup.

"Only slightly. But I'm a great admirer of his, and of the business he built."

"I see. I've come to learn only recently that he had a lot of friends and admirers."

"I'm so sorry for your loss. This must be a terrible time for you."

"It has not been easy. But he's in a better place now."

Both Sachs and Amy were feeling a bit weird at this point, because both were lying through their teeth. Amy had somehow gotten through the charade of the memorial service, but the strangeness of it was beginning to tell on her. Sachs was somewhat better at lying because he practiced it constantly in his business, but this face-to-face fibbing with a supposedly grieving sister made him oddly uncomfortable. He had a faint feeling this meeting wasn't real, but he pressed on.

"He was a good man. He knew that to have a friend, a man must be one."

"Everyone thought of him as a friend, that's true," Amy agreed.

"To him, all people were created equal; he treated everyone with dignity."

"So true. Everyone was equal: men or women, rich or poor, black or white, athletic or disabled."

"He felt that everyone had within himself the power to make this a better world."

"He always looked for the best in people."

"And he had an abiding faith. He used to say, 'God put the firewood there, but every man must gather and light it himself.'" Sachs had read that in one of the papers his assistant had given him.

"You must have known him well. I have never heard that, but it sounds just like him."

"It was a privilege to know him." Sachs did not want to lie right to Amy's face—he had never met the man and, in fact, didn't know him at all. But this statement seemed appropriate.

"I'm glad you came," Amy volunteered, truthfully.

"What's going to happen to his business?" Sachs asked, seemingly as an afterthought.

"I don't know. It hasn't been resolved." Amy deflected the question and stood up to lead the stranger to the door or at least change the subject.

"It will need some attention," Sachs commented off-handedly.

"Yes, I guess. We haven't given it much thought."

"Will the company be for sale?" Sachs asked, trying his best to stay on course with his agenda but not wanting to seem pushy to this person who was still in mourning.

"I don't think so," Amy replied and walked him to the door.

"It must be very valuable."

"I don't know. How valuable would you think?" Amy was in fact a bit curious about this, and here was a businessman who just might have some idea.

"I'd say around five hundred."

"Is that all?" Amy asked, her disappointment clearly showing in her demeanor. For a moment, Sachs thought he had made a serous mistake in saying this number.

"You think it's higher?"

"I'd say it was at least double that."

"I suppose you're right. Yes, maybe it *is* worth a billion."

"*Billion?!* I thought you just said five hundred thousand."

"Five hundred *thousand*? No, no. I meant five hundred *million*! But I agree, the number is more like a billion." Sachs was beginning to think he'd just entered the twilight zone.

Amy was totally flustered now, but did her best to cover it up. "Well, whatever," she said, opening the door to usher Sachs out. "It was so nice of you to drop by like this."

"If you do consider selling, please contact me." Sachs handed her his business card. "A billion dollars is a lot of money."

"No, sir, I wouldn't. Not for all the money in China." Amy glanced at the card. "Have a nice trip back to Toronto!"

When Sachs left, Amy thought a moment and shook her head from side to side. "That's just amazing," she said under her breath as a fond image of her older brother came briefly to mind. Knowing her brother, she had a feeling that within a few years the business would be worth ten times more.

CHAPTER 15

Tom and Toronto headed back to the United States to start their investigation of the suspicious Mini Coopers that were riding the RoadWheels. Tom drove the tractor this time, although Toronto had driven when traveling west from Tom's family homestead to Toronto's house. When they stopped at the US customs station at the border, Toronto looked over and gave the high sign to his US counterpart in the booth. "Alonzo!" the man shouted, recognizing him instantly. "Wazzup?"

"I've got a new job!" Toronto shouted back, smiling broadly as Tom handed his and Toronto's passports to the customs official.

"You mean you quit Canadian customs? For real?"

"Yup! Tryin' something new. But I'll never forget you guys."

"You keep in touch, understand? We won't forget you either, buddy."

Without looking at them, the man handed the two passports back to Tom.

"What's in the back?" he queried, more to Toronto than to Tom.

"My friend here and I live in this rig," Toronto replied. "It's got everything: bedroom, kitchen, office, you name it—and that's just upstairs. Downstairs is the garage with our cars and my Indian motorcycle."

"No kidding?" the man replied, casting an appreciative eye at the huge trailer. "Jeez, that's neat! Life on the open road—I can see why you jumped ship."

"Wanna look?"

"Nah. If we can't trust you, who can we trust? Get going!" The man waved them on through.

"Thanks! But I'll be baaack!" Toronto shouted, mimicking the accent of the Terminator as Tom fired up the big diesel. Tom slowly eased the rig out of the customs area and then accelerated onto the superhighway, heading south.

After traveling a few miles in silence, Toronto spoke. "Would you like to stop and look where they ambushed you? The exit is just a mile or two up ahead."

"Uh, no. I'm not sure I want to relive that . . ."

"Okay. Suit yourself. It might be therapeutic, though."

Tom drove on in silence for a short time and then turned his head toward Alonzo and nodded. "You're right. We should stop." Without another word he eased off on the gas when they approached the exit, drove carefully down the exit ramp, and turned right onto Whitehaven Road. "It was right about there," Toronto said, pointing to a spot up ahead.

"Yes, I think I remember. It's still a bit of a blur in my mind." Tom brought the rig to a halt just short of the place where the attack occurred. "I remember feeling really scared."

The two climbed out of the cab and walked up. Tom stood there silently and took a deep breath on the desolate spot where he was knifed in the chest and left for dead. Toronto gave him an understanding look and stood next to him, saying nothing, waiting for Tom to speak first. It was a full minute that seemed like five before Tom said anything. What he said was a heartfelt "Thank you for saving my life."

If the two had been women, they would have hugged. But they just stood there for a time, looking away from each other, not knowing what to feel or to do.

"I've always wondered," Tom began, somewhat hesitantly. "How did I end up in the Toronto hospital?"

"It was just a hunch I had. It didn't feel right when I saw you turn around that day and head back with those two black cars following. So I asked to be relieved from my post at customs and took off on my motorcycle. When I finally found you it was almost too late. Those guys had knifed you really bad. I lifted you into the back of your van and drove it like crazy to the only hospital I knew: the one in Toronto."

"How could you get me across the border? I didn't have a passport."

"I kind of smuggled you in. On the way I called ahead to my friends at customs, and they let me through. They even gave me a police escort, with sirens and everything, to take us the rest of the way."

"I'm greatly in your debt."

"Sometimes hunches pay off. I'm kind of lucky that way."

"Lucky? I'm the one who was lucky."

"No, I mean I get these hunches sometimes. They just come to me."

Tom looked at Toronto for a beat without speaking, taking this in. Finally, he continued, "Just one more thing—what happened to your motorcycle?"

"I left it right here when I took you in the van," Toronto replied, pointing to a spot right next to where they were standing, "But I called Bonnie right away. She came to the hospital and picked me up. While you were in surgery, she brought me back here and it was still right where I left it. By the time we returned to the hospital, you were out of surgery and in recovery."

"I'm glad no one took it."

"Me too. I love that motorcycle. It's a 1940 Indian Scout in mint condition. They used them during World War II. Indian made a bigger one too, called the Chief, but I prefer this. It's more maneuverable."

"You have to let me ride it sometime."

"My cycle is your cycle."

Toronto eventually dropped his eyes and began looking carefully and critically at the ground. *"Kemo sabe,"* he said, using an expression of endearment he recalled from stories of the Lone Ranger he heard in his childhood. "I've been trained by Canadian customs to look for evidence. Let me see if I can find anything. Anything at all."

"I doubt if you will. Those men were professionals. They wouldn't leave anything behind."

"Still, you never know," Toronto remarked as he began methodically to comb the area.

After a while, however, he gave up the endeavor, but not before asking, "Did you struggle with them before they stabbed you?"

"I don't think so. I don't think I had a chance."

"Whatever signs of a scuffle there might have been, they're long gone," Toronto said, standing at a place on the side of the road where the dirt rippled slightly. "But let me take a look." He drew a single leather glove out of his right pocket and put it on his right hand. He then squatted down and, with his gloved hand, ran his fingers over the earth in the area of the ripples. Parting and sifting the soil he thought he saw something. Clearing the soil away he uncovered a small object. It blended in among the stones, but it was definitely man-made. Toronto carefully picked it up using his fingers as tweezers and inspected it before standing up. "Looks like a Kocopelli, only with a strange head," he said, handing it to Tom.

Tom took a handkerchief from his pocket and held it open in the palm of his hand to receive the object. He stared at it, trying to figure out what it was. It appeared to be a gold lapel pin, although it was dark and tarnished. The shape was a symbol of some kind that neither Tom nor Toronto recognized.

"Maybe there *was* a scuffle," Tom thought aloud. "I really don't remember. I might have accidentally pulled this pin off the man who grabbed me from behind."

"It must have come from one of those men. How else could it have fallen in just that spot?"

Tom pocketed the handkerchief with the pin, and he and Toronto walked slowly back to the tractor-trailer rig, both lost in deep thought about the discovery. Toronto realized one thing from this first day on his new journey: he desperately wanted to assist Tom in bringing to justice those who had attacked him, but they were a long way from finding out who these men were and why they did what they did.

CHAPTER 16

Seymour Schuster, now in his seventies, was less than a year old when a Quaker couple in England obtained his exit from Nazi Germany at the time of the Holocaust. Although his foster parents were working class, they managed to scrape together and pay the British government the required fifty-pound-sterling guarantee and also pay for their trip to Munich, where they received the little baby from the arms of his Jewish parents barely a year after the horrors of the Kristallnacht. Although the Quaker couple continued to write them letters, thanking them for their blessed gift, Sy's birth parents were never heard from again.

Sy knew nothing of this, of course, but his foster parents explained this sad heritage to him as soon as he was old enough to understand. They had also decided that Sy should keep his Jewish name. While this was done out of respect for his birth parents, it may not have been the best thing for Sy, who at a very tender age began to ponder the significance of the Holocaust and what it meant to be a Jew. The more he thought about it, the angrier he grew: angry at Hitler, angry at the Nazis, angry at the Germans, angry at humanity, and angry at God for letting this happen. In the end, he just couldn't believe there could be a God at all, or *he* would have intervened.

Without a God, who were we? If people allowed the Holocaust to happen, who are we? Without God, without humanity, was there any purpose to our existence? In the end, were our lives merely a random event at a random time? From among the six million Jews who were extinguished, why was he allowed to live?

Sy grew up in Liverpool, where his adoptive parents had their modest home. Calling them "adoptive parents" was perhaps a misnomer, because no formal adoption ever came to pass. The moment they received the little Seymour from his tearful birth mother in Munich, the baby became and was treated as their own child. Knowing the dangers of staying in Germany, Sy's birth parents had performed one last act of sacrifice, writing an emergency letter to a friend in England asking to have someone take, protect, and nurture their baby. This friend looked for a suitable family by searching through the public list of conscientious objectors, and this Quaker couple quickly agreed to do their part.

A British citizen thus "by birth" but unsatisfied with his life in Liverpool at age sixteen, Sy Schuster took what little cash he found in his father's pocket one evening and left home, never to return. Booking steerage passage on the very next steamer to Canada, he settled first in Toronto, where he took odd jobs. From there it was a simple matter to cross the border into the United States to seek his fortune in the nearest major city: the city of Buffalo.

Buffalo was struggling at the time to provide services for its citizens and in its run-down condition was sorely in need of renewal. At the young age of twenty-one, Sy found himself his life's work. He was at the right place at the right time to start a construction company, and, to give himself a competitive edge, he decided to undercut the prices of his competitors and call his company Cut-Rate Contracting. It was a winning strategy for a while, but it meant paying his workers no more than minimum wage without any benefits or the possibilities of promotion, and one by one they left him, telling their friends of their bad experience, so that Sy eventually had difficulty in hiring and keeping qualified personnel.

Sy then hit upon a brilliant plan: he would import Spanish-speaking workers from south of the US border and give them steady work. They would be glad to have jobs and would not complain about the low wages or the fact that they had no opportunity for advancement. They would work hard for ten to twenty years while they were in their prime, and, when they reached age forty or fifty and could not continue to do the heavy lifting, they would return to their home country. They received no pension for their old age, but that was not Sy's concern. Because of their limited ability to function in a country that did not understand their language, these men were a captive workforce. They turned out to possess some amazing talents and skills, and, best of all, they were willing to work, and work hard, for the legal minimum wage.

Sy initially called the Department of Immigration to learn how he could obtain work visas for tradesmen from Central and South America.

He then contracted with an employment agency in Mexico to select men willing to spend a few years away from home earning, so he said, "a living wage." The workers who first took the chance to come to the United States sent money as well as messages home reporting on their good fortune. Except during the frozen winter months when there was precious little work and they had to while away their time inside their small apartments, the conditions in Buffalo were much better than those in their home country.

Once this favorable word got back to their families, the employment agency was no longer needed. The workers arrived by themselves, at first in only a tentative trickle but then in ever-greater numbers. Buffalo became a destination of choice, with one family telling another that this was the place to go. The first ones who came were legal, but thereafter most were not; however, this made no difference to Sy. He ran a cash business and paid them off the books to avoid reporting their employment and paying the required withholding taxes. What was important to him was that he had sufficient workers to meet the requirements of the ever-increasing number of jobs he was able to attract, in part due to his reputation for reduced cost and in part because, as he repeatedly told his customer base, "No job is too big or too small for Cut-Rate Construction."

To keep costs down and keep his profits up, Sy became more and more Scrooge-like with his company's money. As far as he was concerned, taxes were money poured down the drain and therefore to be avoided by all possible means. Sy quickly found that if he expensed *everything*, including his and his family's personal expenses and the company's ordinary business expenses, he could substantially reduce the reportable income on his K-1 tax form. Also, by placing cash receipts in his personal bank account rather than the corporate account, he could supplement his income without any tax implications at all. This was a double win for him, and, in his mind, he would be stupid not to do it.

His accountant took a dim view of some of his personal expenses, such as his family's routine living expenses and even travel expenses for family vacations, but he soon learned to hide these. What was the difference between gas for his trucks and gas for his wife's car?

As far as his home was concerned, he was in the *construction* business after all, and who would know or care whether his men worked on a legitimate paying job or worked on his house? If anyone ever asked, and no one did, he could always contend his company worked out of his home office. Over time, his house became bigger and better until, after twenty years of successive "home improvements," it rivaled the homes of many celebrities in Hollywood.

Sy also discovered, to his astonishment, at first, how easy it was to get contracting work from the government. Construction jobs were awarded by politicians, and politicians had a seemingly endless need for money. At the outset, Sy issued company checks as campaign contributions; however, he quickly learned that these were not deductible expenses. He therefore switched to cash contributions, directly to those in the position to assist his company, because these came right off the top from his unreported cash income. He justified this largesse as being quite the same as campaign contributions, but of course he understood that such "gifts" were illegal. He did not really care who got elected, as long as the recipient was aware of what was expected of him. As Sy knew, the recipient preferred the cash because he was free to spend the money as he chose.

Cut-Rate Contacting Inc. thrived for forty years and grew steadily in size until it became one of the largest businesses in Buffalo. Due to its economic importance to the community, not to mention its being a source of financial support for local government officials, politicians fawned all over Sy and he was named Buffalo Man of the Year three years in a row.

One might think that this success would have satisfied this man who grew a bit richer every year, but greed does not appear to have limits and, sadly, Sy became no wiser through the years. In order to increase profits while keeping cost estimates to his customers below what his competitors could possibly charge, he was forced to reduce his labor costs. Since he already paid the minimum wage, the only way he could do this was to "forget" now and then to pay his workers, and when anyone complained, as a few of them did, to punish them by refusing to give these ungrateful little people further work. Since most of them were illegal, they couldn't seek redress in the courts; however, even if they did, a court could only award them their meager back pay.

After forty years of conducting business in the community in this way, Sy felt almost untouchable by the long arm of the law. No matter how far he departed from the rules of fair play, no matter how much he exploited his workers, he felt no guilt or shame. He was smarter than anyone else, so he was *entitled*. And, he was sure, there was no God looking over his shoulder.

CHAPTER 17

Tom and Toronto returned to the superhighway and headed south to the New York State Thruway. Shortly before noon, they pulled into Bonnie's station, where Tom had first learned about the Mini Cooper gang.

When she saw them arrive she ran over to the tractor-trailer and stood on the tarmac, watching and waiting for Tom to shut down the engine and climb down out of the cab. Toronto climbed down on the opposite side and came around the front of the rig. Bonnie shook Tom's hand warmly and then gave Toronto a big hug. "You've got to call me sometime," she said coquettishly. "You're still my boyfriend, you know."

"Well, I uh . . ." Toronto shot Tom a sheepish glance. "I'm kinda busy right now."

"Don't worry. I'm good with it. It's not like you found another girl."

Toronto gave no reply and left the subject unfinished. Expecting none, Bonnie turned to Tom with a suddenly serious expression. "I believe we have a small problem here."

"You want to go inside," Tom said, motioning to the side door of the big rig, "where it's private?"

"That won't be necessary. Everyone knows about this, but there's nothing we can do. We hired a contractor to redo our lounge and bathrooms for our customers here. He was the lowest bidder and had a reputation for excellent work. But now we find out he's hiring day laborers from Buffalo and not paying them."

"Why don't they sue him? If they're owed money, they can nail him in small claims court."

"That's the problem. They can't do that and he knows it. First of all, they only speak Spanish, and they don't know the system. But more important to them, they need the work, desperately. They think they'll never be hired by any contractor if they sued one of them."

"Have you talked to the contractor?" Toronto asked.

"Yes, I told him what I heard, but he denies it."

"Maybe he *is* paying them," Tom remarked. "I can't believe an employer would ever do such a thing."

"Oh, yes," Bonnie said. "These contractors do it all the time."

"What do they tell the workers?"

"They always say they haven't gotten paid for the job yet so they don't have the money. But when they do get paid, after the job is all finished, they never come back to pay the men. They just conveniently forget about what they owe them."

"This sounds like a job for Alonzo," Toronto said. Both Bonnie and Tom looked at him blankly.

"*Alonzo*?" Bonnie quipped. "Who's Alonzo?"

"You know, your old boyfriend? How quickly he's forgotten."

"I didn't mean it the way it sounded," Bonnie backpedaled. "I was just trying to make a joke."

"What do you have in mind?" Tom wanted to know.

"I speak Spanish. I grew up in a Spanish home, remember? That was my first language."

"You'll talk to them."

"I can do better than that. I'll become one of them. I'll hang out on the street where they live and get hired by your contractor. We'll see if he pays me. Then it won't just be his word against theirs."

"You can wear a wire," Bonnie suggested, warming up to the idea.

"You'll have to be very careful," Tom cautioned. "You could end up like I did when he finds out what you did."

"Hey, you can come to my rescue!" Toronto beamed brightly.

Tom cracked a smile. "Right! It'll give me a chance to pay you back," he said but then immediately turned serious again. "Let's first go over to Buffalo and see what's there. I want to try and find out what's going on before I let you put yourself in harm's way."

Tom, Toronto, and Bonnie spent the next half hour unloading Tom's van from the back of the tractor-trailer and then headed toward Buffalo to find out where Bonnie's contractor picked up his workers. "The whole city is desperate for work," Bonnie explained on the way. "Unemployment is way over 20 percent, and in the Hispanic community it's even higher than that.

"There's an area where most of the Hispanic immigrants live. They've been coming up here for some time from Mexico, Guatemala, Honduras, and even from South America to find work, but things are really bad right now, and they just keep coming."

Bonnie sat in the front passenger seat and gave Tom directions as he drove. On the way, Tom broached the Mini Cooper mystery. "Are those cars still coming in?" he asked, hoping the answer would be negative.

"They stopped for about a month, but then they started up again about the time your death was announced and made the front-page news," Bonnie responded matter-of-factly. "We get more cars than ever now. Three or four a day, I imagine."

"Are those black Mercedes still around when they arrive?"

"They don't make themselves obvious, but they're there. I spot them once in a while. Whenever I do, I shudder to think what they did to you."

The mere mention of the black cars caused bits and pieces of the events leading up to the attack to come trickling back into Tom's mind. "I . . . I think I can remember something. Something I'd forgotten before. One of those guys had a really distinctive voice. It was deep and rough like gravel. I believe I'd recognize it if I heard it again. In fact, I'm sure I would."

"Bingo!" Toronto shouted from the backseat. "I've heard a voice like that before too. He's come through Canadian customs with a black Mercedes. I'll bet I can find out who he is. I can ask my buddies there to look in the computer system."

"Much as I hate to say it, you two make a really good team. Am I going to lose a boyfriend here?"

"Whoa! Hold on there. You can't get rid of me that easily."

Bonnie and Toronto both turned to stare at Tom to see where he stood. He let go of the steering wheel for a brief moment and held his hands high in the air. "Don't look at me! I'm hoping to be invited to your wedding."

Bonnie breathed an exasperated sigh. "Wedding? Who said anything about a *wedding*? I just want to know if I'm still entitled to girlfriend benefits."

By this time they were fast approaching downtown Buffalo on the superhighway, and Bonnie needed to focus again on navigation. "Let's get off right there," she said, pointing to the sign for the next exit. "At the end of the ramp, take a right, and it will take us to the street where all the contractors pick up their laborers." Tom followed her directions, and in just a few minutes they were traveling slowly down a relatively wide street in a run-down commercial neighborhood. On both sides of the street stood men in dirty blue jeans, some with hoodies in gray or dark blue, but most in just T-shirts, mostly colored gray, even as a cool wind blew through off Lake Erie. A few of the men were in small groups but most stood forlornly alone, looking anxiously out at each passing vehicle. As Tom drove by, he sensed the longing in the many eyes that were fixed on him. He also felt a sharp pang of compassion for these men who had risked everything to travel this far north to find work to support their families. They had left their homes with nothing but the humble clothes they wore and the determination that comes from desperation: the certain knowledge that life did not owe them a living and that there was no other option but to leave. There was simply no work there. They did not own a plot of land with soil to till, nor did they own a boat with gear for fishing. They had no money and no security—not even a country that cared about them and provided the barest necessities, not to mention medical care when they became injured or sick.

Whatever hope they had, Tom realized, came from people like him and the two passengers in his van who *did* care. They were their only hope.

CHAPTER 18

"We've gotta help these guys," Toronto said from the backseat. "Just look at them. It breaks your heart."

"It's tough enough for them out there, but to work all day and not get paid . . ." Bonnie shook her head sadly. "It's unbelievable, but that's what I heard."

"I'll find out if it's true. And if it is," Toronto leaned forward and spoke directly to Bonnie, "that contractor is going *down*. One way to stop this is to make an example of him. When this gets out, this contractor might as well close up shop and join these poor people looking for jobs."

Tom, who had been silent for some time, finally spoke up. "You might fix this problem temporarily, but it won't help much in the long run. These laborers are so dependent on contractors and landscapers to give them work."

"Yes, but when they do get work, they should get paid. That's not only fair, it's also the *law*," Toronto said.

"Do you think it's safe for you to stay here and talk to these people?" Bonnie asked.

"I'm going to do better than that. I'm coming back here early tomorrow and stand on the street with these guys to beg for work."

"You don't look the part," Bonnie replied. "You're just too . . . too WMC."

"WMC? What's WMC?"

"White middle class. Hate to say it, lover boy, but you couldn't pass for a day laborer if your life depended on it."

"Now that's where you're wrong. Did you know I was an actor in my previous life?"

"An actor? Ha! You never told me you were an actor."

"So? You don't know everything about me *yet*, and it's true. I was in drama groups all through high school and college. I even took acting lessons and scored pretty big in the Toronto theater scene before, uh, settling down."

". . . with a safe government job." Bonnie added sarcastically.

"Well, yeah. A guy's gotta do what a guy's gotta do to make a living."

"And all this time I thought you were just this boring bureaucrat."

"But you loved me anyway, beautiful. That doesn't reflect too highly on *you*, now, does it?"

"I was struck by your boyish charms. What can I say?"

"Don't say anything. You've said much too much already."

"What? That I didn't believe you were an actor?"

"Yes, and also that I was boring," Toronto sniffed.

As usual in these little spats, Bonnie was allowed the last word. "Don't worry your little head about that. If I really thought you were boring, you would have known about it long ago."

Having explored the area to learn where the immigrant workers stood in wait to offer their services to the contractors and landscapers that trolled the streets, Tom turned at the next corner and steered the van back in the direction from which they came. On the way back to the RoadWheels station at the Clarence Travel Plaza, they made plans for Toronto to return the next morning as an undercover laborer.

"You have to pretend you live around there," Tom said. "You certainly can't show up in this van."

"I could ride in on my motorcycle," Toronto suggested.

"How many of these laborers have motorcycles?"

"I would say none," Bonnie replied. "One in ten might own a bicycle. They're extremely poor and most of what little money they earn they send back home to their families."

"Okay, so Tom, *you* ride my motorcycle. You bring me in and it'll look like I'm bumming a ride. You just drop me off and head back to the station."

"I'll drop you off nearby, but I'll stay around just to make sure you're safe. You can walk over to the street and join the job seekers."

"Good idea. I really don't know if they'll like me being there."

"If you get in trouble, just call and I'll come. Otherwise, you can forget about me."

"You probably won't get a job anyway," Bonnie commented. "Most of these guys don't get picked. As a matter of fact, my contractor usually brings in the same guys every day, so chances are he won't pick you. But maybe you can at least talk to some of them."

"Imagine having to stand there every day, in good weather and bad, and beg for work," Toronto remarked. "It's dehumanizing."

"And to think that my contractor might be exploiting them," Bonnie said. "That makes my blood boil."

"I'll find out one way or another. What's your contractor's name?"

"Sy Schuster. And his company's called Cut-Rate Contracting."

"You hired this guy?"

"He was cheap. What can I say?"

"Yeah, He's *cut-rate* because he gets his workers for free."

"Don't get on your high horse, buster. How was I supposed to know?"

"With a name like *Shyster*?"

"Schuster."

"All right, all right," Tom broke in. "We'll find out soon enough if he's a crook. In the meantime there are a couple of things we need to do."

"Two things?" Bonnie wanted to know.

"First, we have to find a motorcycle shop and pick up a pair of matching helmets with a built-in Bluetooth connection so we can talk to each other while we're on the road."

"Roger that. So what's the other thing?"

"We need to find a Walmart and buy a couple gray hoodies."

CHAPTER 19

Early the next morning Toronto unloaded his Indian Scout motorcycle from the back of the tractor-trailer and showed Tom the controls. It had been a long time since Tom had ridden a motorcycle—or even a bicycle, for that matter—so he was a bit apprehensive at first, but his love for adventure far outweighed any thoughts he might have had that riding a motorcycle was possibly more dangerous than sitting behind the wheel of a one-hundred-ton tractor-trailer.

"My Indian Scout was born with a lot of power, but I added a turbocharger," Toronto explained. "You can't beat it now. When this model first came out in 1920, it was the racing bike of choice, and it hasn't changed much since. The 1928 Scout was used by all the stunt riders of its time, and, because of the unique weight and balance, it's still seen on the stunt circuit today."

Tom threw his leg over the cycle and sat on the seat holding the handlebars, grinning from ear to ear. "This is going to be fun!"

"Before I get on behind you, you'd better take it out for a spin," Toronto suggested, half in jest but also half seriously. "It's like riding a horse. You have to get comfortable with it."

"Giddyup, Scout!" Tom shouted as he gunned the engine and roared out over the tarmac on the parking lot. "Let's go with Toronto!" could be heard as he headed away. Tom took a few laps around the lot and then came back to the truck, where Toronto was standing. "Yippee!" he yelled. "I want one of these!"

"You need a bigger one, like the Indian Chief."

"They still make these things?"

"The Indian Motorcycle Company has been through tough times, but the brand survived. They make some great bikes now. You should check out the Chief Dark Horse. They say it's definitely not for the faint of heart."

"Can I get a White Horse?"

"Just get a Dark Horse and paint it white!"

Tom took off again and practiced riding for another ten minutes. When he felt he was ready for the road he stopped long enough for Toronto to climb on behind him.

"Hold on tight. Here we gooo!" Tom spoke into the microphone in his helmet as he released the clutch and the Indian Scout took off like a pebble from a slingshot. Toronto held on to Tom's waist for dear life, wondering if this motorcycle ride with his inexperienced *Kemosabe* would be his last. After traveling a few miles on the superhighway, however, Toronto began to feel a bit safer and relaxed his grip.

When they reached the Buffalo exit on the thruway, Tom suddenly realized they had to pay the toll and didn't have a ticket showing where they had entered the highway. "Uh-oh. What happens now?" he said as they approached the tollbooth. "Are we going to have to pay for traveling all the way from New York City? When I tell them I don't have a ticket, they'll never believe we started this trip from a tractor-trailer parked at the Clarence Travel Plaza."

"I'm way ahead of you. Last night I programmed my EZ-Pass to show we got on at the thruway entrance right before this one. Just keep going. The machine will read the EZ-Pass even though it's in my pocket. You'll see."

"You programmed it?"

"Sure. The system will think we got on the highway ten minutes ago."

"You can do that?"

"Sure. In my previous life, I was a computer engineer."

"You said you were an actor."

"That too, but that was my avocation. I studied engineering at college."

"You have any other talents I should know about?"

"I have a black belt in karate. Does that count?"

"Might come in handy. What else have you got?"

"I'm a pretty good magician, and also—"

"You can stop there. I was just joking. You also saved my life, remember? That counts for everything in my book."

The two men rode through the EZ-Pass gate at the toll plaza, and the green light came on, showing the toll had been paid. As they continued, the secondary road leading to Buffalo became suddenly rougher, and the cycle bounced up and down as they rode along.

"I forgot to tell you, the suspension is not so good on this thing," Toronto said into his vibrating helmet. Toronto's voice vibrated also.

Tom, not used to the rough ride, held tight to the handlebars and managed to utter, "I . . . I'm not so . . . sure . . . I like . . . this, Tonto."

"Name's Toronto. At least it was a minute ago."

"Uh . . . Tonto. It's . . . easier . . . to say." Tom quickly slowed down so the ride was smoother.

"Yeah, well, *Tonto* means *stupid* in Spanish. You can call me Toronto or my real name, Alonzo, but not Tonto. Anything but that."

When they came near to the neighborhood of the day laborers Toronto got off the motorcycle, left his helmet with Tom, and walked the rest of the way. He lifted the hood of his gray hoodie over his head so it covered all but his face and tried to fit in as he sauntered slowly down the street where the laborers were standing, waiting for jobs. He walked up to a small group who were talking together and gave a greeting, *"Buenos dias,"* with a friendly smile. They stared at him strangely, as if he had come from another planet—which he actually did, in a way—and Toronto held his breath.

Time seemed to stand still as the men studied him carefully, trying to figure out whether this newcomer was friend or foe, until finally one of them smiled back and replied in Spanish, "You new here?"

"*Sí.* I came to visit some friends," he said, also in Spanish but with a definite American accent.

This seemed to break the ice, and suddenly everyone was smiling and talking at once.

Toronto told them his real name, Alonzo Sierra, and said he had moved to down the States from Toronto, which was indeed partly true.

After a brief friendly exchange of small talk, the first one who had spoken to him, who seemed to be a leader of the group, eventually volunteered his name and asked the critical question. "I'm Darwin," he said. "You looking for work?"

"I have family back home." Alonzo intentionally avoided saying that his family lived in Toronto. The men nodded. They too had families they supported back home.

"Do they cheat you here too?" Alonzo asked, hesitantly.

The men made quick eye contact with each other, as if to check whether they should open up to this stranger, and then Darwin, the spokesman for the group, replied, "Yes. There is one man. Watch out for him. He has a company, Cut-Rate Contracting. He doesn't pay sometimes. We don't like to work for him, but he gets many jobs and comes here every day."

"You do the work but he doesn't pay?"

"He says he'll pay later when he gets the money, but then he forgets."

"Why don't you remind him?"

"If we say we want our money he gets mad and does not ask us to work anymore."

"Has this happened to you?"

"Yes, but no more. He does not pick me."

"How about the rest of you? He does not pick you?"

Everyone in the group looked at each other and nodded their heads. They had all asked for money at one time or another and now they didn't get work from the Cut-Rate man.

While they stood there talking, one pickup truck after another drove slowly by, occasionally stopping to pick up workers. One of them halted right next to Darwin's group, and the driver asked for two men. The group spoke briefly, discussing who should go; finally, two of the men walked over, climbed onto the back of the pickup, and sat down on the open flatbed amid the clutter of lawn care equipment.

As this truck drove off, a white-panel truck appeared in the distance, coming toward them from the opposite direction and cruising the street like a sleazy John trolling for working girls. Written in red, bold letters on the side of the truck was:

CUT-RATE CONTRACTING, INC.
No job is too big or too small
www.cutratecontracting.com

When he approached, the driver saw Darwin and would have kept on going except that Alonzo ran into the street in front of the vehicle, waving his hands furiously. "I need work!" he shouted in English, but with his best imitation Spanish accent.

The driver stared critically at him through the windshield, seeming to be making a split-second decision whether or not to run him over. He eventually shrugged his shoulders and braked to a stop, just short of where Alonzo was standing. "You do construction?" he barked back, leaning out the window.

"That's what I do best," Alonzo replied proudly and feigned a bow.

"Then get in the back." The driver waived his hand to emphasize that workers rode in the back. Only the privileged white people got to ride comfortably in the plush front seat.

CHAPTER 20

In the Cut-Rate Construction van riding to the construction site, which he knew would be at the RoadWheels station on the New York State Thruway, Alonzo spoke in Spanish with the other workers riding with him. After introducing himself and asking their names, he began, ever so gingerly, to probe into the reputation of Cut-Rate.

"You like working for Cut-Rate?"

The four other men looked at each other. For a moment, it looked as if no one would say anything, but eventually one of them replied, also in Spanish.

"No, we don't. The boss man pays sometimes, and sometimes not."

"That's what I heard. Then why do you work for him?"

"We are very poor. We have nothing. We need the work."

"Aren't there other contractors that hire you?"

"Not so many. Cut-Rate is getting the most jobs around here. Others have gone out of business."

"Maybe that's because Cut-Rate doesn't pay you, so they're cheaper than the others."

"Maybe. But we have seen things."

"What things?"

"The boss man. Mr. Schuster, he has much money. He uses it to get what he wants."

"Have you seen him . . . pay people off?"

Again the workers looked at each other, and hesitated. Finally another one of the four said, "Sí."

"What people? Government people?"

"Sí."

"Have you told anyone about this?"

The men looked at each other again.

"We all know. The man is bad. But we need work."

"I understand. I've heard that if you tell anyone he won't hire you."

"And this man, Mr. Schuster, he is friends with the police. They will do nothing."

"He pays them too?"

Again the men checked with each other before continuing.

"We think. We have not seen."

Alonzo thought for a moment before continuing.

"There will always be work. If Cut-Rate doesn't get the jobs, another company will."

"We have trouble with other companies too."

"You do?"

"Some of them. Some of them pay us well. No problems."

"What happens when you can't work? What if you get hurt or you get sick?"

"If we don't work, we get no pay."

"Do you know a doctor who can help you?"

The men looked at each other and then shook their heads. This time another one spoke. "We have no money for a doctor or anything like that. We must send money home to our families."

"How about clothes? Where do you get your clothes?"

"We go to the Salvation Army. They help us a lot."

"What do you do for entertainment? Do you ever go to a movie?"

The men looked at each other, and then back at Alonzo, all shaking their heads. "No."

"Do you watch television?"

One of the men smiled. "Sí. There is a TV in the place we rent."

"Do you share a place?"

"We live together. It is cheaper that way."

"How many rooms are there, in the apartment building?"

The men talked together and came up with a number. "Maybe twenty," one of them said.

"So there are maybe fifty men just in your building. Are there other buildings too?"

"Sí. Many buildings like ours."

"Of all the people in your neighborhood, would you know how many have worked for Cut-Rate Contracting? Just a guess. Was it maybe one out of ten?"

The men looked at each other again, and one of them replied, "We all have worked for this man, Mr. Schuster. We have no choice."

"Really? Okay, one more question, then. Would you know about how many have not been paid when they worked for him?"

The answer came without hesitation.

"We all have this problem. He gives us work, and sometimes he pays. But many times he does not."

Alonzo thought about this as the van rumbled on toward its destination. The small group of workers also fell silent as they had come to realize the difficulties they all shared. Nothing more was said until the van came to a stop and the driver, who called himself Sam, opened the rear doors to let them climb out.

As he jumped down and trailed the driver and the other workers toward the building with the work site, Alonzo pulled up a number on his cell phone and said, "*Kemosabe*, this is Toronto. We need to talk. *Pronto.*"

CHAPTER 21

During Toronto's lunchbreak, Tom and Bonnie sat at the conference table in Tom's upstairs office in the trailer while Toronto related what he had heard. Tom and Bonnie listened intently without interrupting.

"We have two problems," Tom summarized after Toronto had finished his report. "First, the workers are not getting paid; and second, even more importantly, there is no way they can get ahead. They can't possibly better themselves."

"We can bring Schuster up on charges," Bonnie suggested, "and he'll learn a lesson in civics while he's crammed in the cooler. Today we're due to make a progress payment. He insists on getting paid in cash so he'll have the bucks to pay his workers, or so he says. If he doesn't—"

"*Cash?*" Both Tom and Toronto interrupted her at once, looking at each other, shocked.

"Guess we think alike," Tom noted with a tiny smile. "You pay him in cash? That's a guarantee he cheats on his taxes."

"Like I said, he's cheaper than the other contractors," said Bonnie defensively. "How was I to know he wasn't straight with his workers, and with Uncle Sam?"

Toronto ignored her remark and cut to the chase. "We'll find out if he pays me. If he doesn't, I can testify against him. You can testify you paid him and I'll testify he stiffed me. So we can easily fix the first problem. The second problem, though—that's a hard one. How can we really help these people?"

"Maybe we can link the two," offered Tom, thinking aloud. "Use the first problem to fix the second."

"What do you mean?" Toronto looked at him questioningly. Bonnie wondered the same.

"If Schuster is so heartless that he can stiff his own workers, we can be sure he didn't stop there. He's that kind of a guy."

"A crook, you mean?"

"You know the type. For certain people it's always 'me first.' Ignore what's fair and what's legal and assume nobody will call you on it."

"So how can we use that to help the workers?" Toronto wanted to know.

"Here's how we can do this," Tom replied, beginning an explanation. For the next half hour the three of them huddled together and worked out a plan.

*   *   *

When Sy Schuster arrived at the RoadWheels station at one o'clock to pick up his progress payment, the team was ready. Bonnie invited him into her office and shut the door. As he entered, Tom and Toronto rose from their seats to shake his hand. They were dressed in dark business suits and smiled pleasantly, at least at first, without saying a word. Tom wore the dark mirror aviator glasses that hid his identity.

"This is Agent Peter Burke and his assistant, Agent Neil Caffrey," Bonnie began. "From the FBI. They have been investigating some allegations about the management of Cut-Rate Contracting."

"Uh, allegations? What allegations? I'm not aware of any al—"

"We'll get into that," Tom replied in a firm tone, taking control of the meeting. "But first I'd like to say a few words about how the bureau views the immigrant situation.

"This country was built on the backs of immigrants. Other than the half million or so descendants of the Indians who originally lived here before we came, all of us, and I mean *all* of us, are immigrants or descendants of immigrants. No one is special or privileged or entitled in any way to treat others with disrespect or with anything other than the honor and dignity they deserve. Everyone in this country is *equal* under the law, and if you do not understand that, you have no right to be here and certainly no right to conduct business here.

"With that said, my assistant here, Agent Caffrey, and I have investigated your company finances and have uncovered some serious criminal activity. We're sure you know what I'm talking about, Mr. Schuster, since all of this activity involves you personally. So before filing charges, we're here to offer you an alternative: you will sign over your firm, Cut-Rate Contracting, to the workers you have unjustly and illegally failed to pay, or you will spend the next few years, and maybe even a lot of years, in federal prison."

"How *dare* you! I know my rights. You're trying to shake me down. What kind of FBI agents are you? How do I know you are agents, anyway? I'll bring *you* up on charges! Before I sign anything, you can be damn sure I'll want my lawyer present."

"Be careful what you say, Mr. Schuster," interjected Bonnie. "These two men know everything about you," she said, nodding in Tom's direction. "They have been investigating you for nine months now, and they have enough evidence to put you away for a long, long time. Not just your failure to pay your workers. Your private deals with government officials, your bribes, your tax evasion—*everything*."

Schuster stared alternately at Tom and Bonnie and saw nothing but determination and conviction in their faces. Toronto spoke up now and pretended to mediate.

"We have thought long and hard about what to do with you, Mr. Schuster. You are an enterprising man and could even be a valuable asset to our upstate economy if given a second chance to follow the law and play by the rules.

"But once you fall into the jaws of justice, the system will swallow you up and start digesting. It will turn you into shit and dump you down the toilet we call the penitentiary, with all the other shits of our society."

As if on cue, Tom took over the argument with the full force of his persuasion. "Your company," Tom began, looking Schuster straight in the eye, "has used unfair and unlawful means to compete with other, honest companies and make huge profits. You know that, and we know that. The question for us now is what to do about it. You can roll the dice with the criminal justice system or start over with a clean slate. Knowing you, you'll land on your feet and even maybe build a new company that is far better than Cut-Rate Contracting.

"And this time," added Tom, "you'll do it right and be able to sleep at night."

For the first time, it looked like Sy Schuster was actually listening and paying attention to what Tom was saying. "I uh . . . don't know what you're getting at. What do you want me to do? A 'second chance'? What does that mean?"

"It means you'll get to keep your house, your bank account, and even your fancy car. What you *won't* keep is your company. You can tell your family and friends you sold it if you want. They'll never need to know what went down today. They'll never have to know you gave it to the very same people that you cheated all these years. Unless, of course, you want to tell them what a good guy you are for seeing the light and doing the right thing."

"Gave it? What do you mean 'gave it'?" Schuster almost choked on the word *gave*.

"Well, not exactly 'gave it.' You are going to assign it. For one dollar."

"I . . . I guess I need my lawyer. We have to talk about this . . . to work out the language. Negotiate—"

"There's no negotiation, and the language is very simple." Tom took a single folded sheet of paper from his jacket pocket and placed it on the table in front of Schuster. Schuster opened the paper and read aloud:

"For the consideration of one dollar, duly received and hereby acknowledged, I hereby sell and assign my entire right, title, and interest in Cut-Rate Contracting Inc. ("Company") to each and all of the day laborers who worked for the Company during the five years previous to the date of execution hereof, in equal shares, share and share alike, *per stirpes*."

Schuster looked up from the document. "This is not legal. It is not clear who's getting the company."

"Your company has taken the names, addresses, and social security numbers of all the people it hired and paid, right? You were required by law to do this for tax purposes. But if you didn't, well, who are you to complain that the document is vague on who gets your stock?"

"I don't know, but . . . a lot of them are . . . illegal. They don't have social security numbers."

"If you hired them, you certainly couldn't use that fact as an excuse to void this contract."

"Okay, I'll sign it, but under protest. I'm being railroaded. This is under duress. You'll never get away with this."

"Here's a pen," Toronto said, slipping one from his shirt pocket and holding it out, smiling.

Schuster grabbed the pen, angrily scribbled his name, and shoved the paper back at Tom.

"Thank you, Mr. Schuster. You won't regret this. Oh, and I almost forgot." He pulled out his wallet and selected a one-dollar bill. "Here's your consideration for the company."

Schuster snatched the dollar that was proffered and stood up from the table, about to leave in a huff.

Bonnie, who had been sitting quietly at the table, took the paper from the table. "One final thing," she added. "I happen to be a notary public. I'll notarize this document and testify that you signed it as your free hand and deed."

CHAPTER 22

After work at the end of the day, Toronto rode back to Buffalo in the van with the four men he had come with that morning. Tom rode separately on the Indian Scout motorcycle while Bonnie stayed behind in her office and made phone calls, first to a Mexican caterer she knew and then to a Latin DJ named DJ Mills whom she found on the Internet.

On the way to their destination, Toronto asked the workers to assemble all of their colleagues together on the street for a big celebration. He didn't tell them the reason, but they didn't need one. One of the men had a cell phone and called ahead as they rode. He gave a message to someone, and by the time they arrived, the street was already filled to overflowing with immigrants from south of the border. The catering truck had arrived, and the DJ was in the process of setting up his speaker system. Anticipation was in the air. Word had traveled quickly throughout the neighborhood that this was going to be an evening to remember.

Before climbing out of the van, Toronto paid the four men in cash, time and a half, for their day of labor and told them to make sure that all of the immigrant workers, legal or illegal, came out that evening for food, fun, and fellowship.

Sam, the van driver, the "white boss man" who worked for Cut-Rate Contracting and who had shown less than due respect to these foreign "guest workers," stayed around to watch and see what was coming down. He had no clue that these indigent men, who worked hand-to-mouth— and to the mouths of their families back home—would soon be *his* bosses in the construction company.

Tom pulled up on the motorcycle and parked behind the van just as Toronto was alighting. "Let's find Darwin," he said, looking out over the milling crowd. "These men will need a leader who can speak English."

Darwin walked up to them just at that moment, appearing as if by magic.

"Darwin," Tom began, "I want to make an announcement to all of your men. It's a brief speech I need to make in English and have you interpret what I say in your own language."

"Sí. But we listen to Alonzo. He speaks our language."

"Alonzo could do it easily, but he won't be with you after today. You'll be on your own with no one else to help you, except one other person: you'll need to find a fine lawyer who can also speak Spanish. With that, and with your own native ability, you can do business in this foreign land."

"I will tell the men whatever you say."

DJ Mills had already begun to play upbeat Latin songs, and the crowd was warming to the music when Tom and Darwin walked up. Tom explained that his company had hired him to spark a great street celebration and asked for permission to use the microphone to get the party started.

"Here's a wireless mike," he offered. "You can stand on top of my car." DJ Mills, it turned out, spoke American English and was not Hispanic at all. To promote his business he enterprisingly advertised that he could play any genre of music, from the fifties rock 'n' roll to the latest hip-hop, as well as any type of Latin music, from Brazilian to Mexican mariachi.

Tom and Darwin climbed onto the roof of his SUV, and DJ Mills stopped the music. Everyone on the street fell still and looked their way. Darwin lifted the mike to his mouth and began speaking in Spanish. DJ Mills adjusted the loudness so everyone could hear every syllable.

"My new friends here and I welcome all of you. We have called you together here to celebrate a new beginning for us. To explain everything, I introduce to you this good man who has made this happen!" Darwin turned to Tom and handed him the microphone with a slight bow of his head. Tom took it with a gracious *"Muchas gracias,"* and began, in English. After every sentence, he handed the mike back to Darwin, who translated his words into Spanish. The audience stood silently listening to what Tom and Darwin were saying. They were dumbfounded by what they heard.

"My fellow *hombres*. Each and every one of us has only one life to live. We must make the most of it before it is over, leaving only your memory in the minds of your family and friends. I know that most of you were born into poverty in a place far away from here. I can only imagine what the conditions were like when you grew up, without the barest necessities that we in America take for granted—a shelter from the wind and rain, sanitation, running water, sufficient food, health care when we need it, and security when our hard work is done and we face old age.

"You have come here to seek a better life for yourselves and your families. I know it was not easy to travel this distance. You have taken a chance and endured hardships to come, and now that you're here, you give over a part of yourselves every day—you give us your labor—in the most difficult of conditions. You do the hard jobs that no American wants to do. And what do you get for this? You receive the minimum wage that the law allows.

"Sometimes even you are not paid at all. You know this, we know this, but no one seems to care. Many Americans even resent your being here, forgetting that their forefathers came here from other countries too, many under similar conditions.

"From the little wages you earn, you send half of the money back home. Wells Fargo makes a good business from your generosity to your loved ones. But even if you kept all of your wages and pooled them together, you could not make enough to start your own business and have the slimmest chance to better yourselves.

"Having told you now what you already know, let me tell you something new. As of this day, you *do* own your own business—a thriving business that *you* built with your own expertise and hard work. As of this day, all of you are equal owners of Cut-Rate Contracting. The owner, Sy Schuster, had a choice to go to jail or make things right. He chose to make things right with you and to give you his company."

Tom looked out over the sea of faces as Darwin translated this last sentence. The people looked at each other, some not comprehending what they had just heard and others thinking Tom's words must have been translated incorrectly. Again there was silence, so Tom repeated what he had just told them.

"Let me say it again. You are all owners of Cut-Rate Contracting. The prior owner, Sy Schuster, has given his shares to *you!*"

As Darwin was translating these last two sentences something like a deep roar originated from within the crowd and began to build. By the time Darwin finished these words, a sound erupted and exploded like the crash of thunder that follows a lightning bolt. The men just stood there, overwhelmed with emotion, staring and screaming at each other with tears running down their faces.

Realizing the importance of this moment, the DJ quickly chose a sentimental ballad by Selena, the Queen of *Tejano*, and sent it out through the speakers to wash over the crowd. Perhaps it was just the right song, or perhaps it triggered something within the souls of these men so far from home, but this music spoke to them as nothing else could. The feeling of relief and joy after so much hardship was almost too much for them to bear.

Tom and Darwin climbed down from the roof of the car and returned the microphone to DJ Mills. Toronto was there too, and the four of them looked out at the scene, reflecting for a moment but barely comprehending the forces they had just unleashed. These men, so long oppressed and without hope, could now take control of their own destinies and join in the life of their adopted country. They had a chance to live the American dream.

Darwin could hardly believe it himself even though he had been the one to send the announcement out to the many faces in the street. He turned to Toronto and spoke to him in Spanish, asking about Tom. "Who *is* that man?"

"Un hombre que entiende," Toronto explained. A man who understands.

As he climbed onto his trusty Scout, Toronto reached out and handed Darwin a small token. He then cranked the cycle engine with the kick-starter, and when it caught, Tom threw his leg over the rumbling machine and sat behind him. Waving a farewell to the surrounding throng of well-wishers, the two of them roared off together.

When they finally disappeared down the road, Darwin looked at his hand to see what Toronto had given him. It was a silver memento in the shape of a tractor-trailer wheel.

CHAPTER 23

Dakota Berk sank ever deeper into one of her dark moods. She was used to getting whatever she wanted, and she wanted to own a controlling interest in RoadWheels in the worst way.

The good news was that Gunther Sachs couldn't buy the company. The bad news was that he had found it apparently wasn't for sale to anyone. She would just *have* to find another way.

She had run the numbers and discovered that this business was more of a gold mine than even her own gold mine. The two businesses together, linked in their endeavors as they were, would create an incredible bonanza.

If Tom Smith's sister, Amy, didn't run the company as Sachs had reported, then who *did*? As far as anyone could tell it appeared to be a phantom ship without a rudder, or even a sail.

Berk had been on the RoadWheels website many times, but she found no clue as to the identity of the CEO or the location of the company headquarters. It was possible to contact the company by e-mail at info@roadwheels.com, but no mailing address was listed anywhere. She had called her lawyer and demanded that she obtain this information—the president's name and company address—but all the lawyer could learn was that RoadWheels Inc. was incorporated in Delaware. As a private company it wasn't required to disclose even this basic information. The secretary of state of Delaware accepted legal notices and lawsuits against the company and passed them to a corporate service company called CSC, which, in turn, passed them to their client, the attorneys for RoadWheels. The attorneys were a multinational law firm called Gold & Silver LLC with offices in New York, London, Frankfurt, New Delhi, Singapore, Sydney, Tokyo, and Beijing. Their letters weren't even signed by an attorney. They were signed in behalf of the entire law firm by a handwritten "Gold & Silver" below the bland closing words "very truly yours." Lawsuits required the appearance of one or more of their attorneys, but these men and women were usually either young partners or senior associates, as was the custom from country to country. If there *was* a senior partner in charge of this client, his name never appeared in the external documents of the firm.

Berk pondered the possibilities and came to the conclusion that this secrecy was intentional. Rather than keeping her at arm's length, however, this lack of transparency only increased her determination to break through the information barrier and find out where and how this company was run. Although she rarely stepped outside the secure confines of her office in lower Manhattan, she decided she needed to investigate this matter herself. Even an experienced detective would have difficulty in gaining access, she knew, so it was probably necessary to use some extraordinary measures to penetrate these carefully erected fortress walls. Also, she had her reasons for keeping her interest in the company a secret, and the fewer people she involved in her investigation, the longer she could continue to operate without interference.

She ordered a car and driver. When she received a call that they were waiting in front of her building, she took the elevator down and quickly slipped into the back of the black limousine.

"Take me to the first rest stop in Connecticut off Interstate 95," she told the driver. "It's just a few miles beyond the New York state border."

If there was ever an important station in RoadWheels network, Berk reasoned, this had to be it. Cars coming from the south on the main artery, I-95, could be heading for New York, for Boston, or for Albany and points west. This was the end stop for cars headed to New York. The cars traveling to Albany and beyond via the New York State Thruway had to be unloaded also and transferred across the highway to a tractor-trailer heading in the opposite direction toward the Tappan Zee Bridge. The cars destined for New Haven, Providence, Boston, and Portland, Maine, stayed on board and continued their trip up the line. This had to be the busiest node in the entire system, and besides, it was in Tom Smith's home state of Connecticut, the most logical place for the corporate headquarters.

When the limousine arrived at this station an hour later, the driver pulled up to the small office building located in the back of the facility. Nearby, a trailer was being unloaded, restocked, and cleaned while the RoadWheels customers visited the public rest area and stretched a leg. The driver got out first and opened the car door for Berk. Wearing sunglasses to hide her eyes she stepped onto the tarmac and strode purposefully into the building, focusing straight ahead without a single sideward glance. As far as she was concerned, the building belonged to *her*—or it soon would. She entered the front door and approached the reception desk, where a young man sat entering data into a computer. "Hello," he said, smiling pleasantly. "May I help you?" From his demeanor he was apparently well taught and experienced in handling the company customers.

"I'd like to see your manager," Berk said curtly.

"I *am* the manager. How can I help you?"

"You look barely old enough to drive a car. I want the manager of this facility."

"You're looking at him. My name's Harry, ma'am. Harry Harden, at your service." He got up from behind the desk and came around to Berk, holding out his hand. Berk stood there but didn't take it.

"Who's your boss, then? I need to see him."

"I'm the boss of this facility. Honest Injun. If you've got a complaint, I'm the one to talk to."

"Whom do you report to?"

"Why do you ask? It's my job to handle anything that comes up."

"Let me get this straight, young man. You expect me to believe that a twenty-five-year-old is in charge of this station and all that goes on here? I'm not buying it for a minute. I need to speak with someone in a position of authority."

"First of all, ma'am, I'm flattered you think I'm that young, but I'm twenty-eight, not twenty-five. And second, if you have business to discuss, please do so. I'm here to help you, but otherwise you can be on your way. I have a station to manage."

"I don't think you understand. I want to talk to the man or woman in charge. This is a big company with what I am sure are layers of management."

"There are no such layers here, ma'am. We don't operate that way, but if there were, I wouldn't tell you. It is none of your business."

"I see you have a computer system," Berk snapped, nodding toward the screen on the desk. "Where is the home office that this connects to?"

"That does it, ma'am. I have to ask you to leave."

Berk said nothing in reply. She just turned and walked out of the office. On her way back to the car she speed-dialed a number and barked into the phone.

"It's me, Berk. I'm at a RoadWheels station on I-95 in Connecticut, near the New York border. There's a man named Harry Harden. Says he's the manager here. Take him out and take his computer.

"Oh, and before you kill him, get his password. Do whatever it takes."

CHAPTER 24

Tom called the Indian Motorcycle Company and was placed on hold. Were there so many calls to the factory they couldn't keep up with the volume? When someone finally came on the line, he asked to speak to an engineer. He was put through to Jim.

"Jim MacIntosh speaking. How may I help you?"

"My name's Tom Smith. I'm interested in buying one of your motorcycles, but I'd like to make some modifications and—"

"Whoa, stop right there. We have three models to choose from. That's it. They're on our website."

"Wouldn't you at least be interested in hearing what I have to say?"

"Nope. We don't do modifications. What we make is what you get."

"Can I at least come out to the factory and talk with someone?"

"Nope. Who do you think we are, QVC? We sell through dealers. Tell me where you live, and I'll tell you where there's one near you."

"I need to speak with someone at your company before I make a large purchase like this. Can you please connect me to your chief engineer?"

"Ever buy a car?"

"A car?"

"Yeah. That's a 'large purchase' too, and before you buy one do you always call up the factory and ask to speak to the 'chief engineer'?

"Very funny. Well, I happen to own a tractor-trailer and, yes, I did call Peterbilt, and they made the modifications I want. They charged me a lot for it too. It's good business."

"Tractor-trailer? Listen, uh, Tom Smith did you say? That name reminds me of . . . oh yeah! I beg your pardon, but aren't you supposed to be dead?"

"That was another Tom Smith. No relation, unfortunately. He was a billionaire."

"Yeah. Cryin' shame about him, it was. But why d'you say 'unfortunately'? Uh, he's dead, and you're not. Anyway, I bet you get that a lot with a name like Tom Smith and all."

"You can't even imagine."

"They say he didn't have a home. Didn't need one. Jus' rode around all day in his specially built tractor-trailer."

"Be a lot easier to ride a motorcycle, I would say."

"Yeah, but that tractor-trailer must have been somethin' else. There's a lot of room in those things. Would've loved to see the inside."

"They say he designed the tractor and trailer himself. Now, if you could just let me design my own motorcycle . . ."

"Listen, buddy, Tom Swift, Tom Smith, or whoever you are. You seem like a stand-up guy. I'll try and put you through to Ken Macklin. He's the brains behind this operation. If he's in a good mood you may just get lucky. He's out ridin' most of the time, but I saw him in the office a moment ago. Hold on."

A moment later a gruff voice came on the line. "Ken Macklin!"

"Hello, Ken. Jim MacIntosh put me through to you. I'm interested in purchasing one of your motorcycles, but I want to customize it a lot. I'm willing to pay for the changes, whatever it takes. Is that something you can do for me?"

"What did you say your name was?"

"I didn't say, but it's Tom Smith."

"*The* Tom Smith? I thought he was dead."

"No, not *the* Tom Smith, obviously. It's a very common name, and I'm very much alive."

"Lucky you. Well, we don't do modifications, you understand, but what do you have in mind?"

Tom spent the next fifteen minutes explaining the special features he wanted on his Chief Vintage motorcycle. The cycle came with leather saddlebags, just like the original 1940 Chief, but it needed a few details to bring it into the twenty-first century and beyond. In the end, Ken agreed to work with Tom to build Tom's dream bike if he came out to the factory.

"Where are you guys, exactly?"

"Spirit Lake, Iowa."

"Where the heck is that?"

We're a little town of five thousand people in northern Iowa. You fly in to Sioux City, take I-29 to Sioux Falls, and then hook a right onto I-90. It's all flat out here. Easy."

"I'll be there tomorrow."

*   *   *

Ten days later on a bright, sunny morning Tom rode his brand-new motorcycle out the factory door and headed west on Interstate 90. Before traveling east to Buffalo, where he had parked his home and office, and while he was only one state away, Tom wanted to fulfill a childhood dream and visit Mount Rushmore in the Black Hills of South Dakota. When in the area he could take the time to travel through the Badlands and maybe even see the site of the Battle of Wounded Knee. Now that he had his new bike, he wanted to ride with the wind and experience adventure. He hadn't taken a vacation in the entire eleven years since he started his company, so he thought, *What the heck. I'll take just a few more days off.*

The bike was a stranger at first, but as Tom rode he made a point of getting to know his new riding companion. The longer he rode, the greater the distance the bike faithfully carried him on its back, the more familiar he became with its weight and balance and with its controls. Tom had to go easy on the throttle to hold the speed to within some semblance of legality, because there appeared to be no limit to how fast this bike would go. The bike seemed to enjoy the freedom of the open highway as much as he did, and as the miles clicked by, Tom felt an ever-greater kinship for this sleek machine.

Cruising at seventy-five, he occasionally rotated the throttle open on straightaways and brought the speedometer up past a hundred miles an hour. Even at this speed, the throttle was nowhere near its end stop, and the machine hummed along the endless blacktop as solid and secure as his big tractor-trailer.

The day was glorious, without a cloud in the sky, and Tom rolled on and on, oblivious to the time, much less the weather. By midafternoon, however, he glanced at the gas gauge and knew that he needed to fill up the fuel tank. Pulling in to the next rest stop and idling up to the gas pumps, he felt worry-free and unburdened as though, as he traveled the miles, his cares and concerns had shaken themselves off like sand

and were left on the road far behind him. He switched off the engine, dismounted, leaned the bike on the kickstand, and went inside the building to use the restroom and buy a cup of coffee. When he came out, he looked up at the sky and saw some afternoon thunderclouds billowing upward in the summer heat far in the distance over the plains. He pumped gas into his tank, all of five gallons, paid for it in cash, and was on his way again in less than five minutes.

Not used to traveling without his trailer-truck home, Tom had reserved no place to stay for the evening. His plan was to ride for as long as he wanted each day and, when he felt like stopping, to pull into the next city or town and take a room at a local hotel—or, better yet, a bed and breakfast. He was in no hurry to get back to Buffalo. His new bike, which by this time was becoming a comfortable friend, added greatly to this carefree mood. He had chosen good managers for RoadWheels and could rely on them to run his business well. Tom had not taken a vacation in years, so he allowed himself the luxury of an entire week off.

Looking ahead, Tom saw the sky above had blackened, although the sun continued to shine at his back. As he continued to ride westward, clouds gathered ominously, and he realized that sooner or later he would have to turn off and find shelter. It was sooner rather than later, however, when the first raindrops began to spatter against his windshield, and Tom quickly decided to take the very next exit off the superhighway. He rode on, hoping an exit would come soon, but the rain suddenly increased in intensity, and Tom saw a lightning bolt flash to the ground from a low-hanging cloud off to the left. Within a few seconds he heard the crash of thunder, drowning out the low, steady hum of the bike's engine beneath him, and a rush of wind almost blew him over into the guardrail on the side of the road. Suddenly concerned that he was in trouble, Tom realized he couldn't wait for the next exit to appear and scanned the horizon for shelter from the storm. The sky was almost completely black by now and daylight had dissolved to dark, making it difficult to see. Far ahead, to the right of the highway, Tom could see the warm glow of electric light from the windows of a lonely farmhouse nestled in an oasis of trees and surrounded by open fields. As he approached it was clear there was no exit nearby, so he slowed and veered off the highway through a break in the guardrail, careful to avoid ruts as he headed straight for the light. At the slower speed he could feel the rain pelting down on him, but the wind was at his back and it even assisted in propelling him forward.

"Steady, boy," he said aloud, more to himself than to his trusty machine. Pulling up to the compound he saw a tractor standing, facing outward, in an open shed. He drove in under the roof and stopped next to the tractor, taking care not to allow the handlebars of his bike to touch anything. Although its tires were muddied from traversing the fields, it had brought him safely to this place out of the wind and rain, and was now entitled to a well-earned rest. Tom switched off the big engine and, leaving the bike secured, ran over to the cabin and knocked on the door. The wind raged behind him and showed no sign of letting up as the door cracked open.

"Rather wet outdoors tonight," Tom said cheerfully, greeting the stranger who peered out. "I was coming by on the highway over there and saw the light at your house." The door opened wider and Tom realized the stranger was holding a pistol, pointed straight at his face.

CHAPTER 25

"Name's Jeb Langworth. How can I help you?"

"I got caught in the storm passing through on my motorcycle. Mind if I come in until it passes?"

The man eyed him suspiciously and then, judging him to be friendly, lowered his gun and stood aside so that Tom could enter the country cabin. "An' right welcome y'are too, stranger. Haul over to the stove here an' take the chill outta your hide."

"Many thanks! I don't mind if I do." Tom stepped gratefully over to a small black stove near the corner of the room. "I must admit," Tom said to his host, "I have no idea where we are."

"Yer in the middle of nowhere, Mister. Town of Red Rock in the Badlands."

"Your cabin was certainly a welcome sight."

"I jes' hap'n to be fixin' up some chow. I reckon I better lay on a few more slabs o' bacon, eh?" Jeb holstered his gun and went about adding bacon and eggs to a frying pan that sizzled on top of the stove and starting another pot with baked beans. The aroma was inviting.

"I could sure eat without any trouble."

"Jes' make yourself right ta hum. Whar'd you come from?"

"No place in particular. Just passing through on my way east."

"You lookin' for work?"

"No, sir. I'm good." Tom wasn't about to reveal just how good he was on that score.

"I allow a man's business is his own affair, an' if you got no mind to talk, I ain't one to be askin' questions. Lay off your boots an' stay awhile. Ole Jeb Langworth ain't never turned a man out yet."

"I appreciate your kindness. I'll keep my boots on, though. When the storm's over I'll be on my way."

"That's your own business too. You're free to stay on, if need be." Just then the two men heard the storm outside increase its fierce rage and felt it shake little cabin around them.

"*Geeminy!* Ain't that storm a buster, though?"

"Wild night, all right. You're Jeb Langworth, you say?"

"Yep, that's me. An' deppity sheriff is my callin'."

"So I see by your badge. Who's the sheriff of Red Rock?"

"Name is Obie Cuyler, an' he's as square a man as you'd find in a long ride. Me an' Cal Steward is his deppities, and 'tween the three of us, they hain't much goes on that ain't right an' in the law."

"I see you've got a poster here, advertising a reward for a gunman."

"Yep. I reckon they hain't a sheriff in this part o' the country that hain't a lookin' for that biker dude."

"What has he done?"

"You hain't heard tell o' him? Why they say that he's the most dangerous feller that's ever been out in these parts. Folks call him the Road Ranger."

"Is that so?"

"Speaks like a gentleman from one of them eastern colleges, an' he's some kind o' Robin Hood, he is. Takes from the rich and gives to the poor."

"But why is there such a big reward for him? What's he done?"

"Danged if I knows what he's done. I know one thing though . . ."

"What's that?"

"My brother . . . he was ailin' an' ready for to die, with some biker gang brandin' him and burnin' him one."

"Your *brother?*"

"Yep, an' this here biker, he comes in about that time an' gits my brother scot free."

"How did he do that?"

"Well, it seems he spoke to the other bikers, in their own crazy way of talkin', an' by golly, in less'n a minute they was all bendin' down an' kowtowin' to him like he was some sort of a idol. Then they loosed the ropes that was tyin' my brother, an' they brought roots an' grease an' things an' fixed him all up as good as new an' let him go."

"And you would still capture this guy if you could find him?"

"By gosh, I don't know whether I would or not."

"You know that he saved the life of your brother, but you don't know what he's done that's so terrible?"

"Well, they say that he killed a lot of fellers."

"Do they know that for sure?"

"Mebbe so, mebbe not . . . Say, I reckon this biker must talk a lot like you do . . . you talk might well eddicated yourself, stranger."

"As a matter of fact, I did get a degree. From MIT."

"*Huh?* Then by gum, *you're* the Road Ranger!"

Tom laughed. "No, I don't think so."

"Yeah. You're *him*, ain't ya?"

Tom eyed the gun in Jeb's holster. "You have a gun, Jeb. What are you going to do with it?"

"I'm leavin' it there, stranger . . . whar she belongs. I ain' the man to turn in a feller like you. No, sir. Haul your chair over now an' see how you like my cookin'. I allus said that sometime I'd git a chance to show how much I 'preciated what that biker done for my brother."

"Don't mind if I do. It sure smells good."

"You can spend the night here, stranger. You're right welcome. Your bike gonna be okay?"

"It's safe enough. It's—" Tom was interrupted by a wrap on the door.

Jeb jumped up, startled at the sound. "Gosh. Who could that be, comin' out 'n this storm?"

"Better call out and see who is there."

Jeb nodded and shouted, "Who is it?"

From outside, muffled by the sound of the rain, came the reply: "It's me, Jeb, Cal Steward. Lemme in!"

Jeb froze and looked at Tom, who asked, "Is that your other deputy?" Jeb nodded, but Tom had already guessed the answer. "Did you lock the door behind me when I came in?"

"Yep, an' I reckon you'd better hide, stranger. Cal ain't the kind to see you git away if he can git his hands on you. I have to let him in an' see what he wants."

"Go right ahead," Tom replied. "I'll make myself scarce."

"Git y'self thru that side door," Jeb suggested, "an' hide in the back room." Then, shouting toward the front door, he called out, "Jes' a second, Cal . . . I'm comin' . . ."

Tom did as he was told and found himself in a small anteroom with a cot. Curious, he put his ear to the anteroom door to listen. As he did so, he heard the sound of the storm suddenly increase as Jeb opened the front door and then decrease again as the door slammed shut.

"Golly, what a night this is, Jeb," said a new voice, presumably Cal's.

"Ain't it now? What brings you out on a night like this, Cal?"

"The point is this, I come to borry somethin' from you, Jeb. Hope you can spare it."

"Sure, anything you wants."

"It ain't much that I needs, just a bucket of oil. The heater in my shack is runnin' low, an' this storm's makin' it mighty chilly. I thought if you could lemme take some oil 'til mornin'."

"Sure . . . I'll git it right off. I keeps it in the back of the shed out theah. I'll git you some, Cal."

"That's mighty accommodatin' of you, Jeb. You been out tonight?"

"Who . . . me?"

"They's wet tracks . . ."

"Oh . . . oh yeah, I jes' got in a few minutes ago. Them's my tracks."

"I see."

"I . . . I'll get that oil."

Tom heard the sound of the front door opening again as Jeb left to get the oil. Listening carefully, he could hear Cal walking around the main room of the cabin in Jeb's absence. A few minutes later, Jeb returned, and he and Cal exchanged a few words, with Cal thanking him and then leaving.

"You can come out, stranger!" Jeb shouted. Tom opened the door and rejoined Jeb.

"That was interesting," Tom said. "Do you really think he needed oil so much he had to come out in that storm?"

"I dunno. He's a strange one, that Cal. But no matter. Grub's ready. Le's eat!"

CHAPTER 26

Tom and Jeb sat at the table and enjoyed a supper of scrambled eggs, bacon, buttered toast, and canned baked beans that Jeb kept warm in a pot. Tom hadn't eaten all day, and the hearty food tasted better than if he had dined in a fancy French restaurant. The two men talked and laughed together, enjoying each other's company as if they had known each other for years, not minutes.

Outside, the storm finally wore itself out, and the men turned in early, Tom on the floor by the stove and Jeb on his cot in the back room. They both passed a peaceful night's rest and awoke with the sun the next morning.

After attending to his bathroom needs, Tom turned to go. "I'm much obliged for putting me up for the night, Jeb. I think I'll be on my way. I like to get an early start."

"Okay, stranger. Glad to to be able to do a good turn by you."

"Maybe I'll be able to return the favor someday."

"Don't think nothin' of it at all. Your good company was enough."

"I was wondering, when Cal came last night, what you would say about the wet footprints on the floor."

"I reckon I got through that all right, eh?"

"Very well indeed. That was quick thinking."

"Ya see, that feller Cal Steward, he don't miss nothin', he don't. He's got eyes like a hawk."

"Yes. It sure seems so."

"I reckon it rankled him some in his mind that I didn't tell him whar I went an' what I went out for, eh?"

"Maybe. You don't seem to like him very well."

"Aw, he's all right, but him an' me got different ideas, that's all."

"I can see that. Well, I'll say good-bye to you, Jeb."

Jeb opened the door to the cabin and walked out into the sunlight with Tom.

"G'bye, stranger. I saw yar bike whar you left it when I got the oil. It's somethin' else!"

"It's very special. Just listen." Tom gave a peculiar whistle, like a bird song, and the bike started its engine in the open shed.

"Well, I'll be!"

"It's got a lot of neat features like that."

Tom walked over to the shed and, holding the handlebars, slowly backed the machine out with its engine idling. "Well, I'm off," he said, throwing one leg over the seat and settling comfortably on the soft leather.

"Well . . . bye, stranger . . ."

"Good-bye, Jeb. Thanks again for taking me in." Tom twisted the throttle on the right handlebar, and the bike's engine roared briefly before falling back to a fast idle. He then released the clutch and headed out toward the plain past a small clump of trees in the direction from where he came.

Jeb shook his head somewhat sadly and said to himself, "Well, I reckon I better git in my car an' git in to town. Sheriff might be wantin' me . . ." As he did so, he was caught up short by the sight of a vehicle approaching the house.

"Gosh, I guess he does want me. Thar he comes now."

The blue and white car with *SHERIFF* in large letters on the side pulled up and stopped right in front of Jeb. Two men got out and looked at him with grim expressions on their faces. The older one, the man who'd been driving, spoke first. "Stand right where you are, Jeb Langworth!"

"Hullo, Sheriff. Mirnin', Cal. What's the call for?"

The younger one of the men carried an especially stern face and came around from the other side of the car to face him. "I guess you know what it is, Jeb. Ain't you ashamed now?"

"Who, me? Why, gosh, Cal, what've I done?"

"I'm sorry, Jeb," the sheriff said. "We'll have to search your cabin."

"What for?"

"A gun."

"Whose gun?" Jeb asked, startled and looking from one of the men to the other.

"You're actin' innocent, all right, but it's your gun I want."

"Mine?"

Cal spoke up again. "Jeb, why'd you do it?"

"Say, I don't git this at all."

"Don't you move!" the sheriff ordered. "You go on in there, Cal, an' look around."

"Right, Sheriff! You keep him here whar he can't do no damage more 'n he's done already."

"Shucks, Cal. I ain't aimin' to do no damage. Sheriff, what have I done?"

"Jeb, it's murder. That's what it is. Dan Higgens was shot last night."

"Dan Higgens was . . ." Jeb stood there, stunned, unable to say another word.

"Yep. We know that he had some money hid away in his cabin, an' he was found dead this mornin'. There was a box where he kept a bag with his money in, but the money is gone."

"But gosh, Sheriff, you don't think that I . . ."

"Jeb, he was shot by a .38. An' there ain't many men here uses anything 'sides a .45, 'ceptin' you."

"But I didn't do it, Sheriff!"

"Cal just rec'lected that he come here last night an' found that you was out of your cabin just afore six o'clock."

"An' that's when Higgens was shot?"

"The doc says it was between quarter to six an' quarter past."

"But . . . I . . ."

Cal came out the door of the cabin at that moment, and the sheriff called over to him. "What'd you find, Cal?"

"I found lots," Cal answered, approaching. "Look—here's his gun, all right, an' they's a bullet missing from the magazine."

"I never shot it!" Jeb was almost shaking now, his eyes welling up with tears.

"What's that you got, Cal?"

"A bag. One of the kind of bags that money is kept in, and it's got Higgens's name on it."

"I never see that bag afore, Sheriff," Jeb pleaded. "I swears I didn't."

"Was you out of your cabin last night, Jeb? In that storm?"

"I . . . I . . . oh gosh . . . I didn't kill him, I swear I didn't. I wasn't nowhere's near him last night."

"Maybe, then, you can explain how it comes that we finds *this knife* just outside of Higgens door!" Cal held a knife out in front of Jeb's face.

"Is that your knife, Jeb?" the sheriff asked.

"That's my knife, sure it is—but I—"

"I reckon it's a pretty bad case against you, Jeb," Cal gloated.

"It's a frame-up—that's what it is, Sheriff . . . a frame-up . . ."

"If you can prove that you wasn't out of your cabin, Jeb, but you can't do it, you see."

"I can prove you *was* out of your cabin," Cal said accusingly. "Come on. Shall I put the cuffs on him, Sheriff?"

"I don't need no cuffs. I'll go quiet like. I'm an innocent man."

Sheriff Obie Cuyler opened the back door of the car and motioned for Jeb to get in. He and Cal Steward got in the front, and they headed back to the local town of Red Rock. From behind a bush near the highway Tom watched them go and decided to follow at a safe distance behind.

CHAPTER 27

With Jeb safely locked down in the holding cell in the rear of the sheriff's office, Deputy Sheriff Cal Steward couldn't stop talking about him.

"Puny danged cold-blooded shootin' of Jeb, the way he plugged old Higgens, Sheriff."

"I don' know what to think of it, Cal. It ain't like Jeb at all. He was allus the most peace-lovin' feller I knowed Why, I didn't ever know Jeb to use violence of any sort."

"You cain't never tell about these silent fellers like him. Gosh, ol' Higgens was well liked, too."

"I knows it," Sheriff Obie said ruefully.

"I'm most afeared to let the news get told around about Jeb."

"Why?"

"I reckon the boys here in Red Rock won't wait for a trial . . ."

"You mean they'll think to lynchin' him?"

"Wouldn't be surprised."

"Well, I ain't a goin' to stand for no lynchin'. This here is a civilized community, an' I'm for law an' order. The law says that a man's entitled to be tried afore a jury, an' that's what Jeb's goin' to be."

"I'm for it, Sheriff, but you cain't stop the boys when they gits their minds made up."

"They don't know thet he's been arrested yet, do they?"

"Nope, I done my best to keep it quiet about who we picked up for Higgens's murder."

"You done your best, you say?"

"Yep."

"Did anyone get to know about it?"

"Well, I ain't jest sure, Sheriff."

"*What d'you mean* you ain't sure?"

"I may've dropped a remark that give it away . . . I reckon maybe we better hustle the trial along. Just to be on the safe side."

"Seems to me yore pow'ful anxious to see Jeb get hanged for the killin', Cal."

"I'm jest anxious for to see him tried an' found guilty, afore he get's lynched 'thout any trial. That's all, Sheriff."

"He's goin' to be tried in the due course o' time. Not afore. An' if they's anything like a lynchin' . . . I'll shoot the man that starts it. Them's my sentiments, an' you can pass 'em along to the men in town here."

"Jest like you say, Sheriff."

"And I aims to carry on a little more investigatin' on my own hook, afore I makes up my mind to anything."

"Sho you don't think Jeb didn't do it?"

"I'm reservin' of my opinion."

"Well, that's your privilege, I reckon."

Just then the two men heard a roar of an unmuffled motorcycle engine on the street outside. It was so loud it rattled the panes on the sheriff's office window.

"What in heavens is *that*?" the sheriff asked.

Cal went to the window and looked out. "A mo'cycle rode up . . . stopped right in front of this here office. A biker dude—he's . . ."

The door burst open, and Tom entered with a friendly smile on his face. "Good morning, gentlemen," he said and turned to the older man. "Are you the sheriff?"

Sheriff Obie stepped up. "Who wants to know? We happen to be lookin' for . . ." He nodded toward a poster on the wall, the same one that Tom saw in Jeb's cabin the night before.

"The biker dude—look out, Sheriff! It could be him!" Cal warned.

The sheriff made a move to grab Tom, but Tom was too quick and sprang back toward the wall, hitting the light switch as he did so. All the lights went dark, leaving the room dimly lit by only the single window to the street.

"D'ya see him anyplace, Cal?"

"Cain't see nothin' . . ."

"Whar'd he go?"

"I . . . I reckon he's got away somewheres . . ."

"I'm right here, gentlemen," Tom said from behind them.

"Huh?" Cal backed away, startled.

The sheriff turned and confronted Tom again. "How'd you git . . . Who are you?"

"I came right here while you were looking over there. No—don't go for your gun!"

"I got no need, stranger. Unless you make another one o' them moves."

Cal, becoming bolder after his brief scare and spoke up. "Are . . . are you . . . the biker we're lookin' for?"

Tom laughed. "No, I'm not."

"So wha . . . what are you doing here?" the sheriff demanded.

"I just dropped in to let you know that Jeb Langworth is innocent."

"I reckon you're the one who killed ol' Higgens, then," Cal growled accusingly.

"Wrong again, Cal," replied Tom in an even tone.

"Well, you're under arrest anyway, for the . . . the murders on that there poster. Don't try any funny tricks."

"Under arrest? *Me?*" Tom laughed again.

Sheriff Obie broke in. "I reckon he's right, stranger. We'll have to put you under arrest."

"That suits me all right. Are you going to let Jeb out of jail to make room for me?"

"He stays right there. I reckon the jail is large enough for both of you."

"I just came here, Sheriff, to tell you to let Jeb Langworth go. He didn't kill anyone."

"Humph!" came a loud comment from Cal.

The sheriff pressed on. "You don't think I'll do it, do you, mister?"

"No, but I think your deputy here, Cal Steward, will release him, to prevent me from telling who the real murderer is. Of a man named Higgens, you say?"

"Huh! Why you . . . you . . ." Cal sputtered.

"Don't let me tempt you into reaching for your gun, Cal. You'll regret it if you do. That's all I have to say, Sheriff."

"You're goin' to go, peaceable like?"

"I'm going, all right. But remember what I said, Sheriff. Release Jeb Langworth, because he's innocent. I can prove who did it if you need me to. That's it. Good-bye!" Tom laughed as he disappeared out the door.

"You let that varmint go, Sheriff?"

"I . . . I reckon so . . . dang him. For a minute I thought you was goin' to shoot him."

"Humph! I don't draw no gun again' that feller, less his back is to me. Why didn't you shoot him?"

"I dunno. Jest a hunch, mebbe."

"Look here . . . he's left a little note on my desk . . . he . . ." The sheriff picked it up and paused for a moment while he read it.

"What's it say?"

"Nothin' much," the sheriff said, frowning. "Reckon it'll make a good hunk of paper to light my pipe with, though."

"What's that note say, Sheriff?"

"Nothing!"

Rebuffed, Cal left the sheriff's office, slamming the door loudly behind him. He looked up the street in both directions for Tom and his motorcycle, but all he saw were some tracks in the mud leading out of town. Shrugging his shoulders, he walked over to the adjacent saloon and entered through the swinging doors. Inside, the crowd was noisy, and a skinny man played ragtime on a tinny-sounding piano over in the corner. Cal found a place at one of the poker tables and was dealt into the game. It wasn't long before he started winning—and winning big.

"Well, gents," he said, grinning, "I guess four queens is a good enough hand to win the pot of any poker game, ain't it?"

"By Tunket, Cal," said the man on his left. "I never see such luck with cards as you hev."

"Yep." Cal laughed. "The luck's with me today, all right, Jerimy. How about you, Tim? Want to play anymore?"

"Me?" Tim answered. "I'm cleaned out, Cal. I'd give a month's pay for a run o' luck like you hed."

"An' me too," said Joe, sitting opposite. "I'm washed up."

Cal laughed loudly again. "Well, boys, I reckon I'll stroll over an' see how the prisoner is gettin' on."

"You shore thet, Jeb done the killin', Cal?" Jerimy remarked dubiously.

"You can't say he didn't in face of the evidence, Jerimy."

"I hates to think thet Jeb'd kill a frien' like Higgens," Tim said.

"Higgens was a good feller. Surprises me there's no talk of a lynchin'," Cal replied.

Joe voiced an objection. "Jeb's a good feller too, an' I reckon that one that starts any talk 'bout lynchin'll hev to face *me!*"

"An' me," Jerimy agreed.

"An' me too, by Tunket," Tim said with finality. "Well, I got to be gittin' on."

"Wait, Tim," Jermiy said. "I'll go 'long with you." Joe left with the others, nodding to lucky Cal to pick up the tab for the drinks.

"G'night, boys!" Cal shouted after them.

"Good night, Cal."

Cal collected his winnings and was about to get up from the table when he heard an authoritative but familiar voice behind him.

"Just a minute, Cal Steward!" It was Tom.

"Huh? How—how'd *you* get here?"

"I've been standing back there watching your little poker game."

"What d'you want here? Don't you know that the sheriff'll shoot you on sight?"

"Yes, but I've got to be seen before he does that. In the meantime, I think I'll play some poker with you."

"*Huh?* Play poker? Here?"

"No, not here. We'll go in that little room over on the side. It's more private."

"I . . . I had enough poker."

"I think you'll play a few hands with me."

"How much money you got?"

"I've got enough."

"I . . . I ain't a-goin' to play!"

"Come. Hurry now. This way. You may bring your own cards if you want to . . . I'll make the stakes high enough to interest you."

"But—"

"Right this way." Tom grabbed Cal by the collar and led him toward the room. "I learned that Jeb Langworth is still in jail."

"I ain't got nothin' to do with that. You'll have to see the sheriff."

"I'd much prefer to see *you!* Go right in there. It's nice and private."

Tom pulled the room door closed, blocking the noise of the barroom behind them, and the two men sat down at the poker table. The room was illuminated only by the daylight from the single window.

"Here we are, Cal," Tom began. "Two chairs and one table, two men and a pack of cards. Strange things can be done with a pack of cards."

CHAPTER 28

"Wha—what d'you mean?"

"You can deal, shuffle, and cut all by yourself."

"Say, look here, stranger. Let me go, an' I won't say nothin' about you bein' here in Red Rock."

"Oh, I don't mind. You can say all you want to say after you leave this room. Deal the cards."

"All right, if you want to get skinned."

"You can even name the stakes, Cal."

"They tells me that you killed some men, is that right?"

"That's what they say."

"You said to name the stakes."

"Right."

"All right . . . two hundred dollars."

"Heck, I can't waste my time on stakes like that!"

"Five hundred, then!"

"With your own shuffle, cut, and deal, and the cards marked the way you want them? I'm surprised. I thought you'd be willing to risk more than that."

"All right, you name 'em! I'll meet 'em."

"Life!"

"Wha—what d'you mean?"

"Your life . . . against mine."

"What's that mean?"

"You have a gun, but I trust you. I'll bet mine against yours."

"An' let me deal?"

"Knowing that the cards are marked, I'll even let you deal, Cal."

"It's a go, then. Lay your gun on the table."

"Sorry to disappoint you, but I don't have a gun on me."

107

Cal laughed with relief. "My, my, but ain't that a surprise!"

"Now how about your gun?"

"Here's mine," replied Cal, grinning. "You're lookin' right down it, stranger. Stick up your hands!"

"I didn't think you'd be this much of a cheat."

"Reach for the ceilin', Mr. Stranger! I reckon this is the time that your fast talkin' won't help you none!" Cal laughed again. "This is the time where brains is beatin' speed! Now I've got you right where you should be."

"Well, what are you going to do about it?"

"I'm a goin' to *kill* you—that's what."

"Not even going to give me a trial, eh?"

"The reward is for you *dead or alive.* An' I'm takin' no chances on you gittin' away, see?"

"Yes, I see. But just a minute, Steward. Don't you know that you don't dare to kill me? Not yet, anyway."

"An' why don't I?"

"Because I've written down all about how you shot Higgens. I've told the sheriff how you came to Jeb's place the night of the murder and sent him out for kerosene."

"Huh?" Cal couldn't believe what he was hearing.

"And how you stole Jeb's knife and gun while he was out of the room. I've told him how you shot Higgens with Jeb's gun and left his knife there to be found, and how you came the next day to arrest Jeb and planted his gun in his shack along with the bag that held the money."

"How d'you know all this?"

"I know a lot of things, Cal, and I've written it all down in a note, just so you won't dare to shoot me."

"A note? Where is it?"

"Well, the funny thing is that it is right in the safe at the sheriff's office, and I guess you can't get it there."

Cal laughed out loud again. "That is good!"

"It's all true, isn't it?"

"Yes, it's true. An' it's true that I can open the sheriff's safe an' get out that writin'. So you see, you ain't so smart as you thought. Now I'm a goin' to shoot you!"

"Just one more thing before you shoot me, Cal. Suppose you tell me just where you put the money you stole. That's fair enough, isn't it?"

"I don't mind tellin' you . . ."

"I'd hate to die without knowing that."

"I got it hid under the floor of my cabin, that's where. An' Jeb is goin' to pay for the crime."

"Don't you think you'll be troubled by your conscience?"

"No, and what's more, none of the folks around here are going to be troubled by you any longer. I'm a-goin' to kill you right now, Mr. Biker Stranger . . ."

Just then, Sheriff Obie burst into the room with his gun trained on Cal Steward. "Oh no, you ain't, Cal. Put up your hands!"

"Sheriff!" Cal stared at him and froze.

"Thanks, Sheriff! You came just in time," Tom said, relieved.

"Wait . . . the biker dude. I got him here, Sheriff!" Cal said, still pointing his gun at Tom.

"Put your gun down, Cal. I heard all that was said, and I guess it's you that'll be tried for the murder of Higgens, not Jeb!"

"You see, Cal," Tom said, "I was so sure that you'd take advantage of me when I was unarmed, and so sure you would boast about it, that I left a little note for the sheriff to be outside that window if he wanted to hear the confession of the *real* murderer."

"You stand where you are too, stranger," the sheriff said, aiming his gun between Cal and Tom, trying to hold them both. "This is a great day for the town of Red Rock."

Sheriff Obie called behind him to the bartender and to two other men who were still in the bar. "Come on in, boys, and put the ropes on these two."

"Sheriff, you'll of course let Jeb Langworth go free now, won't you?" Tom wanted to know.

"We ain't got nothin' on Jeb now."

"You see, he did me a favor, and I always do my best to return a favor. If you're sure that he'll be free now . . ."

"What'll you do?"

"I guess I'll be leaving."

"Sheriff, he's leavin'!" Cal called out. "Don't let him go!"

Tom whistled and then took a flying leap and jumped out the open window. Outside, his motorcycle started up by itself and stood waiting for him to jump on.

"Hiyoo! Off we gooo!"

Without kicking up the kickstand, Tom roared off.

"That man's wanted for murder! Stop him, boys! Stop him!"

Tom could be heard laughing as rode off toward the east, never to be seen again in Red Rock.

"Well, there goes the Road Ranger!" Sheriff Obie Cuyler said, his eyes following the rider until he disappeared into the distance. Finally catching his thoughts, he felt something in his hand and looked down at it. It was a little silver road wheel.

CHAPTER 29

When Tom finally pulled into the Clarence Travel Plaza station, everyone crowded around and admired his new Indian motorcycle. The black leather saddlebags hung over both sides of the rear wheel, but all the rest was white and bright, shiny chrome. Tom wore his trademark aviator glasses.

Bonnie and Toronto were both on hand and were joined by all the other RoadWheel colleagues who worked at the station or worked on one of the tractor-trailers that happened to be passing through.

"Do you have a name for it?" Bonnie asked, staring at the majestic machine.

Tom looked at her quizzically. "A name? What do you mean a name?"

"You know, a name. What are you going to call it?"

"I'll call it 'my motorcycle' or maybe 'my bike.'"

"No, no. That's fine when talking to other people, but what are you going to call your bike when you talk to *it*?"

"I don't understand," Tom replied. "I'm not going to talk to *it*. It's a *machine*."

"To other people it's just a machine. But to you," Bonnie said, somewhat mysteriously, "it will be your personal friend and traveling companion that never lets you down."

"It sort of is, already," Tom admitted.

"So give it a name!"

"Hmm. What do you suggest?"

"What's the first thing that pops in your mind when you think of your motorcycle?"

"Uh, the handlebars?"

"Well, you can't call it 'Handlebars.' What else?"

"The dials and gauges and the about twenty or so knobs and switches."

"You mean all that complicated stuff between the handlebars?"

"Yes, it's got a lot of great new features, and . . ."

"How about 'Silver'?" Bonnie suggested.

"'Silver'?"

"Yeah, 'Silver.' Everything is bright and shiny as silver and probably just about as expensive too."

Tom looked around at the admiring audience. "'Silver,'" he called out to everyone. "Shall I name my bike 'Silver'?" The audience responded with a resounding yes, clapping enthusiastically.

Tom looked back at his machine and announced, "Then 'Silver' it is. I hereby dub you . . ."

Bonnie's cell phone buzzed, and she turned away to take the call. No one paid any notice of this until, after standing still a moment with the phone at her ear, she screamed, "Oh my God!" Everyone turned and stared at her.

She hung up the phone with tears welling up in her eyes. She shook visibly and could hardly speak further but managed to say, "There's been a terrible tragedy at the Greenwich station on I-95. Someone broke in and killed Harry Harden so they could take his computer!"

CHAPTER 30

Dakota Berk sat in her office with Harden's computer on the desk in front of her and tried to spy into the financial workings of RoadWheels. As general manager of the Greenwich station, Harry Harden had had full access in the corporate information system to any and all financial data related to his node, but he (and now Berk) was blocked from viewing the financials of any other node.

One node was enough, though. Berk extrapolated from the financials of the Greenwich station to form a consolidated view of all forty-eight nodes of the network, and what she found was astounding. RoadWheels was an absolute cash cow.

Looking back over the records of the past few years, Berk estimated the revenue at the Greenwich station now averaged over $15,000 a day. The company charged only twenty dollars a foot to transport a car from one node to the next, but this amounted to $150 for a seven-and-a-half foot Smart Car. This per car revenue, multiplied by an average load of ten cars in each truck that left the station, netted gross revenue of $1,500. Ten trucks a day, one leaving every hour on the hour, brought in the $15,000, which, when multiplied by 350 working days a year, amounted to an astonishing $5.25 million dollars annually.

If one node earned that much revenue, forty-eight nodes brought in nearly a quarter billion dollars, but that was not all. Berk calculated that expenses—for personnel and station rent, mainly—were less than a thousand a day, or only about a quarter million dollars a year. Missing from Harden's profit and loss statement were the payments to the tractor-trailer owners who she knew were independent contractors.

Berk spent the next three hours researching and figuring the amortized capital expenditures and the cost of fuel and maintenance for the RoadWheels tractor-trailers and came up with a base cost per mile. She added in an average income of $50,000 for each of two drivers per truck and, after running the numbers, figured the total vehicle expenses were at maximum another third of the gross revenue. Even after allocating another 10 percent for corporate overhead, Berk realized that company *profits* were close to *$100 million per year.*

The passengers rode free in the tractor-trailers, but they spent money in the rolling cafés, which also turned a profit for the café owners and for RoadWheels. Harden's computer didn't show these numbers either, but this revenue stream had to be good gravy on top of the great meat and potatoes.

The owner of the company, whoever he or she may be, was earning a cool *$300,000 a day.* To a greedy person like Berk, no matter how wealthy they already were, this created an enormous incentive to grab hold like a bulldog and not let go. Especially because RoadWheels also facilitated her own business of transporting gold across the country and into Canada—and perhaps in the future into Mexico—Berk wanted to own this company so badly she could taste it.

She lifted the phone and called her on-again, off-again business associate Gunther Sachs. "Hello, Gunther. It's me, Dakota," she purred as sweetly as she could muster.

"Berk. I've been thinking about you. Do you know anything about that murder at the RoadWheels Greenwich station?"

"No, do you?"

"All I know is what I hear on the news. The guy was tortured and then murdered. They took his computer. I can't imagine the brutality."

"Must be someone really wanted that computer."

"Why didn't they just take it? They didn't have to torture and kill that guy."

"No witnesses."

"But the torture?"

"May have been after something. The password, maybe?"

"Let me tell you, Berk. If they ever find out who did it, they should torture *him* to death."

"What makes you think it was a man? Could have been a woman."

"No woman could do such a thing."

"You'd be surprised."

"Women don't have the *cojones.*"

"Well, let's just say this came at a very convenient time."

"How so?"

"This will shake things up. There'll be an investigation. It will come out who owns the company. Then we can make our play."

"We already know who owns it, and I already spoke to that person."

"That's where you're wrong. Can't be that Smith's sister owns it. She's still farming."

"So?"

"I figure the company *earns* a hundred million a year. Revenues are three times that."

"How do you know this?"

"I ran the numbers, stupid."

"What numbers? They're not public."

"I have my ways. Corporate espionage. You'd be surprised what you can get, even legally."

"If I ever find out you're stepping over the line, Berk, with so much as a speeding ticket, I'm out. I don't know you."

"Don't worry, Gunther. I'm a good girl," Berk said smoothly.

"You can figure the business is worth over ten times earnings. That's a billion."

"We'll take control. Take it public. Make another billion." Berk wasn't about to tell Sachs why she *really* wanted to own this business. He was too damned squeaky clean.

"So how do you plan to do that?"

"Maybe with this tragedy the owner will want to sell. Cheap. We'll make a play."

"Can you get your hands on a billion dollars? Is your collateral that good?"

"No, but together we can. Me and you, you and me—we're a team."

"I'm not so sure."

"Think about it. We can double our money overnight."

"That's entirely possible. I agree."

"You're in?"

"No, I have to think about it. We still don't know who owns the company."

"We'll find that out soon enough. There'll be a leak."

"I'll bet not."

"You'll lose that bet. There's got to be a company response to this. It will all come out."

"Those station managers must all know. They report to *someone*."

"Yeah, and one of them will talk."

"They haven't up to now. Why should they?"

"Just wait and see. In the meantime, get back to me about our play."

"Seems like low risk. Big upside. Kind of deal I like."

"Hurry, Gunther. It's a big opportunity knocking at your door. I can't wait long."

"Give me twenty-four hours."

"Okay, pardner." Berk hung up and immediately dialed another number.

"It's me. Berk. I've got another assignment for you."

CHAPTER 31

When she'd received the call about Harry, Bonnie had nearly fainted. She emitted an unintelligible primal scream and let the cell phone slip from her fingers. Staggering over to Tom's nearby tractor-trailer, she grabbed on for support while she tried to compose herself. Toronto followed instinctively, putting his arm around her shoulders to keep her from falling.

Tom yanked his phone from his belt and dialed a number. "Amy, it's Tom. What have you heard?"

Seven minutes later the three of them were in Tom's trailer office, sitting numbly at the conference table and trying to understand what had happened. They needed a plan for going forward.

"We've got to come to grips with the death of one of our own," Tom said finally. "Our priority has to be Harry's family, supporting them in any way we can. If they wish to take charge of the funeral arrangements, we follow their lead and provide whatever backup they ask for. If they can't manage Harry's funeral for any reason, it's up to us. In any case, I want all of our managers there. We'll pay expenses for anyone else in the company who wants to attend. I wish like hell I could join you, but I'm supposed to be *dead*.

"Let's make this a fitting tribute. Harry was killed in the line of duty. We don't know the reason, but I'm sure it had something to do with the company. I want the world to know that we are a tight-knit family and we come together at times like this."

"Who do you want to have speak for the company?" Bonnie asked.

"All of you managers will be there. You are all free to speak. If you do, you speak for the company. You *are* the company."

"Reporters will be there," Toronto noted. "And television cameras too. What do the managers say if they're asked who owns and runs the company?"

"They say it's none of their business."

"And what if they're asked where the home office is?"

"They say each manager operates an independent office."

"But the computers at all the offices are networked—"

"Wait! What did you just say?" Tom held up his hand, palm out.

"What? The computers are networked?"

"That's it! That's why Harry was killed!"

Bonnie and Toronto looked at each other, blankly. Neither knew what Tom was getting at.

"Don't you see? Someone wants to find the answers to just those questions. They took Harry's computer, tortured him to get his password, and then killed him to hide their tracks. They thought they could get into the computer network this way."

"Why would they do that?" Toronto wondered aloud. "Why wouldn't they just write a letter or something?"

"Because . . ." Bonnie picked up the thread. "Because there is really no way to find out about our company. A letter with questions like that would not have been answered. The company website doesn't give even a clue to where the headquarters are located. And we never respond to reporters when they ask questions about our management and finances."

"Maybe it's time to provide some answers," Tom said tentatively, thinking aloud. "If our corporate secrecy puts our people's lives in danger, we should go public with the information."

"But *you* own the company, and *you're* dead," Toronto said, stating the obvious. "We can't go public with that!"

"That's where you're wrong. Years ago I put all of my company stock in a blind trust I set up offshore. However, all the profits of the company stay in the United States and are used to open new stations, improve the ones we have, and otherwise build up our infrastructure. We make huge profits, but they're all reinvested in growing the company."

"Okay, that sounds plausible, except that now you're dead. So who owns the stock?" Toronto wanted to know.

"The trust does."

"The *trust*? What the heck is that?"

"It's a separate entity I set up to hold the stock."

"Why did you do *that*?" Toronto was incredulous.

"To make my life simpler. I don't own anything now, except my new motorcycle. The company owns my tractor-trailer home office and everything in it. Also, it keeps me from being a target for lawsuits. I really don't have any money."

Toronto eyed Tom quizzically for a moment, wondering what all this meant, and then asked, "So who runs the trust?"

"A trustee."

"A trustee?"

"Just an attorney in a place called the Cook Islands."

"Cook what?"

"The Cook Islands. It's a country in the South Pacific, near Tahiti. They have strict laws about privacy and secrecy, so the trustees are anonymous."

"Well, okay." Toronto was fast becoming exasperated. "Who does the guy report to?"

"He doesn't actually report to anyone. He just holds the stock."

"But what if you *really* died? Who would he contact?"

"He's been told to turn to my sister, Amy."

"Can we go public with that? That Amy owns the company?"

"Oh no! I don't want anyone to pressure Amy or subject her to publicity. She has her own quiet life, and I want to protect her."

"But, God forbid, if you did really die and she became the owner?"

"What she did then would be up to her. Knowing her, she would probably give all her shares of stock in the company to charity."

"But in the meantime, who do we say runs the company if it's not some trustee on that Pacific island?"

"The board of managers."

"The *what*?" Bonnie, who had been silent the last few minutes, suddenly perked up. "What board of managers?"

"Didn't you know? All forty-eight of you meet every month by videoconference to discuss business, and you meet face-to-face once a year to hold elections."

"Oh, really? That's news to me!" Bonnie said, taken aback.

"To tell the truth, it's news to me too," Tom admitted. "I just thought of it."

"Seems plausible enough, though," Toronto commented. "Is that for publication?" Toronto winked at Bonnie, who held her breath.

"Yes, it is."

"Okay, we can do that. But there's just one more thing . . ." Toronto continued.

Karl Milde

"What's that?" Tom asked absently, quickly turning his thoughts and attention to the real issue at hand: honoring Harry and finding his killer.

Toronto looked at Bonnie, saw her nod imperceptibly, and then asked, "Can the station managers get some stock in the company?"

"Hmm, I'll have to think about that," Tom replied, his mind racing elsewhere. "I don't see why not, but I'll have to ask my trustee. I don't own the stock, remember?"

CHAPTER 32

Harry's funeral service was held at the First Congregational Church of Greenwich, Connecticut. The church was filled to overflowing with Harry's family and friends and all the employees of RoadWheels—all, that is, except Tom and the few who were ill or on vacation overseas. The company's web page announced a shutdown of service for the day in Harry's honor and posted his obituary and the information about making donations in his memory.

The media picked up on this announcement and spread the news so that almost everyone traveling the superhighways on this day knew that they would have to drive themselves. There were a few people, however, who didn't get the word and were bitterly disappointed when they arrived at a RoadWheels station and saw a sign that the service was suspended. Over time, people had come to rely on the company and to take its dependable service for granted.

Although the event generated a media frenzy, with newsmen and women fighting for every scrap of information about Harry, Harry's murder, and Harry's job at RoadWheels, the reporters remained respectfully outside the church during the service and watched the live feed from a single television camera set up on the church balcony. The media event generated renewed interest in Tom Smith, his history, and his legacy, and his absence added to the sadness of the occasion.

Dakota Berk had slipped inside before the front doors closed and watched the service from the back of the church, straining to pick up any clues regarding the operations of the company that was now in her crosshairs. She listened impatiently as the minister spoke about the transience of life on this earth and family members eulogized their offspring, their sibling, and their spouse, interspersed by organ and solo vocal music appropriate to this extremely sad time. All those who spoke and all those who listened were touched by these heartfelt expressions—all, that is, except for the one person who had brought forth this outpouring of grief: the person who had caused Harry's death.

Finally, after what seemed to Berk like an eternity, several of Harry's peers, other station managers at RoadWheels, began to speak about their working relationships with their friend and colleague. Berk listened intently, but nothing at all was said about Harry's position in the management of RoadWheels, and, even before the service was over, she left the church disappointed and angry with herself for wasting a day on this drivel without anything to show for it.

Outside, she briefly watched the reporters go through their motions, and, after standing there a few moments to listen to their spiel, she slipped into her waiting black limousine and commanded her driver to head back to Manhattan. When she was underway she involuntarily opened her computer and typed in the address *www.roadwheels.com* to visit the RoadWheels website—as she had done many times. She was astounded at what she saw.

When the home page came up and she clicked on the tab About Us, she saw a short section she had never seen before, called "Organization and Management."

Organization and Management

RoadWheels Inc. (the "Company") is a corporation of Delaware, certified to do business in all forty-nine of the United States in continental North America.

The Company's mission is to serve its customers in providing convenient and cost-efficient transportation from station to station on the interstate highway system.

The Company is operated by the Board of Station Managers, who have been delegated the authority to set policy and procedure and to conduct business to carry out the mission.

The Company is owned by a private Trust in the Cook Islands.

Berk couldn't believe her eyes. There it was in black and white. She had nearly all the information she needed to take over the company.

She immediately grabbed her phone, selected a number, and called.

"Gunther, it's me, Dakota," she growled. "You'll never guess what I found on the RoadWheels website. The organization and management—it's all there now, plain as day. Check it out. We need to get moving. There's a lot of work to do."

"Okay, just a minute." Gunther brought up the site and looked at the About Us page. "I don't get your point. So the stock is held in trust for the owner. We still don't know who the real owner is."

"Don't you see? We know who to talk to about buying the company. There's a person—the trustee."

CHAPTER 33

Joe Williamson walked with a slight swagger down Ara Tapu, the road that encircled Rarotonga Island and formed the main street in Avarua. As sole trustee of more than thirty trusts, he could finally breath easily financially for the first time in his life. Born of impoverished but hardworking parents in New Zealand, he had to beg, borrow, and steal to afford the legal education from which he now enjoyed the bountiful fruits.

With a population of only fifteen thousand, Avarua was still the largest city and the national capital of the Cook Islands. It boasted an international airport and was the center of tourism for this English-speaking paradise in the Pacific. Attorney Joe, as they called him, could not have done much better for himself. A white New Zealander with the foresight to open a law office in Avarua just when the asset protection provisions were enacted and added to the International Trusts Act of the Islands, he served as a bridge between the arcane judicial system of the indigenous Polynesian Maori people and the outside world of finance and banking.

Joe enjoyed his morning walk into town each morning from his bungalow on the beach. The beams of the rising sun off to his left trickled through the tops of the trees, casting intricate patterns of shadows on the wide street. The buildings that lined the street were dark brown and nondescript, but nearly all of them bore a unique signature: their roofs were shining white. Joe entered the largest building, climbed the stairs to the third floor, and walked down a corridor with doors on each side. At the end of the corridor, toward the side of the building facing the street, was a door with his name on it: "Joseph E. Williamson, Attorney at Law."

He opened the door and entered his office suite. Mary, who had arrived at seven and was already hard at work, looked up from her computer and smiled.

"You're right on time. You got a call about a half hour ago from someone new. I got her name and told her you'd be in about now, but she said she would call back. I put the note on your desk. It's evening where she is, in New York."

"Thanks, Mary. New business is what keeps the lights on."

Joe passed by her desk and entered his office. The door to his office was always left open. If he needed to confer with a client in private, he would bring them into the spacious conference room next to his office and close the door.

Joe pressed the power button on his computer to boot it up and turned his attention to the files Mary had placed on his desk. There was a thin one that caught his eye. The name on the file tab said "RoadWheels." Joe picked it up and glanced through the sheets. It seemed to be in order, so he pressed the intercom button and called out, "Mary, what's this RoadWheels file about? Looks to be in order."

"The woman who called mentioned RoadWheels. Said she wanted to ask you about it. Thought you should have it handy."

"Got it. Thanks."

By this time the computer screen had arrived at its default setting and was playing the screen saver, a constantly moving logo over a dark blue background. Joe had designed the logo himself in his younger days when he was aspiring to do what he was doing now but his clientele were few and far between. He had more time and more ambition then. Now that he had finally "arrived," Joe's ambition had waned. He never thought he would say this, but it would have been quite all right with him if he never made more money than he did right now.

Mary buzzed him. "That woman called back. Her name's on your desk. Pick up line two."

Joe looked for the note and found a yellow Post-It stuck to his in-box. He held it in his left hand as he grabbed the phone with his right and pressed the flashing yellow button. "Hello. This is Joe Williamson. Is this Ms. . . . uh . . ." He looked at the note. ". . . Bell?"

"Yes," came a voice with an odd-sounding southern American accent. "I'm Georgia Bell. I found your name on the Internet, Mr. Williamson. I'm interested in settling a trust for some of my assets."

Joe smiled to himself. He used to have to beat the bushes for clients but now they were calling *him* from all over the world. Life was good.

"Call me Attorney Joe, or just Joe. Everyone does. I'd be pleased to help you with that. It's what I do."

"Well, I don't know just where to start. I've never done this before. I have quite a few questions . . ."

Joe could empathize with this prospective client. Once you made your millions, how do you make sure it is not taken away? Asset protection was a complicated subject, but that's why his clients paid him the big bucks. He ran his mental tape for Georgia Bell as he had done for other clients many times before. At the same time, he jotted down the phone number from the caller ID next to her name on the yellow note.

"Ms. Bell . . ."

"Georgia."

"Georgia, you called the right place. The laws in the Cook Islands are the best in the world for protecting your assets. We were the first country to enact laws allowing you to set up a trust naming yourself as beneficiary. The statute of limitations for challenging transfers of money into your trust is only a year in most cases and if the trust is funded while you are still solvent, the transfer can't be challenged at all. There's also a host of other provisions that protect you against anyone who might make a grab at your hard-earned money. A trust in our country just can't be pierced by a spouse or even one's children."

"I'm interested, Attorney Joe. How does this work? How do I set up a trust?"

"We file a trust instrument with the court to register the trust. Once we have a legal entity, we open an account at a local bank, and you can transfer assets to it. It's that easy. I'd be glad to take care of all this for you."

"Can we transfer stock as well as cash?"

"Yes, of course. You just instruct the corporation to put your stock in the name of the trust. You should check with your accountant, though. The transfer is surely a taxable event."

"Don't we have to have a trustee or something?" Dakota Berk asked, almost too innocently. To Joe it seemed she knew the answers to all questions she was asking and was playing dumb on the pretense of establishing some kind of rapport. He detected a feigned sincerity in her approach and had the distinct impression she considered him to be just another money-hungry attorney.

"Yes, and I'd be pleased to serve as your trustee. We're a one-stop shop here. No need to bring in the trust department of a bank or anything like that."

"That sounds good!" Berk exclaimed, her southern-belle voice conveying a seemingly false enthusiasm. "How much does all of this cost?"

"That depends on the nature and size of the trust," Joe replied. "The trust instrument can be a complicated legal document, depending on the circumstances. I can't give you an estimate of the charges without knowing more about what you want to do."

"Could you give me some references? Names of others I can call to check you out?"

"I'm sorry, ma'am. The names of our clients are highly confidential. I'm sure you understand."

"As I mentioned to your secretary, I know the people at RoadWheels. Is stock of this company in a trust with you?"

"I . . . uh . . . am very sorry, but I can't say." Joe's innate sense of legal ethics was vigorously waving a red warning flag.

"If I got permission of the owners of RoadWheels, could you answer the question then?"

"The owners?"

"Yes, the owners."

"Can you tell me their names?"

"Of course I can."

"You don't really know, do you?"

"What?"

"The *owner* of RoadWheels is technically the trustee. If you mean the *beneficiary*, there is only one."

Berk did not reply for an uncomfortably long time. Joe was sure he had blown the opportunity to land a wealthy new client. He had questioned the woman's veracity and he now regretted being so circumspect about the ownership of RoadWheels.

However, the female voice came back on the line and said simply, "Of course I know who the trust beneficiary is. It's Tom Smith's sister, Amy Lambert."

Joe was now fairly certain there was something false about this woman. Whether she became a client or not, he didn't care. He stood his ground. "Sorry, ma'am. But I'm not at liberty to say."

"Attorney Joe," Berk replied, this time accentuating her feigned southern accent, "ah'd like to come and see you about setting up a trust."

CHAPTER 34

Just as soon as the conversation was over, Joe hung up and dialed Tom's cell phone number. It rang three times before Tom picked up the call.

"Hello! Is this who I think it is? Joe Williamson, is that you?"

"Yes, it's me. It's been a long time."

"What, maybe ten years we haven't spoken? I came to you right after I set up my company."

"Something like that. I've still got your stock, Tom, safe and sound. How are you doing?"

"Well, there's some good news and some very bad news," Tom began. "Someone in the company was killed. The police are investigating, but they don't have much to go on."

"God! That's *terrible*. What did the person do?"

"He was one of my managers. They took his computer. I think they were trying to find out information about the company."

"Did they get confidential information?"

"I don't think so. But I don't want to put my managers in harm's way. Just in case they were looking for information about the ownership, I put it up on our website."

"You did *what*?"

"I posted that the company is managed by a board of our managers and owned by a trust in the Cook Islands."

"That explains it!" Joe exclaimed. "The reason I'm calling is that I just got a strange call from someone who is trying to find out who owns your company."

Dumbfounded, Tom was silent for a moment. "Who called?"

"It was a woman. Let me see, I have a note from my secretary here . . ." Joe picked the Post-It note off his in-box and stared at it. "It's a

Georgia Bell. A 212 number . . ." Joe read off the number he had jotted down.

"That's in Manhattan. What did she say?"

"Not much. She wants to set up a trust. But she says she knows you. Wanted to find out who the trust beneficiary was."

"Knows *me*? I never heard of her."

"Well, not you exactly," Joe said. "She thinks the beneficiary is your sister, Amy."

"That kind of makes sense. I'm supposed to be dead."

Now it was Joe's turn to go silent while he thought about what he just heard.

"Dead?" Joe's day was getting stranger by the minute. He felt like he was entering the twilight zone.

"I was stabbed by some goons and left for dead. I even had a *funeral*, but of course I wasn't there."

"Let me get this straight. I'm the trustee holding all the stock in your company with you as beneficiary, and no one told me you had died?"

"I guess I kind of overlooked that. But, you see, I'm still alive. You just called me."

"Is your sister still alive? She's the backup beneficiary, you know."

"Yes, she's also very much alive. Nothing's changed."

"So how's the company doing? Why would anyone want to kill you and kill one of your managers?" Joe wanted to know. "That's *horrible*."

"That's just the thing. That's the good news. The company's doing fine."

"When you started the company eleven years ago, you said you invested $100,000. That's the value I have on the stock."

"Well, it's worth a bit more now."

"What would you estimate?"

"About one billion."

"A million dollars. Ten times your money. That's pretty good!"

"No, a billion. With a 'B.'"

Joe nearly fell off his chair. "A . . . *billion*?"

"Yes. It's done pretty well."

Joe paused again to gather his thoughts. "Okay, right! That stock certificate is pretty valuable, then. You know, you owe me some more money. I charge by the asset value of the trust."

"Gosh, I forgot about that. Sorry! I'll be glad to pay you what I owe."

"My bad for not contacting you in all these ten years. Let's just say that, going forward, I'll have to charge based on the value of the stock. More responsibility, you understand."

"No problem with that. The company is growing. In a couple of years it should be worth double."

"That's great! But it's dangerous, too. I'm not sure that I should keep holding the stock. It might be safer in a large bank like, say, the New Zealand Banking Group."

"That's up to you. I'd just as soon pay you as pay a bank."

"I like the money, of course. I'll send you a bill for the new honorarium."

"That's fine. You keep the stock safe, and I'll pay the bills you send me."

"Next year I'll send you a letter asking about the company. Hopefully, for both of us, there will be no more problems like the ones you've had, and the stock value will go up."

"I hope so," Tom replied.

"And any time you want to come and visit me, you're welcome you know. I'd like to meet you."

"Maybe someday."

"I mean it. I'll show you around here. The Cook Islands is a great place to take a vacation."

"I'll keep that in mind, but I'm kind of busy right now. Thanks for calling about this Georgia Bell. I'll find out who she is."

"Let me know what you find out. She said she wants to become a client of mine."

"I'll do that. You do the same."

"I will. You have my word, Tom."

Joe hung up and immediately typed "RoadWheels" into Google. This led him to www.RoadWheels.com, and he clicked on it. The home page of the website bore some general information about traveling with the network and listed all of the stations. He clicked on one of the stations and was transferred to a separate page with photos and a map for that location. Joe was amazed. Starting from one well-traveled route on I-95 between Washington, DC, and New York City, Tom had extended the system to cover nearly half the United States.

Joe felt a warm satisfaction and pride that one of his clients had done so well. It was almost as if he had done it himself. The small trust he had settled for Tom ten years ago had turned into a big one. That was a good thing—a very good thing. It would lead to a gusher of money.

*   *   *

After Tom hung up the phone, he sat in his trailer office for a moment and thought about what he had just heard. It was the day after Harry's funeral, and his people were just getting back to work. He started by Googling "Georgia Bell, New York City." This netted over two hundred hits for sites mentioning that name, but none referring to a person in New York City. He then Googled "telephone directory" to find the white pages and did a reverse lookup using the phone number that Joe Williamson had given him. As he had expected, he found the number unlisted. He sat there in silence, pondering his next move.

After a while he opened a desk drawer and took out a little cardboard box. He removed the lid and examined the small gold lapel pin that Toronto had found at the very spot where he was attacked. Using the point of a pencil he turned the object over and looked at it from every angle. He had seen that symbol before, he thought, but where? In a magazine, perhaps? In an advertisement? He forced his mind to comb through millions of images, searching and searching, but for what? He didn't even know what to look for. Yet suddenly, as if by magic, there appeared the image of a full-page newspaper ad he had seen many times. He had seen it recently too, in fact. He grabbed the local newspaper that lay on his desk and opened it up. There in the centerfold was an ad for the purchase of gold jewelry. In the upper left corner was a logo, identical to the symbol on the lapel pin. At the bottom of the page was the name of a company offering to pay cash for gold at a local motel. Tom entered the company's name, "Gold Inc.," into Google and found an address in Manhattan.

Tom next picked up the phone and called Peterbilt, his favorite truck manufacturer. He told the receptionist he wanted to order a new custom-built tractor and she put him through to a sales engineer named Bill.

Tom spent nearly an hour on the phone with Bill, explaining what he wanted. It was a special arm mechanism, arranged one on each side of the tractor behind the cab, to hold the two motorcycles, his and Toronto's, and swing them down onto the road whenever they were needed. Bill listened intently, asked questions throughout the conversation, and, when

Tom was finished talking, he announced his decision. "We can do that," he said and asked Tom to e-mail the exact specifications and dimensions of the two cycles.

Tom then dialed another number and reached out to his faithful companion. When Toronto answered, he said urgently, "Hurry and get back here. You and I are going to New York."

CHAPTER 35

Dakota Berk was in a rare pleasant mood when she spoke to Gunther Sachs on the phone. In fact, Gunther had never known her to be in such a good mood before. She was closer to being normal—almost like other people—than he could ever recall.

"I've hit the lottery," she was saying. "I can't believe my luck."

"Let me guess. You found the trustee."

"I not only found him. I spoke to him on the phone."

"I'll be damned. You really are a lucky SOB. Or should I say 'a lucky B'? What did he say?"

"Nothing, really. He didn't tell me who the trust beneficiary was, but it has to be Tom's sister, Amy Lambert. Who else could it be? He's got no kids."

"I spoke to her. She doesn't have a clue."

"I have to say that's more then weird, but it's a good thing for us. She won't even know when we take over the stock from the Trustee. The statute of limitations will run out and— . . ."

"Whoa! How do you expect to get the stock—legally I mean? And what do you mean by 'we'? I'm not having any part of this shady deal."

"Come on, Gunther! Don't bail on me now! We're *this* close. I can *taste* it."

"I'm still listening, though I'm taking no chances. I don't do that."

"It's a slam dunk, but I need your resources. I can't do this alone."

"What is this going to cost me?"

"I have it all figured out. It won't cost you a dime if things work out. I just need your money until I get the stock. Then I'll pay you back, big time."

"Things never work out."

"This deal will. We buy the company and then take out a loan with company assets as collateral, and I buy you out. What could go wrong?"

"Murphy's law. I don't take risks like that."

"You'll double your money overnight."

"I'll lose my money overnight."

"Come on!" Berk felt her dander rising fast.

"No. You asked for a decision, and that's your answer. I won't do it. Count me out."

"*What?* Why, you *bastard*!"

"Don't use that language on me, Berk. I'm hanging up."

Berk's voice instantly changed and became deadly serious. "If you don't go along with this, I'll see to it that you'll lose everything. I'm warning you, Sachs."

"So shoot me. I don't want any part of this, especially now. I don't like your tone of voice."

"Shoot you? I'll do worse than that. I'll have you rot in jail," Berk warned.

"For what? I buy gold from you. That's it."

"You're forgetting something."

"Oh? What's that?"

"It's called smuggling. All that gold that crossed the border into Canada? You're not a registered dealer."

"Hah! *You're* the one that smuggled. You're more guilty than I am."

"So we both go down. Don't think I won't do it out of spite. And what's more, you know where that gold came from. I don't have to remind you it's dirty."

"So you cheat poor people to get it," Sachs replied. "That *your* business, not mine."

"It was you who thought up the scheme. They bring in their gold jewelry, and we pretend to weigh it. They're happy to get a few pennies."

"You're the one who does that, not me. You have people all over the country collecting jewelry, taking advantage of these hard times."

"Do you think I wouldn't protect myself? We're in this together, you and me. It's called a conspiracy."

"Try and prove it, bitch."

"Don't push me. I will."

Gunther felt sweat on his forehead. This conversation was getting out of control.

"Okay, okay. So we've been working together. I'll grant you that."

"I've made you rich, Sachs, beyond your wildest dreams. I sold you gold at half-price, and you sold it at market."

"It's time to stop."

"You do this one thing for me, and we'll do just that and forget the past."

"So what do you want?"

"We'll form a firm to buy that stock. You and me, equal partners, equal risk."

"I thought you said there was no risk. 'Slam dunk,' you said."

"There's always a risk, Gunther. You know that," Berk said smoothly. She switched to her warm and fuzzy voice once again.

"A firm, you were saying?"

"Just for buying the stock. Nothing else. After we buy it, the firm will take out that loan, and I'll buy you out. You put in half a billion, and you get a billion out. All within a few months."

"Put in half a *billion*? Who do you think I am, Warren Buffett?"

"I know you're good for it, Gunther. Remember who you're talking to."

That scene at the casino, when he bet all the money he had on roulette, played like a video as a flashback in Gunther's mind. Gunther shuddered and closed his eyes.

"That's all the money I have."

"Me too. Do you think I'm richer than you are?"

"We're betting the farm."

"Not really. We're buying stock in a huge company."

"Okay. But after this, you and I are parting ways. Permanently."

"You'll be a billionaire, Gunther. You won't have to ever work again."

"I intend to keep working, just not with you. I don't like your attitude or your methods."

"The feeling's mutual. You're too chicken. No *cojones*."

"I've done pretty well."

"Yeah, thanks to me."

Gunther remained silent for a beat before he continued, changing the subject. "So what do we call our new company? 'Sachs and Berk'?"

"I've been thinking about that. First of all, my name goes first, so its 'Berk 'n Sachs.'"

"Ugh! That's awful. We need a name with a nice ring to it."

"Okay, so what do you suggest?"

"Sachs Fifth Avenue."

"Get real, Gunther. How about 'Gold and Sachs'?"

"'Gold 'n Sachs'? That does sound nice. I like it!"

"So we found this firm, fund it with the capital we need, and head to the Cook Islands to buy the stock. Deal?"

"What makes you think that trustee will sell?"

"He'll sell. I'll make this happen. I've got ways."

"Don't tell me. I don't want to know."

"I wouldn't tell you if you did."

"You sure this deal is risk-free?"

"You can trust me, Gunther."

"Why am I still worried?"

"You worry too much."

"You worry too little."

"I don't think so."

"Someday it's going to come back and bite you in the ass."

CHAPTER 36

Tom drove and Toronto rode shotgun in Tom's big rig. They were heading to New York City as the miles clicked by on the seemingly endless New York State Thruway. They planned to stop at the RoadWheels station at the Palisades Mall and drive into the city in Tom's sports car that, along with the two Indian motorcycles, was stowed in the lower deck of the trailer. Along the way Tom told Toronto he had ordered a new Peterbilt tractor with mechanical arms behind the cab for holding the motorcycles and lowering them onto the pavement.

"Wow, that sounds expensive," Toronto commented.

"The business has revenue to burn. It generates a lot of cash."

"Well, it's good for the economy, anyway."

"We try to do our part."

"I'd say you're doing it pretty well. How much does a tractor like that cost?"

"You don't want to know."

"Yes, I do. Tell me," Toronto implored.

"About a quarter of a million, give or take a hundred thousand."

"How about the trailer behind us?"

"That's another quarter million. Custom fitted."

Toronto was silent for a minute and then asked, "The owners/operators that drive those trucks for you in your business. Do their rigs cost half a million dollars?"

"Yes, but they don't need that much money to start. The bank owns the rigs, and they just make payments. Anyone with a tractor-trailer license can buy a rig and start driving for the company if they can raise as little as a hundred thousand. The company loans them money, too, to help them out."

"That's cool. It's the American dream."

"A lot of these guys started with nothing and worked hard."

"You gave them an opportunity to start their own businesses."

"They love doing what they do. The café owners too. They're entrepreneurs, building their own businesses. Once they have one business going, they can start a second and then a third. They can keep growing with us as we grow."

"I'll bet they're loyal."

"Hope so. I need them as much as they need me."

Tom and Toronto fell silent again and stared out the windshield at the road ahead. They were following a dark green sedan in the right-hand lane that maintained a steady pace at a good roadway speed for a while and then seemed to drift and weave from side to side as it slowed down. It then sped up again and returned to the steady speed. This happened again and again, causing Tom to back off on the pedal each time before accelerating and continuing to cruise.

"That driver's crazy," Toronto said eventually. "Let's go around him."

"I think something's wrong," Tom replied, keeping his semi rolling a safe distance behind the car. "Maybe they're having trouble." His experience with his father when he was just ten years old came flooding back from deep within his memory. His father's car had sputtered several times before it had finally stalled while they were on their way to see a Yankees game.

The car ahead seemed to catch its breath and then kept going for quite a while before it coasted again and drifted off to the right into the breakdown lane. Tom swerved left to avoid the car, passed it, and then braked to a smooth stop in the breakdown lane five hundred feet beyond. As his rig was slowing he switched on the flashers.

"Grab the flares," he commanded Toronto. "They're behind the seat. Quickly go and plant them on the highway way back behind that car. Go as far back as a quarter mile and light them all up. We need to warn the oncoming traffic."

Toronto found the flares, climbed out of the cab, and headed back toward the green sedan. Tom waited for the traffic to clear and then opened his door and followed Toronto. As Tom approached the car he saw an African American woman at the wheel with two small children strapped in car seats in the back. The woman's face was buried in her hands, and she was crying. She looked up as Tom knocked on her driver's side window and quickly composed herself. Tom realized the car was fairly old as she rolled down the window with the hand crank.

"Ma'am, I've been following you and could see you were in trouble. Can I help?"

The woman stared at him for a moment, trying to figure out what she should say, and then blurted out simply, "My car—it . . . it stalled, and I have to get someplace in a hurry."

"Did it stall and start up again back there a couple of times?"

"Yes, several times. I thought it would be okay but now it just . . . died."

"Mind if I take a look under the hood?"

"Yes, my husband is a mechanic and always kept this car going, but he's . . ." She hesitated.

"Pull the latch and I'll take a look."

The woman did so, and Tom went to work troubleshooting the engine. He first pulled a spark plug wire and asked the woman to crank the engine. As the engine turned over he saw a healthy spark jump to the engine block. He replaced the wire and went back to talk to the woman.

"How are you on gas?" he asked.

"I just filled it up this morning before I went to work," she replied. Her eyes were still red from crying. "The gas gauge says three-quarters full."

"It's probably the fuel pump, but they don't usually fail like that—starting and stopping again. I'll get some tools from my truck and be right back."

Tom walked back to his truck and, selecting a key from his key ring, opened a small, hinged door on the side of the cab. Reaching in, he grabbed his emergency toolbox, drew it out, and closed the door. He walked back to the car, set the box down in front of the grill, and opened it. There were tools of every type and description.

Taking a screwdriver from the box he reached into the engine compartment of the car and loosened the band holding the air filter on the carburetor. He removed the filter and looked down the throat of the carburetor.

"I don't see or even smell any gas," he shouted to the woman who had remained behind the wheel. "I'll check the fuel pump to see if it's working."

He took out a three-quarter-inch wrench and unscrewed the copper fuel line from the side of the carburetor. "Crank the engine," he shouted. The woman rotated the ignition key and the starter responded, turning the engine over several times.

Tom watched the free end of the fuel line as the engine cranked. "You can stop. No gas is coming out," he announced.

The woman muttered, "Oh God," and buried her face in her hands again. Tom returned to her window just as Toronto came walking up. "Don't worry, ma'am," Tom said in a calming voice. "We won't leave you here stranded. If necessary, my friend Toronto will take you and your two children where you have to go. If the problem is the fuel pump, I'm afraid we'll have to call a tow truck."

"My name's Molly," the woman blurted out between her tears. "These are my two children, Tyrone and Riana." Tom smiled at the children in the backseat and they beamed back. "We were on our way to pick up my husband. He's in . . . uh . . . jail, and we need to get there by four to see him. Then this happened, and . . . we have no money for a tow truck."

"I'm so sorry," Tom replied sympathetically. "Let's just see if we can find the problem, and then we'll try to find a solution. Don't give up hope."

Tom turned to Toronto and asked him to get a few things from the workshop inside the trailer. He then asked Molly about the gasoline.

"The gas station where you bought the gas—had you been there before?"

"Oh, yes. It's where we always buy gas. It's much cheaper there than anywhere else we know."

"Was there anything unusual about your buying gas this time?"

"No, not that I can think of, except it was especially busy and I had to wait a long time. A lot of other people buy their gas there too."

"How long did you have to wait?"

"It was nearly fifteen minutes this time. Does that matter?"

"Did you leave the engine idling?"

"As a matter of fact, I turned it off to save gas. I even let the children out of the car so they could play while we waited. I remember because they got in a fight. Tyrone picked up some pebbles off the ground and started throwing them at Riana. I was just opening the gas cap when it happened, and I started screaming at them to get back in the car."

Within minutes Toronto returned with a rubber hose and a small, red can filled with fuel. Tom excused himself from Molly and worked with Toronto to connect the inlet of the fuel pump to one end of the rubber hose. Tom inserted the opposite end of the hose into the gas can and asked Molly to crank the engine.

"Try it now," he called. "We'll see if the fuel pump's working."

Molly turned the key in the ignition and the engine roared to life.

CHAPTER 37

"It seems you've got a pebble in your tank."

"A what?"

"A little pebble. It rolls around on the bottom of the tank and sometimes blocks the outlet. When it does, the engine quits."

"Do you think the kids . . . ?"

"It probably flew in when you were getting gas."

"How do I get it out?"

"That's pretty easy. You'll need a mechanic, though. He'll have to remove the drain from the bottom."

Molly stared at Tom wide-eyed for a second and then made a face. Tom could see she was crying again.

"What's the matter?" he asked her tenderly.

"My husband's a . . . a mechanic," Molly said haltingly. "A good one. But he's just been accused of . . . *murder*." The realization of this horrible situation caused Molly to let go completely and cry openly in front of these two men she did not even know. A few moments later, however, she was able to compose herself and reached into her purse for a tissue to wipe her tears and blow her nose.

"Where is he now?" asked Tom with great compassion for this stalwart wife and lady whose life had suddenly come apart in more ways than one.

"He's at the county police station," she replied with deep sadness in her voice. "We were on our way to him. We have to be there by four or . . . they'll lock in him in a cell and we can't see him until tomorrow. He needs to know we're there for him and will help him get through this. He didn't do it. Not my Jim. There's been some terrible mistake." Molly did her best to retain her composure this time as she looked up at Tom. "I . . . I'm sorry. I don't know why I'm telling you this. It's not your problem."

Tom signaled to Toronto to close the hood of the car. Toronto nodded and wedged the gas can between the engine and the fender wall before carefully lowering the hood and pressing it down to latch it. The engine kept running.

"You have only a gallon of fuel in that can. Good for about twenty miles," Toronto told Molly. "You can fill it up if you need to go farther, but you'll have to get that pebble out eventually."

"I can't thank you enough, both of you. You saved my life," Molly said gratefully. She put the car in gear in readiness to return to the highway.

"If you wait a minute we'll get back in our truck and follow you," Tom said. "Your husband is in serious trouble, and he's going to need all the help he can get."

"Wha . . . wha . . . what?" Molly looked at Tom incredulously. "You . . . you're going to help him too? Who *are* you people?" She looked from Tom to Toronto and back again.

"We're kind of . . . uh . . . *rangers*, ma'am. Road Rangers," Toronto responded.

*   *   *

They reached the police station by quarter of four and asked to see Molly's husband, Jim. They were led into a small interrogation room and were told they had fifteen minutes before Jim would be led away to his jail cell in another building. Jim sat at a small table with cuffs on his wrists and tried to stand when Molly, her two kids, Tom and Toronto were ushered into the room by a detective who called himself Michael Weston. Jim was unable to speak at first but his face spoke volumes. He looked extremely tired. His clothes were dirty and hung loose on his body. He had lost nearly all his dignity, but at the sight of Molly and the children he perked up slightly, as if a heavy weight had been partially lifted from his shoulders.

Molly ran to him and held him in her arms. She would have started crying again had she not understood that this time she had to be the strong one. "Jim, I'm so sorry," she began. "I've brought some friends . . ." She realized suddenly she didn't even know their names, so she couldn't introduce them. "We're here to help you. If you're innocent, we'll get you out."

Jim didn't reply but just sat down again. He had lost all hope that his life would ever be the same. Molly, Tom, and Toronto sat down opposite to him at the table.

Molly instinctively held Jim's hand across the table while Tom took the lead in speaking. "Jim," he began with a reassuring voice, "tell us what happened."

Jim looked at Tom and Toronto and then looked at Molly questioningly. He had never seen these men before and was not about to tell them what terrible things had transpired, all on this one day. However, Molly returned his look with such a compassionate face that when she nodded for him to go ahead, he knew he should trust them and tell them everything. Maybe, just maybe, these two strangers could be a lifeline when he needed one most. At this point in time they were his only hope.

"I work at Phil's Classic Cars," he began haltingly. "It's a small shop—just Phil, George, and me. Phil's the owner, and George and I work for him. We fix cars. Old cars, mostly. We call them classics, but they're not really. They're just old, and we keep them running. A lot of people around here are poor and can't afford good cars. They depend on us, and we don't charge much." As Jim continued to talk, his voice became stronger, and the words started to come tumbling out. He needed to tell his story to someone who believed him, and he knew his wife did. At first he wasn't sure about the two men who faced him, but they seemed to want to help.

"Phil installed a video camera in the shop some months ago because some of his tools kept disappearing. He never caught anyone, though. The tools stopped disappearing when the camera went in. I guess whoever saw it knew better than to steal any more.

"Anyway, this morning I was working on the computer in the office, ordering parts for a car, when I heard some shots. I ran outside but couldn't see anyone, so I looked in the shop. The shop door was open, and there was Phil, lying on the floor, shaking like he was dying. I ran up to him and saw blood everywhere, and there was a gun near his feet. Then George came running in from somewhere, saying he heard the shots too. He screamed when he saw Phil and ran out to the office to call 911. The next thing I knew the police were there and started asking questions. I told them what happened, just like I told you, but they didn't believe me. They kept talking about the video and said I should admit I killed Phil."

Jim took Molly's right hand in both his hands and held on for dear life.

"If they had the video I assumed it would show I didn't do it. I said to ask George but they claimed George told them a different story and the video backed him up. So they put handcuffs on me and brought me here to the police station. They let me make one phone call, so I called Molly."

Tom turned to Detective Weston who was standing guard by the door and asked him, "Have you seen the video?"

"Of course, and it shows the killing: two shots to the chest. The gun's thrown down at the man's feet and this man, Jim, comes walking in right after, no more than a second later. The other guy, George, said he was out working on a car in the yard. Said he came running as soon as he could. He shows up about a half minute later, screams, and then disappears from view. He ran to the office to call 911. We got the call at ten seventeen this morning."

"Where is George now?"

"We left him at the shop when we brought Jim in. We left an officer there, too, to wait for the medical examiner. By now they must have taken the body to the morgue so the place is clear, hopefully locked up tight."

"Who has the key?"

"There was a key in Jim's pocket. We took it, along with his wallet. The victim had a key too. We took all the stuff from his pockets and bagged it. Molly can pick up her husband's belongings at the front desk before she leaves."

"Where's the video?"

"We brought the tape with us when we brought Jim in."

"A videotape? Not a disc?"

"Nope, the old fashioned kind. VHS. I understand the guy would run it on slow and then record over it every day. That way he'd always have the last twenty-four hours."

"Where was the recorder located?"

"In the office, next to the computer."

"Did you get a statement from George?"

"We sure did. And he told us all we need to know to hang this guy."

"Did he see Jim fire the shots?"

"That and more. He said he was outside the shop working on a car in the lot when he saw Jim arguing with Phil, the owner, and then start shooting. He said he saw everything because Jim stood outside the open door while the owner was inside. He was afraid that Jim would shoot him too so he ducked down, but then he saw Jim drop the gun on the floor and walk up to stand over the dying man. That's when George thought it was safe to run into the office and dial 911."

"George told you all that? Do you believe him?"

"Sure. What's not to believe? It squares with everything we found at the scene. And he told us something else."

"What's that?"

"Phil told him privately last week he was going to fire Jim because Jim's work was shoddy."

CHAPTER 38

"What about the gun?" Tom asked Weston. "Whose was it?"

"We don't know and couldn't trace it. The serial number was filed off."

"Any fingerprints?"

"No prints. The shooter must have worn gloves." Weston was beginning to show his irritation from all Tom's questions.

"Did you ask Jim what parts he ordered?"

"As a matter of fact, I did." Weston stared at Tom. Who *was* this guy to ask him how he investigated this case? "He told me he didn't have time to order any parts before the shots were fired."

"Thank you, Detective. May I call you Michael?" Tom asked politely. "And can we have a moment alone with Jim before we leave?"

"No, you can't," Weston replied, clearly annoyed now. "As a matter of fact, you're going to leave, and I'm going to lock this perp up for the night."

Molly, who was still sitting and holding Jim's hand, stood up quickly and tried to get to her husband to hug him and reassure him that she would move heaven and earth to prove his innocence. However, Weston grabbed her arm and held her back. "Oh no you don't! Keep away from him. He's going to jail right *now*." With that, he forcefully yanked Jim out of his seat and dragged him out of the room.

"Oh, Jim!" Molly cried out, seeing Jim stumble at Weston's rough treatment yet unable to come to his aid. The deeply sad and helpless look on his face at that moment left its mark on her mind, searing itself permanently in her memory. There was nothing at all she could do.

Like Molly, Tom felt certain Jim was being framed by his fellow employee and auto mechanic, George, but he saw no way to prove it. His thoughts raced, but he couldn't come up with a plan or even a single idea of a way to shed light on what really happened that morning. A man had been murdered in cold blood, and one of the two men at the scene was charged with the crime based on the other man's testimony.

Without further evidence, Jim would be imprisoned for the rest of his life, leaving Molly and their two children destitute.

"I think I know a way," Toronto said. He had been standing quietly in the room the whole time. "What about cookies?"

"Thank you, Toronto," Tom replied gratefully, his mind instantly realizing the importance of what Toronto just said. "Molly, there may be a way to prove your husband's innocence, but it will take time. We'll give you more gas. Drive home now with your children and wait for our call."

*   *   *

Tom knocked on George's front door. Toronto remained behind the wheel of the sports car with the motor running in case they had to make a quick getaway. It was nearly sunset by the time they had seen Molly and the children off. They had taken the car from the back of the tractor-trailer and had finally driven to this man's house. Tom told Molly he would call her just as soon as they had something to report. She said her mother could take care of the children if they needed her, any time of day or night.

The door opened and a heavyset man with tattoos on both arms stood there still chewing some food. They had obviously interrupted his supper. He wore dirty jeans and a black, oil-smudged T-shirt with the message "Go Away" on the front.

Tom got right to the point. "We're investigating the murder that took place at your auto repair shop. We'd like to ask you a few questions."

"And who are you? I'm not answering no questions," George said brusquely and started to slam the door. Tom put his foot on the doorstop so it wouldn't close.

"Do you know about the cookies?" Tom asked the man who was nearly a foot taller than both himself and Toronto. He had to look up when he spoke to him.

"Go fuck yourself!" the man said and tried to push the door shut.

"The cookies prove you did it."

"I don't know what the fuck you're talking about. Now get out of my face or I'll get my shotgun."

"Just beware of the cookies, that's all." Tom removed his foot from the door and started to turn away.

"What's this cookie shit you keep talking about?" Tom finally had his attention.

"They're little fingerprints stored in the computer. They show where you've been on the Internet with the date and time."

"And?"

"They prove Jim didn't shoot Phil. You did."

"Yeah, right! So why am I not in jail?"

"Because no one's looked in the computer yet," Tom replied off-handedly as he turned and walked back to the car.

"What happened?" Toronto wanted to know as Tom settled into the passenger seat. "From here, at least, it didn't look like he knew what the heck you were talking about."

"I think he did," Tom said. "He just killed a man. He's not the kind of guy to be worried, but I'll bet he tries to cover his tracks. It's time to place a call to Detective Michael Weston."

CHAPTER 39

That evening, Tom and Toronto lay in wait, hidden behind one of the cars in the parking area of Phil's Auto Repair. They sat on the ground, which was unpaved but graveled, while they bided their time. Tom's car was also out of sight, parked on a side road a quarter mile away.

"What are the chances?" As the evening wore on, Toronto became more and more concerned. It was fully dark now, although the half-moon in the clear night sky provided enough light to outline black shapes on the horizon.

"Look at it his way. He's got to get to that computer or he'll leave a loose end. But if he doesn't, the cookies will prove Jim was using the computer at the time of the murder."

"There might not be any cookies."

"Oh?"

"Not every website sends out cookies, and sometimes the computer is set to block them."

"Then an innocent man will be convicted of murder."

"Not if we can help it," Toronto said firmly.

Just then they heard the sound of a vehicle driving up and stopping in front of the garage door. Tom and Toronto got to their knees and crouched, remaining out of sight behind the car. Looking out, they saw George and another, younger man get out of a pickup truck and walk toward the office door of the repair shop. Using a flashlight, the two men ducked below a strip of yellow police tape and entered the building.

"Now," said Tom, and Toronto pressed a button on his cell phone. Meanwhile, Tom called the number of Detective Michael Weston.

About ten minutes later George and the younger man stepped out of the office, arguing together as they came.

"That man said there were cookies in there!" George was saying.

"I tell you there weren't. There were no cookies," the younger man said firmly.

"I'm sick of this cookie shit. You'd better be right or you're dead meat."

"Whatever cookies that might have been there are gone now. Don't worry."

"Your ass is on the line."

"Why is it so important to kill the cookies, anyway?"

"Just is. Now shut up. Don't tell anyone we were here . . ."

As George locked the office door a pair of headlights appeared and a black sedan turned into the yard. It braked with a crunch on the gravel and stopped with the high beams on, shining its lights on the two men who stood frozen in front of the door. Detective Weston stepped out and walked up with a swagger. "Hello, George. I thought I'd find you here. Who is this fellow?" Weston nodded at the younger man.

"He's . . . uh . . . a friend."

"What are you doing here this late?"

"I . . . uh . . . just came to look at who's scheduled to come in tomorrow. We didn't get much work done today, and we're running behind. I gotta make some calls to reschedule."

"Is that all you're here for?"

"Yeah. What do you think? I have a business to run. Now that Phil's dead, I'm taking over."

Tom and Toronto stepped out of the shadows behind the car and came forward. "That's not entirely correct, is it, George?" Tom shouted.

"You again! Who the hell *are* you?"

"Let's just say we're interested in seeing that justice is done."

George turned back to Weston and spoke accusingly. "This asshole came to my house yesterday. Do *you* know who he is?"

"Not really. What's your complaint?"

"He says I killed Phil."

"Well, did you?"

"Hell no! But if I did, you couldn't prove it."

"That's where you're wrong," Tom broke in. "Let's go back to the office. I want to show you something."

"You mean those cookies? There *are* no cookies, you son of a bitch."

"Follow me," Tom said. Taking a key from his pocket as he strode to the office door, he unlocked and opened it. "Please come in," he said, holding the door wide until all had entered and then following them in. Once in, he went right to a small TV on the desk and turned it on. As it came to life he pressed some buttons on the video recorder to rewind the tape. He pressed *play* and the TV responded. There were both picture and sound.

"What the!" exclaimed George. "Where's the camera?"

Tom pointed to a hole in the wall between the office and shop. "Right there. Toronto and I came over and installed it in the shop after visiting you at your house. My companion here started the recording with his cell phone when we saw you arrive."

The video showed George entering the office, followed by his young companion, who immediately sat down in front of the computer.

"You gotta get rid of those cookies," George told him. "And be quick about it!"

"Okay, okay, we have to wait for it to boot up."

"I'm telling you, this is top secret. We weren't here tonight, understand?"

"Right. No problem. Mum's the word. By the way, how old is this computer? It's taking a long time to boot."

"Shit, how should I know? Phil bought it a long time ago."

"Oh, here we go." The young man started punching keys and the TV set showed clearly what came up on the screen. After a minute he said, "Are you sure there were cookies in here?"

"That's what the man said."

"Well, I can't find any."

"You sure?"

"Positive."

"That son of a bitch. Well, let's get the fuck out of here."

Detective Weston had seen and heard enough. "George, you're under arrest for Phil's murder." He grabbed handcuffs from his belt and quickly cuffed him. "I'm bringing you in, you vicious creep. And *you*," he continued, looking at the young man who accompanied George, "I'll charge you as an accomplice unless you testify."

The young man was clearly shaken. "I . . . I just came along to help him with his computer. He called me this afternoon. I'm just a friend. He needed me, so I came."

"What did he ask you to do?"

"He said he had a cookie problem. Wanted to purge his computer."

"Did he tell you why?"

"No. I told him there was no need to do that, but he wanted it done anyway."

"You're free to go, but I'll want your statement. Come down to the station tomorrow and we'll have someone take it down."

"How do I get home now?"

"What?"

"George drove me here. I need a ride."

"Toronto," Tom spoke up. "Bring this man home with the sports car and then come to the station. If it's okay with the detective here, I'll go with him when he brings in George and meet you there."

On the way, Tom placed a call to Molly. She picked up on the first ring. "Hello?" she said in a tentative, wavering voice.

"Your husband is free to go," Tom said. "Come to the station and pick him up. He needs a ride home." As he spoke, Tom could almost feel Molly's relief and joy as if transmitted through the phone.

"Oh, God!" was all she could say, starting to sob. After a minute she composed herself and finished her thought with the brief statement: "I'm on my way."

When they arrived at the station, Molly was already there, waiting to greet them and be reunited with Jim. Weston brought George inside and, a few minutes later, brought Jim out. Molly ran to him and embraced her husband, who embraced her back. "Thank you!" Jim kept saying. "Thank you."

"Don't thank me. Thank them!" Molly turned to look for Tom and Toronto, but they had already returned to the sports car and were driving off. "Hey, wait, mister!" Molly shouted as they sped away, but it was too late.

"Who was the one with the aviator glasses?" Jim asked.

"I don't even know his name," replied Molly. "But his companion, the younger one, called him the Road Ranger."

Detective Weston came up to Jim and Molly and said, "I don't know who that man is either, but he asked me to return this key." He pulled Jim's repair shop key from his pocket and handed it to him. "He also asked me to give you each one of these." He reached out, first to Jim and then to Molly, and dropped something in the palms of their hands. They both looked down and stared at silver road wheels.

CHAPTER 40

Tom and Toronto spent the night in Tom's trailer and then fired up the big rig and resumed their trip to New York City before daybreak the next morning. The early daylight seeped in slowly, invigorating them like morning coffee as they rode, perched high in the tractor seat as if in a lookout tower above the highway. The New York State Thruway extended forward like an endless ribbon to the unfolding horizon in front of them. Neither spoke, not wanting to disturb the feeling of mastery that a clear morning brings as the sun creeps up, inch by inch, and washes the landscape with its warm glow.

Heading east, then south, and then east again in the giant backward "S" formed by the thruway, they eventually made their way to the RoadWheels station at the Palisades Mall. When they pulled in they were greeted warmly by the Palisades station manager and his morning crew. Stopping just long enough for a hearty breakfast and to reconnect with everyone, exchanging chitchat interspersed with business information, they continued on their way by motorcycle, leaving the tractor-trailer parked out of the way, near where two other RoadWheels trucks, one eastbound and the other westbound, waited patiently for their turn to be loaded with cars and passengers before heading out on I-87.

Tom was glad to be riding his new Indian Chief again, this time in tandem with Toronto, who rode his Indian Scout. They crossed over the Hudson on the Tappan Zee Bridge and followed the signs for New York City. Since neither carried an EZ-Pass, they had to stop and pay cash at the thruway tollbooths at the end of the bridge and in Yonkers. Continuing on as the thruway became the Major Deegan Expressway in The Bronx, they passed Yankee Stadium on their left and took the exit for the Willis Avenue Bridge across the East River into Manhattan. It was already noon when they drove over the bridge and made the 270-degree right turn to head south on the FDR Drive.

Cruising down the crowded FDR with the East River on their left and Manhattan apartment buildings on their right was an exhilarating change from driving on the open road. Vehicles on both sides jostled for position, and several cars nearly cut them off. Riding single file with Tom leading, they were energized by the pulse of the city but found the traffic somewhat unnerving. They breathed a little easier when they finally eased off the highway at the Forty-Ninth Street exit.

Once in the hustle and bustle of Manhattan, they zigzagged through the blocks of streets to reach their destination: the address of Gold Inc. on Park Avenue. Tom pulled up to the curb in front of the building with Toronto right behind. For the first time they were able to take their eyes off the road and admire the view of the tall buildings all around them. The skyscraper in front of them soared upward with a glass façade reflecting light from the sky with clouds far above. It gave Tom the shivers to look up.

"We'd better find a garage for these bikes," Tom said, "or they might disappear." Toronto nodded and they continued on, exploring several nearby blocks until they found a parking garage and drove in. Leaving their bikes at a special spot reserved for motorcycles that was near the attendant's office, they stepped out onto the street, joining and blending in with the pedestrians walking by. They were finally free to walk about in the magnificent city of New York.

They made their way back to the Park Avenue skyscraper and entered the building. Looking around in the cavernous entryway they spotted the security desk and walked up. Toronto took the lead in speaking to the guard on duty. "We're looking for Gold Inc. at this address. Do you know what floor?"

The guard looked at a computer screen in front of him while moving and clicking a mouse several times. "That's on fifty-nine. Sign in here and then take the elevator bank back there for the floors thirty-one to sixty." Toronto thanked him and he and Tom took an elevator up.

Toronto noticed that Tom felt visibly uneasy as the elevator quickly rose as an express through the lower floors, and he voiced his concern. "Is everything all right, Tom?"

Tom winced, closing his eyes briefly. "I'll be all right. I'm just a bit queasy. I don't like heights."

When the elevator finally slowed to a stop and the doors opened, they alighted at a closed-in lobby area having a wallpapered wall with a cherrywood door on one side and a matching wood paneled wall with a pair of glass doors on the other. On the panel above the glass doors was a sign that read Lawless & Badass LLP, Attorneys at Law. The left glass door bore the names Justin Lawless Jr. and Ian M. Badass.

"I'll bet the 'M' stands for *mean*," quipped Toronto as he pushed open the door and entered the law firm.

Ahead of him was a large reception area with a donut-shaped reception desk nearly at the center, a bit closer to the entry doors than to the enormous windows behind it. The windows, which extended from one side of the room to the other and from the floor to the ceiling, formed a transparent far wall. Beyond that, there was a breathtaking view of the tops of the nearby buildings and the city beyond. In the distance one could see the financial district in lower Manhattan with its cluster of skyscrapers growing like money plants out of the ground.

The windows allowed daylight to fill the room and bathe it in a summer glow.

Toronto walked up to the receptionist, a young, dark-haired woman with a pleasant smile. She wore a microphone headset hooked to a bank of telephone buttons on a panel next to a computer screen, all recessed under the circular counter. He assumed Tom was right behind and would be at his side, but when the receptionist looked up at Toronto expectantly, Tom was MIA. Toronto turned around and saw Tom creeping toward him slowly, head down and staring at his feet.

"I . . . I can't look out the window," Tom said, almost in a whisper.

Toronto signaled for him to stop. "That's okay. Stay right there. As a matter of fact, you head back down. I'll take care of this and then meet you at ground level by the guard desk."

Visibly relieved, Tom quickly turned and walked back to the relative safety of the elevator lobby. He pressed the button and took the next elevator down. Toronto watched him go with an empathetic heart and then turned back and said to the receptionist, "I would like to speak with someone at Gold Inc."

"You're here to pick up the letter?" the woman asked.

"Uh, no. I'd like to speak with a representative."

"Oh, I'm sorry. You are?" The receptionist flashed a smile because she liked what she saw in the handsome young man in front of her.

"My name's Alonzo. Alonzo Sierra. We were given this address for Gold Inc."

"This is a law firm. I can make an appointment for you if you wish."

"Is Gold Inc. here?"

"Gold Inc.? No, this is a law firm."

"We were given this address. Does the firm represent Gold Inc.?"

"I'm not supposed to give out any information," the receptionist said, winking conspiratorially at Toronto. "But yes, it is one of our clients." The receptionist smiled again and added, "As a matter of fact, we're expecting someone from the company to arrive here very soon."

"Can I speak to someone who knows about the company?"

"Like I said, I can try to make an appointment, but I doubt if anyone will speak with you."

"Why not?"

The receptionist leaned forward as far as she could and spoke to Toronto in a low voice. "The company is really hush-hush. The partners never talk about it to anyone. We're just like a . . . uh . . . mail drop or something."

"Do you know where the company actually *is?*" asked Toronto.

"I can't tell you anything. It's super confidential. I'd lose my job if I did." The woman looked around as if to indicate they were being watched.

"No problem. At least I know they exist. That's a big help."

"I guess I've told you too much already . . ."

"Can I make it up to you?"

"What?"

"Would you have a cup of coffee with me?"

"Well, I don't know . . ."

"I'm from out of town, and this is a big city. I could use a few pointers."

"What the heck. You seem like a nice guy. Just coffee, that's all. There are so many creeps in this city."

"What's your name?"

"Barbara. You're . . . uh . . . Alonzo? I like that name."

"Folks call me Toronto, because that's where I'm from."

"Toronto, then. Pleased to meet you, Toronto."

"Pleased to meet you too, Barbara. When are you free?"

"I just started my lunch hour. See you in five on the ground floor by the front desk."

Toronto nodded and offered a silent salute. He then turned on his heels and walked out to the elevator lobby. Before he had a chance to press the button, one of the elevator doors opened. A tall man exited and looked at him strangely before moving past to enter the law firm. Toronto stepped into the empty elevator and headed down.

Arriving at the building lobby, he looked around and spotted Tom standing inconspicuously among the many people who were coming and going. Tom seemed to be his old self again and quickly joined him.

"That man that just went up," Tom said. "He's one of the ones who attacked me."

CHAPTER 41

Toronto sat with Barbara at a small table by the window in a Starbucks. Although she came straight from work, Barbara had clearly taken the time to fix herself up. She looked freshly minted.

"Full disclosure," Toronto was saying as he sat opposite, enjoying the eye candy. "I have a girlfriend back in Buffalo."

"Don't they all . . ." murmured Barbara and then responded with, "It's hard to find a standup guy in this crazy city, so a girl gets realistic real fast. Now I just go for it. After all, life's a competition, isn't it?"

Toronto ignored the remark and changed the subject. "I'm a bit out of my element in this place but I'm a fast learner. Are you from the city?"

"Not really. I grew up in Chappaqua, which is about an hour north of here. But people from Chappaqua either commute to the city to earn the big bucks, or they commute to Chappaqua to earn the little bucks as nannies or housecleaners. I got myself a cheap apartment here now, though, not far from Union Square."

"You like your job?"

"I'm lucky to have one, and it puts bread on the table while I go to law school at NYU at night. How about you? What do you do?"

"I've done a lot of things. I'm Canadian, eh? Trained in the Canadian military. Even worked as a customs officer on the Canada border with the US. Right now I'm helping a friend find some people."

"You mean at Gold Inc.?"

"I don't want to say too much, but—"

"You don't have to explain. There is definitely something fishy going on there."

"Oh, yeah? Like what?"

"Like we are their address. They don't want anyone to know where they are and who they are."

"But they operate out of your office."

"Not really. We're just a mail drop. They send messengers to pick up their mail every day."

"Do you at least know what they do?"

"They buy and sell gold. They just about steal gold jewelry from old ladies and then sell it—don't ask where—at quadruple the price."

"That's probably not illegal."

"The way they do it, it is."

"Yeah?"

"Did you see that guy who came in right after you were there today?"

"He's one of them?"

"Yes, and you don't want to find yourself alone with him in a back alley. They call him the Enforcer."

"You mean?"

"He's in charge of security at Gold Inc. I'm sure they hurt people who get in their way."

"How do you know?"

"I'm in tight with Ian, one of the partners at the firm. He tells me things."

"Ian *Badass*? He sounds mean too."

"Oh, but he's not. Ian's a pussycat. But he makes a lot of money doing practically nothing for Gold Inc. He fronts for them."

"What was this Enforcer guy there for?"

"Came to pick up a letter. I gave it to him after you left."

"Do you know what it was about?"

"No, but I can imagine. They're doing some kind of big transaction, so they need legal confirmation of the bona fides: corporate charter, stock ownership, audited financial statement, that sort of thing."

"Is he the messenger that comes every day?"

"No, but they needed an original, signed by a partner, and they *had* to have it today, they said. I never expected the Enforcer would come."

"Should be easy enough to find out who's behind the company. Just follow the Enforcer when he comes in next time."

"Not so easy. They're totally hush-hush about the location of Gold Inc. I'm sure the Enforcer covers his tracks. He's a real pro."

"What about the mail messengers? You said they come in every day."

"I'm sure they just drop the mail in a safe box somewhere and don't even go to an address. To cover their tracks too."

"You're probably right. But this transaction you mentioned—any idea what it's about?"

"No, but Ian told me it's big. Really big."

"In what way?"

"A lot of money involved. A 'bet the company' kind of thing. That's all I know."

"If you find out anything, would you let me know?"

"I like you, so I'll say yes on one condition."

"What's that?"

"You agree to see me again."

"See you?"

"You know. Come to my apartment, and—"

"Oh! Well, I'm engaged, remember?"

"This is a free country and a free city. Maybe Canada isn't, I don't know, but . . ."

"How about dinner someplace nice?"

"That would do for starters."

"Okay. How about tonight? Seven o'clock? I can meet you right here at Starbucks. We'll go to any restaurant you choose, no matter how expensive. You tell me what you find out about this big transaction and it's on me."

"You're on. We have a deal." Barbara opened her purse and took out a pen and a business card. She scribbled a number on the back and handed it to Toronto. "Here's my cell. I need yours."

"Give me another card and I'll write it down." Toronto took another card from Barbara, wrote down his number, and gave it back.

"By the way," she asked as she got up from the table, "what's your girlfriend's name?"

"Bonnie. Why do you ask?"

"That's a sweet name. Just want to know who I'm up against."

"She's hard to beat."

"Oh yeah? You tell her to watch out for a girl from the big city. Oh, and one more thing . . ."

"What's that?"

"You're taking me to the Four Seasons."

"Sounds expensive."

"It is." Barbara winked and added, "But I'm worth it."

CHAPTER 42

Tom waited in the lobby until he saw the Enforcer exit the elevator. Tom didn't even know the man's name, but he knew he and his accomplices had forced him off the road, knifed him, and left him for dead. He would never forget their faces.

As he now always did when he appeared in public, Tom wore his wraparound aviator glasses. The glasses were just large enough to conceal his identity, even from the most observant and inquisitive, but not so large as to look suspicious to the casual observer. There was nothing extraordinary about Tom's appearance other than the shades. With his average height and average build, he easily blended in with the other people milling in the lobby.

The Enforcer walked out through the front entrance and got into a waiting cab on the street in front of the building. Tom followed briskly but calmly and took the next cab in line.

"Follow my friend there," he told the cab driver, pointing to the car ahead that was leaving the curb. "And please don't lose him. I don't know the address where he's going."

The cab driver started the meter and entered traffic, right behind the taxicab, a yellow Ford Escape that looked like practically every other cab in the city. Tom peered forward to get a good look at the vehicle and committed its license plate number to memory. "My name's Tom," He introduced himself. "I see you're name's Moishe." The driver's name and photo were displayed on the cab's identification card.

The driver glanced in the mirror and nodded. "You're following somebody?"

"As a matter of fact, yes."

"Friend?" The driver flashed a knowing smile.

"As a matter of fact, no."

"Not to worry. I've done this often, and I never lose my prey."

"Often?"

"I'd say maybe once a week someone gets in the cab and says to follow. It's a big, crowded city, and not everyone knows their way around."

"I'm surprised."

"You a detective?"

"No, why?"

"You're following someone. That's what detectives do."

"You don't want to know," Tom said.

"Yes, I do. Maybe I can help."

"Help?"

"Yeah. See that cab? I know that guy. If we lose him in traffic, I can just call him."

"Really? It's that easy?"

"Sure. There aren't *that* many cab drivers here in the city. Most of us know each other."

"You all work together?"

"No. It's cutthroat competition, but we've been known to help each other out."

"Like how?"

"We're the eyes and ears of the city. Not much goes down that we don't know about."

"You help solve crimes?"

"You bet. Are you on to one?"

"As a matter of fact, yes. That man who got in that cab tried to kill me."

"There you go. Why didn't you say so? Moishe and his detectives are at your service."

"I need to know where that guy is going."

"We'll find that out in just a few minutes. Anything else?"

"I need to know who that guy reports to."

"We can do that. Anything else?"

"I need to know where that boss person lives."

"Got it. Check."

"I need to know where that boss person goes."

"Check."

"I need to know what that boss person does.

"That's a little harder, but consider it done."

"You'll do all that?"

"Yup. For a price." Moishe winked at Tom in the mirror.

"So what's the catch?"

"Money talks in this city."

"What is it saying?"

"I'm hearing a thousand dollars." Moishe cocked his head inquisitively as he drove. "What do you hear?"

"I pay cash in advance."

"Cash is king. How about five hundred."

"If you could deliver the info, it would be worth that."

"One hundred now and a hundred each time I answer one of your questions."

"How do I know this isn't a scam?"

"Got your cell phone with you?"

"Yeah, why?"

"Call this number." Moishe placed a card in the slot in the barrier between the front and back and Tom took it. It said "Moishe's Detective Agency" and, under that, "Licensed to Carry." It also listed an address and phone number. Tom dialed the number.

Moishe answered from the front seat. "Moishe's Detective Agency!"

"Oh, well, now I'm convinced," Tom announced sarcastically.

"Seriously. We can do this. You're only risking a hundred dollars. Think of what it would mean if I delivered for you."

"I'd give you a bonus."

"Now you're talking."

"And your name on the card does match the name on your cab's ID."

"I could lose my hack license if you complained."

"You really have a license to carry a weapon?"

"Yup."

"You're going to need it."

"No problem," Moishe said as he slowed the cab to a crawl and pointed. "There's the answer to your question number one."

Tom saw the Enforcer get out of the cab in front of them and run up the steps of a town house. The door of the house opened, and the man disappeared inside.

CHAPTER 43

Tom asked Moishe to bring him back to the side street off Park Avenue where he and Toronto had parked their motorcycles. He paid for the ride and gave Moishe his first payment of a hundred dollars.

"What's a good hotel nearby?" he asked.

"How good?" Moishe wanted to know.

"Need a nice suite. I'm here with a friend."

"Try the Marriott East or, if you can afford it, the Waldorf."

"Thanks. We'll stay at the Waldorf for the night. Call me anytime you learn something." Tom gave Moishe a slip of paper with his cell number scribbled on the back.

Moishe glanced at it and asked, "Where are you from?"

"You eventually may need to know that, but not just yet. Right now I'm just a man from the Waldorf, and don't tell anyone I hired you."

"My lips are sealed." Moishe made a sign of turning a key in his mouth and throwing the key away.

Tom exited the cab and started to walk toward the parking facility. After taking a few steps he stopped and turned around. "And one more thing!" He came back to Moishe's driver's side window.

"Sure. What's that?"

"You don't know my name."

"You mean 'Tom'?"

"That's right. People think I'm dead."

"Oh! Got it. Check. That could be a good thing."

"How's that?"

"This boss character, whoever he or she is, won't know you're coming."

"That's true. And I'd like to keep it that way."

"If anyone finds out, it won't be from me," Moishe replied as he waved and drove away, his yellow cab blending into the virtual sea of yellow cabs in the traffic.

Tom stood on the sidewalk, found Toronto's number on his cell phone, and pressed *send*. After three buzzes of his phone he heard another phone ring on the street. He looked around, and there stood Toronto.

"Well, hello! Waiting long?" Tom asked.

"I just got here."

"Where have you been?"

"Having coffee with the receptionist at Lawless & Badass."

"Really? And?"

"We need to talk. I got some intel. Also, I'm having dinner with her this evening. Hopefully get more intel. How about you? You find out where the Enforcer went?"

"Who?"

"That guy who tried to kill you. They call him the Enforcer."

"Yes, I did. And there's more. I hired the cab driver to find out who runs Gold Inc."

"He can find that out?"

"I hope so. He also happens to be a detective."

"We need to stay in the city."

"I'm way ahead of you. We're staying at the Waldorf right up the street. But first we have to tell the people here at the parking facility to hold our bikes overnight."

"And I have to go out and buy a suit. I'm having dinner with an attractive young lady at the Four Seasons."

"Sounds expensive."

"It is."

"You're buying?"

"No, you are," Toronto said, smiling brightly.

"Why me?"

"We're on a road trip. It's a business expense."

"I guess I'm good for it."

"Darn right. You're rich, remember?"

"I don't own anything. My trustee does."

"That could be a problem."

"Makes life much safer and simpler. However, as long as he lets me, I can sign for company expenses."

"Is there anything you do that's *not* a business expense?"

"I can't think of anything. My motorcycle, maybe."

"You used it to drive here. That's for business."

"Smart thinking. Use your personal credit card and the business will reimburse you."

"Don't you have a business credit card I can use?"

"No, a credit card is traceable. For me it's strictly cash."

Tom and Toronto visited the office of the parking facility to extend the stay of their motorcycles and then parted ways. Toronto headed for Madison Avenue to look for a suit while Tom checked into the Waldorf. When finally ensconced in a suite on a low floor, Tom called the concierge and asked for a laptop computer.

"We have a business office on the ground floor where you can use one."

"I'd like one here in the room so I can use it day or night."

"You'll need to leave a deposit. Can we put that on your credit card?"

"No, I'll come down and give you cash. How much do you need?"

"Fifteen hundred. That's the cost of the computer. Plus one hundred dollars a day for the rental."

"Sixteen hundred. I'll be right down with the money."

Tom visited the concierge, where he traded sixteen hundred dollars cash for the computer and took the laptop back to his suite. Connecting to the Internet through the Waldorf's Wi-Fi, he went to the New York City database for taxable real estate and typed in the address of the town house the Enforcer had entered an hour before. A few seconds later the name of the owner appeared on the screen: Gold Inc.

He was getting somewhere, but not very fast. He needed to know the officers of Gold Inc. His cell phone rang and he picked it up.

"Questions two and three." It was Moishe's voice. "The boss is a woman named Dakota Berk, and she lives in that town house we saw. You owe me two hundred bucks."

"How did you find out so quickly?"

"Elementary. I looked up the owner of the town house and got some corporation called Gold Inc. Albany keeps a record of the officers of its registered corporations, so I searched there for Gold Inc. Dakota Berk is the president. I also went to the town house and read the name on the mailbox. I'm parked outside the building right now, and I see that she and that guy are coming out. Looks like I'll be answering your questions three and four pretty darn quick."

"That's amazing! I'm at the Waldorf. Meet me here to pick up the rest of your money."

"I'll follow them first and then stop by on my way home. Looks like a major trip coming up. The guy is carrying a couple of heavy suitcases, and they're getting into a big black limousine as we speak. I'll call again when I find out where they're going."

Moishe clicked off, and Tom closed his laptop, thinking, *What a shame. I just wasted $1,600.*

CHAPTER 44

Dakota Berk and the man they called the Enforcer rode comfortably in the limo out to JFK airport. While in the car, Berk made a call to Gunther Sachs. The Enforcer half-listened absently and without much interest. Strategy was not his job, and, in any case, he had heard it all before. The phone call took place via Bluetooth, with Berk carrying on the conversation as if Sachs were right there in the limo with them.

"I'm on my way to the airport, Gunther. I'm taking Alex. We'll be gone for a week. The plane leaves at three thirty, and we're running a bit late. There's a stopover in LA and in Auckland, so we won't arrive until four fifteen tomorrow afternoon."

"Keep me informed. I'm in this too, remember."

"My resource limit is half a billion. After that, I'm going to need you. Just as soon as we own the company, we'll take out a loan based on the assets and pay ourselves back."

"Seems like a really safe bet. You *sure* the company has no debt?"

"Don't worry. I researched the shit out of this. If there were ever any debt, it was paid off long ago. It's a cash cow now that just keeps on giving more milk."

"That's my kind of investment. What say I put in half with you and we go fifty-fifty?"

"No deal, Gunther. I'm keeping at least fifty-one. After that, your investment, divided by our total investment, is the percentage you get."

"Okay, okay. It's your baby. But I'm covering you. You couldn't do this without me."

"Have my money ready to transfer. Yours too."

"I'm with you on this one."

"I made you rich. You may forget that, but I won't. You'd *better* come through for me."

"The money's there, ready and waiting."

"I'll call you from Rarotonga."

Berk pressed *end* to terminate the call and shot a fierce look at the Enforcer. "You'd better be ready too," she said sternly.

Outside, a yellow taxicab kept pace with the limo in the adjacent lane to the left. The cab looked like every other Ford Escape Hybrid taxi in the city except that a small antenna protruded from either side of its roof to pick up Bluetooth signals of nearby cars. The received voice sounds were partly garbled but understandable, and Moishe recorded them on his iPhone.

Moishe followed the limo all the way to the Departures lane of the United Airlines terminal at Kennedy airport. He pulled up to the curb right behind the stretch sedan and sat in his taxi, watching inconspicuously as Berk and the Enforcer alighted and the limo driver got out and popped the trunk. The Enforcer took out the two bags and followed Berk with them into the terminal. Moishe looked at his dash clock as they disappeared. It was two thirty in the afternoon.

Moishe called Tom to let him know he was on the way and nearly an hour later called him again from the lobby of the Waldorf Hotel.

"Come on up!" Tom said. "Fourth floor. Suite 451."

Moishe knocked on the door of room 451, and Tom opened the door.

Moishe came in, peered around the elegantly decorated suite, and whistled. "Man, one could get used to this!"

"How do you like your coffee?" Tom asked. "I made a fresh pot."

Choosing a comfortable armchair, Moishe sat down and took a load off his frame, weary from riding the taxi all day. "Double sugar, double cream," he said with a relaxed sigh. As Tom handed him a hot cup of light coffee, he gave his report. "They went to the airport for a weeklong trip. They're booked on a United Airlines flight that leaves at three thirty."

"That's amazing! How did you find this out?" Tom wanted to know.

"It's all recorded right here." Moishe held up his cell phone. "In fact, I know where they're heading. They're flying somewhere via LA and Auckland. Wherever they're going, they're landing at four fifteen tomorrow afternoon."

Tom thought for a beat. "Then I know where they're going," he said, staring at Moishe with a darkened look. "The Cook Islands. I happen to know there is only one flight a day there from Auckland, and it arrives at four fifteen."

"Okay, there's more. On the way to the airport the woman called someone named Gunther. That guy we followed to her house is with her too. Turns out his name is Alex."

Moishe pressed some buttons on the phone to start the voice recording. He placed the instrument on the coffee table in front of him as it played through its tiny speaker.

Tom's jaw dropped. "How did you get *that?*" he asked.

"Bluetooth. Broadcasts for about ten feet. With the right equipment you can pick it up."

"Is there any way we can get the number of the person she called?" Tom asked after hearing the recording.

"I'm afraid not. I only started the recording after I heard she had placed the call. I didn't get the digits she was dialing."

"We know he's wealthy and his name is Gunther. That's a start. And we know her name is Dakota Berk and she's the president of Gold Inc. She's got half a billion dollars at her disposal, and she's asking him to invest his money too. Moishe, I know what's coming down. Those two want to take over a company."

"Oh? What company is that?"

"I can't tell you that yet. But what's important is she's bringing the Enforcer, the man she calls Alex. He's very dangerous. I told you, he tried to kill me once."

Tom's comments were interrupted by a knock. He walked over to the door, looked briefly through a peephole, and then opened it wide. Toronto bounced in, all smiles, carrying two shopping bags in one hand and a garment bag in the other. "I love shopping in New York! When I put these new clothes on I'll be a new man!" Toronto caught himself and stopped in his tracks when he saw Moishe rising from his chair.

"Toronto, this is Moishe, the detective I was telling you about."

"Pleased to meet you." Toronto went over and shook his hand.

"Pleased to meet you too. Glad to meet a friend of Tom's. If there is anything further . . ."

Tom reached in his pocket and took out a roll of bills. As he counted the money out, Toronto headed for the bedroom with his new clothes. "I have to hurry," he remarked. "Got a date with a lady tonight and don't want to be late." He closed the bedroom door behind him.

"Here's the rest of what I owe you," Tom said, handing four one-hundred-dollar bills to Moishe. "And a bonus too. You've certainly earned it. I'll use you again."

"Thank you very much! Whenever you're in town, just give me a call. I give taxi rides, follow people, find missing persons, do undercover work, whatever. You have my card."

"Well, there *is* one more thing," Tom said as he led Moishe to the door. He talked with Moishe briefly, gave him another hundred-dollar bill, and then shook his hand warmly as he said good-bye.

CHAPTER 45

Alonzo Sierra, a.k.a. Toronto, walked over to the local Starbucks at quarter to seven and waited for Barbara. When she walked in, only five minutes late, she took his breath away. Wearing a red chiffon dress with a plunging neckline that revealed the tops of her spectacular breasts and wearing matching bright-red lipstick that emphasized her cute smile, she turned everyone's head as she entered the café.

Toronto proudly stepped away from the crowd of patrons at the counter and walked over to her. Taking her hand, he looked at her admiringly and kissed her on the cheek. "Thanks for coming," he said.

"I wouldn't miss this date for the world," she answered. "We had a deal, remember?"

"A deal? What deal was that?"

"I give you the information you so desperately want and you come back to my apartment and, uh, take care of business."

"Wait just a minute! I never agreed to—"

"Just kidding! Ha! I had you going there for a second."

Toronto revealed a small self-deprecating smile. "I guess you did," he said. "You got me."

"So?"

"So, let's go!" Pulling her by the hand, Toronto led Barbara out onto the street, where he hailed a cab.

Yellow cabs were as thick as bees near a hive at that hour, and within a minute the excited couple were on their way to the Four Seasons. Toronto didn't say much, but Barbara filled the void with bubbly banter. When they arrived, Toronto paid the driver and told Barbara to wait a minute. He then got out, walked around to the other side of the cab, and opened the side door for her.

"How chivalrous! No one's ever done that for me before," Barbara told him as she extended her shapely legs, gingerly placing her high heels on the curb and exiting the cab. "By the way, is that a new suit? You look really handsome, you know that?"

"You're the one who looks terrific. I can't stop staring, and no one else can either." Toronto took her right hand in his left, held her steady as she alighted, and held out his right hand, palm up, to indicate the small crowd of people who had stopped in their tracks to gape and admire.

"This is every girl's dream, to be the center of attention," she said, looking around and beaming like a celebrity. She then tucked her hand under Toronto's arm, and they walked proudly up the steps and entered the Four Seasons. The doorman tipped his hat and winked at Toronto as they walked in.

They were seated at the restaurant's place of honor: a table for two by the huge plate glass window overlooking Park Avenue. Toronto ordered a bottle of Cristal champagne, and they exchanged small talk until the sommelier arrived and performed the ritual pouring.

"Here's to us," Toronto said, raising his glass.

"To *us*," Barbara reached over, clinked their glasses together, and tasted the champagne. "Oooh," she cooed. "That's *reeeally* nice. You did good, my man from Toronto."

They ordered all four courses, from appetizer to dessert, and then settled back to absorb the ambience and get down to business.

"I had a talk with Ian this afternoon," Barbara began. "He must have been in a good mood, because he told me *everything*."

"You have my attention," Toronto replied, turning serious.

"Have you ever heard of a company called RoadWheels?"

"I think so. They're pretty big, aren't they?" Toronto feigned ignorance.

"They're *huge*. It's a billion-dollar company."

"What about them?"

"Apparently they're available for sale, and Dakota Berk—she's the president of Gold Inc.—wants to buy them. She's leaving for the Cook Islands today to make a deal."

"The Cook Islands?"

"They're somewhere in the South Pacific. That's where the stock is held."

"It's owned by someone who lives there?"

"No, the stock's held by a trustee. But the original owner—his name was Tom Smith—died suddenly. Maybe you heard about it in the news."

"So who's running the company, then?"

"Who knows? Maybe this trustee on the Cook Islands, but that's kind of far away. I doubt if he knows what to do."

"What's his name, this trustee?"

"Joe Williamson. A lawyer type. Just a figurehead, but he has the power right now."

"That's very helpful. Did you find out anything else?"

"Not really. That's the scoop. Oh yes, there's one more thing . . ."

"What's that?"

"This Dakota Berk doesn't have the billion dollars it would take to buy the company, so she's teamed up with another rich mogul, a guy called Gunther Sachs, to make the deal. They call themselves Gold and Sachs. Pretty good, huh? Like Goldman Sachs—get it?"

"That's pretty funny, though I'm not surprised she needs a partner. A billion dollars—it's a lot of money."

"Yeah, and not too many people have that kind of bread. It seems that Berk thinks this company would make a good fit for her business. I can't imagine why."

Toronto thought for a moment and then asked, "Any idea how much money Berk can raise by herself?"

"Ian said she's good for about half a billion. She needs this other guy for the other half."

"So Berk is on her way now to the Cook Islands?"

"Yup. And if I don't miss my guess, she's bringing the Enforcer with her."

"Why bring him?"

"He helps her get things like this done. And he'll probably bring the price down."

Toronto leaned back in his chair and thought about what was just said. "That is some information you brought me," he said finally.

"Did I come through or what?" Barbara shot him a cute smile.

Toronto returned the smile and admitted, seemingly grudgingly, "You did good."

"Well, I've delivered, then. Now I'm going to enjoy this place. I don't get to go out on dates to expensive restaurants very often. Like, I mean *never*." Barbara emphasized the last word by inflecting her voice upward.

Waiters appeared out of nowhere and silently served their meals, course after course, while Toronto and Barbara lost themselves in conversation. Barbara repeatedly poked and probed Toronto for information about his past and present, but he was more interested in *her*.

Nothing impresses a girl more than a guy who listens, and she did most of the talking. By the end of the evening, after the champagne bottle was empty, the dessert and coffee were finished and the headwaiter had dropped the leather folder with the bill on the table, Barbara leaned over to Toronto and said quietly, "Excuse me. I have to powder my nose."

Remembering his manners, Toronto stood as she left the table and then sat down again and opened the folder. "Lucky I'm sitting down," he thought as he stared at the check. The tab ran way over nine hundred dollars. He paid with his personal credit card.

CHAPTER 46

When Barbara returned from the ladies room, Toronto noticed she had removed all her lipstick but she had added to her perfume, exuding a combination of flowers and musk. The scent was unknown to him, but he instantly took a liking to it. He stood when he saw her, and together they walked out the door. The same doorman who had greeted them two hours earlier winked again at Toronto as if to say, "You've got the right moves, man. You're sure to get lucky tonight!"

The doorman waved his hand and a yellow cab pulled up at the curb. He opened and held the rear door for Barbara while Toronto walked around to the other side and got in. Barbara gave the driver the address of her apartment and the cab pulled out onto the busy city street.

"It's been a magical evening," Barbara cooed as she snuggled up close to Toronto in the privacy and darkness of the backseat. She took his right hand in her left and pressed gently.

"I've enjoyed it too—a great one for my memory book. But all good things must come to an end," Toronto said with a sigh.

"It's not over. The best is yet to come."

As she said this, she lifted his right hand and placed it squarely on her rounded left breast. Keeping her hand on top of his, she squeezed down so Toronto could feel the soft, large bump. With her right hand she reached around Toronto's neck and pulled his head close, at the same time moving her mouth toward his lips to present him with a deep kiss. Her moist mouth found its mate and, caught off guard too quickly to resist, Toronto found himself in a deep embrace. Barbara's tongue darted in his mouth, exploring every nook while Toronto tasted an outpouring of her sweet saliva. All of Toronto's senses were awakened suddenly, but he knew it was wrong for him to let these events unfold. He took his right hand reluctantly from her breast and then pressed her gently away with both hands.

"We can't do this," he said. "I have another girl back home."

"But you have a girl right here who wants you," Barbara said softy. "And she wants you real bad."

With that she reached behind her back and pulled down the zipper that held her chiffon dress together. It slipped like silk off her shoulders and revealed her black lace bra. She next unclipped her bra from behind and it fell with the top of her dress onto her lap, revealing the all of her rounded breasts. Toronto tried but couldn't resist feasting his eyes.

Barbara next reached over with her right hand and cupped it over Toronto's crotch. "Ooooh," she said. "I can feel you want me too." She massaged the area gently but firmly, a bit harder with each stroke, and then pulled his head toward hers and kissed him again, this time passionately and aggressively, giving Toronto neither the time nor the space to resist. "I want you," she murmured between deep French kisses, holding his face tightly between her two hands. "My panties are so wet, I could use them to wash this taxicab."

By this time, Toronto was fast losing his grip and his ability to make a rational decision. The effects of Barbara's musky perfume mixed with the taste and smell of her saliva was intoxicating. Again he tried to push Barbara away, but she was undeterred. With her right hand she unbuckled his belt, and when it was free she quickly took both hands and unclipped the top of his pants and unzipped the zipper. Underneath his white underpants was a large bulge that excited her even more. She slipped her hand beneath the elastic top and squeezed the hard shaft.

All of this activity had taken a mere ten minutes to unfold but, because of the light traffic, the taxicab had already reached Barbara's address near Union Square. The taxi pulled over next to the line of parked cars and stopped.

"We're here already?" Barbara looked up and saw the steps leading into her brownstone. She hastily attached her bra again and pulled up her dress while Toronto closed his pants.

"Pay the man and let's go," she said urgently.

Toronto sat there dumbly, clearly torn by indecision.

"I can't," he finally said.

"No, no, no. You *must*," Barbara pleaded, opening the door with her right hand and pulling at him with her left. "You need to come!"

"I . . . I have another girl . . ."

"You have *me*!"

"I'm not coming with you," Toronto said firmly.

"You *creep!*" Barbara shouted. "You led me on."

"No, I didn't."

"Yes, you did!" she screamed and slapped his face, hard.

"But . . . but I told you—"

"Boys don't say no and mean it! You *bastard!*" In an instant she got out of the cab and slammed the door.

Toronto just sat there, stunned. When he recovered he looked up and saw the driver looking at him through the rearview mirror.

"You did good, kid," came a familiar voice.

"Moishe?"

"Yeah. I've been watching out for you."

"But how . . . ? Did Tom . . . ?"

"Yeah, he did. The Moishe Detective Agency at your service."

CHAPTER 47

By the time Toronto was awake the next morning, Tom had already been up for three hours and had ordered breakfast to be delivered to their suite. Tom was famished, and, when he called his order in, he had asked for the works: two full American breakfasts with eggs, sausage, and hash browns, and two full Continental breakfasts with croissants and an assortment of cheeses and deli meats, together with two carafes of juice, both orange and tomato, and a pot of coffee. When the breakfast cart arrived, Tom went into the bedroom and shook Toronto awake. "Time to get up," he said. "We have a big day ahead."

Toronto just lay there and said nothing while he cleared his head.

"You hungry? Breakfast is here."

Toronto finally woke up enough to move his mouth. "What time is it? I must have overslept."

"It's nine. I let you sleep in because we'll probably be up for a long time. We're going on a trip today."

"A trip? To where?" Toronto perked up, stared blankly at Tom, and threw his legs over the side of the bed.

"The Cook Islands. We're going to pay a visit to my trustee."

"To save your company?"

"Yes, if it's not too late. Dakota and the Enforcer had a one-day head start."

"Does he know we're coming?"

"Yes, I called the man. His name's Joe Williamson. He told me she called ahead too and said to expect her."

"Does he know what she wants?"

"She's pretending she wants to set up a trust fund, but Joe knows her real agenda. He can stall and hold her off for a day until we get there.

He'll give her a tour of the island, take her to dinner, show her some hula dancing on the beach at night, that sort of thing."

Toronto was wide-awake now. "I'd better get going!"

"We have time for breakfast," Tom said. "Then we'll get our motorcycles and ride them back to the trailer at West Nyack. I ordered a limo to be there at noon and take us to JFK. We're on an Air New Zealand flight via LA and Auckland to Rarotonga, leaving at three thirty."

"Wait! Hold it. We're *flying*? I thought you couldn't stand heights. We'll be at forty thousand feet!"

"Flying doesn't bother me at all. Yet I get scared just climbing up two rungs on a ladder or coming close to a window on the third floor."

"That is so *strange*. Maybe if you pretend the window is on an airplane . . ."

"I tried that. It doesn't work because I know it's not."

"Okay, just a thought."

Over breakfast Toronto told Tom what he had learned from Barbara the night before. "This Dakota Berk thinks you're dead and can buy RoadWheels on the cheap from your trustee. She has about five hundred million and a rich partner, a guy named Gunther Sachs, who can put up whatever else is needed."

"That's important to know. The best way to get to even with rich people is to take their money away. Short of converting all their money into a pile of dollar bills and making a bonfire, that's hard to do. Money is an asset that just keeps on sticking to them no matter what happens. They can buy their way out of pretty much any problems that come their way."

"So what's the plan?"

"The plan is to take *all* of Berk's money away."

"Well, I'll be! How do we do that?"

Just then Tom's phone rang and he looked at the screen. "It's Moishe," he said and pressed *answer* to take the call. He put the phone on speaker and placed it down on the breakfast table between himself and Toronto.

"'Morning, Moishe. You're on speaker."

"Is he there?"

"Yes, thanks to you."

"No, I can't take any credit. He managed to do it all by himself."

"And it was one of the hardest things I've ever done!" Toronto shouted into the little black instrument. "I was *that* close."

"Bonnie trusts you, and so do I," Tom said with calm assurance.

"So you hired Moishe to check up on me?" Toronto replied sarcastically.

"You guys leaving today?" Moishe wanted to know, changing the subject.

"Yes," Tom said. "We're on a three-thirty plane."

"You're lucky you're getting out of town. We're having a big demonstration today."

"Oh? Is there a problem?"

"It's a problem that's been going on for years. We just can't take it anymore, so we're going on strike."

"On strike? You'll cripple the city."

"We hope so! A few big companies own all the yellow cabs. They've been bidding up the price of the medallions to the point where they're over $1 million now—$1 million to operate a cab! The little guys can't afford them anymore, so independent cab drivers are practically a thing of the past. Now the rich owners of the cab companies are getting richer, and they're squeezing us drivers. We're lucky if we can make twenty grand a year. You can't support a family on that!"

"So what's your plan? When you strike, what are you asking for?"

"We want the city government to do something. *Anything*. They've got to bring the price of the medallions down to one or two hundred grand."

"You're asking the government to fix the price?"

"I'm aware that's unrealistic. They can't do that. Too many people paid a million dollars for a medallion, and fixing the price would confiscate their property."

"So what can the city do?"

"That's just the trouble. There's no real fix for this thing. The cab companies are hiring immigrants from third-world countries to drive for slave wages. They're taking jobs away from hardworking Americans, and these coolies barely know how to steer. It's getting dangerous out there."

"Have there been accidents?"

"Damn right! And the cab companies don't care. They insulate themselves from liability by creating a separate corporation for every single cab and by carrying the minimum liability insurance the law allows. That way if someone gets hurt and sues, they only lose an old, beat-up cab worth about $1,000 and whatever the insurance company pays, maybe ten thousand total. That's it!"

"So what's your leverage?"

"Our *what*?"

"Leverage. What have you got that will force the cab companies to change?"

"We're striking! We're refusing to work! That's what we've got."

"You're just hurting yourselves and hurting the city. People won't be on your side for very long when they can't get a cab."

"So, Mr. Smartass, what do you suggest we do?"

"What time is the strike?"

"The demonstration is at four o'clock. After that, we're all going home and refusing to drive."

"We have a little time. By then I'll have a solution ready to bring to the drivers."

"What? A *solution*? You have a solution to our problem?"

"Yes, I do. There aren't many disputes between people that can't be resolved fairly."

"I thought you were going to fly out today."

"I was, but this is more important. We have to save the city."

"What can we possibly do?"

"You've got one thing going for you that you didn't have just a couple of years ago."

"What's that?"

"Nearly everyone has a modern cell phone."

CHAPTER 48

Tom explained his plan to Moishe and Toronto and they both agreed it was worth a try.

Tom extended the reservation for his suite at the Waldorf and changed his airline reservations for the planned trip to the Cook Islands to the following day. He then called the one person in RoadWheels who wasn't a station manager but who reported directly to him: his chief engineer for information technology, Tom Swift.

"Tom, it's me, Tom."

"Yo. I recognize your voice, like a voice from the *grave*, ha ha."

"That's very funny. How are you doing?"

"Doin' well. How're *you* doin'?"

"I need your help."

"Anything, boss."

"Don't say that."

"Say what? 'Anything'?"

"No, 'boss.' We're all equal in this world and in this company."

"But you *are* my boss. You tell me what to do and I get it done."

"That's just the point. Once you know what to do, you do it without involving me. Everyone in the company has a job to do, and everyone does it well."

"But someone has to lead the charge. In this company that's you, boss."

"I get the ball rolling, but once we know where the ball's supposed to go, we all work together to keep it moving in the right direction. No one's more important than anyone else."

"What about the bumps in the path? This Find-Me Project I'm working on? It's your solution to a pretty big bump."

"It was as much your idea just as it was mine. We brainstormed it together, remember? *You* came up with the phone app solution."

"Okay, so that's a bad example."

"So what do I call you? 'Mr. Smith' sounds a bit stuffy."

"'Tom' will do just fine, thank you."

"Okay, Tom."

"So how's it coming, Tom?"

"What, the Find-Me Project?"

"The phone app."

"It's in beta test and it works great."

"Is it ready for prime time?"

"How prime?"

"About fourteen thousand medallion cabs in New York City and about two million people who use them."

Tom Swift whistled. "That's prime, all right. When do you need it?"

"We need it today. At four o'clock."

The software engineer whistled again. "We have a couple of glitches to tweak out yet."

"Can you make the tweaks in the next hour?"

"Heck no! A couple of *days*, maybe—that's if we can find the glitches right away."

"You have a whole hour. Do it."

"You're kidding, Tom. Right?"

"I'm not kidding. And I'm the boss. You said so yourself."

"Now admit it—you're playing Steve Jobs and his reality distortion field."

"It worked for *him*."

"Thy will be done."

"Good, and I need you to make a few changes also."

"Tell me."

Tom Smith spent the next fifteen minutes explaining what he had in mind. Swift listened intently and asked a few probing questions to clarify several points.

"We can do that," Swift said finally. "How much time do I have?"

"You have until four o'clock."

"Today?"

"By four today."

"Okay." Swift sighed. "We'll do that too."

"Downloadable from the app store?"

"That's a bit harder. Apple has to approve it."

"Send it in. Then call Apple."

"Gimme an hour and the tweaks'll be done. The changes will take a bit longer. But getting the approval will be out of my control."

"Okay, then I'll take care of that. And by the way, it just occurred to me . . ." Tom Smith said.

"What?"

"The president of Apple is Tom Cook. All three of us are called Tom."

"Strange, huh?" Tom Swift said.

"Maybe more than a coincidence," Tom Smith mused.

Tom Smith rang off and placed a call to a fellow chief executive, iPhone to iPhone: the president of Apple. He had to explain to Tom Cook that the reports of his demise had been greatly exaggerated but that he liked it that way and that this fact was to remain completely confidential between them. Tom took off his aviator glasses and used the Facetime feature to reveal his face. Once Tom Cook was sure that he was who he said he was, the deal was struck. The phone app would be uploaded at four and then tested, approved, and made ready for free download by five o'clock that day.

*   *   *

Meanwhile, Toronto was making an important call of his own. The first two times he called, the phone rang and went right to voice mail. The next time he tried it rang longer. *Third time's the charm,* thought Toronto, hoping against hope that Barbara would pick up. After four rings she answered.

"I don't ever want to speak to you again, you . . . you . . ." The phone went dead in his hand.

Toronto tried a fourth time, and, when Barbara answered the call, he immediately started talking before she could hang up. "I need you desperately. Give me another chance. I'll make it up to you. *Please!*" Toronto waited and held his breath while he listened to the phone. There was silence. She didn't hang up this time.

"Can we meet at Starbucks at lunchtime again?" he asked.

CHAPTER 49

At about noon a tractor with a flatbed trailer pulled up on the edge of a grassy area in Battery Park at the tip of Manhattan and stopped. The driver got out and lowered the stilts on either side of the trailer to support its front end. He then unhooked the tractor and drove away.

A short time later a white panel truck drove up and parked next to the trailer. The driver and two carpenters got out and started unloading lumber and other parts for a stage. The three men carefully lifted down two small staircases and placed one at each end of the trailer. Next they unloaded a podium, carried it up one of the sets of stairs, and set it down in the center of the trailer bed, facing the open grassy area. Finally they unloaded a large number of two-by-fours, and, with saws, hammers, and nails, they proceeded to construct a safety railing around the perimeter of the trailer, which now formed a stage.

When they were nearly finished a van drove up and stopped near one side of the stage. The driver got out and unloaded fifty-five folding chairs. He threw ten of these onto the trailer bed and then climbed up and opened them, placing five in a row on each side of the podium. The remaining forty-five he set up in front of the stage in three rows of fifteen.

Another panel truck arrived next, and two technicians began unloading sound equipment. They installed eight large loudspeakers at the tops of long poles that stood firmly on tripods and placed them strategically around both sides of the grassy area. One loudspeaker was placed on each side of the stage, facing outward, and the remaining six were distributed in a semicircle facing an imaginary audience at the center. Together the technicians next unloaded a heavy DJ "coffin," a controller containing turntables, mixers, and power amplifiers, and set it up on legs behind the stage. They strung a microphone cable straight back from the podium to an input jack on this box and connected a laptop computer to another input via USB cable. Finally, they daisy-chained the right and left sets of speakers to the right and left outputs of the box and connected the whole system to a power cable that tapped free electricity from the mains. When done, they tested the system using the podium mike, with one of the technicians saying, "Testing, one, two, three," over and over again as the other one went from speaker to speaker adjusting its volume. When they were finally satisfied, they selected a tune on the laptop and the speakers rocked the area with the reggae beat of "Red, Red Wine."

While these men were working, a pink van drove up with the words "STAR'S EFFECTS" painted on its sides and rear in bright-colored lettering, superimposed on background images of exploding fireworks. Two young women wearing overalls and cowboy boots alighted and walked back to open the rear panel doors and access their equipment. They proceeded to decorate the stage with red, white, and blue banners hanging from the railing and bouquets of yellow, helium-filled balloons tied with black ribbons at each corner of the stage. Next they brought out launching tubes for fountains of fireworks and confetti and affixed them firmly to the trailer, business end up, at the back of the stage.

At first the only people who saw this activity were the occasional passersby. Some curious souls stood and watched, but most walked right on past as if this were a normal occurrence in New York, as indeed it actually was. Demonstrations happened all over the city, some small, some large, for all kinds of reasons, mostly in an attempt to attract media attention. A few demonstrations, like the Occupy Wall Street movement, continued for days, while other, mini demonstrations erupted seemingly spontaneously, communicated rapidly by viral tweets and text messages, and often died before they had a chance to materialize. Some relied on the presence of a celebrity to attract an audience, while others relied on a constituency for a popular—or wannabe popular—cause.

This particular demonstration was a bit different. The political pressure had been building and gaining steam for a long time, and the date and time of the demonstration had been announced far in advance. A license had been duly applied for and obtained by the New York City Taxi Drivers Association, also known as the New York Hack Association or NYHA, affectionately called Nia (rhyming with *Leah*). All the pertinent politicians had been invited, and nearly all had agreed to come. Some, who relied on the New York City Taxi *Owners* Association for campaign contributions, apologized for "schedule conflicts" and declined the invitation, but they regretted their hasty decision after learning that many of the taxi owners intended to show up themselves and be heard. Knowing that by this time any pretense of suddenly freeing their schedules would reveal the real reason they declined to attend, they stayed away, hoping no one would notice. Members of the press, always alert to point out the hypocrisy of politicians, called to ask for their schedules that day and made public the fact they had no other place to go.

People started to arrive as early as two in the afternoon. They came walking over from the Wall Street area and by riding the buses and subways. By three o'clock people were literally pouring out of the Bowling Green Station, coming in waves as train after train pulled to a stop in the narrow cavern below and unloaded its passengers before continuing on through the tunnel to Brooklyn. With the exception of those who came by chauffeur-driven vehicles, very few people came by car, knowing the problem of space at the tip of Manhattan. Two lucky taxi drivers were asked to bring their yellow cabs and park them on either side of the stage as symbols of solidarity. These two cabs and the stage itself were soon surrounded by a sea of people of all races and nationalities that extended outward in an ever-enlarging circle until by four o'clock a crowd of close to thirty thousand was assembled and ready to hear and take part in the political push and shove that was the New York City equivalent of a town meeting.

By this time, the television vans and crews had set up and were sending live feed to their respective networks for use in the evening news programs. The politicians arrived punctually at the appointed time via chauffeured black SUVs and made their way through the crowd toward the stage, reporters with microphones in tow, following them to capture every precious sound bite that fell from their lips. When they finally reached the stage they climbed the steps and took their designated seats at the dais on both sides of the podium.

At precisely four o'clock Moishe stepped forward, front and center, and spoke into the podium microphone. The music, which had been blaring popular tunes all afternoon, suddenly stopped, and the crowd swiftly hushed itself and slid into silence. The atmosphere was crackling with anticipation. Moishe felt the heat of sixty thousand eyes on him, and he trembled inwardly, imperceptibly to the onlookers, strangely energized in a way that he had never experienced before.

"My fellow New Yorkers," Moishe began, "we have come to this meeting place from all over the five boroughs to debate and to deal with an issue that has slowly become more and more acute to our many taxi drivers in particular and to our city's transportation system in general. Driving a taxicab in this city used to be an honorable and fairly compensated profession. Since the dawn of the automobile age, and up to fairly recent times, it has been possible to own and operate a taxicab and make a decent living doing so. Many young men, and even a few young women, were able to obtain a taxi license from the city, purchase a vehicle like our beloved Checker cab, and earn a living for themselves and their families by driving eight hours a day, six days a week, year in and year out. It was a simpler world then: a world when you could start your own business and, through hard work and long hours, earn a fair income. Because of the medallion system in New York City, that is no longer possible. Medallions simply cost too much for the average hardworking Joe, so the only way for him to drive a cab is to work for somebody else.

"We all know that New York City is a magnet for people around the world. They come here, sometimes out of desperation, to try to better themselves. We who are lucky enough to have been born here wish fervently that all of them could have the same chance at life that this great city has afforded us who preceded them. It used to be if you could drive a car, or learn to drive one, you could make a living with a taxicab, but that promise is gone. No longer can a taxi driver start and build his own business.

"It would be fine with us taxi drivers to work for someone else—to work for a large enterprise, even—if we could receive fair compensation, such as wages above the poverty level and health and retirement benefits. But we don't. We are entirely dependent on the fares we are able to attract by cruising the streets day and night.

"In order to survive, many of us have had to take on second jobs in addition to driving a cab. I started a detective agency; others work construction jobs where the pay is much better but the work is not steady. Many aspiring actors and actresses drive cabs when they cannot find work.

"The point is, driving a cab is no longer a profession. It has been cheapened and demeaned to the point where only the down-and-out see any benefit. We, the taxi drivers of New York City, cannot take it anymore! We are taken for granted by the taxicab companies and by the people of this city. We are underpaid and forgotten. We have pleaded our case to the taxi owners and to the city, but no one listens. There is no other way to get their attention and the attention of the public. We must and we *will* go on strike!"

At the conclusion of this rousing speech, the crowd roared its approval.

CHAPTER 50

Next came the rebuttal of the Taxi Owners Association, explaining their position in this economic give-and-take. A wealthy cab company owner named Bill Ryan made the case for maintaining the status quo.

"My fellow citizens of this great city, we'd like you to know we *have* listened and listened repeatedly to the taxi drivers. They have not been shy or otherwise unable to make their complaints known to us, and complain they have. Again and again they raise the same issues: not enough pay and not enough fringe benefits for the work they are doing.

"Let me tell you, it is easy work they do. They ride around the city in air-conditioned comfort all day while policemen, firemen, trash collectors, and practically all other workers in the city lift heavy loads and sweat the heat. There is a reason why so many people apply to work for us as taxi drivers. We turn away twice as many applicants as we hire!

"When drivers are hired they know what the pay scale is, and no one complains. It is only later, after they have heard the grumbling of other cab drivers, that they start with their complaints. It is never enough money, never enough benefits, never good enough working conditions, whatever! They are never satisfied.

"Allow me to explain the cold, hard economics of the taxi business. First, there is this permit to operate a cab that we call a medallion. There are only so many, so the price keeps going up. We don't need more taxis than the fourteen thousand we have now. There are only so many fares on an average day, so if we allowed more cabs, there would be less work for everyone.

"There are other fixed costs too: the cost of the cab and the cost of insurance are the main ones. Then there are the operating costs: the gasoline and the maintenance of the cars. Finally there are soft costs, such as legal fees, city parking fees, and on and on. It all adds up.

"At the end of the day, there is not much money left for the driver.

"A medallion now costs a million dollars, give or take. If one invested that sum in a low-risk bond, it would earn interest at 5 percent, or about $50,000 a year. We should expect no less from our investment in a yellow cab.

"The amortized cost of a Ford Escape hybrid, which costs thirty thousand and lasts five years, is $6,000. Insurance is another four, so we must carry the cost of another ten thousand per year.

"Gasoline at four dollars a gallon for twenty-five thousand miles divided by twenty-five miles per gallon is four thousand dollars. Maintenance is another thousand.

"Adding all this up, we have fifty thousand plus ten thousand plus five thousand equals sixty-five thousand. Those are our annual costs that have to be covered.

"A good driver earns a hundred thousand in fares in a year if he drives six days a week. That does not count the tips he takes in, and which belong to him. Subtracting the sixty-five thousand in costs of operation, this leaves only thirty-five thousand to split between us cab owners and our drivers. We can afford to pay a driver twenty to twenty-five thousand, but anything more cuts into our very thin profit.

"So you see, you can strike, but if you do, it will not change the economics of the taxicab business. You will only hurt yourselves, and, more importantly, it will hurt the riding public. I therefore urge you to be realistic and stop this nonsense. I ask you—I beg you—not to strike!"

The crowd remained quiet as Bill Ryan spoke, but when he concluded they erupted and showed their displeasure with loud boos and catcalls. They were a very tough crowd and definitely on the side of the drivers.

Next came the politicians. They posed as the peacemakers, the wise ones who tried, unsuccessfully, to satisfy both sides. The economics just didn't work, and there was nothing they could do to forge an agreement between the parties. Like Bill Ryan, they were booed by the electorate, and it seemed as if a strike were inevitable.

The mayor of New York City spoke last. Of all the speakers, he was the most well known and the most respected, and it was hoped by all that *he* could, and would, provide *the answer*. He, of all men, was the only one who could illuminate a path to that most elusive of all solutions: an agreement by which everyone gained something. The drivers, the cab companies, and the riding public—all should be able to walk away satisfied from this impasse with a positive financial gain. Higher pay for the drivers, more profits for the cab companies, and lower fares for the public. It was up to Mayor Hizzonor now to work his magic miracle.

As the mayor addressed the crowd, it fell suddenly silent. Everyone listened intently to his sonorous, monotone voice as it reverberated throughout the area via the eight huge loudspeakers. By this time, it was nearly five o'clock on the East Coast, and the mayor's face appeared on almost every television screen in New York City and on the television screens of the major networks throughout the nation, no matter what their time zone. As far as the news media were concerned, everyone should have an interest, and everyone should *care*. This *was* important. As goes New York City, so goes the entire country.

What they heard shocked everyone, and it enraged the taxi drivers.

"My fellow New Yorkers," the mayor began.

CHAPTER 51

"I truly sympathize with the taxi drivers of New York City. It is very hard to make do and to raise a family on $20,000 a year. And no matter how hard you work, you cannot earn more money. Your pay does not even keep up with inflation.

"But what about the taxi fleet owners? They are stuck too! If they pay their taxi drivers more money, they will earn less. That is the reality we must accept. The taxi drivers cannot expect to receive a handout from the fleet owners.

"Yes, it is true that the fleet owners earn much more money than do their drivers. They make ten or maybe twenty times more than what a driver makes. But if we didn't have rich people—if we all earned the same—we couldn't aspire to better ourselves. That is the fuel that accelerates this fire of commerce we call capitalism.

"I grew up here in the city, in the borough of Brooklyn, on a third floor walk-up. My father eked out a living, as did so many other New Yorkers. At five o'clock every morning, he rode the subway to Grand Central Station, where he shined shoes for the wealthy executives who came in by train from the suburbs on their way to work. Most of his customers paid only the basic fee for their shine, but sometimes, especially at Christmastime, they would leave him a handsome tip.

"As a young boy, I thought about this a lot. I thought it wasn't fair. My father worked so hard at what he did and got paid so little. He would stay at his shoe shine stand all day, mostly biding his time, waiting for customers, to catch a few stragglers who came to work late and in hopes of shining shoes for the wealthy ladies who came into the city to shop. The ladies seldom needed a shoeshine, though, because they frequently bought new shoes. I could not help but wonder why my father made so much less than the people he served.

"Well, let me tell you, that motivated me. I worked hard at school and then took out loans to go to college. I 'burned the midnight oil,' as they say, to study, and study I did. I studied finance because, to paraphrase Willie Sutton, that's where the money is. I got a job on Wall Street and I worked—I clawed—my way up.

"I had a fire in my belly because I did not want to be like my father. I did not want to stay poor. I worked longer hours at my job than anyone else in my firm, and the hard work paid off. My salary and bonus exceeded a million dollars a year before I was thirty-five. By the time I was forty I was taking out outrageous sums of money. Don't ask me where that money came from, and don't ask me if it was fair. No one on Wall Street ever thinks that way. They just take, and they take as much as they can get away with.

"It was as if I could never make enough. The more I made, the more I wanted.

"But then came the downturn. My firm laid off nearly half of its employees, including me! I thought I was invulnerable—the master of the universe—but I realized later what had happened. There were others in the firm who were jealous of me and wanted to have what I had. So they conspired to take over my accounts. They stabbed me in the back.

"Revenge! That is the best motivator of all, and I wanted to get back at those guys who fired me. I had plenty of money saved up by that time. I could have retired then and lived a comfortable life, but no. I had to get back at them.

"So I took a gamble. Having worked on Wall Street, I knew what their needs were. Those guys were working long hours and making gobs of money, so they never saw their families. Their kids were growing up and their wives were growing older, but that was all happening at home in the suburbs. They were never there. I realized that what they needed was better communication. The technology was available. Everyone had a computer on his desk. We could use it to bring a man's home to his office.

"So instead of going quietly into the sunset, I risked a lot of my money to hire a computer company and develop the system. You know it well by now. A man's wife wears a lapel pin with a built-in video camera, so wherever she goes, her husband and the father of her children can go with her. He can see what she sees on his computer screen. He can watch while she takes the kids to soccer practice, and, when they have games, he can watch them with her. If he wants, he can listen in while she schmoozes with her women friends over coffee. And best of all, he can make sure she isn't flirting with the appliance repairman.

"When I started the company, I had no idea whether I could sell this service. Sure, I had focus groups tell me they would buy it if it were available, although some women objected, but you never know. Well, the rest, as they say, is history. Husbands are clamoring to watch their families, even if only on their computer screens. They're insisting that their wives wear their pins at all times and some even order pins, expensive as they are, for their teenage children.

"I'm a billionaire now, and the money just keeps rolling in. Getting fired was the best thing that ever happened to me, and my Wall Street friends are eating their hearts out."

By this time, the crowd was getting restless and starting to make some sounds of disrespect. What was this speech about? What did it have to do with them? However, the punch line was not much longer in coming. The mayor droned on:

"So you see, capitalism works! You have to trust it. The system may not be fair, but it is the best system we've got to create business and provide jobs for everyone. If you don't like your job, if you are overworked and underpaid, you had better not complain. Go out and get another, better job. I'm talking to *you*, our taxi drivers of New York City. The city is *not* going to come to your aid, even if it could. Like I said at the outset: that's the system we have. Deal with it!

"One final thing: Don't you dare go on strike. If you do, the city will go to court and seek an immediate injunction to forbid you from striking. And if you still refuse to drive, a judge will send you to jail for contempt of court. I mean it. Driving a taxi in this city is a privilege, and we expect you to honor it.

"A strike would result in damages for our fleet owners, for which they will seek redress, I'm sure. I know I would. And worst of all, a strike would inconvenience the riding public. As mayor, I cannot stand by and allow you to tie up the people of this city. There *will* be harsh consequences if you strike! I will not allow you to sit comfortably at home while Rome burns . . ."

The anger of the audience had been welling up, like the pressure of magma building in a volcano, until it erupted in a fiery blast. The people roared their disapproval as the mayor spoke these last words and stood at the podium staring defiantly. Moishe, who had been standing behind him on stage, pushed his way forward to the microphone and tried to mollify, or at least moderate, the effect on the crowd.

Someone shouted "Strike!" and the crowd responded repeated the yell. This quickly evolved to a repeated chant: "Strike! Strike! Strike!"

Moishe held his hands out, right and left, palms out, to try to get the attention of the revelers. "There is a way!" he shouted into the microphone, but the chanting kept on.

Moishe looked nervously at his watch. It was after five o'clock. Where were Tom and Toronto? This entire demonstration was lurching out of control.

Just then, out of the corner of his eye, he caught a glimpse of something bright and shiny. He looked out toward the edge of the crowd and saw a silver motorcycle, followed by another, gold-and-white-colored motorcycle, making its way toward the stage. The astonished crowd followed with their eyes where Moishe was looking and paused in their chant. The people in front of the motorcycles parted like the Red Sea to make a path, and the machines slipped slowly by, engines idling between revs, avoiding even an appearance of danger to the startled souls but nevertheless pressing inexorably forward to their destination. An aviator-glasses-masked man was mounted on the first motorcycle, and a handsome young man drove the second. An attractive woman rode behind him, with her arms tightly wound around his waist.

After switching off their engines and setting their steeds on their kickstands, the three dismounted and walked up the steps to the stage.

Moishe, meanwhile, had no more trouble with the crowd. They silenced themselves out of curiosity when they saw the new arrivals. Turning again to the microphone, Moishe introduced the final speakers of the day.

"My fellow taxi drivers," he said, "before we go on strike, I would like you to lend an ear to my two friends who have just arrived. You will be amazed at what they have to say!"

CHAPTER 52

Tom stepped up to the microphone and looked out over the audience. After an initial rustle of murmurs that quickly died down, he spoke with a clear, authoritative voice. "There is a way that everyone can make more money," he began. "You just have to increase the number of taxi rides every day. And starting today you can do that."

There was another rustle of murmurs, this time louder than the last, as people whispered to each other: "No way, Jose!" and "Who is this guy, anyway?" After the murmurs died down again, Tom continued.

"There are three modes of public transportation in this city: subways, buses, and taxicabs. Subways are fast and inexpensive, but they don't go everywhere, and you have to walk to and from the stations. Buses run on many streets, but you have to take about three of them to get where you want to go. Taxis are available everywhere, except when you try to hail one in Manhattan in the rain or you happen to be in one of the outer boroughs, and they are much more expensive than either subways or buses.

"Manhattan has the greatest concentration of riders, so that's where most of the subways, buses, and taxis are. The outer boroughs are left to fend for themselves.

"However, it's even inconvenient to get around Manhattan. There's lots of ways to get uptown or downtown, but to go across town on the grid you pretty much have to take a taxi. There's the shuttle from Grand Central to Times Square, and there are a few cross-town buses, but that's about it.

"So you see, you don't just have a taxi problem here in New York City. You have a *transportation* problem."

Tom paused a moment to give the audience time to think about what he had just said. This time, rather than talking among themselves, they remained strangely silent and stared at the stage, waiting and wondering what would come next.

Tom reached into his shirt pocket, pulled out a small black object, and held it up high. "This is a cell phone," he shouted. "This one happens to be an iPhone, but they come in all types. If you have one of these, I want you to take it out now and hold it up."

There was a grumbling sound in the audience, but about half of the people did as they were told and held up their cell phones. It was a strange sight with so many hands in the air, holding the tiny video screens, some illuminated and some dark, aimed in all different directions. Those that did not hold up phones looked around and were amazed at the numbers of these little instruments. Those who did not have a cell phone made a quick decision to head to the nearest telecom store to buy one. The others just stood there, as if in Missouri, thinking *Show me*, and stared at the man on the stage, expectantly.

"With these phones," Tom said, still holding his high, "we are going to solve the transportation problem in New York. Here's how.

"Taxis presently roam the streets looking for passengers, wasting fuel and adding to the limited capacity of the grid. The fleet owners do not have complete control over the movement of their cab drivers, since they use a bidding system for on-demand requests. Even when prospective customers call in from remote areas, like from the outer boroughs, you drivers don't always want to bid on these trips, and these requests are left unfulfilled or have a long response time.

"Furthermore, because you drivers earn money per trip, it is in your best interest to maximize the number of trips.

"Finally, as you all know, taxi customers do not like to share cabs, because the trip takes longer, and it is difficult to divide up the cab fares.

"As a consequence, taxicabs are not being utilized to their maximum capacity, and the people of this city are not receiving the door-to-door service that these taxis can provide."

Tom paused once again to let the information sink in before continuing.

"Suppose that a transportation system were available that offered the convenience and flexibility of taxicabs at the efficiency and lower price of buses." Tom looked earnestly out at the crowd and they looked back at him, their mental wheels turning. The audience was starting to connect the dots.

"Suppose a transportation system were available that saved fuel and freed the streets, since the cabs did not travel around looking for passengers, leading to a smaller carbon footprint per cab as well as per customer.

"Suppose a system were available that reduced the response time to a customer request yet was cheaper to use than the current taxi system due to higher utilization of cabs and cost savings.

"Such a system is available *now*!" Tom held up his cell phone again. "Ten minutes ago, a phone app became available for download that can provide this system for all of New York City—not only in Manhattan but throughout the five boroughs. It's called Find Me. Everyone who wants a ride in the city should get it from their phone app store. It's a *free* download!"

Quite a few people in the audience pressed the phone app store button and began typing "Find Me" to access the app. Others just continued to listen as Tom explained how the application worked.

"What you'll see when you use the app as a customer is a map of the grid with a red dot showing your location and green dots showing the cabs that are available nearby. You type in the address or just tap on the spot where you want to go and a cab appears. It's that easy!

"You indicate whether are willing to share a ride, and if you have a time limit in getting to your destination—within fifteen minutes, say— you indicate that too. Sharing a ride will reduce your cab fare but getting to your destination by a particular time will increase it, so you have a choice. It is sometimes possible to do both—share a ride and get to your destination on time—depending on where the other rider in the cab wants to go. Sharing a ride cuts the fare in half, so most people will want to do that.

"When the system is up and running, the ridership in taxis will increase, because a lot of people will use taxis instead of buses. They will get you right where you want to go and, by sharing rides, they won't be much more expensive than buses.

"The increased ridership will lead to increased revenue for both the fleet owners and the taxi drivers. The system will also benefit the public because they will be getting door-to-door service throughout the five boroughs. In this way, everybody benefits!"

Tom ended his speech with these words, and, realizing he was finished, the assemblage in Battery Park let go with an enormous roar of approval. The DJ behind the stage quickly put on a Boston Pops rendition of "Star and Stripes Forever," which rang out over the eight loudspeakers and enhanced the celebratory mood. As it was playing, Moishe took Tom's place behind the microphone and waited patiently until the song came to its triumphant conclusion. When it was over, the park fell silent again and Moishe addressed the crowd one more time.

"My fellow New Yorkers, you have heard the future. Do we still need to go on strike?"

There came a resounding response of *"No!,"* almost in unison, from all corners of the park.

"In that case I'd like to introduce Barbara, an intelligent, energetic, and pretty young woman who will fill you in on the important details. Fleet owners and taxi drivers alike, you will need to know how to use this system. She will be your go-to person to explain how the system works and to operate the computerized call system. You will be using a different cell phone app that directs you where to pick up customers and where to take them."

Barbara came forward to the podium and stood at attention, bathed in resounding applause from the audience. As the applause died down, the sound of two motorcycles could be heard over the sound system. Tom, followed by Toronto, threaded his way out through the crowd and nearly reached the street at the edge of the park before most people realized they were leaving.

"Hey, wait a minute!" someone shouted near the stage. "Who was that guy?"

"I don't even know his name," replied Barbara, speaking through the microphone, her voice echoing throughout the park. "But I've been told by his friend that they call him the Road Ranger."

CHAPTER 53

Imagine an island paradise in the South Pacific, and you will picture Rarotonga Island in the Cook Islands.

Rarotonga is an almost perfect oval, seven miles long from east to west and four miles wide from north to south. Like a green pendant of Victorian jewelry, it adorns the navy blue sea sprinkled with whitecaps. The rough-surfaced emerald stone at the center is outlined in white gold—a continuous sandy beach around the island.

The native population of about twenty thousand live, work, and play near the edge of the island in an encircling band of flat land close to the beach only a quarter mile wide. To get from one place to another, they travel by bus, car, or bicycle on the Ara Tapu, or main road, that runs completely around the island perimeter, a round-trip distance of some twenty miles. The cars and buses are all small in size, and their protocol is to drive on the left.

No roads run across Rarotonga from one side to the other, but there are wondrous hiking trails. The lush green heart of the island is an unspoiled and uninhabited rain forest with rugged hills, waterfalls, and a volcanic peak, Te Manga, that juts twenty-one hundred feet above sea level.

Dakota Berk sat in the first class cabin with Alex at her side, gazing out the window as the single daily flight from Auckland descended and entered the landing pattern for Rarotonga International Airport. They flew parallel to a single east-west landing strip for several minutes before banking left for the base leg of the landing pattern and then banking left again for the final approach. It had been a long trip with only fitful sleep, and with her internal clock turned upside down, Berk already felt a throbbing headache coming on. The sooner she could get her business done and return home from this godforsaken place, the better, as far as she was concerned. This was definitely *not* a pleasure trip, as it seemed to be for all the other annoying, chatty passengers on her plane. The next time, if there *was* a next time, she would hire a private jet, she told herself.

At Joe Williamson's suggestion, she had reserved two nights at the Paradise Inn in Avarua. The hotel did not count itself among the luxury resort hotels that surrounded the island, but it was within walking distance of Joe's office on the main strip of Avarua. All Dakota Berk wanted to do was to conduct her business as quickly as possible and *leave*.

When she and Alex landed, they quickly passed through customs, collected their bags, and took a taxi to the nearby hotel. While checking in, the desk clerk handed them a sealed envelope, addressed simply to "Ms. Georgia Bell, Paradise Inn."

When she and Alex were settled in their suite, Berk opened the envelope and read the message:

> *Dear Georgia:*
> *Welcome to the Cook Islands! Please call me when you arrive.*
> *Cordially,*
> *Joe*

The message, written on Williamson's office stationery, gave his contact information.

"I'll be damned if I'll call him," Berk snarled. "I want to have a bite to eat and go to bed."

"Maybe you should make an appointment to meet him tomorrow," suggested Alex.

"He's expecting us," Berk replied. "We're going to appear at this office at ten tomorrow and get this done."

"I have a few persuaders with me. Should I bring them?"

"What have you got?"

"Only the stuff I could get through security: ropes, plastic clamps, drugs, ceramic knives—that kind of thing."

"Bring your briefcase. I doubt if we'll need them, but we're going to do whatever it takes."

"Understood." Alex grinned in anticipation of what Berk wanted him to do. And to think she was *paying* him to come with her all the way to the Cook Islands and to use his talents to persuade this guy.

The only problem was the kind of thing he was expected to do for his employer after their dinner tonight. Torturing and even killing people were enjoyable, but for that he had to provide stud services too? It was such an undignified and disgusting part of his job. Someday he would force her to pay dearly for it.

*　　*　　*

Attorney Joe sat in his office the next morning, wondering if his new client would show up. She had said to expect her today, but if she had arrived on the four-fifteen plane the afternoon before, she had not called him as he had asked her to. Should he call *her*? He did not want to seem anxious, but he also knew that if she was on the island now, his job was to stall her for at least a day. He knew her real name and her hidden agenda, which was to take over the ownership of Tom Smith's company. His task, as he had discussed with Tom on the phone, was to keep her happy and stall for at least two days until Tom had a chance to fly there. When he arrived, the two of them would execute their plan of action.

Keeping her happy would not be a problem, he thought. This was a beautiful island with lots of things to see and do.

At precisely ten o'clock Joe's secretary, Mary, announced her arrival. "Georgia Bell is here," she said over the intercom, "with another man she calls Alex."

Joe came out from his office to greet them. He was all smiles and held out his hand to the lady, a short, stocky woman with dark brown, bobbed hair and without lipstick. She wore a plain brown tailored suit and only minimal jewelry. *Incredibly nondescript,* he thought. He would never notice her at a party.

"Pleased to meet you, Ms. Bell," he said, carrying on the charade although he knew her real name. "You brought a friend?" Joe turned and addressed Alex, who backed away slightly and said nothing.

"His name is Alex. He's my associate," Berk said. "And my name is not Georgia Bell. It's Dakota. Dakota Berk. I just used that name on the phone when I first talked to you to remain incognito while checking your references. You can call me Dakota."

"All right, Dakota," Joe replied, still smiling, inwardly glad that she had cleared *that* up. He didn't like the pretense of calling her Georgia while knowing her real name was something else. Dakota it was, and Dakota it would be.

205

"Please come in to my office so we can get to know each other and plan your stay with us here on Rarotonga Island." Joe led the way and walked behind his desk while inviting them to sit down in the two chairs in front. "People who come here usually stay two weeks, but I'll tell you a secret. The island is not that big, and you can see everything there is to see in about a week. If you are a member of Rotary, we meet for a sunrise breakfast every Thursday, so you can do a makeup. There's biking, hiking, kayaking, sailing, snorkeling—"

"Cut the crap, Joe. We're here to do business," Berk snapped, but keeping her temper in check. "We're not *tourists*."

"Oh, I know. But you should do yourself a favor and stay awhile. It's a beautiful place to relax."

"We're from New York," Berk said, as if that explained it all. "We don't *relax*." She said the word as if it were not a part of her active vocabulary, which indeed it wasn't. "Let's get right down to business if you please."

"May I get you both a cup of tea? Coffee? Soda?" Joe was doing his best to place his new clients at ease and to slow their pace down to something closer to the usual hands-and-knees pub-crawl for doing business on the Cook Islands.

"We'll pass, thank you," Berk said. Alex nodded in agreement.

Joe stared at them a moment, wondering what to do next, and then said finally, "I understand you want to set up a new trust for your assets. Well, you have come to the right place. How may I be of service?"

Berk looked over at Alex, quietly signaling him to be ready, and began.

"Joe, we're not here to set up any kind of trust. We're here to buy out RoadWheels. As trustee, you're owner of the stock, and you're going to sell it to us. We're not leaving until you do."

CHAPTER 54

"The business is not for sale. And if it were, I'm not the person to talk to. I'm the trustee; a fiduciary for the real owner. I can't help you, I'm afraid."

"Now, that's a problem, isn't it? Because I *will* buy the company." Berk glared at him.

"Well, then, you'll have to speak to the real owner."

"*You* hold all the stock in the company."

"I hold it in trust. Do you know what that means?"

"Yes, it means you can sign over the company to me, and that you'll hold the money you get for it in trust for the owner."

"Money? You couldn't possibly pay what it's worth."

"I'm prepared to pay you today, as a matter of fact." Berk cracked a rare simile. She was in her element. Money did talk, and she knew it.

"Really? How much?"

"Five hundred million. And not a penny more."

"Five hundred million? The stock is worth twice that!"

"Who knows what it's worth? That's what I'm willing to pay."

"And I'm not willing to sell," Joe said with finality.

"Ever heard of the carrot and the stick?"

"What about it?"

"You are about to experience the stick. Alex, close that door."

"Wait just a minute! You can't—"

Alex lifted his big frame off the chair and headed for the door. Joe pressed the intercom button in a panic and spoke to his secretary, "Mary, call the police! Right away!"

"Tsk, tsk, you shouldn't have done that," Berk said, shaking her head. "Now we have to bring Mary in here too. Such a shame."

Following Berk's cue, Alex quickly sprang out the door and grabbed Mary before she had a chance to make the call. Holding her arm in a vice grip, he brought the terrified woman back into Joe's office. She cringed and whimpered softly, with a pleading look at Joe for assistance. Joe was horrified himself, however, and sat frozen in his chair. He couldn't have stood up if he'd wanted to. "What . . . what are you going to do?" he asked in a small voice. Alex forced Mary to sit in one of the side chairs.

"That depends on you, now, doesn't it? Are you going to sell me the stock? I have offered you a huge sum of money."

"F—fi—first of all, that's only half what it's worth, and second of all, if I sell the stock to you, it would be under duress. The owner could sue you and get it back."

"You let me worry about that."

"And what if I don't sell it?"

"You don't want to know. Then again, maybe it will help to give you a hint." As if rehearsed in advance, Alex picked up the briefcase he brought with him, placed it on the desk and snapped open the two latches, one on each side of the lid. He lifted the cover and, with a flourish, revealed his tools of torture. Joe stared at them in horror. Mary stood back, shrinking from the evil sight. The reflection of this evil on Joe's face told her not to even think of looking in the direction of the briefcase.

"Well?" Berk said expectantly. Her menacing look contrasted with Alex's obvious pleasure at what was to come next.

"Uh, I have to make a call and speak to the owner."

"No calls. He or she will obviously say no."

"It's a he."

"Oh, it is?" Berk was clearly surprised. "Who is it?"

"Tom Smith."

"He's dead."

"No, he's not."

"Yes, he is. Alex here killed him months ago. There was even a public funeral."

"*You* killed him?" Joe stared at Alex, who gave a confirming nod while maintaining a strangely pleased look on his face. This conversation was going in the right direction, as far as he was concerned. The more Joe and Mary knew, the less chance they had of living to tell about it. And it would be his pleasure to take care of this loose end.

"He's still alive," Joe uttered, almost imperceptibly.

"*What?*" Berk was incredulous.

"I thought you knew."

Alex's jaw dropped at the news. Berk looked over and glowered at him. It was his turn to stammer. "I—I killed him. I swear!"

"We'll see about that. But it doesn't matter now. *You*," she said, turning back to Joe, "are going to sign over the stock to me."

"You . . . you said you would pay . . ."

"Oh, yes. You'll get your pay. And you'll live long enough to put the money in the bank here on Cook Islands, in your trust account for *Tom Smith*." She spoke the words "Tom Smith" with great disgust, to emphasize the fact, to Alex, that he was still alive. Alex felt the heat rising in his face in reaction.

"How?" Joe prodded again.

"How what?"

"How can you pay? There are capital controls. You can't smurf that amount of money. The banks catch on quickly to structuring."

"So? I don't use banks."

"Then how . . . ?"

Berk got up from her chair and walked to the window of the office. Looking north over the palm trees and out to sea, she could see a large freighter ship edging its way toward the harbor at Avarua. "It's out there," she said, pointing.

Joe and Mary both looked out into the distance and saw the ship.

"On that ship," Berk said, "there are five Mini Cooper cars. I chose to provide them in different colors so you could tell them apart. They are red, blue, green, black, and white."

"Five cars?"

"Yes, that's it. They will be unloaded today. They will be yours when you sign over the stock."

"But . . ."

"I know what you're thinking—that's not the five hundred million dollars."

"Yes."

"Oh, but you're wrong. Each car has been specially built and weighs about five thousand pounds."

"So, where's the money?"

"With the exception of the parts that are made of steel, those cars are worth their weight in gold."

CHAPTER 55

"The bill of lading for those cars is made out to you as trustee for RoadWheels Inc. When you present your personal identification and the original, notarized trust document appointing you as trustee, those cars will be released to you. I suggest you do it quickly before anyone realizes their value and steals one of them."

"So what am I supposed to do with them?"

"For starters, I'd lock them in a very secure garage. Each car carries exactly 3,906.25 pounds of gold. At $1,600 an ounce, that's one hundred million dollars."

"Locked in a garage? What the hell good is that?"

"Each time the price of gold goes up by one dollar, those cars are worth three hundred thousand dollars more. Not a bad investment, I'd say."

"That won't even buy a loaf of bread if it's not in cash."

"Gold is legal tender in every country in the world. You figure it out. Now it's your turn to deliver. You're going to issue me a certificate for all the stock in RoadWheels." Berk looked over to Alex, and he bared a devilish grin, showing two rows of ragged teeth. Joe looked over at Mary, and they both shuddered. Fear and shock drained all the color from Mary's face.

"All right, I'll do it. But don't say I didn't warn you. It's voidable."

"Do it!" Berk said menacingly.

Joe nodded and asked Mary to get the stock book. She rose from her chair and slowly headed for the door with wobbly steps. Alex walked right behind her into the front office and watched while she opened a file cabinet and pulled out a black bound volume with "RoadWheels Inc." embossed on the binding in gold lettering. Mary brought the book back to Joe's office and laid it down gingerly on his desk in front of him. Joe flipped through the pages to find the next blank stock certificate and ripped it out along the serrations.

"Here, Mary," he said gently. Type in the amount of outstanding shares, and we'll void all the old certificates." Turning to Berk he asked, "What did you say your name was?"

"Berk. B-E-R-K. Dakota Berk."

Mary took the book and the certificate back to her desk to type in the name and number of shares. Alex followed and stood lurking over her to prevent her from calling the police. Joe stayed seated the whole time, trying in vain to figure a way to get help. He kept his mouth shut and just stared blankly at Berk.

"How long are you going to stay?" he asked finally, stalling for time and not knowing what else to say.

"What difference does it make?"

"Tom is coming in on the four-thirty flight tomorrow. You should talk to him."

"I'll be long gone by that time, believe me."

"You should talk to him. Maybe learn something about running his company. If he doesn't sue you to get the stock back, that is."

"He won't be suing anyone. He's supposed to be dead."

"Well, he's not. He's—"

Berk cut him off. "He will be. Alex is going to finish the job."

The moment she mentioned Alex's name, he returned to the room with Mary, who carried the completed stock certificate in her trembling hand. She laid it down on the desk in front of Joe and he examined it.

"It's correct," he said after a beat, looking back at her appreciatively.

"Now sign it!" Berk growled. Joe took a pen and signed his name as trustee at the bottom of the certificate. Berk grabbed the paper off the desk, examined it carefully, and, for the first time, showed a hint of a smile. This simple sheet of paper was worth a billion dollars. The moment passed quickly and her face returned to a scowl.

"Now give me the signed trust agreement," she growled again.

"The original?"

"Of course the original, you idiot! You're not going to need it anymore."

"We, uh . . . don't have it here. It's in a safe-deposit box at the bank."

"Well, that complicates things, doesn't it? You kept a copy?"

"Yes."

"Let me see it."

Joe nodded to Mary and she went out again with Alex to look for it in the front office. She came back again a few moments later with a file, Alex following her like a shadow. Berk grabbed the file out of her hands and looked through the papers. "I'll need an extra copy of this," Berk demanded, pulling out and holding up one of the documents.

"I have a scanned copy in the computer. I can just print it out," Mary replied, reluctantly. She looked over hesitantly at Joe as if to ask him for permission. He nodded his agreement and she turned to leave again.

"Are you a notary?" Berk glared at Mary.

"Y—yes," Mary acknowledged.

"Then notarize a true copy a give it to me. But scan the copy and also send it to my lawyer."

"What's his e-mail address?"

"Imbadass@lawless.com."

Mary stared at Berk with an incredulous look. Joe couldn't help from smirking in spite of himself and the dire situation they were in.

"What's so damned funny?!" Berk screamed. "Send the fucking e-mail!"

Mary left the room again, followed by her shadow. A few minutes later she returned with the notarized copy and handed it to Berk.

"All right, that's the end of the road for you two."

"Wha—what do you mean 'end'?"

"You know too much. I don't leave loose ends."

With that simple statement, Berk walked out of the room with the paper file in hand and shut the door behind her. Alex remained in the room with Joe and Mary.

Joe looked from Alex to Mary with terror in his eyes. However, Mary remained strangely calm and began to speak, the words spilling out rapidly in an odd, high-pitched voice. "You're going to kill us now, aren't you? I don't really mind, but when you do, I want you to please make it quick. I can't stand pain and suffering. Joe has given you everything you asked for. There's no reason to torture us, right? Oh, and could you please give me and Joe just a few final moments to savor this life before our lights go out? You will do that for us, won't you? What is your name again? Alex? That's a nice name. It has a strong, masculine sound to it. And you're a real tough guy, aren't you? I have always liked men who are real men, ready to stand up to anything. I won't mind dying at the hands of a guy like you. Kick the old proverbial bucket. Sing my last song—"

"SHUT THE FUCK UP!" Alex dove into his briefcase that lay open on the desk and grabbed a ceramic knife. Joe jumped up and backed away with a start, tipping over the chair on which he sat. It crashed to the floor with a loud thud just as Alex lunged and plunged the knife into his chest.

Mary shrieked. "Joe! Oh my God! Stop it, you evil man!" She came at Alex, whose back was to her, and started punching and kicking. Alex turned around with the bloody knife in his right hand and came at Mary menacingly. She backed away, horrified, as Joe grabbed and held on to the top of the desk in an attempt to keep from falling. "You murderer! You tried to murder Tom Smith, but you failed miserably. Now you're trying to murder us! Well, let me tell you, *Alex*, you son of a bitch, you won't get away with it. Do you hear those sirens?"

Alex hadn't been listening, but sure enough, off in the distance he could hear the wail of police sirens getting louder and seemingly heading their way. He froze for a moment, not knowing what to do.

"You stay right there, Mr. *Alex*, or whatever your name is. Yes, I e-mailed the police when I was sending the trust agreement to your Mr. Badass! You're too stupid to notice. Well, they're coming for you right now, and you'll get yours."

Mary ran to the door and tried to open it. Alex dove for the door too and held it shut, trapping her and Joe in the room. Joe turned to take a quick look out the window to see if help were really coming, and in that moment, Alex threw the knife at him. Alex's aim was sure, and the knife whizzed through the air with the point forward like a spear, but in twisting toward the window, Joe's body no longer presented the same target, and it took a glancing blow to his back. The knife deflected but kept flying and smashed against the pane of glass, which broke with a loud crash.

Down below, two police cars arrived at the same time and four uniformed men got out. Hearing the crash of glass, they looked up, saw exactly where they needed to go, and rushed into the building.

Meanwhile, Mary made another dash at Joe's door and this time made it out to the reception area, where she immediately opened the main door to the office and called to the policemen. "We're up here, officers! Please hurry!"

This time it was Alex who felt trapped. He looked around for a second door to Joe's office and found none. Pushing Joe out of the way, he grabbed Joe's desk chair, which had fallen on the floor, and used it as a club to complete the job of clearing the window. Looking out and seeing no other policemen, he grabbed his briefcase, climbed through the shattered glass, and jumped from the second story down to the ground.

By the time the police entered the room he was gone.

CHAPTER 56

Dakota Berk was walking over to the Paradise Inn when she heard the sirens. *No way could they be heading for Joe's office,* she thought. *How could they know?* Nevertheless, it was time to leave—and leave quickly.

She had paid cash for two nights in the hotel room. She had half a mind to stop at the front desk and get her money back for the second night.

But then there was Alex. By now he had dispatched Joe and Mary, yet he still had to finish off Tom Smith when Tom flew in that afternoon. Alex might need the place to stay for one more night.

Berk rushed to the room, grabbed her bag, and walked out of the hotel. She took one of the taxis out front to the international airport. The ride lasted only five minutes, but when Berk stepped out of the cab with her bag, she had blonde, flowing tresses instead of bobbed brown hair and bright red lipstick instead of plain lips. Her clothes looked different too, although all she had done was remove her beige-ish brown jacket to reveal a white frilly blouse and remove her pants to reveal a light blue miniskirt. And she now wore glasses with a light blue frame.

Alighting at the departures area for Air New Zealand, she walked briskly to the airline counter with her bag in tow and presented her open return trip ticket and a US passport for Georgia Bell.

"We can have you on the next flight to Auckland, Ms. Bell," the female clerk said cheerfully. "It leaves in an hour. Just go to gate five."

By the time Berk passed through the security check and reached gate five, the first-class passengers had already started to board. She entered the aircraft, placed her bag in an overhead compartment and settled in to her assigned seat. She always chose a window seat so she could see out and visualize her surroundings. She hated the closed-in feeling she got when she sat near the aisle and, without the visual cues, felt like she was locked inside a flying building.

The coach passengers boarded, and the hatch door closed in preparation for leaving. The chief flight attendant announced the procedures for an aircraft emergency, and they were ready for takeoff. However, the aircraft remained standing at the terminal without a pushback. Something was amiss, and it made Berk very nervous.

After what seemed to be an interminable ten minutes, the pilot made an announcement. "Sorry for the delay, folks. We'll have to open the hatch for just a few minutes and let a security team aboard to check our manifest. It won't take long, I'm told. We'll soon be underway."

Berk slumped in her seat and pretended to stare out the window. Out of the corner of her eye she saw two men enter the aircraft each holding sheets of paper. They examined their papers and then looked carefully at the rows of passengers before proceeding down the aisle with one man looking left and the other right. As they approached her row Berk saw both men were holding a police sketch—of *her*. They were about to pass by when one of them, the man scanning the passengers on her side of the plane, stopped and stared at her. "What's your name, ma'am?" he asked.

Berk almost forgot who she was. "Who me, officer?" she replied, assuming her best southern accent. She batted her eyelashes and feigned a cute smile.

"Yes, ma'am. What's your name?"

"My name's Georgia Bell," she said politely. "From Atlanta." Her southern accent appeared almost authentic. It could fool even a native-born southerner, let alone plain-clothes policemen in the Cook Islands.

"I'd like to see your passport."

"Certainly, officer." Berk reached into her purse and took out her US passport. The officer opened it, looked at the picture and then back at her.

"Thank you, ma'am," he said as he handed back the passport and continued down the aisle. The men soon finished their security check and gave the chief flight attendant the all-clear sign to take off.

* * *

Alex landed on the sidewalk, hard, and twisted his right ankle. Excruciating pain caused him to bend over for a moment, but he ignored it and started walking briskly, briefcase in hand. He started heading for the Paradise Inn, keeping to side roads and alleys to avoid being seen, but when he arrived, he saw an empty police car in front and knew they were investigating his room. He had no access to his luggage that carried his passport, his spare clothes, or even his razor. All he had with him were the tools of his trade in his briefcase.

He placed his briefcase on the ground, opened it and took out two ceramic knives. Placing the knives under his belt he closed the briefcase, picked it up and walked over to the taxi stand in front of the hotel. After waiting his turn he climbed into the backseat of the next cab in line. "Go," he commanded. "Take the circle road."

"Which way?"

"Either way. I'm going to the other side of the island."

The driver made a right turn out of the hotel entrance onto the Ara Tapu and headed east out of town. Alex sat back in the seat and thought of what to do next. Agenda number one was to finish the job of killing Tom Smith. Agenda number two was to get rid of that attorney, Joe, and his snotty secretary, Mary. Agenda three was to get home to New York, but how he was going to do that without a passport he didn't have a clue. Maybe he could borrow someone's identity, possibly after he killed that person and took his passport. Right now, he needed to get as far away from the police as he could in this little godforsaken hellhole.

To do his job he needed two things. He needed shelter, and he needed a car, both of which his taxi driver had. He leaned forward, wincing in pain from his swollen ankle, and asked the man, "Got any kids?"

"No, sir. I don't have a woman."

"Why not? You're a good-looking guy. You can get yourself one."

"Had a wife once. It didn't work out."

"What happened?"

"She left me. Caught me with another woman."

"Can you blame her?"

"Well, yeah. Here on the island everyone fucks around."

"Everyone?"

"Men do, anyway. Women are so good-looking."

"You live alone?"

"I live with my cat."

"Where?"

"Where I live? I have a bungalow on the far side by the beach."

"Take me there."

"To my house?" The taxi driver suddenly perked his antennae up.

217

"Yes."

"Listen, mister. I don' know who you are, but I'm not goin' there."

"Yes, you are." Alex drew a knife from his belt and brought it forward so the taxi driver could see the blade. "And don't even think about using your cell phone to call for help."

The driver nearly froze with fright but managed to keep on driving. Ten minutes later he pulled up in front of a one-story cement home with shuttered windows.

"Get out and let's go in," Alex said in his deep gravelly voice. "And don't do anything funny. Try it, and that's the last thing you'll ever do."

The driver got out of the car and walked up to the front door with Alex right behind. When the driver opened the door with his key and walked in, that *was* the last thing he ever did.

CHAPTER 57

Tom Smith sat in the first-class cabin with Toronto at his side, gazing out the window as the flight from Auckland two days later descended and entered the landing pattern for Rarotonga International Airport. They flew parallel to the single east-west landing strip for several minutes before banking left for the base leg of the landing pattern and then banking left again for the final approach. It had been a long trip with only fitful sleep, and with his internal clock turned upside down, Smith already felt a throbbing headache coming on and did not relish the thought of dealing with Dakota Berk and her attempt to take over his company. The sooner he could take care of this matter, the better, as far as he was concerned. This was definitely *not* a pleasure trip, as it seemed to be for all the other happy passengers on the plane.

As they disembarked and entered the holding area for international passengers to await their baggage, Tom and Toronto executed their plan of action. As far as they knew, the man they called the Enforcer could recognize Tom but not Toronto, so they separated. Toronto first collected his bag and went through customs as if traveling alone. Tom lagged behind and eventually went through the same process five minutes later. The Cook Islands was a separate country from New Zealand although, it was joined with New Zealand in "free association." Its citizens carry New Zealand passports, they use the New Zealand dollar as currency, and they share a common language, English, although the natives speak an ancient native language called Cook Islands Māori.

The customs official glanced at Tom's passport and the declaration sheet he had filled out in advance and compared Tom's picture with the live visage in front of him. "Business or pleasure?" he asked pleasantly.

"A bit of both," replied Tom, looking around for Toronto, who had disappeared at that point. The official paused.

"Is this your first visit to the islands?"

"No. Actually I was here once about ten years ago."

"Well, welcome back!" the official said, smiling, as he stamped the passport with a loud thunk.

At just that moment, Tom spied Toronto near the main doorway to the building, signaling a warning with a gesture they had agreed upon in advance. Toronto ran his hand through his bushy, ash-blond hair and at the same time pointed secretly with his fingers toward the drive-up area outside. Tom looked where Toronto was pointing, through the glass doors, and the saw the Enforcer standing on the curb next to a taxi. Tom nodded, almost imperceptibly, and walked briskly to the left inside the building with his suitcase in tow. Toronto followed with his own suitcase, seemingly separately from Tom, staying several steps behind.

Tom walked to the end of the long lobby and exited at the far end, continuing to the left in the direction of the arriving cars and buses. If the Enforcer happened to see them, he would be unable to follow in a cab against the flow of traffic. Seeing an empty taxi heading their way, Tom flagged it down. The taxi pulled over to the curb, and the driver got out to assist in loading luggage in the trunk. Both Tom and Toronto handed over their luggage and jumped into the backseat.

"The Paradise Inn, please," Tom said as they sped away.

As they passed by the Enforcer, both Tom and Toronto just happened to be looking out the left window, resisting the urge to gaze in the Enforcer's direction.

"How long are you staying?" asked the driver.

"A week. Maybe more. We haven't decided."

"Vacation, then?"

"Yes."

"You came to the right place. I can show you around if you like."

"Do you have a card? Can we give you a call?"

The driver took out two cards from a slot in the dashboard and handed them back. Tom and Toronto each took one. "My name's Tepaeru. I'm native Māori. I grew up on this island. I know all the nooks and crannies. You want a good time? You call me."

"You can give us a tour?" Tom asked.

"I can do more than that. I come with you and explain things. I speak *Te Reo*, the native language. There is much to know."

Tom looked at Toronto and Toronto looked back at Tom. "Are you thinking what I'm thinking?" Toronto asked.

Tom grinned and said to Tepaeru, "What is your charge?"

"One hundred dollars a day or five hundred a week. That includes my taxi, but other expenses are extra."

"Are you free for a week?"

"Yes, indeed, sir!"

"Tepaeru, you have a new client. My name's Tom, and this is Toronto. Pick us up tomorrow morning at nine."

"Count on me, Mr. Tom. I'll be here. And by the way, my friends call me Tepae."

Saying these words, Tepae drove to the entrance of the hotel. Tom and Toronto got out and watched as Tepae handed over the luggage to a bellhop and spoke to him briefly in *Te Reo*. The bellhop loaded the luggage onto a cart and disappeared with it into the hotel.

"What did you say to him?" Toronto asked, curious to learn whatever he could about the native Māori.

"I told him to take good care of you," replied Tepae. "You are my special clients."

"We are lucky to have met you!"

"The luck is mine, Mr. Toronto. I will take care of you. And this taxi ride to the hotel—it's on me."

"No, no, Tepae," replied Tom while handing Tepae a hundred-dollar bill of New Zealand currency. "This is called commerce. To our mutual benefit. We will take care of each other."

"You will have the best week of your life! I guarantee it."

Tepae shook hands with his new clients, grinning from ear to ear as he did so, and returned to his taxi. As he drove off, Tom exclaimed to Toronto, with a note of irony in his voice, "I'll be happy if we still *have* a life in a week."

CHAPTER 58

The next morning, promptly at nine, Tom and Toronto stepped out of the hotel entrance and saw Tepae standing next to his taxi, waiting for them and grinning. He waved them over and, after the pleasantries, they all climbed in the cab with Tom and Toronto in the in the back.

"Any particular thing you like to see?" Tepae asked, turning to look at his passengers.

"We have a business meeting today," replied Tom. "It won't take long. After that we're all yours."

Toronto handed Tepae a piece of paper bearing Joe Williamson's office address and they were off. Tepae glanced at the paper as he drove and then suddenly jammed on the brakes and stopped the vehicle while still in the hotel driveway.

"You can't go in there," he said, his face turning instantly dark.

Toronto stared at him. "Why not?"

"Because the police are investigating. There's been a . . . uh . . . an incident."

"What kind of incident?"

"Some kind of a knifing. It was awful. Reported in all the news."

"A knifing? Who?"

"It was an attack on an attorney. I don't know his name."

"Could it be that man, Joe Williamson?" Toronto pointed to the paper Tepae was holding.

Tepae looked at it and shook his head. "Can't recall exactly. There are a lot of attorneys in that building."

"Did they catch the guy who did it?"

"No. He's still out there. They know who it is, though."

"They do?"

"He tried to kill the attorney's secretary too, but she outsmarted him. She got a message to the police. When they came, the guy jumped through a window and got away. She was able to give them a description."

"Did the attorney die?"

"No. Hurt badly, though. He's in the hospital. Owes his life to that secretary."

"Are they thinking the guy might try again? Is there a guard on him?"

"Yeah, there is. And they're guarding the secretary too. There's not much crime here on the island. When something like that happens, makes you wonder. No one is safe anymore."

"Let's drive there anyway. Maybe it wasn't Joe."

"Sure," Tepae agreed. "I'd like to see the building. They say he smashed a front window on the second story and just jumped out. Had to be a long way down."

It took just a few minutes to reach the building. Two police cars were parked outside, and the second-floor window facing the street was boarded up. A uniformed policeman stood guard at the front door limiting access to the building.

Tom and Toronto got out of the cab and walked up to the man. "Pardon me, officer," Tom said politely. "We have an appointment this morning with a Joe Williamson. Flew in last night from New York. Can we go in and see him?"

"No, you can't. He's not seeing anybody."

"Why not?"

"Guess you haven't heard. He was stabbed. Stabbed bad. He's in the hospital. Be there a long time."

"Yes, we did hear that someone was hurt, but we didn't know it was him."

"He's under guard round the clock. No one gets to see him but the immediate family."

"Did they catch the man who stabbed him?"

"I can't tell you that. You'll have to leave now. I guess you'll just have to fly back to wherever you came from."

"New York."

"Okay then, New York. It's a long way. I'm sorry."

"Can we speak to the detective in charge?" Tom asked, finally. "We think we know who did it."

"You *what?*" The policeman eyed Tom suspiciously.

"We know of someone who had a reason to kill him."

"Well, *blimey*! When did you say you came from New York?"

"We arrived yesterday."

"Can you prove that?"

"Yes, of course."

"You may have to. This is the biggest crime of the century around here. The chief's very nervous. Everyone's a suspect."

"We have information that can help."

"Okay. I'm calling the chief right now." The policeman keyed his walkie-talkie and spoke to someone at the other end. "Get me the chief. There's a guy here who he should speak to." He clicked off and turned back to Tom. "He'll be down here in just a minute."

"Thanks," replied Tom. "We'll wait."

While they waited for the chief of detectives to arrive, Tom and Toronto looked up at the boarded-up second-story window from which Alex had jumped. It was a good twenty feet off the sidewalk level—quite a distance for a big man to fall. They walked over to the spot where they assumed Alex had landed and inspected the sidewalk, but they found nothing. As they were looking around for clues, the chief walked up.

"Gentlemen," he said. "I'm Detective Hardwick. You are . . . ?"

"Tom Smith and Alonzo Sierra," Tom introduced himself and his colleague. "We had an appointment today with the attorney Joe Williamson. We come to find out he's at the hospital."

"Very tragic. Nearly stabbed to death. Missed the vital organs, thank God. He'll survive, they say, but barely. We have him under surveillance in case the perpetrator tries again."

"How about his secretary? I believe her name was Mary?"

"She's safe too. Under guard night and day until we catch the guy. My policeman said you have some information?"

"Yes. We believe we know who did it and why."

"All right, I'm game, Mr. Smith. Tell me what you think you know."

"The man's name is Alex, but he's called the Enforcer for a woman by the name of Dakota Berk. He's more dangerous than you can ever imagine. He kills the people she wants out of the way. You have got to find him and stop him as soon as you possibly can. He's out there waiting to strike again—and believe me, he will."

"How do you know all this?"

"Because he stabbed me, too, and left me for dead."

CHAPTER 59

The detective's eyes widened as he looked at Tom with sudden interest. "But how do you know it's the same man?"

"Joe Williamson is—no, *was*—my trustee to hold the stock in my company. Dakota Berk had an appointment with Joe two days ago. That much we know. She wanted to get control of my company, and I assume that's what she came for. I also assume she was successful in getting Joe to sign over the stock ownership. Once that was done, she wanted Joe as well as his secretary, Mary, out of the way so they couldn't testify that the transaction was under duress. She gave orders to her Enforcer—this man, Alex—to dispatch them both. I should have gotten here sooner or at least alerted you to the danger. I feel so sorry! Those two were like . . . like Mary and Joseph." The names Mary and Joseph hung in the air for a moment with holy significance.

As Tom was speaking, Toronto reached into his pocket and brought out his phone. He pressed the app for photos and brought up some pictures. "Look here," Toronto said. "These are pictures of Dakota Berk and Alex on their way to Cook Islands. They were taken at JFK airport as they were about to leave." Toronto held out the phone so Detective Hardwick could see as he cycled through a number of pictures Tom had received from Moishe. The pictures were of Berk and Alex as they got out of the limousine, retrieved their bags from the trunk, and walked into the terminal building. "These two are the ones you should be looking for."

Hardwick stared at the faces of the man and woman and said, finally, "That's very helpful. I'll need copies of these pictures."

"That's easy," Toronto said. "What's your e-mail?"

"Hardwick@RarotongaPD.com."

Toronto typed in a few letters and pressed *send*. "Done," he said. "Was that quick enough?"

Hardwick's mobile phone buzzed in his pocket, and he pulled it out. "Here they are!" he said, amazed. "We can catch these people now. I'll put out an APB. This island is not that big."

"Have you checked the hotels?" Tom asked.

"Yes, we did," Hardwick replied. "We didn't have much to go on, but we found one thing. A woman called Georgia Bell checked into the Paradise Inn with a male companion and didn't check out."

"That's her. Joe Williamson told me that's the name she gave when she called him. She probably has a passport with that identity."

"That's too bad, because she's gone. A woman with that name left on a plane two days ago, within hours of the time the crime was committed. The other guy—this Alex, I presume—is probably still on the island, though. We found a passport of a William Berk in the luggage left in their hotel room."

"He couldn't leave for two reasons: he was ordered to kill Joe and Mary right away and then wait on the island and kill me."

"But the police interrupted him, and—"

"He jumped out the window. He's definitely out there, waiting to finish the job with Joe and Mary and then finish the job with me."

"We'll catch him. Don't you worry. But first I'm going to tighten the security around Mr. Williamson and his secretary. Just a minute, please. Don't go away." Detective Hardwick pressed a few buttons on his mobile phone, put it up to his ear, and spoke rapidly. Turning back to Tom and Toronto, he said, "Thanks. That was a close one. Both of them are still safe, but we had no idea of the danger. We've buttoned things down a bit."

"Can I talk to Joe?" Tom asked.

"As far as I'm concerned you can. You'll have to see what the doctors say. I'm told he was hurt real bad."

"I need to speak to him about my stock. I may not own a business anymore."

"I needed to speak to him, too, about the stabbing. But maybe now I don't have to, thanks to you."

"As long as he's safe, I can wait," Tom said agreeably.

"Might be a few days. Maybe a week."

"We have a taxi waiting with a driver that's going to show us the island."

"If what you say is true, I'm afraid we'll need to keep you under guard."

"I have Toronto here, Detective. He saved my life once before."

"Now just a minute, Mr. Smith . . ."

"Tom."

"Tom. If this man is as dangerous as you say, why aren't you afraid?"

"Here we are on this beautiful island, and you want us to do what? Stay in a hotel room?"

"Yes, sir. That's what I recommend. Until we catch him and lock him up. Then you'll be free to move about the island."

"Suppose we help you catch him. It would speed things up."

"You mean use you as bait?"

"That would make it easier for you."

"Quicker, maybe, but certainly not easier. Then I'd have you two to worry about. If anything happened to you, well, I wouldn't want that on my record or my conscience. You're not law enforcement. We are."

"You can't hold us, Detective Hardwick."

"No, but if you want me to beg, I'll beg. I want you to stay at the hotel for now. I can put a guard on your room, 24-7, but I can't spare the three bodyguards it would take to keep you safe while running around on the island."

"If we do go out, we'll need only one thing."

"What's that?"

"Your mobile number to put you on speed dial."

Hardwick complied, and Tom and Toronto both stored Hardwick's number in their cell phones.

"You're free to go now," Hardwick said, "but you'll have to give me your numbers too." Tom and Toronto complied, and the detective tapped in their numbers to his own phone. "You two keep in touch. I want you to have a good time here and go home *alive*."

Both Tom and Toronto shook his hand and then headed back to Tepae, who was sitting and waiting in his taxi.

Alex was sitting and waiting in his taxi too, some distance back, watching Tom and Toronto climb into Tepae's taxi.

CHAPTER 60

"Is that Detective Hardwick?" Tepae asked, staring at the man as Tom and Toronto settled into the backseat. Hardwick was talking to the officer who stood guard in front of the building.

"Yes," Tom replied. "They called him the chief."

"I *hate* him," Tepae said in a matter-of-fact tone.

Tom glanced over at Hardwick and saw him disappear into the building. "Why?" Tom asked simply.

"He's holding my sister for something she didn't do," Tepae said, still staring straight ahead at the policeman left standing in front of the door.

"He arrested her?"

"He charged her with murder."

"She didn't do it?"

"I know my sister. When there's a fly in the house, she captures it and lets it go outside. She couldn't possibly."

"Who did Hardwick say she murdered?"

"Her husband."

"How did he die?"

"They think it was poison. Arsenic, they say."

Toronto gave Tom a face as if to say, "She probably did it." Tom returned the look with a thoughtful gaze.

"Do you have any idea who did it?" Tom asked.

"I know who did it. I just can't prove it. It was the other woman."

"Her husband cheated?"

"Sure. All the men cheat on this island. The women are so sexy. It's what we do."

"And the wives allow it?"

"They don't like it, but they don't kill their husbands. If they did there'd be no men left."

"Have you spoken to your sister?"

"Hardwick won't let me see her until the investigation's done. He says I should get her a lawyer."

"Did you do that?"

"All the lawyers are in that building there," Tepae said nodding toward the building Hardwick went into. "And I can't get in to see anyone."

"Then we should do some investigating of our own," Tom suggested. "Do you happen to have a key to your sister's home?"

"No, but I know where she hides the spare key."

"Let's go there first."

Tepae started the engine and pulled out onto the Ara Tapu. He drove west past the airport and followed the oval along the coast. White sandy beaches could be seen through the palm trees, glittering invitingly in the sun.

"Come evening these beaches are crowded," Tepae remarked. "The women and girls dance the hula. You won't believe what you see."

"Is that why so many men cheat?" Toronto asked, curious to know why the men were so unfaithful in this island culture.

"Partly. If the single women would show some respect for the rights of married women, all this cheating would disappear. But they think it's a game, luring the men. If they don't have a husband of their own, they go after someone else's."

"You don't blame the men?"

"The men? Not really. We're pretty much putty in women's hands."

By this time the road had turned eastward, and they were following the road around the southernmost part of the island. Tepae slowed and turned left onto a cross street and then angled through a maze of narrow streets and stopped in front of a cute home with a thatched roof. "Here we are," he said.

The three got out and examined the property from the outside. The house was dark and still, and its front door was marked with yellow police tape. The tape had a repeated message—"CIPD—KEEP OUT"—along its length. Tepae walked up two steps to the front door and lifted a loose tile on the side. The key was underneath.

Entering the house, Tepae took the lead and at first stepped forward carefully and quietly, as if someone were there. Tom and Toronto followed in turn and branched off to check the various rooms. Upon determining that the house was empty they realized they could talk together normally.

"My sister, Serena, came home and found him dead. She immediately called the police."

"Where was he?" Toronto asked.

"I don't know—living room, maybe. All I know is that his lips were blue and his blood tested positive for some kind of poison."

"Did they find any poison here in the house?"

"I don't think so. Not that they told me about."

"They don't have any evidence?"

"Well, yes. They asked around and learned about Venus, my sister's rival."

"Did they talk to her?"

"Must have. They arrested Serena."

Tom nodded, indicating he understood, and suggested they split up and give the house a thorough search. They did so, but after two full hours of searching they had nothing to show for it. They checked under the kitchen sink, in the pantry, and in every corner of the basement for rat poison and found only rat droppings. They looked in the man's bedside table and found only girlie magazines. They looked in the medicine cabinet in the bathroom and found only prescriptions from a pharmacy. They looked in all the kitchen cabinets and in the refrigerator and found only food. They found no poison anywhere.

"Damn!" Tepae said when they reconvened. "I was sure we could come up with something."

"Maybe we can pretend we did," Tom said.

"What do you mean?"

"Whether we found something or not, the perpetrator won't know. He or she will have to come back here."

"But what if there's no evidence here to come back for?" Tepae wanted to know.

"Now that would be a problem. Let's hope there is."

The three men left the house, and Tepae carefully locked the door behind them. He replaced the key under the tile, and they walked together back to Tepae's taxi. None of them noticed there was another taxi parked a block away but within the line of sight, with a large dark figure behind the wheel.

As Tepae drove away, the other taxi pulled out and followed, frowning, at a safe distance behind.

CHAPTER 61

Tepae drove straight to Venus's house, which was only a few blocks away. He pulled over and stopped on the side of the street right near the path to her front door. "She is the one who did it. I'm sure of it," Tepae said. "It makes me so mad I could scream!"

"Toronto and I should speak with her alone," Tom told him. "If she's smart she won't want to talk to you. Wait here in the car."

Tepae started to object, but Tom insisted, and both he and Toronto got out and headed up the stone path. Before they had a chance to ring the bell, the door opened, and a woman stepped out, dressed in a two-piece bathing suit. She carried a large cloth bag and was apparently on her way to the beach.

"Uh, who are you?" After closing and locking the door behind her, she turned and came suddenly face-to-face with the two men. She stood there, as close to naked as a woman can be in public and still be legal, her narrow bikini stretched thin over her contour, barely covering her private parts. She almost took Toronto's breath away.

"We're from the United States. I'm Tom, and this is Toronto. We're investigating a possible murder," Tom replied truthfully.

"Well, can't you see I'm on my way to the beach? And I don't need to answer any more questions about Randy's death. I've already talked to the police."

"We have just come from Serena's house. We found something that may interest you."

"I doubt that, but I'd still like to know. What did you find?"

"Can we go inside and talk?"

"I'm in a hurry. I'm meeting someone at the beach, and I'm very late."

"I'm sure he'll wait."

"He's used to wait—Hey, wait a minute! How did you know it was a *man*?"

"Just assumed. We just want to ask you a few questions. It won't take long."

"All right. You look like nice guys. But you promise to leave in five minutes? I really have to go."

"It won't take even that long."

Venus turned around again and unlocked the door. She led the two men into her house. Although her skimpy, sun-worshipping outfit seemed almost appropriate outside, it lent an odd feeling to the seriousness of the interview that was about to take place. Venus waved her hand toward the couch in the open living area in front of them. The wide windows in the rear revealed a landscaped swimming pool in the backyard shaded with palms. "Have a seat," she said.

"Do you mind if I use the bathroom quickly?" Toronto asked. "It's been a long morning."

"Sure. Help yourself. There's only one bathroom. Go through that door and you'll find it," Venus said, pointing toward the bedroom.

Tom sat, uncomfortably, on the narrow couch while Venus briefly followed Toronto into the bedroom and came back, moments later, with a light robe draped over her shoulders and hanging almost to the floor. She then reclined on an easy chair and looked at Tom with raised eyebrows. "Five minutes, max. That's all you have," she said.

"And that's all I need. What I'd like to know, if you don't mind telling me, is where you were when Serena's husband died."

"That's easy. Where I always am during the day—on the beach."

"You go to the beach every day?"

"Every day. I love it there."

"You don't have a job?"

"With *this* body?" She smiled and opened her robe to reveal her female curves. "Not hardly."

"Men pay you?"

"What! You think I'm a whore? That's insulting! They give me *gifts*." Venus feigned shock.

"No, I'm just trying to figure out why this man died. Did you know him?"

"Yes, I knew him. Everyone knows that. I liked him a lot. And no, I didn't kill him."

"Do you know how he died?"

"They say he was poisoned."

"What kind of poison?"

"Is that a trick question? How should I know?"

Tom ignored the comment. "They say it was arsenic."

"Oh. So you want to search my home for arsenic? Be my guest." Venus waved her hand as an invitation to look around.

Toronto reappeared in the bedroom doorway, back from his visit to the bathroom, and his eyes met Tom's. Tom responded to him with an inconspicuous nod.

"That's all I have," Tom said to Venus, standing. "Thank you for your time."

"That's *it*? That was nothing."

"If I may," Tom continued. "I do have one more question."

"Of course. What do you want to know?"

"Do you have other men friends? Other than the man who died, I mean."

"That's very personal, Mr.—uh, what did you say your name was?"

"Tom. Tom Smith."

"Mr. Smith. I'm not going to answer that."

"The police will want to know."

"I've answered all their questions already."

"They'll be back."

"All right, if you must know, there was someone else, but I don't like him anymore. He has money and gave me some really nice gifts, but he's too nerdy. Now get out of here! Both of you!"

With that, the woman walked purposefully to the door, opened it, and stood there, holding it open, in effect shooing the two men out. They left quickly.

"Good-bye, and don't come back. I won't be so accommodating next time."

Tom and Toronto walked back to the waiting taxi and climbed in the backseat from both sides.

"Okay, guys." Tepae was excited to hear what they had to say. "What did you find out?"

"She didn't do it," replied Tom flatly, seemingly disappointed.

"But we know who did," added Toronto, smiling from ear to ear.

"You *do*?"

Before Tom or Toronto could answer, Tepae, who had turned in his seat to look at his passengers, caught sight of Alex's taxi through his read window. "My God! Who is *that*?" Tepae exclaimed as if to himself. "That's my friend's taxi, but the guy in the driver's seat is definitely *not* my friend."

Tom and Toronto turned around to look and saw Alex glaring fiercely at them. *"Go!"* they shouted together.

CHAPTER 62

Alex had waited at the airport for Tom to come out, but when he didn't appear, he drove directly to the Paradise Inn to see if he could stop him before he checked in. He had telephoned the hotel service earlier to confirm he had a reservation.

Not seeing him anywhere, he sat in his taxi and called the hotel with his cell phone.

"Paradise Inn," came a singsong voice. "How may I connect you?"

"I'd like to speak with one of your guests. A Tom Smith." He clenched his fist while the receptionist looked up the name.

She finally came back on the line. "Just a moment, I'll connect you."

Alex pressed *end* to terminate the call before it rang in the room, started the car, and drove away. He reasoned the man would stay in the hotel for the remainder of the evening, as he had done with Dakota two days before, and would venture out the next morning. He preferred finishing the business he had with him in a less public place, preferably while he was out walking about on foot.

It was time for Alex to explore the island and prepare a plan of attack. He needed to do the job the very next day and get off the island with the passport of the taxi driver he had killed before the man's death was discovered and reported to the police. At that instant, his taxi would become toxic and the object of an island-wide search, so he had no time to lose. Killing Tom Smith could be quickly and easily done in a drive-by shooting, but he had no gun and, unlike in the United States, guns were a rarity in this third-world country. He had no idea how to get his hands on one, so he would have to make do with his ceramic knives.

He often preferred the use of knives anyway. Death by knife wound was slower and more painful than a bullet to a vital organ, and he liked to see his victims squirm in agony and realize their mortality before their lights went out. It was no fun to kill someone who didn't know he was about to die and wouldn't experience the throes of death.

He needed and wanted to isolate his prey and engage him in hand-to-hand combat, a fight he knew he could win. His professionalism gave him confidence, and his confidence made him more proficient at extinguishing human lives. He was the best in the business.

Alex's first step was to procure and study a map of the island. Upon viewing the map, he was surprised to see no roads at all traversing the island from one side to the other. The center of the oval-shaped region of land was filled with the natural forest, without roads or buildings of any kind. This meant no humans were there, which meant it would be an ideal place to lure his prey. He could attack and torture Tom with impunity.

The map did show walking trails through the forest leading to the main points of interest: Te Rua Manga, a needle shaped rock; Papua Falls, a giant waterfall; and Raemaru, the flat-topped volcanic mountain. Although some tourists would surely be seen here and there along the trials, Alex thought, there would be no one to interfere with or be a witness to the death of a man who strayed from the trail, intentionally or not, into the dense foliage.

The very next morning Alex sat in his taxicab and watched the hotel entrance. He saw Tom Smith exit with another man, whom he assumed was a friend, and walk directly to a waiting cab and ride off. He followed with his own taxi a safe distance behind and eventually realized they were heading for Joe Williamson's building. When their cab stopped and Tom and the other man got out, he parked out of sight and waited patiently for a chance to draw them away from the inhabited areas of the island.

Shortly thereafter the two men returned and again climbed in the back of the waiting taxicab. After a few moments, the cab started up again and headed west, following the main road counterclockwise as it paralleled the coast, leading around in a semicircle to the southern side of the island. Alex followed far behind but never let the cab out of his sight for more than a few seconds. He was careful to drop behind other cars and blend into the traffic, yet he needed to tail Tom and his friend so he could dispatch them without delay. It was a difficult balancing act: he had to see without being seen, and at the same time he had to somehow lure these two men deep into the rain forest, all by nightfall that evening.

When the cab ahead arrived at its destination, Alex parked on a side road out of sight. He got out of his cab and walked over so he could watch from behind a bush. He saw the cab driver lead the two men up to the house and unlock the door with a key he took from under a tile. Alex saw the yellow tape, identical to the tape at the door of Joe Williamson's building, but the three men stepped right through it and walked into the house as if it weren't there.

Alex looked at his watch. It was nearly eleven o'clock, and he urgently had to take care of business and be on his way back to the United States. He touched the knives he had inserted in his belt to make sure they were there and waited for the three men to come out. Fifteen minutes elapsed, and then a half hour. It was time to get moving, but Alex couldn't just go into the house and start killing. The three unarmed men would not pose a problem for him, but the yellow tape could signify that a policeman was stationed inside. The policeman's gun could easily trump his knives.

Patience was often necessary in his line of work, but Alex was not a patient man. The time ticked by as he watched and waited. He began to think the men must have gone out the rear door, but their taxicab remained parked on the street, and they would have to come back to it eventually. One hour elapsed, then one and a half. He became ever more anxious and was fast on the way to becoming furious. Finally, when Alex could stand it no longer and felt he should storm the house and take his chances, the men emerged, got back into their cab, and quickly drove away.

Those *bastards*! Alex ran back to his cab, started the engine, and sped off in the direction the other cab had headed, but it was no longer in sight. Alex was pissed to no end. What if he'd lost them? He sped faster down the narrow road. Where did they go? He looked right and left into the side roads as he raced by them. There were several parked cars but no taxicab—and then, finally, there it was, parked on a side road in front of a small house, and the two men were walking up to the front door. Alex slammed on the brakes and stopped his car, pulling over to the side as he did so. He was within the line of sight of the other cab, but Alex no longer cared. He was not going to lose them again. The taxi driver remained in his cab this time and was facing the other way. The man had not noticed him, but that hardly mattered now. He had to get on with his agenda. It was already afternoon.

Tom Smith and that other man came out of the house and climbed into the back of the cab. Alex could see the driver turn around and talk to them and, in doing so, the driver saw Alex through the back window of his taxi. The two men in the backseat turned also and stared at him. Alex stared back with a message to them: "I am coming for you."

The cab with the two men sped off, and Alex followed.

The cab in front knew the roads on the island. Alex didn't. The cab zigged and zagged through the local streets, but Alex managed to remain in close pursuit. Without the two passengers in the back, Alex's cab was more nimble and could negotiate the corners, tracking the turns without understeer or oversteer and thus maintaining its forward momentum. After several minutes of this it became clear that Alex could follow the runaway cab as if towed behind with a rope. The cab in front needed to change its tactics and did so. It turned left onto the Ara Tapu, the main road, and headed straight, gathering speed as it sped away in a counterclockwise direction around the island. Alex made the same corner and floored the accelerator.

Thirty, forty, and fifty miles an hour, Alex's speedometer kept climbing, and the cab in front kept pulling away. The two taxis were racing as the scenery on both sides flew past: beaches and beach resorts on the right and gardens and the rain forest on the left. The two cabs dodged right and left around the slow-moving traffic and startled the occasional pedestrian that tried to cross the street. Up ahead the main road split into two, with the Ara Tapu bearing right and an equally important road, the Ara Metua, bearing left. The cab in front slowed for a moment, allowing Alex to catch up and come closer to its rear. Looking ahead, Alex saw the fork in the road and realized he would have to make a choice. He would have to guess which road the cab in front would take and, if he guessed wrong, he would lose them.

The cab in front kept racing straight ahead until, at the very last instant, it swerved left onto the Ara Metua. It was all Alex could do to keep from ramming the fork divider, but he had guessed correctly and turned left. He continued to follow closely behind.

Up to this point Alex had concentrated on following the speeding cab, but now that he was certain he could keep up in this chase, he began to formulate a plan. As he sped along, it eventually dawned on him that the cab in front should be following *him*, not the other way around. By this time, one of the men in the cab would certainly have called the police from his cell phone, so he could not expect this race to continue for very long. He had to act, and act quickly, to turn this chase around. Up ahead he saw the town of Avarua fast approaching. He remembered seeing a trail into the rain forest there. That would be his turning point. Seeing the trail ahead on his left, he quickly braked to a stop, jumped out, and ran to the trail entrance. Before doing so he honked his horn to catch the attention of the cab ahead. Out of the corner of his eye as he ran into the woods he saw the other cab come to an emergency stop and turn around. The man he was after as well as that younger man had emerged from the backseat and were heading his way.

CHAPTER 63

Tom and Toronto followed Alex down the cross-island trail as he ran south toward the Needle, a prominent rock that jutted so far in the air it was visible from nearly everywhere on the island. Tepae stayed with his cab to assist the police when they arrived. While they were racing up the Ara Tapu, Tom had called Hardwick on his cell and the man had promised to send his entire available security force. Tepae called again when he stopped his cab at the trailhead and told Hardwick his location. Hardwick assured him his men were on the way.

"Do you know where this trail goes?" Toronto asked Tom, both running full tilt as they raced after Alex.

"We must be heading due south, straight through the middle of island."

"So what's our plan?"

"We need to follow him so the police can find him."

"You think he has a gun?"

"I don't see how he could bring one into the country, but there's no way to be sure."

"We know he has a knife. He used it on Joe. And on you too!"

"Don't remind me."

"So let's get this guy."

"We need to be careful," Tom warned. "This forest is so dense you could be standing two feet away and not know he's there."

Tom and Toronto could see Alex up ahead, running fast but not so fast that they couldn't keep up. Apparently Alex wasn't concerned about being caught, or he would have run faster or ducked into the dense foliage.

"Looks like he's heading for the Needle," Toronto said, looking ahead and seeing the spire pointed upward and piercing the sky. "I wonder what he's going to do there."

"Whatever it is, I can't go there," Tom replied. "I'm no good with heights, remember."

"We just need to keep him in sight. The police will do the rest."

"It would be better if we didn't have to climb. Let's stop here."

"What? *Stop?*"

"He wants to *kill* me, remember? That's what he's here for!"

As if reading their thoughts, Alex suddenly jumped into the foliage on the right side of the trail and vanished. Both Tom and Toronto stared at the spot up ahead where they had seen him last, just a few seconds before, and stopped dead in their tracks.

"Damn!" Toronto shouted. "He's gone!"

They moved carefully forward and slowly approached where Alex had entered the woods. A few leaves were hanging down with their stems broken, and the bushes showed evidence of having been recently parted. Tom and Toronto stood there for a moment, wondering whether to follow.

"Let's go back!" Tom said loudly.

"Good idea!" Toronto agreed, winking at Tom, and the two began walking back on the trail in the direction from which they came.

"He won't follow us all the way back," Tom whispered. "The police are there. So let's head to that mountain." Tom pointed to the huge volcanic mountain off to the right that soared upward in the middle of the rain forest. "We passed a trail up ahead that leads over in that direction."

"That's a plan," Toronto agreed, pulling out his phone and pressing the button for an app called Mirror. He held the phone in his palm as if he were dialing a number while using the mirror surface created by the app to see behind. Just as the trail was about to bend around a corner he saw Alex emerge and look in their direction. "He sees us," Toronto said secretly. "Keep going and he'll follow."

Tom and Toronto retraced their steps on the cross-island trail until they came to its intersection with the trail that led to the mountain. They paused there a moment to make sure Alex was following before turning off onto this new trail. As soon as they turned the corner and were out of sight for a moment, Tom made another call to Hardwick.

"Where are you? We need your policemen *now.*"

After a brief exchange during which Tom explained where they were going with Alex in tow, he ended the call and told Toronto, "They're assembling near Tepae's taxi. Hardwick said they'll head this way in just a minute or two."

"They'd better hurry. This guy Alex is only interested in live bait. Once we're dead he'll lose himself in this forest and disappear."

"That's one good reason for them to hurry. And there's this other reason, too," Tom commented in a self-deprecating tone.

"I know," Toronto replied, rolling his eyes. "We'd like to *remain* live bait."

The two men looked ahead and saw the mountain looming large in the distance. It had the appearance of a huge tree trunk covered by rough bark that grew upward out of the dense, green surroundings. The trunk was cut off at the top as if by a chain saw.

"Wow!" Toronto exclaimed. "That's something!"

"That's pretty high, all right," Tom said, looking upward.

Toronto followed his gaze, squinting in the bright sun. "Can we get all the way to the top?"

"I can't go up there," Tom replied flatly.

"Are you kidding? There's a madman stalking you. All we have to do is stay alive until the police come."

"I know, and he's got knives but we don't. Let's just keep moving and see where this trail goes."

They continued on, following the trail toward the base of the mountain. Every so often Toronto took out his cell phone and looked behind with his phone app mirror to check if Alex was gaining on them. "We'd better hurry," he warned Tom as they ran along. "He's about a hundred yards back."

When the trail reached the mountain it curved to the right and began a continuous left-turn spiral ascent to the top. The trail was cut into the side of the rocky mountain surface and had a railing along the outside edge that fell away abruptly.

"Uh-oh," said Tom, staring at the trail leading upward. "I can't do that."

"We don't have much of a choice," Toronto replied. "Unless we take our chances off the trail."

Tom looked around at the surrounding rain forest. The vegetation was so dense that movement through the underbrush would be almost impossible. If they blazed a trail, however, Alex could follow.

"If we pressed through that brush, Alex could easily catch up," Tom agreed. "I'll just have to grin and bear it. This won't be pretty!"

Toronto nodded in sympathy. "You go first. I'm right behind, watching your back."

Tom gritted his teeth and half closed his eyes. "Damn it all!" he shouted and ran up the steep incline, ignoring all of his senses that were screaming loudly at him, "Danger! Danger! Danger!"

Tom continued following the trail on its upward reach along the side of the mountain. He hugged the rock solid side of the trail, keeping as far away from the railing as he could and all the while staring only straight ahead. One look to the right at the drop-off from the edge, Tom knew, would cause him to freeze with fear. By avoiding this view he was able to move swiftly up the trail, and he and Toronto stayed well ahead of the man who kept following. As they climbed higher and higher, Tom realized, somewhat to his surprise, his vertigo abated rather than strengthened. The added height didn't seem to matter at all, Tom found, and the anticipation of reaching the relatively safe top of the mountain made racing upward even easier.

The tops of the trees in the forest were already far below. Here and there a hardy tree grew out of the side of the mountain, but the volcanic rock was inhospitable to biological growth, and these trees were stunted and craggy. The view of the island was therefore unobstructed, and when Tom and Toronto reached the top of the mountain and looked out, the beauty of the scene took their breath away. They could see into infinity.

Far in the distance, beyond the green forest that surrounded the mountain, they saw the Ara Tapu that ringed the island and beyond that the white sand of the continuous surrounding beach. Beyond the beach the water shimmered in light blue, deepening into a darker blue out to sea, extending out to the sharp line of the horizon, again light blue. Moving upward from the horizon, the color of the sky transitioned almost imperceptibly from light blue to a transparent deep blue overhead, interrupted here and there by cloud patches of pure white.

This place at the very middle of the island was a spot where all visitors were expected to come, but at this moment there were no tourists in sight. Tom and Toronto stood alone on the mountaintop looking out as Alex arrived at the head of the trail, a knife in each hand.

CHAPTER 64

Tom and Toronto looked at each other. "Uh-oh," Toronto said with a swashbuckling grin on his face. "Bad guy, coming on fast."

"Let's do this!" Tom shouted to his friend. It was time to stand and fight.

They had no plan, but they were two against one. On the other hand, they had no weapons, and Tom was afraid to go near the edge of the walkway. Not exactly a level playing field.

The top of the mountain had a deep hole formed by the ancient volcano, surrounded by a wide, circular walkway. The walkway was bounded on both sides by a railing to protect pedestrians from falling, either into the hole in the center or over the cliff at the mountain edge, but Tom could not go near either side without feeling faint.

Tom and Toronto both charged at Alex just as he stepped onto the pedestrian platform and caught him off guard. Like two Davids colliding with a Goliath, Tom and Toronto landed as one against Alex's huge frame, and he stumbled backward from the blow. He dropped one of the knives but kept the other, and, managing to right himself, he lashed out viciously with this remaining knife. Tom and Toronto jumped back in fear and avoided the slash, but Alex came forward now, fierce anger on his face.

Tom dodged to the left and Toronto to the right, leaving Alex with a man on either side. Alex turned from Toronto and headed straight for Tom.

Seeing his chance, Toronto rushed forward bravely, dove down, and threw his body against the rear of Alex's legs, causing Alex to trip and fall toward Tom. Alex dropped the other knife as he held out his arms to break his fall and landed squarely on his hands and knees. Before he could stand, Tom jumped up like a coil spring and flew himself blindly onto Alex's head and shoulders, descending on the huge form with his full weight.

Alex remained down for only a moment. With both Tom and Toronto on top of him he slowly stood up, not unlike King Kong, and shed his attackers. Tom and Toronto fell to either side and scrambled back, but not before kicking away the two knives that lay on the ground. One knife flew through the railing and over the edge of the mountain. The other skittered along the pavement and remained on the pedestrian platform. Toronto ran after the weapon, but Alex was too quick. Before Toronto could reach it, Alex grabbed him by the collar, lifted him up and threw him off to the side as if he were just a brief annoyance. Alex bent down and retrieved the knife, then turned to face Tom again with his fierce look.

Toronto had landed hard and was hurt in the fall. He lay there, stunned and in pain.

Tom took several steps backward, drawing Alex away from Toronto, and finally turned on his heels and ran. Alex jogged after him in a lumbering gait, apparently unhurt from the mild encounter with these two lightweights. In fact, he had a smile on his face. He was enjoying the battle. These were the moments he lived for!

As Tom made his escape around the walkway that encircled the deep depression in the middle of the mountain, he realized that if he kept going he would lead Alex right back to Toronto. When he reached the opposite side, farthest from the place where Toronto lay, Tom knew it was time to face and deal with his attacker. Tom stopped running near an overlook, where the platform and railing bowed out over the edge of the cliff, and turned toward Alex, who was running toward him. A coin-operated binocular viewing device stood on a post near the railing, and a small trashcan stood nearby for use by tourists.

Initially standing his ground in the middle of the walkway, he looked at Alex, staring straight in his eyes without flinching, and shouted, "Stop! Let's talk."

Alex did stop abruptly and stood there, ten feet away from Tom, glaring so fiercely Tom could scarcely keep himself from visibly trembling.

"I've got something to tell you," Tom continued, staring straight at his adversary while stifling his fear as best he could.

Alex brandished the knife in his right hand and momentarily paused from dispatching the man he had tried unsuccessfully, twice, to kill. As Tom watched, his face contorted into a grin that grew wider and wider, finally reaching from ear to ear. Eventually his body began to shake as laughter welled up from deep within.

"Ha, ha, ha!" Alex let go with a belly laugh. He held on to his sides and howled.

"I'm glad that I'm amusing you, Alex, but now that you've had yourself a good laugh, I'd like to tell you something."

"Tell me something? *You?*" Alex burst out in laughter again and then suddenly became deadly serious. "You, who are about to die, what can you tell me?"

"The woman who employs you, Dakota Berk, will not be able to pay you anymore."

"*What?*" Alex bellowed. The statement apparently took him by surprise. This was a time that a victim of his violence would normally be begging for mercy.

As Alex spoke, Tom instinctively backed slowly away. "I'm guessing two things: Dakota Berk came here to buy my company, and she took out a loan to get it. She's now broke and can't pay you."

"How do you know this?"

"Not many people have a billion dollars."

"She didn't pay a billion dollars."

"How much did she pay?"

"Half that."

"She stole my company, then. But I'll bet that's all the money she had."

"She owns your company now. She's rich."

"She has nothing."

"She has the stock certificate. I saw it."

"Just a sheet of paper. It's worthless."

"What do you mean?"

"The corporation is worth nothing. It's an empty shell."

These last words, Tom saw, had the opposite effect from what he intended. Instead of explaining to Alex that the person he worked for could no longer afford his services, Alex had apparently assumed that Tom somehow cheated Dakota Berk into buying a nonexistent company. Suddenly enraged, Alex took quick aim with the knife in his hand and threw it straight at Tom. The knife sped through the air with the point forward.

Tom quickly reached out and snatched the nearby trashcan. Bringing it up, he deflected the knife and caused it to go flying over the railing into empty space. Seeing this happen, Alex came charging toward Tom like an enraged bull.

By this time Tom had edged backward to the point where his back contacted the railing. Although he kept his eyes on Alex, he could feel the presence of the cliff behind him, and he struggled with his rising fear of falling. As Alex rushed toward him, he crouched down to the level of Alex's groin, and, when Alex made contact, he pushed upward with his legs, lifting the enormous man, who was now on his shoulders. With his feet off the ground, Alex's forward momentum carried him outward over the railing.

Falling downward, Alex made a grab for whatever was there and caught hold of a scraggly tree that grew tenuously out of the rocky cliff wall. Its tree roots held fast, but its thin trunk snapped and supported Alex by a thin thread as he hung in the air.

Looking down from the railing, Tom saw what had happened and tried quickly to think of a way to rescue the hapless man. Toronto, who in the meantime had picked himself up and run to Tom's side, was the first to have the answer. "Our belts!" he shouted. "Let's use them."

Both men ripped off their belts with one quick pull. Tom wrapped his belt around the pole that held the viewing device and threaded its free end through the buckle to hold it fast. Toronto coupled the buckle end of his own belt to the last hole of Tom's and then dropped its free end down to Alex. Alex, who was holding on to the small tree with both hands, let go with one hand and grabbed the strap.

As the two men stood there at the railing, looking down, they were joined by Hardwick's policemen: first one, then two, and then five altogether. They all pressed forward to the railing to have a look at the man below, dangling from the two belts connected end to end, attached securely to the post at the top.

"Somebody do something!" Alex screamed.

Tom and Toronto backed away from the railing to make room for the police officers to pull the man up.

"Uh-oh," Toronto said, looking at Tom with a sheepish grin. The pants of both men were falling down about their legs, revealing their white underwear.

CHAPTER 65

Tom and Toronto could see Tepae standing next to his taxi, waiting anxiously as they approached from their walk back along the trail from the mountain. Tepae's face lit up like a streetlight when he spied them, and he spread his arms wide in a warm, welcoming gesture. "Hey, you guys, thank God you're here." His eyes were moist and he could hardly speak. "You just took a year off my life!"

"We're really glad to be here," Tom admitted. "I'm still numb from the shock. It'll take me at least one good night's sleep to feel normal again."

Tepae opened the taxi door for his new friends. "Forget about sleep," he said. "It's time to celebrate! There's *one* beach where everyone goes at night to party. Tonight you're going to see what Rarotonga has to offer and *enjoy.*"

"We still have some unfinished business," Toronto reminded him. "Your sister. We have to prove she didn't kill her husband."

Tepae turned suddenly serious. "You never told me what you found out."

"We think we know who did it. But now we have to prove it," Tom said.

"Who? Who?" Tepae was all ears.

"You said that your sister's husband died of arsenic poisoning."

"They think so. Yes."

"We couldn't find any source of arsenic in your sister's home," Toronto explained. "No rat poison. Nothing in the kitchen. So we looked in the medicine cabinet in the bathroom."

"You found it? You found arsenic?"

"No, nothing like that. Just regular prescriptions for your sister and her husband."

"Oh."

"But when we went to Venus's house I saw prescriptions in the bathroom too," Toronto continued.

"So?"

"They were for unusual drugs. Things you can't get a doctor to prescribe unless there's a good reason. And we noticed something else."

"You did?"

"They were from the same pharmacist your sister and her husband use."

"And?"

"Opportunity and motive," interjected Tom.

"I'm not sure I—"

"A pharmacist is one of the few people who has access to arsenic, and he provided drugs to both your sister's husband and to Venus. That's opportunity."

"That's possible. Then what about motive?"

"Suppose the pharmacist was jealous of your sister's husband."

Tepae tried to follow. "I don't understand."

"Your brother-in-law's night with Venus may have cost him his life."

"I see! The pharmacy guy has the hots for Venus. So when he learns she's offering her body to someone else, he acts to eliminate the competition."

"That could be his motive. But we have to prove it."

"How do we do that?"

"Venus told us she often goes to the beach."

"So?"

"You said everyone goes to this one particular beach?"

"Everyone goes there, including the kids, to watch the hula dancing at sunset."

"Okay, then, here's what we'll do . . ." Tom spent the next five minutes explaining his plan to Tepae and Toronto. When he finished the two nodded in agreement.

"The dancing doesn't start for a couple of hours," Tepae said. "I can bring you back to your hotel for a change of clothes and pick you up later."

"No," answered Tom. "There's somewhere else we must go first. Drop Toronto and me off at the hospital. We need to talk to Joe Williamson if he's awake."

* * *

When Tom and Toronto arrived at the hospital, they learned that Joe was conscious and was expected to eventually recover from his knife wound. However, he had lost a lot of blood and was extremely weak. After the attending physician heard they had come all the way from New York to see Joe on business, he allowed them to enter his room as visitors but warned they should limit their stay to fifteen minutes.

Joe blinked blankly at Tom as they walked into the room, apparently not realizing at first who he was. Then his face suddenly brightened to a smile so wide it radiated pure joy.

"Tom," he said with a shallow but happy voice.

"Hello, Joe. It's been a long time." Tom stood by the bed and looked down with sympathy at the man who lay there connected to wires and tubes.

Joe tried to straighten himself up in bed, but winced in pain. "Too long," he said simply.

"Doctor says we can stay only a few minutes, but I just wanted to reassure you, I'll take care of everything financially. This is all my fault."

"Your fault? That the bad guys are after us? I don't *think* so." Joe tried to wave his hand for emphasis and received a stab of pain for his effort. He winced again.

"As it happens, the same guy that attacked you knifed me too. This fellow saved me." Tom motioned to Toronto who stood by his side. "His name's Alonzo, but I dubbed him Toronto."

"Like the city?"

"Yup. Toronto, Canada. That's where he's from."

Joe looked at Toronto and shot him a smile, this time without moving a muscle. "You did good, young man. This guy's worth saving."

"So we're members of the same club," Tom continued. "People who've been knifed by a man named Alex."

"Tell you the truth, Tom, I didn't want to join your darn club. Did my best to stay out of it, but now I'm in, I consider it an honor."

"We're both in it for life."

"We're blood brothers, my friend. Pun intended."

"The police caught Alex, by the way."

"Now that's a bit of a relief! In my worst nightmares I imagined he would show up here to finish the job."

"Rest easy, Joe. You'll never have to see him again."

"I might visit him in jail. Just to see him behind bars and thank him for doing a lousy job of killing me."

"He would like that. He's not going to get many visitors in your Rarotonga prison."

"If he survives, that is. They torture prisoners here when they get out of line. It's not like your Club Fed back in the States."

"If he ever serves out his time here, he'll be brought back to be tried in Connecticut. My RoadWheels manager in Greenwich wasn't so lucky as you and me."

"Another club member, rest his soul. This Alex wasn't exactly Mr. Nice Guy, was he?"

"No, but he's not even the worst. Our next step will be to go after his boss, Dakota Berk."

"Oh God, I almost forgot! I sold her your company. I'm so sorry." Joe seemed to sink into the pillow in shame for what he had done.

"No, no! That's all right, Joe. Selling the company was for the best."

"What?" Joe struggled again to sit up despite the pain. He pressed down with his arms to raise himself and stared at Tom. "How can you say that? You started your company and built it brick by brick over these many years that I've known you, and now—"

"Joe, I'm forty years old. It's time to move on."

"Move on? And do what? Start another company?"

"Help people. Toronto and I will have a lot to do."

"What do you mean, 'help people'? Like who?"

"Wherever we go, we find people who need our help. We'll travel all over the States and Canada too."

Toronto grinned and spoke up for the first time, "I call this guy the Road Ranger. He's got a custom tractor-trailer that can take us anywhere. He also rides a silver motorcycle."

"You mean . . . kind of like the Lone Ranger or something?"

"Never thought of that, but yes, the Lone Ranger and Tonto. And I'm Tonto."

"The Road Ranger and Toronto. I get it." Joe allowed himself to sink back in the bed with obvious relief. "Well, at least you won't have to ever worry about money," he noted with a sigh. "I got five hundred million from that evil woman who bought your company."

"Invest it wisely. You're still my trustee, you know."

"My trustee fees are pretty high, but I'll cut you a special deal."

"We can share the interest."

"Interest on five hundred million? There'll be plenty for both of us, and I'll be satisfied with just a small piece."

"You've already earned your fee, in advance."

"There is still a bit of work to do. I'll have to get the money into your trust account at the bank."

"Where is it now?"

"It's in five Mini Coopers worth a hundred million each, sitting on the dock at the port right here in Avarua."

CHAPTER 66

The sunset cast a golden glow over the beach that bordered the western side of the island. Palm trees, silhouetted against the horizon, stood up like canopy umbrellas with their stems stuck in the sand. Children laughed and shouted as they played tag, threw balls, and ran about helter-skelter to the ever-present background sounds of peeping seagulls and ocean waves washing ashore.

This beach was always the place to be at sunset on Rarotonga, but this evening was extra special. The island was abuzz with news of the capture of a very bad man from America, that faraway place filled with so many people and so many problems. The man had traveled nearly ten thousand miles from New York City, bringing a brush with evil to this peaceful place. Before anyone even knew he had arrived, he had spewed death and near death upon innocent inhabitants of the Cook Islands. He had killed a taxi driver in cold blood and had attempted to kill two other innocent islanders, Joseph and Mary.

There was a collective sense of relief as well as celebration in the air that the evil had been challenged and contained. Their own chief of police, Captain Hardwick, and his brave officers of the law had captured and arrested this foreign invader. In due time, the man would be brought up on charges to answer for his actions. They were safe now, thanks to Hardwick, their real live hero and protector.

If there was one thing the people of this island paradise knew how to do, and do well, it was to celebrate. So on this evening and on this beach, celebrate they did. Men came from all corners of the island with their fifes and guitars, their bongos and traps, to play music along the mile-long stretch of sand. Women donned their coconut-shell bras and grass skirts and came out to swish their hips in the special Cook Islands way of hula dancing, while young girls looked on with awe and tried to imitate their impossible moves. Some men brought driftwood and built bonfires while others brought torches and set up long tables at intervals along the mile-long beach. Women brought local dishes of food they had prepared at home and presented them proudly on the tables for all to enjoy. The music wafted in the wind, blending with the ocean sounds and calming the spirit, while at the same time exhorting the island inhabitants to live their lives in a way that made every moment memorable.

As the sun sank slowly behind the sea horizon, the golden hour transitioned to the blue hour, the time when daylight is sucked out of the air until it is empty. In the light of the torches and bonfires, the people on the beach merged into one large, loving family, eating, drinking, singing, and dancing together beneath the black canopy sky.

Tom and Toronto arrived with Tepae in his taxi while it was still possible to see and recognize faces. They were astounded at the number of people on the beach.

"We'll never be able to find her," Toronto said with concern. "This beach goes on and on."

"Don't worry. Venus has her favorite spot. Over that way." Tapae pointed to a cluster of palm trees set back from the water's edge. Nearby, people were crowding around an open-air bar covered by a thatched roof, talking and laughing, meeting old friends and making new ones as they sipped a powerful island punch called the Captain Cook.

Toronto and Tom scanned the crowd but could not see anyone who looked like the Venus they had met earlier that day. Tepae corrected them, "No, no, not at the bar. Over there—she's dancing the hula."

And there she was, swaying and vibrating to the *rata-rata* sounds of the nearby band, her hips serving as a hanger for her loose grass skirt with just enough grass to pass muster under the Cook Islands' version of a moral code. A group of onlookers stood nearby, enjoying the entertainment and clapping with excitement in time with the drumbeat.

Toronto stood mesmerized, his mouth open in astonishment. It was the sexiest sight he had ever seen.

Tepae led the way toward the dancing woman, attracted to the flame, the heat increasing sharply as they came closer. Toronto was definitely in danger, his thoughts of Bonnie crowded out by the vision of Venus swinging her hips in the firelight.

"One of us will have to serve as bait," he said to Tom. "I'm willing to do it."

"Okay, just watch out," Tom cautioned. "We don't even know what the pharmacist looks like. He might show up when you least expect it."

"I'll take my chances," Toronto replied without taking his eyes off the woman.

"I know what he looks like. He's probably out there in the darkness right now, watching her," Tepae said. "His name's Rick Perry. He owns Rick's Pharmacy. I'll drive you there tomorrow—that is, if he hasn't attacked you already. I've heard he's crazy in love with her." Staring at Venus as she kept time with the faster and faster drumbeat in a frenzied finale, he commented, "I can maybe even forgive my brother-in-law for being tempted."

When she finished the dance, the three men walked up to Venus. Never shy about his good looks, Toronto was the first to speak. "Hello, I'm Toronto. Remember me?"

"Sure, I remember you. You were in my bedroom today."

"Your bathroom, actually."

"My bedroom on your way to the bathroom."

"Hope you didn't mind."

"No problem. You were a perfect gentleman."

"You're a terrific dancer."

"You liked my dancing?" Venus smiled coquettishly.

"Loved it. Can I take you home with me?"

"In your dreams, maybe. I prefer a guy like your friend here." She moved toward Tom and looked up at him with big eyes.

"But I'm smitten. You can have *me*," Toronto protested.

"Plenty of young girls around here. Take your pick."

"But I want you!"

"Not interested. Not when I can have a *real* man." Venus looked at Tom again, who said nothing.

"Oooh, that hurts!" Toronto replied, clutching his heart with both hands.

Realizing Toronto was getting nowhere, Tepae interrupted. "Let's all go over to the bar and have a drink."

As they headed toward the bar, Tepae walked along next to Venus and asked her, "Have you heard about my sister? She'll be going on trial for murder soon."

"I'm sorry to hear that."

"They say she poisoned her husband because he went with you."

"The police asked me about that. I had to tell them the truth."

"You don't feel the least bit guilty? The man's dead because of you."

"It's not my fault he was killed."

"Do you think my sister did it?"

"I don't know. She had a reason to, I suppose."

"The reason was you."

"Listen, if every man on this island was killed for screwing someone besides his wife, there'd be no men left."

The crowd at the bar was getting louder by the minute, and as the group arrived, they were greeted warmly. Tepae went to the front, paid for a pitcher of Captain Cook punch, and grabbed four glasses. "You gotta try this," he said, pouring it out and handing the first glass to Venus. Tom and Toronto took their glasses, and Tepae held his up.

"To my sister!" he shouted over the din. "She didn't do it!"

"To your sister!" everyone around them responded in unison. "She didn't do it!" Other than Tom, Toronto, and Venus, only one other person knew what he was talking about. That person, Rick Perry, stood in back of the crowd, watching intently.

Tom and Toronto each took a sip of the Cook Islands elixir. "This is terrific!" Toronto exclaimed. "What's in it?"

"You don't want to know," Tepae replied. "Just be careful. It packs a punch."

Venus looked up at Tom with doe eyes and quaffed her drink. "Ooooh," she cooed. "It makes me feel so sexy."

Tom scanned the crowd and noticed the man in the back staring at them. Guessing who he was, he asked Venus, "Is that Rick Perry watching you?"

"Yes, he's always doing that. It creeps me out."

"He must be crazy about you."

"So?"

"You don't want to go to him?"

"He's a real loser, compared to you guys."

Tom ignored the comment and said to his friend. "Toronto, would you please take care of this young lady?"

"I'll do my very best," he replied. Bending down, he kissed Venus sweetly on the cheek.

Venus pursed her lips, grabbed him by the arm, and dragged him away into the surrounding darkness. Tom and Tepae watched them go.

They also watched Rick Perry see them disappear, his eyes so intense they burned like coals.

"Looks like our plan is working," Tom said. "Tomorrow we can set the trap."

CHAPTER 67

The next morning, Venus placed a call to her pharmacy. Rick Perry answered.

"Rick, it's Venus."

"I know."

"I've been awake all night."

"Oh?"

"Yes, and I need some medicine."

"What kind of medicine?"

"Something to make me sleep."

"I can do that."

"I'll just throw something on and come over."

"I'll have it ready."

Venus arrived an hour later with her hair mussed and without makeup. She wore loose fitting jeans and an overlarge T-shirt that hid all of her curves. "Hello, Rick," she said flatly as she approached the counter. "Have you got something for me?"

"You look terrible."

"It's been intense, if you know what I mean."

"Not really."

"Just lying wide-awake in bed."

"So?"

"So I'm all twisted around, and my head's throbbing. I need something to slow down."

"Why?"

"Why what?"

"Why did you go with him?"

"With who?"

"With that man, last night." Rick glared fiercely at Venus.

"Him? Toronto? He refused to go with me."

"What?"

"He said he couldn't betray his, uh, girlfriend. I was sooo frustrated I couldn't sleep."

"Well, I've got something for you that will solve your problem." Rick handed her a bottle. "Take one of these every night before bedtime. There's enough for a month."

"Will I sleep then?"

"You'll sleep so well it will be hard to wake up. Just keep taking them every night."

Venus looked at the bottle in her hand. "Thank you, Rick. You're a lifesaver."

"Good-bye, Venus."

Venus turned and walked out of the pharmacy. She felt a strange twinge of sadness for Rick. He had been such a good friend to her these past two years. She had allowed herself to have sex with him off and on, but a girl had to move on, didn't she? She wasn't getting any younger.

Outside, she handed the bottle of pills to Captain Hardwick.

*　　*　　*

Tepae picked up Tom and Toronto from the Paradise Inn and drove them to Joe Williamson's office. Their suitcases were stowed in the trunk, ready for the trip back to the United States.

"There is just one more thing I must do," Tom had said. "Before we go, I need to stop in and thank Mary."

He got out of the car and entered the building, leaving Tepae and Toronto to wait while he made this one last important call on a woman who had saved Joe Williamson's life and at the same time had saved him from losing everything he had worked for over the past ten years.

He walked upstairs to the second floor and opened the door. Mary was at her reception desk, talking on the phone when he entered. Seeing him, she interrupted her conversation and covered the receiver with her hand. "As I live and breathe, Mr. Smith!"

"Mary. I've come to thank you."

Mary quickly finished the call and stood up from her chair so she could embrace Tom warmly.

"I visit Joe every day," she said. "He told me you'd been in to see him."

"Yes, just yesterday. It looks he's going to make it, thanks to you."

"All's well that ends well, as they say."

"I asked him to take care of my assets. And I know you'll be the one who's doing the caring."

"Well, we're a team, Joe and I."

"I assume he pays you a good salary, but I want to give you something to put away for your retirement, when that day comes far in the future." Tom handed her a sealed envelope.

Mary looked at it and then back at Tom. "I don't know what to say . . ."

"It will give you a feeling of security, against the unknown."

"Thank you, Mr. Smith." Tears welled up in Mary's eyes as she buried her face in Tom's shoulder and hugged him tightly. "God bless you."

Tom hugged her back and then turned to leave. "Sometimes it takes a sudden jolt, like what just happened, to make one stop and think about the future."

"Even though I'm on the opposite side of the globe, you can still call, you know."

"I know. I'll call. Many times. And I'll come back. I promise."

"Joe tells me you're going to take to the road to help people in trouble. Sort of a 'Road Ranger,' he said."

"I've found there's a need."

"Well, my heart will follow you wherever you go. Joe and I will stand watch over your trust account and keep it safe and sound."

Tom gave a brief wave and walked out the door. Mary stood there a moment, holding the envelope. She eventually opened it and found a little silver wheel with a check, payable to her from Tom's trust account. It was for one million dollars.

*　　*　　*

Tepae continued on the way to the airport with his two passengers. "Captain Hardwick told me he'd call just as soon as he got the results. He said he'd let my sister go if the pills test for arsenic."

"I have an idea they will," Tom said. "But I hope they go easy on Rick Perry. His love for Venus became an obsession and spun out of control. She was just too much for him."

"I can see how that could happen," added Toronto. "She was some siren."

"She's not the only one," Tepae said. "Practically all the young women on the island are like that."

"I never imagined that beautiful women could be such a problem," Toronto replied.

"It's an island paradise here," Tom said. "Beautiful weather, a beautiful rain forest, beautiful beaches, and beautiful women. Who would have thought you'd have any problems?"

Tepae thought about this for a moment and then commented, "I guess there'll always be someone you can help, no matter where you go."

"We'll be back, Tepae. Whether you need us or not."

"Next time, plan to spend a week or two. There is a lot to enjoy here."

As he said this, Tepae pulled up at the curb at the departure area for Air New Zealand. All three men got out of the cab, and Tepae opened the trunk so Tom and Toronto could grab their bags.

"Well, my friends, this is it," he said, standing on the curb. "The more you know and like someone, the harder it is to say good-bye." Tepae's eyes glistened slightly from the tears that were forming.

His two passengers hugged him and then headed for the door of the building, their bags in tow. As they went, Tepae's phone rang, and he grabbed it out of his pocket. He looked quickly at the screen and yelled, "It's Hardwick!" Tom and Toronto stopped and turned to face him for a moment to wait while he took the call.

Tepae put the phone to his ear and listened for just a few seconds. Then his face spread into a wide grin, and he jumped up in the air, shouting, "They're letting my sister out of jail! She's free to go!"

Tom and Toronto both waved that they understood and then continued on into the terminal. "Let's go home, Toronto. This is not really where we belong."

CHAPTER 68

When Dakota Berk landed in New York, she immediately called Gunther Sachs. He picked up on the first ring. "I did it!" she gloated. I bought the company."

"How much did you pay?"

"It was a *steal*. I got it for half-price."

"Five hundred million?"

"Exactly."

"How did you manage that?"

"I had a little help from Alex. As a matter of fact, he's still there, cleaning things up."

"I don't like the sound of that."

"Don't worry. Alex is very careful. He's a professional."

"That's not what I mean."

"I know what you mean. Everything was aboveboard. Alex will be back here soon, and he can tell you himself."

"He's a bigger liar than you are."

"What can I say?" Dakota sounded annoyed and exasperated.

"So you didn't need my money."

"No, but I had to really stretch to close this deal. It took all my assets. I need a loan."

"A loan?"

"Yes, I need cash to tide me over."

"Let me get this straight. You asked me to put up money for an equity share of the company worth a billion dollars. You managed to buy it, God knows how, for all the money you had, and now you want me to give you a *loan* that just pays interest?"

"Who said I'd pay you interest?"

"You son of a bitch, Dakota."

"What's the matter? Your money is safe with me. I own a giant company now. I've got a notarized stock certificate right here."

"And?"

"So I need a hundred million on account. My own money's tied up."

"Then go to a bank."

"You know I can't do that. They'll have to do their due diligence."

"So?"

"I've got some, uh, skeletons in the closet."

"I figured. Maybe it's not such a bad thing you didn't need my money to partner with you."

"*Christ,* Gunther! Give me the line of credit. I know you have it. I made you rich."

"If you own RoadWheels now, use that asset. You can borrow on it. Better yet, you can have the company borrow the money and loan it to you so the money's tax-free. Otherwise, just keep screwing poor women out of their gold jewelry like you've always done."

"You *bastard.*" Berk slammed down the telephone receiver. She was fuming. She sat there brooding for a moment and then she picked up the receiver again. She speed-dialed Alex on his cell phone. The call went right to voice mail.

"*This is Alex. Leave a message.*"

"Alex, this is Berk. I need you. Call me as soon as you get this message."

Berk slammed the receiver down again so hard it nearly broke in two. She had credit cards like everyone else but no longer any ready cash. She had taken from Peter to pay Paul to come up with the five hundred million. To maintain her lifestyle she had to spend at a burn rate of, conservatively, fifty thousand a month. Her gold business generated more than that, but she had loaded it down with obligations that absorbed cash. In a word, Dakota Berk was now *insolvent.*

She needed to draw money out of RoadWheels *fast,* but, oddly, she didn't know whom to call. She went online to the company website and got the general number. An attendant answered, "RoadWheels. How may I direct your call?"

"I'd like to speak with someone in charge," she replied, not knowing what else to say. The she realized how stupid that sounded and was about to explain the reason for her call when the attendant said, "Which station would you like?"

"Uh, Greenwich." That was the only station that came to mind.

"I'll connect you."

Berk waited only a moment and the call went through. "This is RoadWheels in Greenwich. How may I help you?"

"I'd like to speak with the manager."

"Just a moment. I'll see if he's in."

"Before you go, can you tell me his name?"

"Yes, it's Mister Raskin. Peter Raskin."

"Oh! That's a new name for me. Was he hired recently?"

"Yes, but I'm sure he can take care of you."

"What happened to the previous manager?" Berk was suddenly curious to find out what RoadWheels would officially say about his untimely death.

"Did you know him?"

"Yes, in a way."

"Well, I'm sorry to say he passed away."

"Oh dear," Berk faked sympathy and concern. "How did he die?"

"It was in all the papers. He was murdered. It was tragic." The attendant's voice dropped an octave to a funeral-like level.

"Did they catch who did it?"

"I'm not at liberty to say. It's under investigation."

"Oh, I see. Well, please put me through to Mr., uh, Raskin."

"Just a moment."

A second later a new and authoritative voice came on the line.

"Peter Raskin speaking."

"Mr. Raskin, my name is Georgia Bell," Berk lied. "I'm an investor in your company based in Atlanta and I'd like to speak with someone at the central office."

"That couldn't be. There are no investors in the company. All the stock is held in trust. And there is no central office."

"No central office?"

"That's correct. What are you, a reporter? If so, I can give you our public relations department."

Berk was taken aback by this answer. She realized that if she was going to get anywhere with this Raskin she had better level with him. "This may surprise you, young man, but I really am an investor. I bought the company from the trustee."

"Really? What did you say your name was?"

"My name is Dakota Berk. I'm based in New York."

"That's not what you said."

"I know. I gave you a different name. So sue me. Now I want you to put me in touch with the central office."

Ma'am—Dakota Berk, or whatever your real name is—I told you," Peter said icily. "There is no central office. There is just a board of managers."

"Well, you let me tell *you* something, Mr. Peter Raskin." Berk strung out the word *Raaaskin*. "You tell that board of managers that I want to meet with them *right away*. I've got something very important to tell them. I will give you my name and number and will give you twenty-four hours to get back to me with a date and time. I want *all* the managers there. This meeting is *mandatory*. Do you understand?"

"I don't think—"

"You *will* do this, or you will be the first manager that is fired when I take over the company."

"Oh, well, let me get your name and number, then. I'll get back to you."

CHAPTER 69

The news of Berk's takeover spread like wildfire among the RoadWheels station managers. They were shocked. How could their leader, Tom Smith, have sold out?

Within minutes the news also leaked to the media, which picked up the story and ran with what scraps of information they could. Berk had operated in secrecy for years and was a complete unknown. A Google search of "Dakota Berk" turned up nothing, so the reporters and journalists made desperate calls to her home office. These calls were unanswered and went to voice mail. No one was able to connect her to any business or organization. Her ownership of Gold Inc. was unknown and untraceable, and her lawyer, Ian Badass, bound by the canons of ethics and the attorney-client privilege, said nothing to anyone.

Berk kept trying to reach Alex on his cell phone, without success. She was not in the least concerned that something might have happened to him. Instead she was furious.

However, Bonnie had been keeping in daily contact with Toronto by phone, text, and e-mail. On that fateful day, when she had learned about Berk from one of her colleagues, she immediately called him again. It was evening in Rarotonga when he received the call.

"Alonzo, it's me! What's going on?!"

"Uh, hello, Bonnie! Um, what do you mean?" At that very moment Toronto sat in the backseat of a taxi with Venus, heading for her home. Did Bonnie have ESP? How could she possibly know?

"What are you doing?"

Toronto let go of Venus's hand and concentrated on the call. "Uh, nothing. I'm on my way to the beach." Venus stared at him, clearly signaling she didn't appreciate that he was lying.

"Tell me one thing: Did Tom sell the company to a woman named Dakota Berk?"

"How did you find that out?"

"She has summoned all the managers to a meeting. Claims she owns RoadWheels. It's very bizarre!"

"It's sad, but it's true. It's hers now. Like I told you, Alex almost killed Tom's trustee. Now, it turns out the trustee sold the company stock to Berk at knifepoint. The trustee could sue her to get the stock back because he was under duress, but Tom doesn't want him to do that."

"*What?* Tom's going to let her keep the company? Why?"

"He's moved on, Bonnie. Nobody knows he's still alive, and he wants to keep it that way."

"Why? And why didn't you tell me?"

"I found out only a couple of hours ago. Tom and I went to see the trustee at the hospital, and he told us everything. Turns out the trustee got paid a lot of money. Half of what the company's worth, but it's still a lot of money. Tom is set for life, and he has other priorities now."

"Other priorities? Other than the company?"

"That's right. He wants to help people."

"Help people? What people? Alonzo, I'm not sure I like the sound of this."

"People who need help, like those Hispanic workers for Cut-Rate Contracting. They own that company now, thanks to Tom."

"Well, maybe not. Sy Schuster is suing them to get his company back, but that's another story. What about us? We're supposed to work for that woman?"

As this conversation continued, the taxi drove up to the curb in front of Venus's house and stopped. Venus waited a moment, becoming more and more annoyed, and finally said, "Toronto, let's go!"

"What's that?" Bonnie asked suspiciously. "Who said that?"

"Just a woman at the beach."

"I heard that!" Venus said, her voice louder so she would be clearly heard on the phone. "I'm *not* 'just a woman on the beach.'"

"Alonzo, what's going on?!" Bonnie was beginning to sound frantic.

"Nothing, Bonnie. I promise. I gotta go now. Tell everyone it's true. Dakota Berk does own the company." Toronto ended the call and left Bonnie hanging, holding the telephone receiver to her ear. When she realized he was gone, she slammed it down.

"That two-timing bastard!" she screamed out loud.

Meanwhile, Toronto said good-bye to a very disappointed Venus and told the taxi driver to take him back to his hotel, the Paradise Inn.

*   *   *

The RoadWheels managers all arrived in New York City a day ahead of the scheduled meeting with Dakota Berk and met privately as a board to consider what to do next. This was the first face-to-face board of managers meeting since they had come together with Tom in his hometown and learned of his "death." However, in the meantime, they had conducted numerous meetings by conference call and videoconference to make decisions for the company. To run the business efficiently, day-to-day, they had elected a management team in Tom's stead. Bonnie, who was closest to Tom by virtue of being engaged to Toronto, had been elected to serve as the first chairperson of the board. Especially since the managers wished to be part owners of the business they ran, they had been able to quickly make a decision on how best to proceed.

The meeting with Berk took place in a meeting room at the Sheraton Hotel in Times Square. A female clerk stationed at the door took down the name and contact information of each manager as he or she arrived and asked the person to take a seat. When she had logged in and accounted for the manager of every RoadWheels station, she notified Berk, who was in her room waiting for the call. The managers turned to see Berk for the first time when she finally appeared at the door in the back of the room. All eyes followed her as she walked to the front and stood there, facing them, dressed in a black business suit. Her hair was in a bun, and she wore black-rimmed glasses on her scowling face. The room was so quiet one could've heard a pin drop.

"Good morning. My name is Dakota Berk and I have just purchased your company. I now own 100 percent of the stock. I am your new boss."

Bonnie raised her hand to speak.

"Yes, what is it?" Berk snarled, annoyed at being interrupted.

Bonnie stood up and said, "Ms. Berk, I have here a letter of resignation, signed by all of us. We are leaving the company as of today."

"You're *quitting?*"

"Yes. We are all loyal to Tom Smith, and since he is no longer with us, we no longer want to work for the company."

Berk's face turned bright red. *"You can't do that!"*

"Yes, we can. And the truck drivers with their trucks and the café caterers are all independent. I'm sure that when we start our competing business, they'll want to come with us."

"If you leave and try to compete, I'll sue your asses off. You'd be breaching your employment contracts."

"Not so, Ms. Berk. None of us employees signed anything. The independent contractors did sign contracts, but they're terminable at will. Tom Smith always treated us right, so we wanted to work for him, but we have a right to walk at any time."

"I'll hire all new people and get new trucks and drivers, you bitch, but believe me, you're going to *pay*." Berk was so furious now she was nearly apoplectic.

"It won't be so easy to buy new trucks. The trailers are all custom-made. If you ordered them today, they wouldn't come in for at least six months."

"I won't need those trailers. I'll buy whatever they use now to transport cars, and I'll hire buses to carry the people."

"There's another problem. You're going to have to set up new stations, too, because we're going to take over the ones the company has now. We're the managers, remember, and we have good relationships with the people we rent from."

"You'll destroy my business! You can't do that!" Berk screamed. She had paid half a billion dollars for a company that was disappearing before her eyes. Without a workforce and without the relationships that made the business run, she would receive nothing for her money. It would be just an empty corporate shell with a well-known trademark that was about to lose its valuable goodwill.

"Yes, we can," Bonnie replied. "This is America. There are laws against involuntary servitude, you know. It's even in the Thirteenth Amendment."

Berk stood there speechless in front of the RoadWheels managers, trying to think of what to say or do. Her first instinct was to call Alex, but the bastard was not answering his phone. As she processed what had just happened, her face flushed with anger, her cell phone rang. She yanked it out of her pocket and looked at the screen. It was Alex!

"Alex," Berk began. "Where have you been?" Berk felt greatly relieved and was able to control her voice. She was talking to the one man who could save the day.

"I'm still here on the island."

"Did you get them?" Berk was fully aware that everyone in the room was listening to her. She had to be careful of what she told Alex, but they couldn't hear what *he* said, and she desperately wanted to know if he had done his job.

"Yes, I got them all: that trustee, Joe, and his damn secretary. Tom Smith came in, and I finished him off too, along with his annoying friend, Toronto, or whatever his name is."

"That's excellent. Now come back here right away. I need you."

"That's why I'm calling. I like it here. I'm going to stay for a while."

"Oh, no, you're not. If you want to get paid you'll take the next flight out."

"This is an island paradise. I've never had it so good. And anyway, I really don't need the money. I have some savings. If I run out, I can always rob a bank."

"That's not funny. As it happens, I've got an important job for you here. Your business there is finished, so come home."

"Sorry, Dakota. I'm not coming. You're on your own on this one."

Berk hung up and did her best to mask the forlorn look on her face. She looked out at the managers again, saw their many faces staring at her, and burst into tears.

With his wrists in handcuffs in the Rarotonga jail, Alex terminated his cell phone call to Berk. Captain Hardwick took the phone from him and patted him on the back. "That was well done, Alex. You did good."

CHAPTER 70

Sy Schuster was furious—furious with the Latinos who now owned his company and furious with himself for giving it to them. His attorney, Candace Sharpe, Esq., was about to fix this problem and take the company back from them. What they did was outrageous!

Sharpe had filed suit in Buffalo in the New York Supreme Court for Erie County. The complaint alleged fraud, duress, and lack of consideration for the transfer of stock, and it asked the court to order the defendants to return their ill-gotten gains to the plaintiff. Discovery was practically nonexistent, because the supposed FBI agents, Peter Burke and Neil Caffrey, did not even exist. The new owners of the company, Cut-Rate Contracting, had no knowledge of how they had come to own the stock. They had assumed it was a gift from the plaintiff who had suddenly repented and wanted to make amends for not paying them for their work.

What discovery there was centered principally upon the value of the company, both its present value and its value at the time of the stock transfer. The company business had skyrocketed when the workers took over, because they had ploughed every spare cent of their earnings back into the business, rather than sucking out profits as Schuster had done. The business was now worth nearly twice what it was less than a year ago when they had received their shares.

It normally took years for a civil case to come to trial. However, a plaintiff seeking a court order required a court to sit in equity before a judge and without a jury, making it possible for Schuster to receive an early trial date. His attorney, Sharpe, had made a motion for summary judgment based solely on Schuster's affidavit, but her motion failed, because the underlying facts were in dispute.

The attorney for the defendants, a young Latino named Marco Domenico, who usually handled domestic disputes, had never tried a case like this before. He had successfully countered the summary judgment motion by simply challenging Schuster's factual allegations, but he was now faced with having to prove the negative, based entirely upon cross-examining the plaintiff. This was a daunting task, since Schuster could say whatever he wanted to bolster his case and lie with impunity. Bonnie Salerno, who had notarized the contract for sale of the stock, was his only witness, but if he put her on the stand she would have to testify that she knew about the fraud. Not only would this damage his defense, but it might also subject Bonnie to a criminal charge.

The judge, Jane Marshall, was well respected at the local bar for being tough but fair. She was known as "the truth detector," and, if an attorney failed to ask the right questions of a witness, she would ask the questions herself. Nevertheless, Domenico clearly understood the difficulties he faced. Assuming that the judge had some latitude in the law to decide the case in his clients' favor, which was doubtful, she had not a clue of the hardships faced every day by the minorities and by the poor, much less the *minority poor* who had retained him to defend them. Domenico was not at all sure she would understand or care about his clients' entry-level positions in the social order. She would apply the law without concern for the consequences on the litigants.

The spectator seats in the courtroom were filled with the many defendants who stood to lose their American dream. Only Darwin sat with Domenico at the defendants' counsel table. Sy Schuster sat stone-faced at the plaintiff's counsel table with Candace Sharpe.

Judge Marshall entered the courtroom, and everyone clamored to stand. When all were on their feet and had stopped talking, she slammed the gavel down once, and they all sat down again. The court was in session. "Ms. Sharpe, do you have an opening statement?" Judge Marshall asked, pointedly staring at plaintiff's counsel over the top rims of her eyeglasses.

"I do, your honor." Sharpe, dressed in a dark blue pantsuit and white blouse with a regimental ascot, stood and stepped forward to the lectern with a legal pad. She looked at the judge for a moment, making brief eye contact, and then dropped her eyes to her notes.

"Your honor," she began, authoritatively but respectfully, "my client, Mr. Seymour Schuster, is a Holocaust survivor who came to this country as a very young man without a penny in his pocket. He got his first job as a day laborer in the construction industry in New York City, where he learned the trade and saved his pennies. Through hard work and much perseverance, he eventually founded his own construction company, called Cut-Rate Contracting, right here in the city of Buffalo. No job was too small for this little company that could, and it eventually thrived and paid its owner a handsome profit year after year.

"Then, one day, Mr. Schuster was visited by two men who called themselves FBI agents. In fact, they were impostors. Not only weren't they FBI agents, they disappeared soon after and have never been seen nor heard from again. There is no telling who they were or why they posed as federal agents, except to scare Mr. Schuster half out of his wits. And scare him they did. They told him that unless he signed over all of his ownership in Cut-Rate Contracting, the company *he founded*, they would charge him with some unspecified crimes and he would be arrested and go to jail.

"Mr. Schuster was so intimidated by these fake FBI agents that did just that. He signed a piece of paper on the spot without even giving it to his lawyer to look at first. This piece of paper, which was then notarized by a woman who happened to be present, assigned all the stock in his company to a bunch of people he didn't even know.

"Mr. Schuster is now suing to get his stock back, the stock that was taken from him by trickery and fraud, and by the mistaken fear of incarceration, which in his mind was extreme duress. These are facts that we will prove and which, under the law, render the assignment of his stock invalid, *ab initio*.

"Mr. Schuster's property rights have been clearly violated, your honor. We are therefore requesting a court order to restore Cut-Rate Contracting to its rightful owner."

As Candace Sharpe said these words, she made eye contact again with the judge, gave an almost imperceptible bow, and returned to her seat.

Judge Marshall waited for her to sit down and then stared at Marco Domenico, inquiringly. Marco sat there a moment, not knowing what to say, and eventually stood and announced, "Your honor, I would like to waive my opening statement and reserve the time for closing."

"Very well, then. Ms. Sharpe, you may call your first witness."

"Thank you, your honor. The plaintiff calls to the stand the plaintiff, Mr. Seymour Schuster."

Sy Schuster stood and walked forward to the witness chair. He was sworn in by the bailiff and sat down. The defendants, sitting at the counsel table and in the courtroom gallery, thought they saw a faint smile, but if it were there at all, it quickly faded to a serious demeanor. Schuster was ready to plead his case.

CHAPTER 71

Sharpe stepped forward to question the witness. Stopping six feet away from the witness box, she smiled pleasantly and said in an almost conversational tone, "Mr. Schuster, please state your name and address for the record."

"Seymour Schuster. I live at 421 Old Lake Shore Road."

"Is that right on Lake Erie?"

"Yes, and the sunsets are amazing."

"I'm sure they are from there. How long have you lived in Buffalo?"

"Some thirty-five years now. Time sure flies."

"You were an immigrant to the United States, were you not?"

"Yes, I came over from England shortly after the Second World War. I left my foster parents there and took a steamer."

"Foster parents?"

"I was on one of the last ships out from Germany, along with a lot of other Jewish children. We came to England, and they assigned us to childless couples there."

"Why did you leave England?"

"To seek my fortune. This was the land of opportunity at the time."

"Would you say this was still the land of opportunity?"

"You can get ahead if you work hard, like I did."

"What happened when you arrived?"

"We docked at the port in Brooklyn. I had no money but I did have the names of some Jewish families I could contact. I remember walking across the Brooklyn Bridge and finding an address on the Lower East Side. I knocked on the door of an apartment, and my future mother opened it."

"Future mother?"

"Myra Schuster. She and her husband Ira took me in and they eventually adopted me. That was my first real home."

"How old were you then?"

"I was fifteen. It was the mid-fifties, and I had hit it just right. There was plenty of work in New York City at the time."

"So what happened then?"

"I went to school and picked up odd jobs. I liked construction, so I worked on crews renovating buildings in my spare time."

"How long did you stay in New York?"

"About ten years, until I graduated from CUNY. The old tenement we lived in was run-down, so it was time to leave anyway. I decided to head north to virgin territory and start my own company."

"What about your parents? Did they move here too?"

"And enjoy the snow? No, they moved to Florida." There was a twitter of laughter in the courtroom. Judge Marshall frowned and the twitter stopped.

"Why did you choose Buffalo?"

"Like I said, it was virgin territory. The economy was down up here, and a lot of people needed work. Besides, it was as far away from New York City as you can get without leaving New York state, where I knew the rules."

"The rules?"

"The construction business is full of rules, written and unwritten. I knew what you could get away with. I also knew quite a few New York politicians who were on the take."

"Where'd you get the money to start your business?"

"My parents never asked me for any money, so I could save everything I earned for those ten years. They also cosigned a loan for me."

"They gave you a head start?"

"Jewish parents, you know. They do whatever they can."

"When you started your construction business, did you have competition?"

"Oh yes. I was the new guy in town, and competition was fierce. There wasn't much business to begin with, and what little there was went to old guard companies with friends in high places. I decided early on I had to take the little jobs and quote lower prices than the others."

"Did that strategy work?"

"Worked like a charm. Everyone likes to save a buck."

"How were you able to beat the prices of those other construction firms?"

"I knew some people in New York City whose business it was to bring in cheap labor from south of the border. I contacted them and they took care of my needs."

"You mean labor from Mexico?"

"Mexico and farther south too. Those people needed work, and I needed labor. It was that simple."

"How did 'those people' get here?"

"At first they were sent up from the city by the truckload. Once a group of them were here, they told their friends. We soon had so many Latinos here in Buffalo that people complained about them."

"But you gave them work."

"I was the only one that hired them at first. Eventually everyone started using them for construction work, landscaping, farm labor, and whatever. Restaurants hired them to wash dishes and clean tables. Anything you wanted done, they'd do it. I guess you could say I started something here in Buffalo—something that works well for us and for those Latinos too."

"So how did it happen that you gave them your company?"

"Over a year ago now, I landed a construction job out at the Clarence Travel Plaza on the thruway to build a station for RoadWheels—you know, that company that'll transport your car from city to city? I went out to check on this job and was nearly scared out of my wits."

"Tell us what happened."

"There were a couple of guys there who told me they were FBI agents investigating corruption in the construction industry. They even gave me their names, but, like an idiot, I didn't ask them to show their credentials. At first I didn't realize they were trying to *scam* me. I just went along with them, assuming they were who they said they were."

"What did they say?"

"They said that they had enough evidence to throw me in jail. Naturally, I panicked. They also said they would give me a pass if I cooperated and signed over my company to the Latinos who worked for me."

"Didn't you find that strange?"

"You have to understand, I was under a lot of pressure. I wasn't thinking straight."

"So what happened next?"

"They handed me this piece of paper some writing on it. It was just a few lines long and stated I would transfer my stock to these . . . these workers."

"Did you sign it?"

"Yes, I did."

"Why didn't you show it to your lawyer first?"

"I . . . I don't know. It was very stupid. I figured I'd just sign it and then get this whole thing straightened out later."

"Was your signature notarized?"

"Yes, there just happened to be this other woman there who notarized my signature."

"Were you paid anything, anything at all, for the sale of your company?"

"Yes, they gave me a dollar. *One dollar* for signing over my whole company!"

At this point, Sharpe stepped back and returned to her counsel table. She picked up a piece of paper and approached the bench. "Your honor," she said, "I would like to offer this assignment in evidence as exhibit A."

She handed the paper up to the judge for her inspection.

"All right," Judge Marshall said. "You may mark the document."

Sharpe handed the document to the court reporter and waited while she placed a yellow exhibit sticker in the upper right corner. Sharpe then gave the document to the witness and resumed. "Mr. Schuster, is that your signature at the bottom of the page?"

Schuster examined the document and looked up sadly. Yes," he said meekly.

"Would you please read aloud the words that are printed there?"

Schuster read aloud: "For the consideration of one dollar, duly received and hereby acknowledged, I hereby sell and assign my entire right, title, and interest in Cut-Rate Contracting, Inc. ('Company') to each and all of the day laborers who worked for the Company during the five years previous to the date of execution hereof, in equal shares, share and share alike, *per stirpes*."

"Were you in your right mind when you signed this document?"

"Of course not. I would never have signed it if I knew those guys weren't FBI agents."

Attorney Sharpe looked over at the judge. "That's all I have, your honor," she announced and returned to her counsel table.

"Mr. Domenico"—Judge Marshall looked at the defense attorney over the rims of her glasses—"you may cross-examine."

CHAPTER 72

Marco Domenico just sat there. His mind was empty. He didn't know where or how to begin his cross-examination. He looked blankly at his notes of the direct testimony. Finally, he slowly and reluctantly got up from his chair and walked forward to the witness, taking his legal notepad with him.

"Mr. Schuster," he began hesitantly. "You said you lived on Old Lake Shore Road. Isn't that the most expensive area to live in Buffalo?"

"I suppose it is," Schuster replied. "With my business, I can afford it—or should I say *could* afford it. I get bubkes now that they stole my business. That's why I'm suing."

"We understand. Now, you testified that you came over to England on the last ship from Germany—"

"I said *one* of the last ships," Schuster corrected as if to say, "Lawyers always try to put words in your mouth."

"One of the last ships. Was that to escape the Holocaust?"

"Yes. My parents and practically all the remaining Jews were . . . were killed."

"Those were terrible times. And you were among the very few that survived, is that right?"

"I was lucky, what can I say."

"I would think that after that experience you would want to help other people in difficult situations—like you were helped by your parents who put you on that ship, by your foster parents in England who took you in, and by your adoptive parents in New York."

"Is there a question there, Mr. Domenico?" Judge Marshall prompted.

"I'll rephrase it. Is it your desire to give back to the community, thankful for the support you received?"

"Objection!" Sharpe shot up from her seat in an instant. "What kind of question is that? Are we looking into the plaintiff's personal philosophy?"

"Sustained. I agree. You can't go there, counselor," the judge ruled.

"The relevance will become clear, your honor."

"Objection sustained. Move on, Mr. Domenico."

Domenico looked down at his notes and started again. "The people who worked for your company as day laborers, when did they expect you to pay them?"

"*They* wanted me to pay them the same day. That wasn't always possible," Schuster added, knowing full well where Domenico was headed.

"Did you always pay them when they worked for you?"

"Not always on the same day, no."

"Did there come a time when men worked for you and you didn't pay them at all?"

"Not to my knowledge."

"Did you keep accurate time records of the hours people worked?"

"We are—we *were* a cash business."

"You didn't keep time records?"

Anticipating a demand for the records if he replied with a yes, Schuster answered no.

"Then how did you know if you paid everyone for the work they did?"

"The workers would complain."

"And what would you do if they complained?"

"We would pay them, of course."

"Would you hire them again, the ones that complained?"

Schuster felt trapped. If he answered yes, Domenico could prove a lie, so he answered no.

"Let me get this straight. It seems to me you have had a rather charmed life, with people helping you at every turn. You were running a successful business, living in the most expensive part of town, and you didn't always pay your workers?"

Schuster looked at his lawyer for help. Sharpe stood up and offered, less than convincingly, "Objection, your honor."

"On what grounds?"

"Argumentative. He's badgering the witness."

"This is cross-examination, Ms. Sharpe. You should know better. I'll allow it."

Everyone looked at Schuster to answer. "No, so I must have missed a few payments."

"And you fired the ones that complained?"

"I didn't fire them. I didn't hire them back. There's a difference."

"They were day laborers, Mr. Schuster. So what's the difference?"

"All right, there is none."

"Did you feel in any way responsible for these workers that you brought up from New York to work for you?"

"Why should I?"

"I'm just asking, Mr. Schuster. When they arrived, did you feel responsible to hire them so they could pay for their food and shelter?"

"Of course not. I would hire whatever workers I needed to do the jobs I had. There were good times and lean times. Especially in winter."

"You didn't give them work in the winter?"

"I closed business during the months of January and February. I spent the winter in Florida."

"How much did you pay your workers—when you *did* pay them, that is?"

Schuster bristled at the innuendo but kept his temper and said simply, "Minimum wage, of course."

"How much was that?"

"It kept going up. I don't know, five dollars an hour? Whatever."

"*If* you hired them, and *if* they worked forty hours a week, that would be $200, would it not?"

"You just did the math."

"The most they could earn was $200 a week?"

"Whatever."

"For forty weeks, that's eight thousand dollars a year?"

"So? What's your point?"

"And you admitted you did not always pay them?"

"I said I forgot a few times, but I always paid them if they complained."

"But then you wouldn't hire them again. Now I ask you: how did you expect your workers to survive the winter?"

"I object to this entire line of questioning," Sharpe interjected. "Mr. Schuster paid his workers, period. That's all he was obligated to do."

"How should I know?" Schuster responded, notwithstanding his attorney's objection. "That wasn't my problem."

"You brought these men up here to the frozen north and then left for the winter. And you say that wasn't your problem?"

Judge Marshall broke in. "All right, Mr. Domenico. That's getting pretty far afield from the contract issue. Let's get back on track."

Domenico looked at his notes again. "You testified that the FBI agents scared you out of your wits. Is that correct?"

"Yes, they did."

"Why is that? Why were you scared?"

"They said they were going to arrest me if I didn't cooperate."

"Arrest you for what?"

"They didn't say."

"You had no idea?"

"No."

"Then what were you afraid of?"

"I . . . I don't know."

"Had you committed any crime?"

"Objection! The witness doesn't have to answer that!"

"Your grounds?" Judge Marshall asked with a quizzical face, almost revealing a small smile.

"Self-incrimination. Fifth Amendment."

"Then the witness should say that," the judge suggested. "Mr. Schuster, do you refuse to answer on the grounds that your answer might incriminate you?"

"Uh, yes, I do!" Schuster replied quickly with obvious relief.

Domenico paused for a moment to emphasize the significance of the testimony and then continued with his cross. "Mr. Schuster, do you watch television?"

"Objection! Relevance?" Sharpe was out of her chair again in an instant. Judge Marshall gave Domenico a withering look.

"Just give me a chance, your honor. The relevance will become clear very quickly."

"All right, Mr. Domenico, but the line had better be relevant, or I'll have it stricken."

"Mr. Schuster?" Domenico prompted the witness to answer.

"Of course! Don't we all?" Schuster sneered and the courtroom twittered again briefly before it fell silent. The tension was palpable. One could've heard a pin drop.

"Do you recall the names of the two FBI agents you said scared you out of your wits?"

"Uh, just a minute. One was Burke, I remember. Peter Burke, I think. The other was Neil something."

"Neil Caffrey?"

"That's it. Caffrey."

"You didn't recognize the names?"

"No. Should I have?"

"They're the agents in a TV show called *White Collar.*"

"What! They're not even real people!" Schuster responded indignantly. The courtroom erupted with raucous laughter. Judge Marshall gaveled the gallery to silence again.

"You had no inkling that the FBI agents were fake?"

"No, of course not!"

"You thought they were real?"

"Yes."

"You thought they could arrest you if you committed a crime?"

"Yes."

"And what crime was that?"

"Objection!"

"No further questions, your honor."

CHAPTER 73

"Is there a redirect?" the judge asked, looking straight at Sharpe.

Sharpe came forward, ready to rehabilitate her witness. "Yes, your honor, just a couple of questions, if I may."

"Proceed."

"As a *business owner*, you were an equal-opportunity employer, were you not?"

"Yes, indeed," Schuster answered. "We never discriminated against anyone."

"How many people worked for your company?"

"Eight people full time, if you count both supervisors and administrative staff."

"The rest were day laborers?"

"Yes."

"How many would you say?"

"It varied, but we've employed as many as fifty at a time."

"Fifty workers? How many were there in the labor pool, would you say?"

"There were times when we hired practically all of the Latinos."

"Did your company advertise in the community?"

"You would see our ads all around: on billboards, in phonebooks and local magazines, and on the Internet. We spent a lot of money to get the word out."

"Did you pay taxes?"

"Absolutely. Federal, state, and local taxes. We did our part as good citizens."

"No further questions, your honor." Sharpe walked back to her seat, and Domenico stood up.

"I have just one question on re-cross, your honor."

"Go ahead, counselor."

"Mr. Schuster, did you ever cheat on your taxes?"

"Objection!" Sharpe shouted. "What kind of question is that?!"

"Objection sustained! Mr. Domenico, you should be ashamed of yourself. I direct the witness not to answer. You may sit down, counselor, and the witness is excused."

Sy Schuster climbed down from the witness stand and returned to his seat at the plaintiff's counsel table.

The judge looked expectantly at Sharpe and prodded, "You may continue with plaintiff's case."

"We have nothing further, your honor. Plaintiff rests."

Looking surprised, the judge turned to Domenico. "Mr. Domenico, your turn to proceed. You may present your defense."

Domenico replied, "We have no witnesses, your honor. The defense rests."

"Well, that's it, then. We can move on to your final arguments, unless you want me to rule now."

Sharpe stood. "Rule now? Your honor, do you have a ruling?"

Domenico stood, too, not knowing what else to do.

"Yes, I've made up my mind based on the undisputed facts. I don't think my decision will change no matter what you two may say."

Sharpe smiled knowingly. "Thank you, your honor. The plaintiff waives a closing argument," she said and sat down again with her arms folded.

Domenico wasn't sure he should waive his right to argue, but if the judge had already made up her mind, that meant he had lost. "I'll waive too," he said dejectedly and took his seat.

"This trial only confirmed the facts that, if true, make my decision very easy based on the law," Judge Marshall announced.

"Let's first dispose of the issue of consideration. Mr. Schuster was given one dollar for all the outstanding shares in his corporation. This wasn't much consideration for his valuable company, but under the law it was adequate. The law of contracts requires only that there be *some* consideration, as there clearly was in this case. The consideration can be as small as a peppercorn, if that was the bargain.

"Second, let's deal with the issue of fraud. Mr. Schuster assumed wrongly that Mr. Burke and Mr. Caffrey were FBI agents and acted accordingly. But had they been real agents, *he would have acted in just the same way.* The nature of the charade did not change the result. Mr. Schuster would also have signed over his company had he not been defrauded.

"Third, duress may have been involved in this transaction, but, if Mr. Schuster felt under duress, this fear was of Mr. Schuster's own making. Had he committed no crime, he would have had nothing to fear, and he would not have been motivated to sell his stock.

"We won't ever know whether Mr. Schuster committed a crime. He chose to assert his right against self-incrimination under the Fifth Amendment of our Constitution. But Mr. Schuster knew himself what he had done, and the transaction that he now asks this court to reverse was the result of whatever that was.

"It is said that equity abhors a forfeiture, but it is also said that one who seeks equity must do equity. Equity does not require a plaintiff to have led a blameless life, but a defense of unclean hands is available to a defendant when there is a nexus between the plaintiff's actions and the very right that he seeks to enforce.

"I rule that such a nexus exists in this case. Plaintiff Schuster may or may not have always paid his workers. He may or may not have reported all the cash he received as income on his tax returns. He may or may not have been corrupt in some way. But in his own mind, his prior actions resulted in his selling his entire company to his workers for one dollar. Consequently, this court will not void this transaction."

When Judge Marshall concluded with these words, Darwin, who had been sitting solemnly at defendants' counsel table, stood up and turned slowly around to face his fellow Latino defendants in the gallery. They were not fluent enough in English to understand what the court had just said. Therefore he quietly spoke to them in Spanish, and, after a pause following his brief explanation, the courtroom erupted with shouts and screams and shrieks of joy. The workers, God bless them, had won!

CHAPTER 74

Dakota Berk was not happy. She had paid $500 million dollars for an empty corporate shell. *Five hundred million!* Forget that the company had been worth a billion at the time. It was worth next to nothing now.

Furthermore, what she perceived as Alex's outrage left her devastated. There was no one to confide in and no one to do her dirty work—and no one to clear her pipes in bed.

"I want to undo the purchase of RoadWheels," she demanded of her lawyer Ian Badass.

Berk had made a rare appearance at the offices of Lawless & Badass and was sitting alone with the man at one end of a long mahogany conference table in a conference room high up over Park Avenue. Windows formed one entire wall, from top to bottom, and expensive modern art dressed the other three. Berk and Badass were both small of stature and actually looked somewhat alike. Badass was featureless, but he exuded a masculine toughness belying a pussycat inner nature that was attractive to clients. Berk exuded a masculine toughness too, but as a woman this was not so attractive. She had cropped brown hair and wore no makeup, not even lipstick, and she bore a perpetual frown. At this moment the frown had morphed into an angry scowl that was not at all pretty. Fortune was not going her way, and she wanted it turned around.

"What's the problem?" replied Badass. "I thought you wanted to own that company in the worst way."

"I bought a pig in a poke. Everybody's quitting, and there'll be no one to operate the company. No stations and station managers, no trucks and truck drivers, no catering and food service, *nothing!*"

"That's unbelievable! Aren't there any contracts in place?"

"No. Everyone's working 'at will.' They were there because they wanted to work for that son of a bitch Tom Smith, but now he's dead and they're walking en masse, taking the operations with them. I've even heard rumors they're starting a new company to do the same thing and compete with RoadWheels."

"Contracts are implied. They can't use company trade secrets."

"And there's another problem." Berk appeared almost desperate now.

"What's that?"

"I spent every last cent I had to buy the company. I have no assets except my town house here in New York, and now I can't even pay the mortgage."

"What about Gold Inc.? It's a going business, making money . . ."

"No, I borrowed from Peter to pay Paul. I raided that company, and I can't even pay those people. As soon as they find out, they're going to walk too."

Badass looked at Berk sympathetically. "What do you want me to do?"

"*Sue!* I want my money back."

"On what grounds?"

"You're the lawyer. You tell *me.*"

"Were any representations made to induce you to buy the company?"

"No. It was a going concern. I just assumed . . ." Berk bit down on her lip, ignoring the hurt, causing it to bleed.

"Was the paperwork in order? Did you receive a notarized assignment of the stock?"

"Yes, I did."

"Did the person who assigned the stock to you have the legal authority?"

"Uh? I don't know." Berk thought about this for a moment. She began to see a glimmer of hope.

"You didn't check this?"

"No, I didn't. Should I have?"

"It might not be too late. You bought the company from a trustee. The trustee may not have had the power to sell the company. We'll have to check the trust instrument."

Berk was getting more hopeful by the second. "You think there is something we can do?"

"We can ask a court to void the sale and order a return of the proceeds."

Berk's dark frown was dissolving like the mist in sunshine. "Yes. I want to do that."

"But I have to tell you: if we go to a court seeking equity, you must have clean hands."

"Clean hands?" A cloud suddenly intervened, blocking the sunshine. "What's that?" Berk demanded, hesitantly regaining her confidence and control.

"A litigant who seeks equity must do equity. When you purchased the company, did you act honorably? Did you deal fairly and honestly with the trustee?"

"Well, not exactly . . ."

"What do you mean?"

"Let me ask you," Berk began, "as my attorney. Is this conversation privileged?"

"Of course. What you tell me will never leave this room. My lips are sealed."

"All right then. Just between you and me. Only one other person knows this, and he's not telling."

"Knows what?"

"I had Alex eliminate that trustee and his secretary."

*   *   *

"Gunther," Berk said as sweetly as she could muster. "I have a company to sell and I'm willing to let it go for half-price."

"I thought you paid only half-price for it."

"I'm willing to take a huge haircut. I'll sell it for two hundred and fifty mil."

"And why is that?"

"You know damn well why. I'm overextended. I'm broke. I'm less than broke. The beggar on the street has more money than I do. At least he's even. I'm way negative."

"So if I offered you a hundred mil, you'd take it?"

"I'm against the wall. I'd hate you forever, but I'd take it."

"For a company worth a billion?"

"You crunched the numbers. You know what it's worth."

"Is there something you're not telling me? The deal smells fishy."

"No, Gunther. There's no risk in this deal. It's guaranteed."

"Okay, so I'm offering. One hundred mil."

"Sold. It's yours, you damn vulture. I'll have my lawyer talk to your lawyer."

Berk hung up the phone with a feeling of great relief. She could survive on $100 million, but it would be difficult. She was high maintenance. At least she could keep Gold Inc. going, and it would throw off a money stream. Sachs would find out too late that everybody in RoadWheels was about to leave and open a competing business across the parking lot at every station.

Now all she had to do was to bug her Badass lawyer to act quickly so she closed on the money before the proverbial shit hit the proverbial fan.

CHAPTER 75

Tom and Toronto landed at JFK Airport and were greeted by Moishe as they came through customs. "So, how was your island paradise?" Moishe had a huge ear-to-ear grin that belied his feigned envy.

"It was a nice place to visit," Tom replied, "but I don't think you'd like to live there. It's much too quiet."

"I could stand some quiet," Moishe winked. "And I don't think I'd miss the New York traffic."

Moishe helped load Tom and Toronto's luggage into his cab. "Where to?" he queried.

"Our tractor-trailer is parked at the Palisades Mall in West Nyack," Tom said. "Take us there. Our home is wherever that truck is."

"You've got to show me this rig. I'll bet it's really something."

"It's comfortable, it has a built-in garage, and you can take it on the road."

"Garage?"

"It's for a sports car and a van," Tom replied. "And a couple of motorcycles too."

"So what happens next? Where are you guys going to go?"

Toronto spoke up. "I've got to see my honey in Buffalo. And soon! Tom, you sit in front with Moishe and tell him about Tepae and the dangers of cab driving in Rarotonga. I'm going to stretch out in the back have a nice long talk on the phone with my honey."

They all climbed in the cab and Moishe punched "West Nyack, New York" into his navigator. As he headed out on the Van Wyk Expressway in the direction of the Whitestone Bridge, Tom began telling Moishe about the events of the past week.

Toronto selected his girl friend's number from the list and pressed *call*. Bonnie answered on the first ring.

"Hello, lover!" she said with a cheerful, upbeat voice. "You're back safely?" She revealed no trace of her concern over Toronto's temptations.

"Yeah, and I can't wait to see you. We're heading up there straight away."

"I'd like that, more than you'll ever know. But I can't let you come here just now."

"What?"

"You have some work to do down there."

"I don't understand. We just landed, and . . ."

"I know. But there is a Mini Cooper headed *your* way this time. It should arrive in about four hours."

"Wait just a minute. I want to put you on speaker so Tom and Moishe can hear this."

Toronto interrupted his friends and told them to listen. "Okay, Bonnie. Go ahead."

Bonnie continued with her explanation. "Do you remember when we got suspicious of cars going to Canada, so we started weighing the Minis that came off the tractor-trailers? Some of them were way overweight, so we figured they were smuggling something? Tom followed one of those cars and got himself, um . . ." Bonnie hesitated. ". . . killed."

"Almost killed," Toronto corrected. "People just *think* he's dead."

"Yeah, well, originally all of those cars were heading *north*. The Minis never used our system to take them back again to wherever they came from."

"That's right. But we did log them both ways through customs. Whatever Minis came into Canada also came back to the States."

"Right! Except now we have a car that's done just the opposite. It's a gold-colored Mini that came down from Canada. We'd never seen it before, so we ran it over our scales while loading it on the trailer. It weighed about five thousand pounds!"

"What do those cars normally weigh? About a thousand pounds?"

"If that. And you told me Dakota Berk smuggled five cars filled with gold to the Cook Islands that way?"

"Yeah, and the gold's still there," Toronto replied. "It belongs to Tom now."

"Well, this gold is coming *from* Canada. And we figure it to be worth about $100 million."

"It must be coming back to Berk for some reason. Where's this car heading?"

"The driver paid for the trip to the Palisades Mall."

"That's just where we're going!"

"I know. And it's too bad."

"Too bad? Why?"

"That means you won't be coming up to see me anytime soon. Like I said, you've got more work to do down there."

CHAPTER 76

Tom and Toronto stood with Moishe and watched from a distance as the cars were unloaded from the tractor-trailer. One after another the small cars were backed out and carefully eased down the ramp to the tarmac by the RoadWheels valets. The very last car was a gold-colored Mini Cooper, and the ramp seemed to give a little under its weight.

As the cars were being off-loaded, their owners came down from the upstairs passenger lounge and stood by and waited. They took possession of their cars as they were backed out by showing a ticket to the valet, and then climbed in and went on their way. A prominent sign posed near the pick-up point said No Tipping, but some of them tipped anyway and received appreciative smiles from the valets. However, the man who waited for the gold Mini wasn't the sort who tipped anyone. He clearly had no interest in either his appearance or his grooming, as they had no relevance to the serious business of transporting a car worth a $100 million from someplace in the vicinity of Toronto to a destination in the vicinity of New York.

The man handed the valet his receipt and settled into the driver's seat. Before he started the engine and left, he sat there and made a cell phone call. Within seconds, two black Mercedes appeared out of nowhere, and, when he drove off, these Mercedes were close behind.

Tom and Toronto started their motorcycle engines and bid Moishe farewell. Moishe had driven them to the Palisades Mall Station in his yellow cab, and his taxi stood out in the mall parking lot like a bright tropical fish in an aquarium full of gray and white guppies. Following the gold car without detection would not be at all possible unless the Mini just happened to wind up in the streets of Manhattan where every third car was a yellow cab.

As the Mini and the Mercedes headed for the entrance to the New York Thruway going south, Tom and Toronto followed suit, after allowing a number of cars to pass them and take a position ahead. Since they could easily pass cars with their cycles whenever they wanted, losing sight of their quarry was not a concern unless a traffic light happened to intervene.

As Tom and Toronto approached the crest of the hill on the road to Nyack that ran parallel to the thruway, they could see up ahead that the light had turned green with a separate left arrow pointing toward the thruway entrance. The line of cars in the left lane veered off toward the entrance, the gold Mini and the two black Mercedes among them, but just as Tom and Toronto approached the light, the arrow turned red, and a line of cars coming in the opposite direction streamed forward. Too late to make the left turn, Tom and Toronto sped forward through the light on the parallel road and ran right into the busy traffic in the town of Nyack. Passing cars right and left, they made their way through as best they could, keeping the expressway in sight on their left and hoping against hope they could reach the second Nyack entrance in time to enter the thruway and forge ahead to catch up.

The traffic on their road came to a stop at another traffic light, but they took advantage of it by passing all the cars on the right and sped out ahead when the light turned green. The road passed beneath the thruway, so, to keep it in sight, Tom and Toronto turned right at the next intersection and passed under it again. This road took them south, running alongside the thruway on their left, until they saw another sign for the Nyack entrance and Tom slowed to enter the expressway. Toronto kept speeding ahead, however, and waved to Tom and he passed by, heading south on Route 9W that paralleled the west side of the Hudson.

"What gives?" Tom radioed, speaking into his helmet microphone.

"There's another way onto the thruway up ahead," Toronto replied. "You take this entrance, but I'll keep going."

"No, this is the last entrance before the bridge over the Hudson."

"The last *official* entrance. I know another way."

"What's wrong with this way?"

"We should split up. It'll attract less attention."

"You're right. We'll take turns following."

Tom took the access lane to the expressway and quickly came to an abrupt halt. The traffic had come to a standstill before reaching the Tappan Zee Bridge. Tom was unable to move forward along the breakdown lane on the right, because even that space was filled with a line of stalled and impatient drivers trying to get ahead. He looked around him but couldn't see any one of the three cars he was following. The Mini had to have been blocked by the traffic too, but as soon as it reached whatever it was that was causing the traffic tie-up, it would speed on ahead and take any number of routes heading east, north, or south. Once he reached the bridge there was no breakdown lane on either side that he could use to pass, and he couldn't squeeze between the cars when all lanes were full. Tom's spirits sank.

Meanwhile, Toronto drove south along Route 9W and then doubled back on South Broadway, heading north. This road led him back to the thruway, where he passed under it again, took the next right and headed south once more on Piermont Avenue. Eventually he came upon the precise point where the thruway left the land and struck out across the Hudson River. Toronto entered the expressway through a gap in the siding and saw, right in front of him, the gold Mini Cooper.

"They're here!" he shouted ecstatically into his microphone. "They're right at the entrance to the bridge."

"Thank goodness! I thought we'd lost them."

"I'll stay on 'em. Don't worry."

"When this traffic loosens, I'll catch up."

Within a few minutes the traffic did start to move, very slowly at first, but Toronto soon saw what was causing the backup: a car had stalled on the bridge in the right-hand lane, reducing the three available lanes to two. Cars were shifting lanes to get around the obstruction while at the same time staring at the unlucky wretch who sat morosely in the vehicle. Most were annoyed at the inconvenience and at the same time felt sorry for this man—most, that is, except for the drivers of the gold Mini and the two black sedans right behind it. The driver of the Mini cursed loudly out his open windows as he passed. "You son of a bitch! Get the *fuck* off the road."

Traveling right behind, Toronto heard him over the roar of his motorcycle engine and winced. "Sorry, buddy!" he shouted as he came alongside the stalled car. "That guy's an ass."

The man in the disabled car, visibly touched by Toronto's message of empathy, responded with a heartfelt "Thanks, buddy!"

After the blockage, the traffic surged ahead, but Toronto had no trouble keeping the Mini and the Mercedes in sight. Tom caught up easily too but kept his distance so as not to appear to be riding with Toronto.

The three cars in the lead took the very next exit and headed south on the Saw Mill River Parkway. When they reached Yonkers they turned off and made their way through city streets. Within a half hour they had arrived at their destination: a one-story industrial warehouse in the center of a poor residential neighborhood called Nodine Hill.

The paint was peeling from the cement walls of the warehouse. Glass panes filled the windows, but they were fairly opaque with brown grime. The windows were covered with rusty bars, an eyesore that added to the ambiance of desperation and despair in the already run-down neighborhood.

To avoid detection Tom and Toronto pulled up short a block away from the warehouse, at a spot with a good a view of the building, and switched off their motorcycle engines. They took off their helmets and as they watched, a gray garage door raised automatically, forming a large, gaping opening through which the Mini entered and disappeared. The two black Mercedes parked in front of the building, remaining outside as the door slowly lowered itself back down. A man with an assault rifle got out of each car, and, after clearing the area, they took up posts on either side of the door. Without knowledge of the value of the gold Mini Cooper inside, one would wonder why these men needed to stand guard.

"What's the plan?" Toronto asked after surveying the place with his eyes.

Tom nodded toward the warehouse. "We need to find out what's in that building. It's practically a fortress."

As he spoke, another black Mercedes sedan drove up and stopped in front of the building. The driver jumped out and opened the rear door. Out stepped a woman in her midforties. She was quite short in stature, seemingly half the size of her driver, and had cropped brown hair that made her look almost boyish. She wore a gray pantsuit with a white blouse and carried a shiny black purse.

Tom stared at the woman with intense interest, his eyes glowing hot with rising anger. "I believe that's Dakota Berk," he said, almost under his breath, trying to keep his voice under control. "She ordered her men to kill me."

CHAPTER 77

"Let's go talk to her," Toronto said eagerly, oblivious to Tom's sudden reaction at seeing Berk. He pressed the *start* button on his motorcycle, and, as soon as his engine sputtered to life, he immediately took off, heading straight in the woman's direction.

Tom didn't move. He watched but kept out of sight as Toronto quickly sped the short distance to her car in front of the warehouse.

Berk looked up, startled, as Toronto rode up. The two guards in front of the building cocked and aimed their weapons, but Berk held up her right hand. They froze in place but kept their weapons trained on the intruder.

"What's this?" she demanded. "Who are you?"

"I live in the neighborhood," Toronto replied, with a slight Spanish accent. Toronto's Latin origin appeared a perfect match for what Berk surmised was the ethnic makeup of the surrounding community. "What's going on here?"

"None of your damned business," Berk said curtly. "Be on your way."

"Don't fuck with me," Toronto pressed, ignoring her demand that he leave.

"Nothing's 'going on,'" Berk responded with increased annoyance. "Now beat it, or there'll be trouble." Berk emphasized the word *trouble* by motioning toward the guards with guns.

"You won't want to do that, bitch, or my gang and I will burn this warehouse down."

"Your gang? The police haven't told me about any gang . . ."

"We run this neighborhood. Nobody does shit without unless we say so. Not even the pigs."

"What's it called, this *gang*?"

"We're the Diablos. Now call off the dogs." Toronto nodded toward the guards.

Berk made a split-second decision. She could either make this guy instantly disappear, or she could play along and hope that he'd crawl back into the woodwork. Lucky she happened to be there just at that moment, or her guards would have made the decision for her—the wrong decision.

"Okay, *el Diablo*. Done. What do you want?" Berk asked, sourly.

"I want to see what you've got in there." Toronto pointed to the closed garage door.

"Not going to happen. What else?"

"You pay. We stay away."

Berk had assumed all along that money was what this was about. Extortion money. "I *don't* pay, and I call the police. How's that?"

"Not the right answer, bitch. This is our territory. Try again."

"It's just a warehouse. We keep our inventory here."

"Inventory of what?"

"We're in the food business," Berk lied. "We supply restaurants."

"My people are hungry. They could use some food. What kind you got?"

"All kinds. What do you want, a checklist?" she said sarcastically. "Now, I've work to do, so fuck off." Berk turned to enter the warehouse.

"Hold it right there, bitch. Or we'll take what we want."

Berk was very close to the end of her patience. "You just *try* and steal from us. The police will be all over you and your gang, and it won't be pretty."

"You think you've got the police in your pocket." It was a statement, not a question.

"I pay them enough. That seems to work around here."

"You think the police would be interested to know you're transporting *gold*? I'll bet if they did, they'd ask for a lot more hush money."

With the mention of gold Berk turned and stared at Toronto, her eyes flashing. "What gold? Who said anything about gold?"

"My gang and I've been watching you. We know you've been transporting gold into Canada with those little Mini Coopers. And that gold-colored Mini that just went into the warehouse? That one that *came* from Canada? It was painted the right color because it was carrying about a $100 million worth of the stuff."

"You son of a bitch. *Guards!* Come here, *now!*" The guards quickly surrounded her and pointed their guns at Toronto.

"Whoa, boys!" Toronto put up his hands in mock surrender. "I thought we were beginning to understand each other. Looks like I hit a nerve. Go ahead, shoot me, and my gang will be right on your asses."

The guards looked at Berk for orders to shoot. Berk held up her hand again. This man had to die, but not before she found out more about him and his gang. She finally said, "So I'll ask you again: what is it you want?"

"We can make a mutual arrangement here. Like I said, I want a look inside."

"Okay, you win. Stand *down*," she ordered her men. They lowered their weapons but kept them cocked. "I'll give you one quick look, and *that's it*. Then we'll talk."

"Okay, bitch. We'll see what we see. Lead the way," Toronto replied, putting his hands down.

"We've got nothing to hide. Just follow me and I'll show you." Berk signaled to the guards that she was going into the building with Toronto. Her limo driver took up the rear as she and Toronto walked to a side door around the corner from the garage door. Berk knocked, and the door opened a crack, held by someone on the inside. Satisfied that it was Berk who wanted in, the door jerked open all the way. Berk entered, followed by Toronto and Berk's driver, in that order. Toronto had the distinct feeling the driver also carried a gun. He could almost feel the muzzle in his back.

From the distance, Tom watched as Toronto disappeared into the building with the others and the door slammed shut behind them.

CHAPTER 78

Inside, Toronto thought he had descended into hell. A half dozen men were already tearing the gold Mini apart, large piece by large piece. The two side doors and the rear hatch were already off and lying on the floor. The front hood had been removed, and a cable with a hook on the end was being lowered into the engine compartment from a winch immediately overhead. Two men were on creepers underneath the car with only their feet showing. Toronto assumed they were unbolting the engine.

But the main attraction that caught Toronto's eye was a huge furnace in the center of the warehouse. It stood there, ominous and silent, while the air around it buffered the heat with transparent vibrations. Every so often a man opened a large, thick door near the top, revealing a fierce orange glow inside, and tossed in a metal part.

Toronto shuddered. The furnace could just as easily swallow an entire human body.

Behind the furnace, in the rear of the warehouse, were several more Mini Coopers in various stages of disassembly. Another half dozen men were working there with wrenches and hammers, all of them wearing leather gloves and dressed partly in leather to protect themselves from the hot furnace.

Toronto noticed the sweat on all the men's faces, wet and shiny, and felt the sweat on his own face too. Only Berk didn't seem to sweat for some reason.

"We're a legitimate business," Berk explained. "We reclaim gold from jewelry, electronic parts, or wherever and deliver it to our customers—banks, mostly—here and in Canada. That furnace is set at the exact temperature required to melt the gold. Other metals have a higher melting point, so the gold comes off, and we tap it from the bottom."

Just at that moment a man lifted a small plate near the floor of the furnace, allowing a glowing liquid to ooze out and form a small rivulet in an open ceramic trough. Toronto followed the orange glow with his eyes and saw it flow into a cavity in an elongated mold. Another man stood near, and, when the cavity was nearly full, he moved the mold to align the next cavity with the end of the trough. Toronto stood there, mesmerized by the sight of the bright liquid metal.

"We can make five to ten gold bricks a day," Berk said, breaking into his thoughts. "Each weighs about five pounds, so on a good day we produce fifty pounds, or well over $1 million worth of pure gold. At the end of the day, we bring it to the bank by armored car and receive a certificate of deposit."

As if on cue, the garage door rolled upward, a gray armored truck drove in and stopped in front of them, and the door automatically rolled down again. Two men jumped out of the front side doors, and one of them walked around to open the rear door, allowing two more men to come out the back. All four men wore holsters with handguns. Seeing Berk, one of the men came over and asked, "Whadda you got for us this time?"

"Hold it a minute," Berk said to him. "There's something we have to take care of first."

She snapped her fingers and a pistol suddenly appeared in the hands of the limo driver, pointed at Toronto. The other three armored car guards walked up and surrounded him, waiting for orders to take action.

"Tie him up!"

As she spoke, one of her workers opened the door at the top of the furnace and threw in a large piece of the gold Mini Cooper. Toronto shuddered as he saw an orange flame burst briefly out and felt a blast of heat before the door was shut again. He decided it was time for him to leave, but not before giving Berk a parting shot.

"I heard you had people killed."

"*Wait!* What did you say?" Berk, about to turn away, did a double take.

"You had people *killed.*"

"*What* people?"

"People who got in your way."

"You've heard altogether too much. How did you know about the gold in this Mini? Where are you getting your information, el Diablo— or whoever you are?"

"My gang gets around. We hear things."

"Not good enough." Berk turned to her driver and snarled, "Before he dies, we'll make him talk."

Toronto suddenly broke loose and sprinted as fast as he could toward the armored truck. Before Berk's driver or any of the armored truck guards realized what was happening, Toronto reached the driver's side door, opened it, and jumped up to the driver's seat. He rapidly scanned the controls and noticed a red button on the dash. He pressed it and all the doors locked with a thunk.

"Get him!" screamed Berk. She was so angry her voice cracked. The sound was piercing, nonetheless.

"Don't worry. He's not going anywhere. I've got the key." The driver of the vehicle reached in his pocket and felt for the key. "Shit! I must have left it in the . . ."

Berk watched, incensed, as Toronto cranked the engine. The instant it came to life Toronto put the transmission into reverse and popped the clutch. He turned the steering wheel as the truck roared backward, veering away from Berk and her men. The rear of the truck crashed into some auto parts that lay on the floor, making a clanking sound and causing Toronto to brake, stopping just short of the opposite warehouse wall. Toronto then shifted into first gear and reversed course, this time surging forward while turning the wheel the other way.

For an instant, the truck was headed straight in Berk's direction, and the men around her scattered, leaving her standing alone, staring in horror and frozen in fear. Toronto ignored Berk and kept turning left until the truck had turned completely around and headed back in the direction from whence it came. He then accelerated forward toward the closed garage door. The door was made of reinforced steel, and, not knowing whether the truck would make it through, Toronto braced himself for the crash.

What happened next surprised everyone, especially Toronto. The garage door began to lift itself up.

Toronto instantly hit the brakes to avoid slamming into it. The armored car jerked to a stop an inch away from the rising door while Toronto peered forward through the thick, bulletproof glass of the windshield. There in front of him stood an entire row of black youths mounted on motorcycles with an assortment of AR-15s and AK-47s pointed in his direction. Off to one side, also on his motorcycle, sat Tom with a seriously concerned look on his face.

"What the f—!" screamed Berk.

CHAPTER 79

At first Toronto did not know what to do, so he did nothing. He just sat in the armored car with the doors locked and stared at the array of men on motorcycles in front of him. Then a curious thing happened. One of the gang members, dressed all in black and seemingly a bit older than the others, waved to the others to get out of the way and leave a space for Toronto.

Toronto looked over at Tom, and Tom shrugged, almost imperceptibly, indicating Toronto might have safe passage, at least for now. Toronto could almost see Tom's mind racing to formulate a plan of action. For the moment, Tom was apparently unsure how the scene would play out.

Toronto gunned the engine and shot out of the building, stopping short right next to his own motorcycle. The group of youths quickly rode their bikes around, surrounding the armored car. Toronto felt oddly safer among these gang members whose intentions were unknown than he did with Berk. Glancing in his rearview mirror, Toronto saw the steel door of the warehouse slowly closing behind him, separating him from Berk and her armed men.

The two men with guns whom Berk had posted outside to guard the building stood with their hands up, held captive by two members of the gang. They looked at each other, unsure of what action to take. Being overpowered and stripped of their weapons was not in their playbook. One of them, who had been forced at gunpoint to operate the garage door, suddenly lunged at his captor and grabbed for his gun. The instant he did this, his head blew apart, spattering blood in all directions, and he slumped to the ground. The youth, who just seconds before had stood guard over him, backed away involuntarily and stared, stunned and horrified at the sight. He was covered in blood. Everyone looked over at the man in black who had fired the shot.

"What the fuck's the matter? You never saw a dead man before?" he said caustically. Tom had seen enough. It was time for Toronto and him to leave and leave fast. He started his motorcycle and put it in gear, letting the engine idle for just a split second while Toronto scrambled out of his vehicle and reclaimed his cycle.

"Thank you, gentlemen!" Tom shouted politely, as if he were talking to a group of suits at a business meeting. "We'll be going now."

"Not so fast!" The man in black shouted back. "Who the hell are you and what are you doing here?"

Without replying, Tom roared up the road, following Toronto, whose cycle burned a ribbon of rubber as it accelerated away. The man in black, not used to being left behind, screamed, "You're dead!" and took off in hot pursuit. The rest of the gang followed, leaving Berk's remaining guard standing there alone with his hands still high in the air. He looked around, slightly embarrassed, took his hands down gingerly and ran inside the warehouse through the side door to tell Berk what had happened.

The pack of motorcycles roared up the road after Tom and Toronto, creating a wall of sound that echoed between the apartment buildings on either side. The man in black rode a customized Harley with elevated handlebars and a low-slung seat. The other members of the gang rode mostly two in the saddle, because many were too young even to drive.

The noise of the passing cycles could be heard throughout the neighborhood. People looked out their windows, some even rushing out of doors, to witness the sight.

Tom and Toronto sped in the lead back toward the Saw Mill River Parkway, the direction from which they had come. "Head south to the GW Bridge!" Tom screamed. Neither he nor Toronto had taken the time to put on their helmets before their fast exit, so he used the old fashioned way to communicate over the roar of the engines: he shouted at the top of his lungs. "I know just where to go!" Toronto gave him the high sign to show he understood.

The two turned south on the Saw Mill and followed the twists and turns of the road as it wended its way into Riverdale and over the Henry Hudson Bridge. As they approached the bridge tolls, Toronto waved to Tom to catch up and they rode side by side in the right-hand lane signed for EZPass. They slowed as they approached the toll bar, giving it time to lift itself out of the way after electronically reading the EZPass device on the front of Tom's bike, and then quickly accelerated down the hill on the West Side Highway in the borough of Manhattan.

The man in black didn't pay the toll. He roared through the tollbooth at full speed, his handlebars snapping the toll bar off the base, leaving an open path for his gang to follow.

Tom and Toronto sped onward, easing over to the left lane exit under the sign George Washington Bridge. Passing under the bridge itself they took the ramp off the highway and doubled back, slowing briefly to make the sharp right U-turn, and headed up the hill toward the entrance to the bridge with the sign for the Upper Deck.

The man in black was unprepared for the tight U-turn. He suddenly realized he was going too fast and braked hard as his motorcycle leaned sharply to the right. Without the full weight of the bike on the road, his wheels lost their grip and locked up. Without rotating wheels, the bike fell on its side, creating sparks as the handlebars and the safety bar below the seat scraped on the pavement. The man held on, keeping his legs in tight and gripping the handlebars, riding the fallen machine as it skidded to a stop at the left side curb. To his amazement, he wasn't hurt, but that was the least of his concerns. He, the fearless leader, had taken a fall in front of his gang members as they all brought their bikes safely to a stop behind his mangled machine and stared at the sight. He stood up, red-faced, trying not to reveal his embarrassment, lifted up his heavy machine, and climbed back on. The right handlebar was bent at an angle, and the chrome safety bar was badly scraped, but the engine came to life again when he pressed the *start* button.

Up ahead, Tom and Toronto slowed to a stop and waited on the edge of the ramp for the gang to follow. Looking back at the sorry sight, Tom shook his head and laughed. "You can take the gang out of Yonkers, but you can't Yonkers out of the gang!"

When they saw that the man in black had righted his bike and was underway again with his gang members in tow, Tom and Toronto took off, somewhat slower this time as if daring the gang to catch them, and at the fork for the upper and lower decks of the bridge, they stayed left for the ramp to the upper deck. Following the ramp around to the right in the three-quarters of a corkscrew turn and ending up parallel to the bridge traffic on the upper deck, they merged into the right-hand bridge lane. Looking in their rearview mirrors they could see the motorcycle gang just entering the bridge as they had progressed halfway across.

Tom and Toronto accelerated forward, weaving in an out among the cars and trucks that were lumbering along, but always returning to the right lane. They pretended to be afraid for their lives but actually had to hold themselves back for the motorcycles behind that were doing their best to keep up. When they reached the end of the bridge, Tom led the way to the Palisades Parkway, and, after making sure the gang was following, he and Toronto accelerated northward through the Palisades Park along this limited access highway. Within minutes they had traveled the nine miles to exit two for the Alpine Approach Road. Following the exit ramp around under the parkway, they turned right at the traffic light onto Route 9W and rode north again for another mile until they came to a green and brown sign on their left for the Alpine Boy Scout Camp.

Tom gave a nod to Toronto and they entered, followed closely by the noisy pack of motorcycles. They came first to a parking lot with a nearby lodge, but they continued on up a trail, rattling the birds out of the trees as they rode, until they arrived at an open field with a flagpole at the center. There in front of them was a troop of boy scouts, aligned in rows and in full uniform. Standing in front of this group was a young African American leader, also in uniform, who wore the badge of an Eagle Scout.

CHAPTER 80

All the scouts turned their heads and stared as Tom, Toronto, and the gang from Yonkers made their noisy entrance and braked to a stop, turning up a dust from the dry earth in the field.

The scout leader held up his hand in a welcoming gesture as Tom, who was first to arrive, dismounted from his cycle and walked up to him. "Hello!" he said pleasantly, still showing his annoyance at the invasion by the noisy trespassers. "My name's Jason. What's going on here?"

The gang from Yonkers sat warily on their cycles with their engines idling and couldn't hear what Tom was saying to Jason. Toronto had surmised what Tom had in mind when they rode into the camp but wasn't at all sure if the plan would work. He remained on his bike and watched in readiness to assist Tom and the scouts if the gang caused trouble. The boy scouts in troop formation giggled among themselves at the interesting interruption of their routine.

As Tom spoke with Jason, the Eagle Scout nodded knowingly, and his face slowly brightened into a broad smile. When he finished explaining the situation, Tom asked the scout for his cell phone number, and, as Jason turned back to address the assembled young men in front of him, he tapped the number into his own cell phone. Speaking loudly and clearly over the noise of the motorcycles, Jason took command. "A warm welcome to you all. Please turn off your engines and come forward. We need to hold a powwow."

Jason's announcement was so matter-of-fact and so obviously the right thing to do that, to Toronto's astonishment, all of the gang members responded—all, that is, except the man in black, who remained on his cycle and glared angrily at Tom. The rest of his gang dismounted and walked up, mixing with the other scouts who immediately held out their hands and introduced themselves with words of welcome. It was a strange sight, the black gang from Yonkers, dressed in ragged T-shirts and jeans, joining the troop of scouts in their pristine uniforms, representatives from all over the globe—white, black, Latino, Asian, and American Indian—and feeling the kinship with their fellow youths. It was clear to Tom, Toronto, and Jason that new and important friendships were being formed right before their eyes.

The man in black sat on his cycle, fuming and aghast at his losing control. "You son of a bitch!" he screamed at Tom. "You're destroying my gang!" Aiming his bike straight at Tom, he suddenly accelerated toward the man who had caused him twice now to lose face in front of his men. Quick as he was, Toronto was quicker, and he sped forward from the side, his front wheel slamming into the front wheel of the attacker's motorcycle and deflecting it so that the man in black had to stop to prevent the bike from falling onto its side. Seizing the moment, Tom ran full tilt to his motorcycle while at the same time giving a whistle to cause its engine to automatically start. With one swift motion Tom jumped onto the seat and zoomed off with Toronto closely behind. The man in black scrambled to right his bike and followed in hot pursuit.

The remainder of the gang stayed behind and watched them ride out in a cloud of dust. As soon as they disappeared from sight, Jason put his leadership skills to work and met the challenge of bringing an undisciplined gang of boys from the streets of Yonkers into the ranks of the Boy Scouts of America. "Gather around, boys," he commanded, his voice authoritative yet friendly. The boy scouts jostled each other for position in front of him, leaving the gang members in back, forming a rear flank. "There's enough of us now to have a game of football," Jason said. "We'll make two teams." He held one hand out straight in front, palm vertical. "We'll divide the group here," he said. "Everyone on your right of this line is on the red team, and everyone on the left is on the blue team . . ."

Racing northward on the Palisades Parkway, Tom and Toronto were careful not to go so fast as to leave the man in black behind. Their only difficulty was to make it seem as if the man was catching up while they, pretending to fear for their lives, were desperately fleeing. To execute this charade, Tom and Toronto took turns bobbing and weaving around the man in black and occasionally grimacing when he tried unsuccessfully to run them off the road. At one point the man in black pulled a handgun out of his pocket and pointed it at Toronto when he come alongside, but, while speeding along the narrow, two-lane parkway, the two had to continually dodge other traffic, and the man had to keep both hands on his handlebars. He angrily stowed the gun for later use and followed Tom and Toronto as best he could.

After twenty minutes they reached the exit for Route 59, a main road that paralleled the New York State Thruway. Tom, in the lead, turned off and headed west one mile to the parking lot of the Palisades Mall. With Toronto and the man in black close behind, he pulled into the RoadWheels Station and stopped next to the men who were unloading cars from a waiting tractor-trailer. The passengers to whom the cars belonged were climbing down the stairs from the upstairs lounge. Other passengers with their cars were waiting patiently to come aboard and be transported to some distant city.

Tom dismounted and walked back to face the man in black, who was just pulling up. Toronto braked, letting the man pass, and stopped right behind him. The man stayed on his cycle with the engine running as Tom approached.

"Get off that bike," Tom ordered.

"Who the fuck *are* you? Some kind of a law man or somethin'?"

"No. Just a biker, like yourself, except I don't have a gang. I ride with my friend, Toronto, here." The man in black sneered and turned to look at Toronto, who also stayed on his cycle, ready to chase after him if he took off. The man snatched out his handgun again and aimed it at Tom's chest as he came close.

"Take one step closer and I'll blow your ass away."

Tom held out his hands to show he was unarmed and put them down again. "I don't carry," he said. "No need for that."

The man in black slowly put his gun back in his pocket. "So what you doin' on my turf?"

"You don't know what goes on in that warehouse?"

"Little cars keep going in an out. So what? I don't give a fuck."

"Those Mini Coopers are worth up to a hundred million dollars."

"That's *bullshit*." The man-in-black took out his gun and aimed it again, thinking Tom had insulted him by lying to his face.

"It's true. Those cars are loaded with gold. Real gold. Up to four thousand pounds of it."

"Sayin' that don't make it true."

"Go in there and see for yourself. There's a woman in charge, Dakota Berk, who runs the operation. She takes gold jewelry from desperately poor women all over the country and melts it down."

"So?"

"She cheats them and gets her gold almost for free."

"So? And you care *why?*"

"Call me a champion of justice."

"Yeah, right! So what's with the cars?"

"She hides gold in them to transport to Canada."

"And she's allowed to do that?"

"Not hardly. There are laws against smuggling."

"How do you know all this?"

"I've been following her. Her enforcer almost killed me, *twice.*"

"You too? She woulda got your friend here if we didn't show up." The man in black used his thumb to point backward at Toronto, who was still behind him.

"Glad you did. Thank you for that."

"You owe me."

"You didn't come to help him. You thought there was a rival gang in there."

"You *lied* to me, you son of a bitch!"

"Guilty as charged."

"The cops know about this woman? Why don't they take her down?"

"The locals are paid to let her alone. The FBI knows about her, but they can't get the evidence they need for a conviction. She's really smart."

"So why don't you and your friend here go in there with guns blazing and clean her out?"

"Much too dangerous. She's got an army. If we don't end up dead she'll have us arrested. The police are on her side, remember."

"So what's your plan?"

"I call it plan A. Here's the idea . . ." Tom held out his hands inquiringly. The man in black nodded his assent, and Tom stepped closer so he could speak quietly over the sound of his idling engine. As Tom explained the plan, a wry gin spread across the man's face.

When Tom finished, the man shot him a conspiratorial look and said, "Okay, that's cool. I want in."

"So let's start again. My name's Tom, Tom Smith. And my friend's name is Toronto. What's yours?"

"Name's Manny. Manny Fresh."

"I think I've heard of you," Tom said, vaguely recognizing the name from some news item he'd read or heard. "Of all the gang leaders, you're the one the police want most."

"Yeah, I know," Manny acknowledged with a mock sigh. "I'm a legend in my own time."

CHAPTER 81

Manny Fresh had grown up without parents in the streets of Yonkers, and more particularly the streets of the most dangerous section of Yonkers, Nodine Hill. His African American mother, herself a product of a broken home, had avoided the existential hurt by spacing out on crack cocaine. It was expensive, to be sure, but it was well worth selling her body to buy. Five years after giving birth to Manny she died of AIDS.

Manny's father, simply said, was a no-show. His mother had no idea whom to call the father of her beautiful child. He could have been one of her many patrons at the time, black or white, or one of her freebie boyfriends, mostly black, who briefly flickered on in her life and went out.

Manny survived by street smarts. Since as early as he could remember he was aware of the high demand for crack cocaine, a commodity of greater value per ounce than gold. Without a home to support him, getting and selling crack cocaine became his lifeline. He started very early as a runner, or delivery boy, and worked his way up the hierarchy to his current coveted position near the top.

Having experienced no mercy as a child, he had no knowledge of the concept. He was heartless and ruthless in his dealings with others, particularly those who interfered with the way he earned a living. Disputes with Manny were decided in only one manner: his adversary would not live to enjoy another day. Over time, smart adults learned to give him a wide berth. Also over time, he developed a following among other disadvantaged young boys in his neighborhood, and they coalesced around him as their natural leader. He was known as "the man," and eventually "Manny."

Enter Tom Smith. Manny first saw him sitting tall in the saddle on the most beautiful motorcycle he had ever seen. He wore aviator glasses to hide his visage, but he seemed to be staring intently at a young Latino in front of a warehouse building. He was arrestingly handsome, his unruly crop of sandy hair framing his striking facial features, and he wore an open black leather jacket over his blue shirt and jeans. Tom was a vision of the man Manny would have wanted his father to be, if only he could have had a father.

Manny approached this man with the mean attitude he always took with a trespasser on his turf, but, deep down and perhaps unconsciously, Manny wished he could make a connection. He rode up and stopped next to him, followed by his motorcycle gang, and demanded to know what Tom was doing there.

"That guy," Tom raised a right middle finger without removing his hand from his handlebar to aim at the Latino youth, "is from a rival gang, and he's trying to make a deal with that woman to protect her operation." Manny saw the woman lead the young man through the side door into the warehouse, leaving two men outside to stand guard.

"Fuck!"

Manny was about to lead his gang to take over the building when he saw an armored car drive up, the garage door open, and the truck disappear inside. When the garage door closed again the gang charged forward and took the two guards by surprise. They had just disarmed these guards and were ready to invade the building when the garage door lifted again, revealing the armored car with the Latino staring out through the windshield at them from the driver's seat.

So, when Tom sought his assistance in bringing down this woman who was operating a gold smuggling business right under his nose, Manny agreed to take part. There was something about this man that garnered his respect, and, at least until he caught a whiff of any betrayal, Manny was willing to go along with the so-called plan A.

Manny liked plan A—getting evidence of this evil woman's crimes—because he and his gang would be doing what they did best: scaring the shit out of some bad people.

"Where *you* from?" Manny asked Tom, now that they were exchanging names.

"Over there." Tom pointed toward a huge tractor-trailer.

"That yours?"

"Yeah. That's where we live. Toronto and I."

"Yeah, right. I mean where's your home."

"That's it. You're looking at it."

"No *shit*! You can go anywhere you want."

"Would you like to take a look?"

"Fuck yes!"

Manny's eyes grew bigger and bigger during the next half hour as Tom and Toronto invited him into the back of the big semi and showed him everything, upstairs and down. When finished, Tom explained all the features of the tractor and let him climb up and sit in the driver's seat. Manny was quiet during the entire tour, but when they returned to their motorcycles, he said simply, "Lead the way."

The three men headed back to Nodine Hill to carry out their plan. On the way Manny called one of the members of his gang to find out what they were doing, but he got no answer. He tried another one of his gang members with the same result. No answer. It was not like them to ignore his calls, but he wasn't at all concerned. He was their leader and would remain so no matter what shit life placed in their path. They were all born without a fair chance, but by supporting each other they could and would survive.

As Tom, Toronto, and Manny rode up to the warehouse, they saw the garage door wide open. The building was totally vacant, its occupants gone.

Tom pulled out his cell phone and made a call. "Moishe, it's Tom. Plan A is not going to happen. Let's go to plan B."

Chapter 82

They stared through the open garage door at the cavernous space. "Let's go in," Tom said simply. The three dismounted and walked in through the wide entrance to look inside.

Tools, equipment, and various cars parts were everywhere, strewn randomly throughout the warehouse where the workers had dropped them. The furnace was still hot, but it was strangely silent with its flames extinguished. All of the occupants had disappeared, as if beamed up to a remote spaceship, leaving the space eerily quiet.

"Who owns this warehouse?" Tom asked as he walked around, examining the leftover items and looking for clues. He noticed that, oddly, there wasn't a single scrap of paper in the building. To that extent, it had been scrubbed clean.

"It belongs to Guido," Manny responded. "Guido Spano. Same last name, but he's not related to all those other Spanos around here, those blood-sucking politicians—Mike, Nick, Andy, and whatever."

"Suppose Guido let you use it . . ." Tom continued, his mind sifting through the possibilities the warehouse offered.

"Use it for what?"

"Anything—anything that you wanted to do. Anything that needs to be done in this community."

"You mean store drugs for distribution?" Manny quipped sarcastically. His entire gang, who were gathered around and listening intently to the conversation, stifled a laugh. Toronto cracked a smile too.

"Sure, if you call liquor a drug. Assume you could do whatever you want in this space, as long as it's legal."

"Guido owns it. That's it, man."

"Assume Guido would give you the building; what would you do with it?"

"That's not going to happen."

"What would you do?"

"I don't know. Work on our bikes?"

"That's a start. How would you make money? Legally, I mean."

"Work on other people's bikes?"

"Sounds good. What if you don't get enough business? What if there aren't enough motorcycles around that need fixing?"

"We could customize them . . ."

"And?"

"And *fuck*. Cut the crap!"

"Humor me," Tom pressed. "You're stuck on bikes. What else needs fixing?"

"Bicycles. There's a lot of 'em around here."

"What else?"

"Cars. There's a lot of old cars. They always break down."

"That's the idea. Start a business. Do great work, keep your prices reasonable, and they will come."

"Get real, man. Like I said, Guido owns the building."

"He let Berk use it."

"And maybe she sucked his dick, I don't know. Guido won't let us use it."

"Why not?"

"I just know."

"Promise me something, Manny." Tom looked squarely at him, deadly serious now.

"I don't make promises I can't keep."

"Promise me you and your gang will start a business here, any kind of business, as long as it's legal, if I get you this warehouse."

"That won't ever happen, so yeah, I can promise. But there's this little problem you should know."

"What problem is that?"

"If I stop doin' what I'm doin', I'm a walking dead man."

"Is it drugs?"

"Yeah, it's drugs. How do you think I've supported myself since I was a kid?"

Tom looked sympathetically at Manny. "You know there's no future in that."

"It's the future I got."

"You deserve better."

"Tell me about it, Mr. Rich Man. My whole gang deserves better."

"You can put an end it."

"Fuck you."

Tom ignored the remark. "Who pays you?"

"We sell, we collect the money, and we pass it up. We keep a small percentage."

"Whom do you work for?"

"I wouldn't tell you if I knew, which I don't."

"Whom do you give the money to?"

"Just a runner. I used to be one myself."

"What does a runner do with it?"

"Drops it off. Gets more drugs."

"Where?"

"How the shit do I know? It changes all the time. You wanna get yourself killed? Go follow one sometime."

"Have the police ever tried to find out?"

"No, man. The police, they're scared too. They don't do shit."

Tom thought a moment and then, grabbing his cell phone, made another call. "Moishe, it's me again. I need a contact at the FBI to tell them about money laundering. Big time!"

CHAPTER 83

Tom, Toronto, and Manny entered the FBI Field Office at 26 Federal Plaza in downtown Manhattan. They were cleared through the building security, a process more rigorous even than the security at airports. They were patted down and required to surrender their cell phones. When finished they were told to wait in a holding area for their contact person.

Within minutes, a man in a dark suit appeared and greeted them warmly. "Hello, gentlemen. I'm Special Agent Danny Lester. Please follow me. I'll take you up to the twenty-third floor."

Tom winced. "I just realized I shouldn't go up there. I don't want to chance it," he whispered to Toronto so that Danny and Manny wouldn't overhear. "You go and talk with them. I'll stay down."

"Remember Rarotonga? You made it all the way to the top of the mountain."

"That was different. I was on solid ground. This is a . . . a *building*."

"You were scared there at the beginning too. Maybe you can press through this now."

"I don't think so."

"You won't ever know unless you try."

"I know, but . . ."

Following Danny into the elevator, Toronto nudged Tom forward over the threshold.

Tom held on to the side rail of the elevator as it rose. He closed his eyes, hidden behind his aviator glasses. When the elevator slowed and stopped at the twenty-third floor, he opened them again, took a deep breath, and stepped out onto the landing.

He was relieved to find there were no windows in sight. The elevator lobby was completely enclosed and sealed off at the center of the building. The walls and doors of the lobby were painted solid white, giving the incongruous appearance of the inside of a hospital. Danny used his ID card to unlock one of the doors and led the group down a narrow hallway to a small internal room. Tom, Toronto, and Manny took seats on both sides of the conference table, and Danny sat in a chair at the head. "Can I get you anything? Water? Coffee?" he asked. No one requested it, so he continued, "So why are you here?"

"We've come from Yonkers. Do you cover that area?" Tom asked.

"We're the New York Field Office. We cover the City and the surrounding five counties. Westchester's one of them."

"Are you aware of the drug problem in Yonkers? The local police are ignoring it."

"There's a drug problem everywhere. And yes, we have information about the special problem in Yonkers."

"You do?" Tom thought it was odd the FBI knew about it but weren't doing anything.

"We have a CI," Danny said, as if reading Tom's mind. "We're trying to get evidence."

"A confidential informant? Who?"

"If I told you, the person wouldn't be confidential, now would he . . . or she?" Danny added, checking himself.

"Do you know who's involved? In the drugs, I mean."

"Yes, there's a whole youth gang. The kid at the top is the worst. He's been running drugs for years, and he kills anyone who gets in his way."

"Oh!" Tom was shocked. "Do you know who he is?"

"I can tell you the name. It's a guy they call Manny, Manny Fresh. He's practically a legend up there."

Tom shot a sideways glance at Manny and caught him staring fixedly at the FBI agent. Tom thought he could detect smoke coming out of Manny's ears.

"Do you know what he looks like? Have you ever seen him?"

"We have pictures in the file someplace. Never saw him in person, no."

"Well, actually you have," Manny said, speaking up for the first time. "I'm Manny Fresh."

This time it was Danny's turn to be shocked. He stared at Manny, his face fading even further from its normal pasty look. "You . . . ?" He couldn't say more.

"Yes, and I resent you calling me the *worst*. You have no idea who I am."

"I . . . I'm sorry. I didn't mean . . ." Danny almost choked on his words.

Tom intervened and explained, "Manny's here to make a deal. He'll come in as a CI to collect evidence against the top drug lord. For that, he wants immunity from prosecution."

"He's not the top guy? Our information says otherwise."

"I'm not," Manny said emphatically. "I'm just the messenger, but I can get to the top. They trust me."

"Trust you? If they suspect anything, they'll kill you. You know that, don't you?"

"Believe me, I know," Manny replied grimly.

"And you're doing this why?"

"This is my shot—my one chance to go straight. Tom here convinced me I could do that. Now can we make a deal, or am I wasting my time?"

Danny sat back in his chair and looked at Manny and then at Tom and Toronto in turn. He smiled warmly. "This is just amazing," he said finally. "Yes, maybe we can make a deal, but this is way above my pay grade. We'll need to get the DA involved. The FBI can't make deals like this. We can only recommend. But considering the file we have on you, I think it could be arranged."

"Okay then. Let's do it," Manny said firmly. "The sooner the better." Tom noticed a sense of relief in his new friend. His shoulders looked straighter, his face a bit less tense.

"I need to leave the room a minute to make a call," Danny said. "But there needs to be someone with you at all times while you're here in the building. Can I have my assistant give you a brief tour while you're waiting? You might even enjoy seeing our small museum."

"A museum?" Toronto perked up, suddenly curious. "An FBI museum?"

"Very few people get to see it, but we have one. There are artifacts from some of our famous cases, that sort of thing."

"Let's go see it!"

Danny pressed a button on an intercom and said a few words. The door opened, and a woman entered. She wore a beige pantsuit and looked very much like a man while still being female.

"This is Betty. We call her 'Brown Betty' because she always wears brown. She'll lead you up to the top floor. I'll call her when I'm ready, and she'll bring you back down."

Tom stared at the woman. "Top floor?" he said aloud but almost to himself. "I can't go."

"I'll be with you," Toronto said tenderly. Tom rose and allowed Betty to lead him, Toronto, and Manny to the elevator.

To Tom's relief, the museum on the top floor was without windows also. But when he finished looking at FBI artifacts and entered the museum store, the feeling of vertigo came over him once again. He stood in the doorway of a room filled with T-shirts, coffee cups, plush toys, and souvenirs and froze in place. On the opposite side of the store was a huge picture window.

CHAPTER 84

Manny had run his business successfully for so long that he had become the go-to person in his territory for any kind of illegal drugs, guns, or ammunition. Manny also carefully guarded his territory. Violence had been necessary at one time, but it took surprisingly few killings to send the message to potential suitors who might wish to challenge him. The word on the street was to stay away, and stay away they did. Manny had become "the man," and over time he had assembled a gang of younger men, from as young as age twelve on up through their teens, who had similar backgrounds to his own in this area of Yonkers, where families were fragile. Although Manny had achieved a manner of success in this way, he knew full well that his operation rested on shifting sands. Taking the long view, he and his gang really had no future. Therefore, Manny realized, this was his moment. He was ready to risk it all and step forward through the door that Tom had opened for him.

Manny tried again to phone a member of his gang. This time the young man picked up on the first ring. "Wazzup?" came the voice over the phone.

"Where the fuck were you? You didn't answer my call."

"Playing football. We parked our phones so we wouldn't break 'em."

"You still playing?"

"No, we're on the way home, but we want to go back there. Those prissy-assed scouts have challenged us to another game. The whites against the blacks, and you know who's gonna get their butts kicked in."

"You Yonkers guys did good, right?" Manny kidded.

"You should've seen us, Manny. Next time, don't run away."

"I didn't run. As a matter of fact, I've been real busy. I need to see you."

"We'll see you in half an hour."

"We'll meet at the warehouse."

The gang converged on the warehouse just as Tom, Toronto, and Manny arrived. They found the garage door closed and the building locked up tight. No Trespassing signs were now posted in front.

"Guido's been here," Manny explained, frowning.

Toronto noticed Manny's concern. "What's the matter?"

"Don't know. Maybe nothing. Not like him, that's all."

"To lock his building?"

"He never cared about it before. It was pretty much open for anyone to use, until that woman showed up and took it over a couple of years ago. I heard he bought the place for a dollar."

"A dollar?"

"Yeah. The prior owner was killed, and Guido grabbed it. It was kinda sudden, but I've got no problems with that. He was in the right place at the right time."

"I need to speak to him," Tom broke in.

"'Bout what?"

"About letting you use the building now that it's vacant."

The entire gang, assembled tightly around Manny, Tom, and Toronto, listened intently to every word and wondered what all of it meant. What were Tom and Toronto doing here with them? Why was Manny playing nice with these people? "Use the building for what?" one of the gang members asked finally. It was what the others were thinking too.

"Anything we want to do as long as it's legal," Manny replied almost casually. The word *legal* fell from his lips as easily as if he were a lawyer.

His gang members were still confused. "Uh, what do you mean by 'legal'?" one of them said. "Since when do you care?"

"Since about an hour ago. Tom, Toronto, and I have been to the FBI."

If they were confused before, now the gang members were stunned. "The FBI?"

"Yeah, the FBI," Manny spat out. "And if you don't like it, you can fuck off. Right now."

Nobody moved. "So what's going down, Manny?" The last word was emphasized with disapproval. "Are we losing you or what?" The person who spoke reflected the concern of everyone in the gang.

"We made a deal with the DA," Manny continued, maintaining an even temper.

"A *deal*? What kind of deal?"

"We're getting some kind of immunity if we bring down the drug cartel in this area."

"I thought that was *us*! We're the drug cartel. We own these parts."

"The FBI wants us to find the source of the drugs and get 'em evidence to put those guys away."

"The *source*?"

"The guys who bring in the stuff from wherever."

"But we don't even now who they is."

"Yeah, I do. I know the top guy."

"You do?" Tom interrupted.

"I wasn't about to tell the FBI and have them screw this up. That son of a bitch is crazy, but he's fuckin' smart. That's how he stays alive."

"Who is it, then?" Tom wanted to now.

"Nobody you know. And I wouldn't tell you if you did. He kills for a living."

"You're planning to do this alone?"

"I'll just talk to him. Wearing a wire."

"I can't let you do that. It's too dangerous."

"I'm willing to chance it for the sake of all the guys here. I owe it to them. They deserve better. When it's over we can all work together on something *legal* without worrying about the cops." Manny had barely used the word *legal* before in his life. It felt strange to him, but that was the path he was going to take, and he'd stay with it.

The gang members looked at each other, wondering what new spell had come over Manny. Had he gone soft on them? Did these new friends of his, Tom and Toronto, have something on him? Some dirt he couldn't shake? Was this some kind of game he was playing?

"What if we don't go along?" one of the gang members said. "What's in it for us?"

"A new life," Manny replied. "If you would like that, climb on board. We'll be free to go our own way."

It sounded too good to be true. Every gang member had heard the old adage that, if something was too good to be true, then it surely wasn't true. Warily, the young men, one by one, agreed to join Manny in his quest to clear the Yonkers streets of drugs and crime in this most dangerous part of the most dangerous city in the State of New York.

CHAPTER 85

Tom and Toronto assisted Manny in installing the wire they has been given by the FBI. It was small and thin and when held flat against his body with skin-colored tape, it was wholly inconspicuous. In fact, only a doctor or a nurse would notice it if Manny stood in front of them, stark naked. An untrained person would have difficulty finding it.

"Do you know where I can find Guido?" Tom asked when they were finished testing the device.

"No idea. I haven't seen him in years," Manny replied. "I wouldn't even know where to look."

Manny stood by his motorcycle and checked the weapons in one of his saddlebags in the back. Tom gave him a disapproving look. "Don't worry. I don't plan on using these. They're in case things go bad. I'm just gonna go meet my boss, peaceful like, and talk some business. I've been working for this guy for years now. It's time he gave me a promotion."

"You sure you don't want us there? We can stay out of sight."

"That's the last thing I want. This guy's surrounded by men with guns. They smell I'm not alone, and I'm a dead man."

"At least tell us the man's name."

"Not going to happen. I don't want you anywhere close." Manny threw his leg over his motorcycle and sank into the seat. "Wish me luck," he said as he started the engine.

All the members of his gang crowded around him to wish him well. Manny flashed them all a wide smile and roared off.

"What next?" Toronto asked as he and Tom walked back to their cycles.

"We find Spano and buy his warehouse."

"How do we do that?"

"Let's try the obvious," Tom said, dialing 411 on his cell phone and putting it to his ear.

"Yonkers, New York . . . . Guido Spano . . . . Business or residence, either one . . . . Well, thank you anyway." Tom ended the call. "There were about fifteen Spanos but no Guido," he said. "Probably uses only a cell phone."

"So how can we find him?""Anyone who owns real property has an address," Tom replied. "They send him a tax bill."

"Right! So where do they keep the land records?"

"The County Clerk for Westchester County. It's got to be in White Plains."

Tom and Toronto climbed on their bikes to make the trip. "We'll be back," Tom promised the gang. "Let's meet here again in three hours."

At the county clerk's office, Tom and Toronto perused the tax map of Nodine Hill in Yonkers and found the lot with the warehouse. Tom gave the lot number to the clerk and asked for a printout of the recorded deed. It was a single sheet that conveyed a fee simple title to the property to one Guido R. Spano for the sum of one dollar. Tom next asked the clerk for the current address of Guido Spano and wrote it on a piece of paper. He thanked the clerk, and they left with the copy of the deed. All of this took only an hour.

"Before heading back to Yonkers, there's one more thing we need to do," Tom said. "We'll go to Kinko's and scan this in."

At Kinko's, only a few blocks away, Tom and Toronto used the service to scan in the document. Once in pdf, it was a simple matter to change the name and address of the assignor to Guido R. Spano at the address they now had. Finally, they blanked out Spano's name and left a large blank space to insert a new name and address for the assignee. After inserting Spano's name on the signature line and inserting a new jurat for a notary public to sign, the document was complete. Tom paid the bill at Kinko's and they returned to their bikes for the trip back to Yonkers.

Tom typed Spano's address into his navigator, and they were off.

The address turned out to be an old Greek revival mansion on the fashionable north side of the city with a great view of the Hudson River from the upper windows. The house was surrounded by a walled-in courtyard, the walls ten feet high and covered with ivy. Tom and Toronto parked their bikes just outside a massive iron wrought gate and walked up to it.

"Wherever I look there's a video camera," noted Toronto. "This place is a fortress."

"But where are the guards?" Tom said cautiously. "Someone must have noticed us by now."

Seeing the gate was unlocked, they pushed it open and stepped in. They immediately stopped short, shocked by what they saw. The inside surfaces of the walls were splotched dark red. Blood was everywhere. Bodies lay strewn on the ground in awkward positions. The carnage, like a battlefield after hand-to-hand combat, was palpable. The area was deathly quiet, but it screamed out with pain. Even the odor was offensive to the senses.

Quickly assessing the situation and gaining their bearings, Tom and Toronto moved stealthily forward to reach the door of the mansion. No one intervened or tried to stop them. They pressed the door open a crack and peered in. The vestibule was clear, but they assumed they would meet with armed resistance if they entered the house. Tom held his index finger to his ear as a signal, and they listened for a sound—any sound that might reveal if there was a person inside. At first they heard nothing, but after a minute their ears became attuned to the quiet, and they heard muffled sounds of someone speaking, somewhat animated and angry.

They cautiously opened the door and crept through it, entering first a foyer and then an adjacent room, moving gingerly in the direction the sound. They walked on the balls of their feet to soften their footsteps, one step at a time. Up ahead was an open doorway, allowing them to look inside from their vantage point without being seen. They observed a man, speaking obscenities and aiming a handgun at someone lying on the floor, a man covered in blood who appeared to be dying. The man with the gun was injured also, but there was no question he had won the fight. He was about to fire another shot when Tom, who was moving along the wall on one side of the adjacent room, came close enough to see the face of the man on the floor. It was Manny!

"Stop!" Tom shouted, both he and Toronto still hidden from view inside the adjacent room.

Startled, the man fired a shot in Tom's general direction. The bullet buried itself in the back wall of their room.

Feeling his life oozing away, Manny saw a final chance. With his last ounce of energy he pulled a small handgun from beneath his prone body, aimed it at Guido Spano, and fired a single hot. The bullet missed its intended mark but pierced the man's shoulder, ripping through his flesh and opening an artery. Spano screamed in pain and fired three shots back at Manny, finishing him off. Blood spurted from Spano's wound, causing his body to go into shock. His vision became blurry and then faded to white. Unable to see, he looked about aimlessly. Momentarily panicking, he fired the remaining few shots in his gun in Tom's direction until the gun clicked harmlessly.

Seeing the opening, Tom and Toronto rushed forward. Tom yanked the weapon from Spano's hand while Toronto grabbed the handgun from Manny's lifeless form.

"You're finished, Mr. Spano. Hold it right there," ordered Tom.

"I'm bleeding. Call the medics, *now!*" Spano demanded.

"We'll do that, but there's something we want you to do first." "What's that?"

"Sign over the deed to your warehouse on Nodine Hill."

"The warehouse on . . . ? Fuck you! Why should I do that?"

"You'll have no need for it where you're going. You'll be spending a long time in prison."

"For shooting that guy?" Spano spat at Tom and nodded toward Manny, who lay lifeless on the floor. "He attacked me first. He came in here guns blazing and killed all my men. He would have killed me too but I got the draw on him."

"Did you know who he was?"

"Damn right I knew him. He's Manny Fresh, the double-crossing son of a bitch."

"Did you speak to him before you shot him?"

"We had a conversation, yes. What's it to you?"

"Did he tell you why he was here?" "We talked business, and then I shot him. Now call the fucking ambulance! Can't you see I'm bleeding out?"

"Sign this deed first." Tom handed Spano the piece of paper and a pen.

"What's with the goddamn warehouse? You can't make me sign that."

"Like I said, you won't be needing it."

"Says who? The Feds have been on my back for years, but they've got nothing."

"They do now, Mr. Spano. Manny was wearing a wire."

"A what?"

"He recorded your conversation. Knowing Manny, my guess is he got enough evidence to put you away.""That lying son of a bitch!" Spano's anger only made his blood spurt faster from his wound.

"Sign this and I'll call the EMS."

"I'm signing! So there." Spano used his free hand to sign the deed. As he did so, Toronto made the call to 911 and asked for the police.

"Thank you, Mr. Spano. Oh, and one last thing. Here's a dollar." Tom reached into his wallet and produced a bill. "I understand you bought the place for a dollar. Here's your money back." Tom held out the dollar, but Spano spat in his face for the second time.

"It's only fair," commented Toronto. "The last thing we want to do is to cheat you."

CHAPTER 86

When Tom and Toronto arrived back at Nodine Hill, they were immediately surrounded by all the members of the gang—all, that is, but their leader, Manny. Tom and Toronto dismounted from their motorcycles and stood there solemnly for a moment among the group of youths, sadness etched on all their faces.

"Manny didn't make it," Tom began. "He was killed in a firefight."

The young men said nothing. They only looked at Tom and Toronto and shuffled their feet. Tears welled in their eyes.

"He died to set you free," Tom said. "It was a new life he wanted for himself and for all of you."

The words only made the gang members feel more forlorn. Their lives, what little lives they had, were at an end. What were they supposed to do now? They had come from broken homes. Two of them had no homes at all. They had no places to go and no lives to look forward to. Manny, the one who had given them both hope and a purpose, had been taken away. They did not want to be "free." They wanted to follow their leader—the one person they could rely on and could trust would have their interest at heart. He was their anchor with the rope to hold on to, to keep together in the churning seas. Now, for reasons they couldn't comprehend, he was gone.

Tom stood grimly in the center of this gang of youths and saw deep sorrow reflected back at him. He could feel the pain of these young men—some of them still boys—who had no families and no future.

Tom quietly pulled his cell phone from his pocket and placed a call. When it was answered, Tom said, "Yes, it's me again. Now is the time. Please come as quickly as you can. We need you." Finishing the call, he said to the assembled young men, "Let's take a walk inside the building."

Tom led the members of the gang into the building through the side door. Toronto brought up the rear. When Toronto stepped inside he turned to the right and pressed the button for the big garage door. The door slowly raised itself, letting the outside light fill the open hall.

"This building is yours to use from now on," Tom said as he took a piece of paper from his pocket. "I bought it from the prior owner for a dollar. This is the property deed. I'll have it notarized by Toronto's girlfriend, who lives up near the city of Buffalo. When that's done I'll have it recorded with the county clerk in White Plains."

The young men looked up in silence and in awe at the cavernous space. After a few moments of reflection, they began to walk around and investigate, looking in all the nooks and corners of the building. It was an enormous warehouse, filled with interesting things: workbenches, storage shelves, wall closets, an overhead crane, and even the huge furnace placed right in the center. The uses of the building were limited only by one's imagination.

"You can do pretty much anything you want here," Tom said, "as long as it's legal. Call this your home away from home."

The youths could not believe their eyes and ears.

As Tom spoke, a motorcycle could be heard in the distance. The sound became louder, and all the young men looked to see Jason, the Eagle Scout, ride straight into the building through the open garage door. Jason braked to a stop in the middle of the dirt floor and jumped off his bike. He stood there like the hero he was, ready to lead this group of young men into the future.

CHAPTER 87

Tom and Toronto were fast asleep in Tom's trailer at five in the morning when Tom's cell phone rang on his dresser. Tom remained in a deep slumber, however, and didn't respond to the incessant buzzing sound. His phone finally fell silent, and Toronto's phone rang near his bed in the next room. Toronto, ever the light sleeper, immediately picked up.

"It's me, Moishe," the phone voice said. "Berk's on the move! She's headed for Queens, and I'll bet JFK. I'm sticking to her like the barnacles on a boat."

Toronto sat up, instantly awake, and threw off the bed covers. "We're on our way! I'll wake Tom, and we'll meet you there."

Toronto knocked loudly on Tom's bedroom door and then opened it and peeked in. He could see Tom's eyes open a crack, and then, after a beat, they opened wide and stared at him expectantly.

"Berk's headed for the airport. We've gotta hurry," Toronto announced. That was all he had to say. Tom jumped out of bed even faster than Toronto had done and began pulling on his jeans.

"Get the bikes ready. I'm good to go."

Toronto hit a button on the wall, and the side door to the trailer opened outward, hinged at the bottom, and dropped down, forming a short staircase to the ground. Toronto hit two more buttons, and arms on both sides of the tractor just behind the cab swung out, each arm tightly gripping a motorcycle and setting it gently on the tarmac. As soon as the cycles touched down, their engines started automatically as if inviting Tom and Toronto to ride.

The two men bounded down the stairs and jumped into the saddles of their cycles. As they sped away, the gripping arms returned slowly to their default positions behind the cab, and the trailer side door lifted itself and closed, sealing the opening so well that even a trained eye could not see that the door even existed.

"Where are you now?" Tom eventually asked Moishe using the hands-free headset in his helmet as they raced along Interstate 287 toward the Hutchinson River Parkway.

"I'm right alongside Berk's limo on the Van Wyk, on the way to JFK, listening in to her phone calls. She checked on some Emirates flight—I wrote the flight number down here—to make sure it was leaving on time, and she's been speaking with some guy in Dubai about a place to live!"

"She's finally bailing. We knew she would eventually."

"Our plan had better work or that's it. She's out of here."

"It'll work. I'll alert Hardwick on the Cook Islands. Toronto is contacting his friend at the FBI. Remember how she's dressed when she steps out of the car."

"I'll do better than that. I'll take a photo."

"That would be great."

"It's showtime!" Moishe shouted excitedly over the phone. "Camera, action!"

In the limousine, Berk was busy changing clothes and putting on bright red lipstick and her blonde, flowing tresses. When her driver finally pulled up at the curb in front of the air terminal, she had become Georgia Bell, the girl from the antebellum South, complete with a charming southern accent. She had on her white, frilly blouse and her light blue miniskirt that matched her glasses with the light blue frames.

Moishe, who had parked his yellow cab right behind the limo, thought at first that she was someone else. It seemed Berk had somehow eluded him and switched places with another woman. He nevertheless snapped away with his camera just to document the moment, taking picture after picture of her arrival through his windshield. His concerns were allayed, however, when he saw how she treated her limo driver. Instead of seeing a sweet southern belle with a charming smile and courteous manner, he watched the woman micromanage the livery with a New York attitude as he unloaded and struggled with four large suitcases, three from the trunk and one from the passenger seat in front.

"Yup, that's her, all right," he said to himself, snapping a telephoto image. She cleans up real nice." *Snap.* "She could've fooled me." *Snap.* "The holy bitch." *Snap.* "We've got one chance"—*snap*—"to bring her to justice." *Snap.*

The limo driver handed over the bags to a skycap at the curb and returned to his car. As he opened the door to climb into the driver's seat, Moishe thought he saw relief on his face. He was finally rid of that woman. If he only knew what Moishe and his friends had in store for her, he would have been smiling from ear to ear.

Moishe pulled away from the curb and headed down the ramp to the ground-level parking. As he did so he pressed a button on the steering wheel to make a call. When asked by the automated voice whom to call, he announced, "The Road Ranger."

Tom picked up on the first ring. "We're almost there," he said without waiting to be asked. "We'll meet you in the parking lot."

When Tom and Toronto finally pulled into the parking facility, Moishe was standing there waiting. After parking their bikes, they walked over, and he showed them the pictures on his camera. The two smiled broadly, amused at her disguise; then their faces morphed suddenly to seriousness. It was time to execute plan B.

All three walked into the airport terminal and looked around for Georgia Bell, a.k.a. Dakota Berk. "She must have gone through security," Tom remarked with some concern in his voice. "Let's find the office of the FBI and have a talk with the agents."

CHAPTER 88

Berk sat stone-faced near a window in the rear of the first-class section of the aircraft as the other passengers filed in and passed by down the aisle. She hardly dared take a breath. The seat next to her was vacant, and as time passed, she began to hope that it would remain so. However, just before the airplane doors were to close, a red-faced, heavyset man rushed in with two bags in tow and took ownership of the space. He created places for his bags in overhead bins on both sides of the aisle by noisily shifting carry-ons of others out of the way. He grunted as he lifted his own bags up and then finally sat down heavily in the empty seat. Berk pretended to pay no attention and ignored this intrusion.

"Attention, passengers," came an authoritative female voice over the loudspeaker system. "Please stay in your seats while we make a final check of the manifest. A couple of police officers will be passing through the aisle with a police dog. Don't be alarmed; it's just routine. We'll be on our way in just a few moments."

A police dog? Berk freaked out silently. If they didn't recognize her by appearance, the dog might detect her scent. Moving her hands slowly and imperceptibly, she opened her purse that she had wedged tightly between her hip and the window side of the plane. She reached into a plastic bag inside her purse and wrapped her fingers around a bottle of cologne. Bringing it up carefully above the rim of the purse, she uncapped the top and pressed the plunger several times with her right index finger. She felt the cold spray on her bare legs and soon thereafter detected the fragrance of the eau de toilette as it permeated the air. Would it fool the dog?

Up ahead, three plainclothes policemen entered, one of them guiding a dog by a leash. Two of them took the lead and walked slowly down the aisle, one looking at each passenger on the right side while the other did the same on the left. The third policeman followed, allowing the dog to sniff the seats and the floor near the passengers' feet.

As the three men and the dog came down the aisle and approached her row, Berk sat motionless but followed the men with her eyes. The officer who wore mirrored glasses and was checking the passengers on her side of the plane stopped and stared at the face of the man next to her. He carried several sheets with names and photos, and, as he studied the man's face, he compared it to the photos. Apparently satisfied, he shifted his attention to Berk. He looked at her and then looked down at his sheets. Shuffling through them, he seemed puzzled for a moment but then saw something. He stared at Berk again. She froze, not even moving her eyes. She thought her head would explode. The man shrugged and moved on. She still didn't move. The dog was coming.

The German shepherd had a large head with a black pointed nose that he poked into openings between the legs of the passengers and the seats in front of them. When the dog came to Berk's row it checked the opposite side briefly before turning in Berk's direction and began sniffing the legs of the man next to her. The dog tried to squeeze through to get closer to Berk, but the large man blocked its way. The dog appeared ready to jump on the man's lap to reach Berk, but the officer held it back with a jerk on the leash. "Steady, boy," he said and moved on.

Berk exhaled and closed her eyes, her face pale from fright.

The next ten minutes were a blur to her as the officers completed their check of the passengers and left. The door of the plane closed with an audible thud and locked with a clank, sealing the cabin. The airplane was its own separate jurisdiction now, tenuously separated from the agencies controlling the ground on which it sat. But it would be airborne soon and free entirely from governmental interference.

The voice of the flight attendant came over the loudspeaker system, reminding the passengers to fasten their seatbelts. The flight attendant went through her routine but the words were a blur to Berk.

"You will now need to switch off your cell phones for the duration of the flight. Switching to 'airplane mode' is not sufficient. Switch off your phones. They can interfere with navigation.

"You also need to switch off all other electronic equipment. I'll make an announcement when we reach our cruising altitude and you can switch them on again. But leave your cell phones off until we land in Dubai."

Passengers all around Berk began to settle in for the long flight. They switched off their phones, took off their shoes, spread their blankets over their laps, and inserted their tablets and books in the seat pockets in front of them, but Berk just sat stiffly and stared blankly out the window as the plane taxied toward the active runway. Her cell phone in her purse remained on.

The flight attendants took their seats and strapped themselves in. The aircraft stopped for a moment, waiting its turn to take off, and then crept forward and stopped again. Each time the aircraft stopped, Berk squeezed her eyes closed and held her breath, thinking the men in black might yet grab her and pull her back from the brink. But the aircraft moved forward again.

Berk could see the runway outside her window. The plane inched forward once more, and instead of stopping, it continued on to a point where she could briefly look down the entire length of the runway. As the plane rotated slowly clockwise to line up with the runway, she could no longer see into the infinite distance, but she felt a bit safer.

She thought she caught a glimpse of some black cars off to the right heading rapidly their way, but she was not sure. The aircraft engines spooled up, and the pilot released the brakes. They were moving down the runway, slowly at first but then faster and faster. Berk leaned back, closed her eyes, and breathed deeply, but only for a moment.

She looked out again and saw the two black cars. They were traveling in her direction on a parallel road. They were speeding, initially moving as fast as the aircraft, but as the aircraft continued to accelerate, they fell back. *They can't stop the plane now,* Berk thought, *even if they reached the pilot by radio. We were committed to takeoff at this speed, this far down the runway.*

An instant later she could feel the wheels lift off the runway, and they were airborne. For the first time in years she felt entirely free—free from the long arm of the law.

As the aircraft floated upward, Berk felt her spirits soar. She was on her way to Dubai, never to return. She would get herself a beautiful apartment, on the hundredth floor or even higher, and start a new life. Her tremendous assets were safely tucked away in a Dubai bank. She could look forward to many years of independence—or maybe even marry an Arab sheikh. The possibilities were endless. As she lay back in her seat, dreaming of the future, the cell phone at her side came alive, buzzing and vibrating at the same time. She looked down at it and saw a face photo of Alex. She imagined him sunning himself out there on that sunny Pacific island and became instantly annoyed. What could he possibly want? She picked up the phone and placed it close to her left ear so it wasn't visible to other passengers or to the flight attendants. "Alex," she said quietly so as not to be heard by the red-faced man on her left. "As I live and breathe. What the hell do you want, you bastard?"

"Is that any way to speak to an old friend? Don't our good times in the sack mean anything to you? They did to me."

"I can't believe this. Where the hell are you?"

"I'm on the Cook Islands. On the opposite side of the earth from you."

"Well, that's fine, then. Let's keep it that way."

"Oh, come on. I'd like to come and see you someday. For old time's sake."

"Yeah, right!" Berk said sarcastically. "Well, I don't need you anymore. I'm out of the business. I'm starting over."

"No more gold?"

"I've seen all the gold I can stand. I'm into green now."

"You'll need an enforcer. Every rich person does."

"Those days are over. I'm getting a new life."

"You can't escape your past."

"Oh, yes, I can. I'm on my way to Dubai where I can't be extradited."

"What about those killings we did along the way? You think they'll give you a pass on that?"

"You did the killing, not me."

"You told me to do it. I did your bidding."

"That's true, but let them try and prove it. It would be your word against mine, and you know what I would say.""What's that?"

"Go fuck yourself, you son of a bitch. I hope they skin you alive." Berk pressed *end* to the call and, finding the settings, followed the menu to turn the phone off.

Over the loudspeaker came a deep male voice: "Ladies and gentlemen, I'm sorry to interrupt. This is the captain speaking. A red light has come on here in the cockpit. I'm sure it's just a faulty sensor, but we're turning around. When we land we'll swap out the navigator unit and be on our way again. We could fly this way, but since we're only a few minutes out, we decided to come in with an abundance of caution."

Everyone, including the flight attendants, looked around, startled, wondering if they had heard correctly.

"One more thing," the captain added. "It's a long flight. When we're airborne again we can easily make up the time. We'll be landing right on schedule."

The aircraft did a slow turn and bank and headed back to JFK. It received priority in the landing pattern and was brought quickly to a segregated part of the airport. A stairway vehicle drove up to the side of the plane. Four men dressed in black opened the main cabin door from the outside and rushed in. They came down the aisle with their hands at their hips, ready to draw their holstered weapons, and stopped at Berk's row. "Dakota Berk," the most senior-looking man said, invoking her real name, "you are under arrest."

Chapter 89

Tom, Toronto, and Moishe stood in front of one of two black SUVs and watched as the FBI officers escorted Dakota Berk off the plane. The SUVs were parked on the tarmac a safe distance away from the JFK terminals. When the aircraft had landed, it was directed to taxi to this remote area of the airport.

Berk's face was grim. She walked unsteadily down the steps to the ground with her hands cuffed behind her. One of the officers walked at her side, holding her arm. The most senior officer led the way, and the two others followed behind.

When Berk reached the tarmac, she looked up and saw Tom and his two companions. Her face reflected a glimmer of recognition, unsure at first where she had seen them before, until she spied the German shepherd through an open window in one of the SUVs. They had boarded the plane with the dog just before takeoff. Her face then flushed angry red, and she glared fiercely at Tom as she walked past him to climb into the nearest SUV. Who was this man in the aviator glasses?

One of the FBI agents opened the door to the driver's seat of the SUV with the dog while waving for Tom, Toronto, and Moishe to join him. Moishe gave a quick signal with his hand, and the dog obediently jumped into the empty space in the back. He and Toronto then climbed into the backseat while Tom walked around and took the passenger seat in front. The remaining three agents climbed into the other SUV with Berk, one on each side of her in the backseat and the third one driving.

The aircraft door was closed and locked again, and the vehicle with the steps pulled away. Once cleared, the huge aircraft shuddered and moved forward on the ramp, its engines spooling up and whining loudly, to return to the active runway. When the sound eventually subsided in the distance and the airplane was safely out of the way, the two SUVs headed back to a terminal.

"Great timing, I must say," the FBI agent driving the SUV said to his passengers, Tom, Toronto, and Moishe. He was following the other SUV that carried the other agents and their prize passenger. "To have that guy Alex call her just when he did was critical to our execution. We needed him to make the call while the aircraft was still under the US jurisdiction."

"I was nervous about only one thing," Moishe replied. "Berk could have turned off her cell phone when she was told to do so."

"I wasn't worried at all," Toronto said. "A woman like that never does what she's told."

"If she had turned off her phone, she'd be on her way to Dubai right now where she could live like a queen—or should I say a 'sheikess'—on her gold reserves," Moishe added.

"It was important to scare her like we did," Tom said. "She was so spooked I'll bet she didn't even hear the announcement to turn off all cell phones."

"Yeah, you should have seen her face when you stared at her twice while pretending to look for her in those photos," Moishe said. "I was holding Shep here, trying to keep him from licking the passengers, and I could hardly hold myself from laughing out loud."

"I missed that, dammit!" Toronto said, with a mock touch of regret. "I was pretending to work the other side."

"And when I got to her row, I gave Shep some leash, and he almost jumped into her lap!"

"I did see that. I looked back and saw you pretend having trouble keeping your dog under control. Berk almost freaked out! It was priceless."

The FBI man smiled in spite of himself. "We don't usually arrange for others to pose as policemen, but this time the charade worked beautifully. All I can say is, you've got a friend on in the Cook Islands—what's his name, Hardwick? Not every law officer will cooperate like that. And what puzzles me still is why Berk's enforcer, Alex, was so cooperative. It's one thing for Hardwick to tell the man in his custody what to do, and it's another for the man to do it."

"Hardwick found out that Berk had some kind of a hold on Alex, and Alex hated her for it," Tom said. "Once Alex was in custody and figured he wasn't going anywhere, he wanted to help us bring her down in return for whatever benefits he could get while doing his time. Hardwick got the recording system ready to go, and the rest was just timing."

"Isn't he wanted for murder here in the United States too?" the agent asked.

"For starters, there's attempted murder—of Tom!" Toronto pointed out. "There is also the murder of one of Tom's station managers. I'm sure there's a string of others."

"Then that's another good reason why the man is cooperating. He's resisting extradition to the US," the agent said. "Under the law, the Cook Islands can have him serve out his term in prison there before they have to acquiesce to his extradition."

"And by cooperating, Alex sees to it that he doesn't serve hard time in his prison," Toronto added. "Alex wouldn't get such a pass in a US lockup."

"The other prisoners would see to that," the agent noted. "Extradition or not, he helped us nail the one we really want. He handed us the proof that Berk was the mastermind."

The two cars eventually reached an unmarked outbuilding, close by but segregated from the airport terminals, and stopped near a steel doorway. After Tom, Toronto, and the FBI agent alighted, Moishe reached back and grabbed the leash for his dog. "Come on, Shep," he commanded, and the dog jumped out of the car onto the tarmac. All four men stood there with the German shepherd at their side and watched as Berk was removed from the other SUV.

She climbed out awkwardly from the vehicle and stood there uncomfortably for a moment with her hands restrained behind her back. Her eyes locked on Tom's face. "I've seen you somewhere before. You're . . . you're the man they call the Road Ranger."

"Yes, ma'am."

"No one knows your real identity," Berk said, more as a statement than as a question to Tom.

"That's right. It's better that way."

"You know, mister, you're kind of a legend in your own time," Berk said, with an odd sense of admiration. "You've been in the news. You help others who can't help themselves."

"I do what needs to be done," Tom said matter-of-factly.

"So who the hell are you?" Berk suddenly grew curious. She looked carefully at Tom, trying to recall where she had seen him without his aviator glasses.

Tom thought for just a moment and then reached up and slowly removed his glasses, revealing his face.

She stared at him, not believing what she saw when the recognition hit her. "You! You're . . . you're Tom Smith! You're supposed to be dead! I ordered Alex to kill you. Twice!"

"I just thought you should know," Tom replied. "Yes, I'm Tom Smith, but if you try to tell anyone I'm still alive, they won't believe you."

Toronto took a silver RoadWheel from his pocket and held it up for everyone to see. "I'd like to give her this," he announced to the four FBI agents, "as a memento from Tom." The agents stared at it, and they all nodded their assent. Toronto walked up and placed the coin in Berk's right hand, which was still cuffed behind her back. Her fingers closed around it.

"I don't get it," she said, sneering. "I try to have you killed and you give me a gift. Well, you can shove it up your ass." She spitefully flipped the coin in the air with her thumb. It landed somewhere out of sight with a soft tinkle.

The FBI agents looked at each other and then at Toronto. One of them asked, "Can we have one too?"

"Of course!" Toronto replied as he reached in his pocket for more and handed one to each agent.

They could barely hide their excitement as they examined their shiny coins and each responded with a heartfelt thank-you. As they turned to go, one of them added, "Your identity is safe with us, Tom. We agents are very good at keeping secrets."

CHAPTER 90

Bonnie came running out of the RoadWheels office when she saw Tom's black tractor-trailer pull into the Clarence Travel Plaza and ease to a stop, air brakes hissing. She reached the eighteen-wheeler just as Tom's lanky frame swung down from the tractor on the driver's side. Her boyfriend, Toronto, who rode shotgun, jumped down on the other side and came racing excitedly around the front of the cab to greet her. "Bonnie!" he screamed, giving her a bear hug. Bonnie hugged him back and they kissed. It was as if they were the only two people on earth.

"I've waited a long time for my benefits," Bonnie said when they came up for air, scrunching her mouth into a pouting smile. "You're supposed to be my *boyfriend*, you know."

"I've been, uh, kinda busy. Catching criminals."

"I know. It's all over the news! You finally got the bitch!"

"The FBI deserves a lot of the credit."

"Yeah, right! It was all *their* idea."

"Seriously. We asked for their help."

"Seriously nothing," Bonnie objected. "You two even posed as FBI agents. Who needs them?"

Tom winced. "That's a sore point. The FBI gave us a pass on that, but we won't be doing it again anytime soon."

"It's against the law," Toronto reminded her, rolling his eyes in mock disapproval. "But it worked like a charm!"

"Well, now that you're back, safe and sound, lover boy, we have some catching up to do. We can finally get on with our lives."

"You mean . . ."

"You know, the, uh, next step . . ." Bonnie hesitated to say it.

"Next step?"

"Now what do you think that might be?"

"I'm not quite sure . . ."

"Our wedding plans, you idiot!"

"Um, Bonnie, I've been meaning to talk to you about that . . ." Toronto did not know quite where to begin.

"About?" Bonnie looked at him, frowning.

"About the future. Now that Dakota Berk is behind bars, Tom and I are going to take to the road."

"Take to the road?"

"Yes. We can go anywhere in Tom's tractor-trailer, and—"

"And do *what*, may I ask?"

"Whatever comes up. People out there need our help."

"You'll just roam the highways like a couple of nomads, looking for people who need help? You're getting that I'm being sarcastic, right?"

"Well, when you put it that way, it sounds kind of dumb."

"It *is* dumb. It's the dumbest idea I've ever heard. Now come to your senses and marry me!"

Toronto looked helplessly at Tom for assistance, but Tom said nothing. Toronto looked back at Bonnie apologetically. "But Tom and I are a team," he said finally. "We're the Road Ranger and Toronto. Kind of like the Lone Ranger and Tonto."

Bonnie slapped his face, hard, with a resounding smack. "You bastard!" she said angrily. She turned abruptly around and headed straight for her RoadWheels office.

As she walked, face flushed wet with tears, a long black limousine with tinted windows and Canadian license plates pulled up and stopped in front of the office door. A middle-aged man, neatly dressed in a gray flannel suit and a red striped tie, stepped out the back of the limo and stood there a moment, looking about as if he owned the place. In fact, he did.

"My name's Gunther Sachs," he said politely and offering his hand as Bonnie walked up. "I'm looking for the station manager. A Bonnie Salerno."

"I'm she," Bonnie replied in a wavering voice, ignoring the hand and wiping the tears from her face. Still in shock from her boyfriend's rejection, she tried to compose herself. "What can I do for you?"

"If this is a bad time . . . I . . . I see you're upset," Gunther said sympathetically. "I can come back." He turned to go.

"No, no. I'm okay. It's just . . . just my crazy boyfriend. He dumped me . . . for now."

"I'm sorry."

"Don't be. The guy's gotta do what the guy's gotta do." Bonnie took a handkerchief out of her jeans pocket and blew, clearing her passages. "Okay, where were we? What can I do for you?" she said, feigning a smile.

"For starters, you can show me around. Then we need to talk. You see I just took over this outfit from the previous owner, a Dakota Berk?" He inflected the *Berk* upward as if asking whether the name was familiar, although it surely was.

"You . . . you're the new owner?" Bonnie's mouth dropped open and she looked the man in the face for the first time. "I . . . I thought . . ."

"I know it must come as a surprise. Berk sold all her shares in the company to me before she was arrested, but it has taken this long to complete the transaction—lawyer stuff, you know. I'll be making an announcement to the media, but before I do, I'd like to meet all the station managers, you in particular. I understand you're kind of their leader."

"I'm chair of the managing board right now, yes. But if you bought the company, there's something you need to know."

"Oh? What's that?"

"Everyone, and I mean everyone, is leaving this company. We're starting our own company to do the same thing in competition with RoadWheels."

Gunther looked at Bonnie, clearly taken aback at first, but then his mouth turned up in a curious smile. "Well, I'll be darned," he said. "That explains everything."

"Explains what?"

"That explains why she sold the company to me for a tenth of what it is worth. I knew there was something wrong with the deal, but I couldn't figure it out. I guess you could say I was a sucker."

"We told her we were going to leave."

"I'm sure you did. But tell me, young lady—why do you want out?"

"Well, I have this boyfriend—er, did. He tells me everything. I found out how that woman took over the company from a trustee. It kind of showed who she was, but we had no idea of how corrupt and vicious she really was. Anyway, we wanted to own stock in the company we worked for, and we saw this as our chance. It was a no-brainer."

"Hmm. You want stock, huh?"

"Yes. It's a great business with great potential. We can keep expanding to every city on the interstate highway system in the US and Canada. We could even start opening stations in Mexico."

"Have you founded your new company yet?"

"Our lawyer is working on it. I'm sorry to have to give you the bad news."

Gunther cocked his head. "I have an idea that will make you very happy," he said with a wink and that same curious smile as before. "Save you some lawyer's fees, too."

"Okay. Try me."

"You want stock? I'll give you 49 percent of RoadWheels if you'll keep managing the company. I have no idea how to run a company, particularly this company, so I won't interfere."

"That's not fair."

"What?"

"You said you bought the company for a tenth of what it was worth. What did you pay, a hundred million?"

"Yes, that's it exactly. How did you know?"

"Well, how about this. You keep 10 percent ownership with a right to a dividend payout of 10 percent of the company profits. We employees get the other 90 percent. I can tell you, this business is a cash cow. You'll make 15 to 20 percent on your investment every year."

"Now, why would I want to do that?"

"Because you have no alternative. Either you do, or we walk and you have nothing."

"Hmm. Now that you put it that way, I'll concede the deal is fair— one hundred million for a 10 percent stake in a billion-dollar company and a nice cash kicker to boot. You can guarantee you'll all stay put?"

"Not only that, but with stock as our incentive, we'll work our tails off to grow the business. Within a few years the company will be worth twice what it is now, and that's just the beginning. You'll see."

"I'm quite aware of the potential, young lady. I've wanted to own a piece of RoadWheels for some time now. Owning 10 percent is not exactly like owning a 100 percent, but I'll take what I can get. And keeping everyone on board reduces my risk practically to zero. You have a deal. You get this approved by your other station managers, and I'll have my lawyer call your lawyer."

Gunther held out his hand, and this time Bonnie grasped it in her own. She looked her new partner in the eye and liked what she saw. "You'll have a seat on the board, of course. It will be a pleasure to work with you."

"The pleasure is all mine," Gunther said, holding on to Bonnie's hand for just a second longer than necessary. She had the distinct feeling that he was sending a message other than strictly business. She knew nothing about this man, and she was not giving up on Toronto, but if this love of her life had other paths to follow and other places he had to go, she thought, a girl's just gotta do what a girl's gotta do.

In the distance, she and Gunther heard the sound of a diesel engine cranking over and rumbling to life. Tom's big rig turned slowly and then moved out toward the interstate. Gunther followed the sleek black machine with his eyes as it gathered speed and headed west into the evening sun on the horizon. "Who are those guys?" he asked, suddenly curious, realizing Bonnie had spoken to them just before she walked up.

"There goes the Road Ranger," Bonnie replied, trying to keep her emotions in check, "and my ex-boyfriend, Toronto."

THE END

THE ROAD RANGER RIDES AGAIN!

BOOK 2

KARL MILDE AND FRIENDS

OF THE ROAD RANGER

PROLOGUE

"I have some great news," Sylvia whispered excitedly in the ear of her lover, her body flushed with the afterglow of lovemaking. "I'm pregnant!"

The young man looked down at her, wide-eyed, and said nothing.

Sylvia's hair spilled outward over the pillow like a golden stream. Her face was farm fresh without any cosmetics or adornment. She held her breath, expecting some reaction from Billy, but none came. However, after a moment's pause he swung his legs off the bed, stood up and walked over to a chair next to the dresser.

"Where are you going?" she asked hesitantly, her voice tremulous. "What are you doing?"

Billy didn't answer. He grabbed his clothes from the chair and disappeared into the bathroom. A short time later he emerged, fully dressed in blue jeans a red cowboy shirt with white suede fringe.

She saw him go to the dresser and grab a lamp off the top. It was plugged into the wall behind the dresser and resisted being taken. Billy yanked at the electric cord but the plug held. Cursing, he shoved the dresser out of the way, yanked the cord again and pulled it loose from the wall. Holding the lamp tight against his body with his left hand, he wrapped the cord around his right and tried to pull the two apart.

The cord held on stubbornly to the lamp at first. Billy jerked it several times but it held fast. He finally pulled angrily with greater effort until it let go and slipped out of the hole in the base of the lamp. Brandishing the cord in his right hand, Billy headed back toward the bed, letting the lamp to drop to the floor with an ominous thud.

Sylvia lay on the bed, aghast at what was happening and frozen in fear. "Billy!" was all she could manage to utter as he came toward her, his eyes glazed, with the lamp cord dangling from his right hand. He was on her in an instant and wrapped the cord around her neck. He held fast as she struggled, her arms and legs pressing against him, trying to push him away. Her death throes only seemed to make him stronger as he leaned in against her with his full weight. She felt the agony of her closed airway, unable to breath, as he pulled the cord ever tighter. Eventually she blacked out and her struggles ceased.

On his way out, Billy noticed the lamp on the floor. He picked it up and took it with him.

CHAPTER 1

Interstate 80 is a limited-access highway that runs from Teaneck, New Jersey, across the Hudson River from New York City, all the way to San Francisco. The second-longest highway in the United States after I-90, it follows the route of the historic Lincoln Highway, the first automobile road across America.

Tom Smith and Alonzo Sierra, the Road Ranger and Toronto, were heading west on I-80 in their all-black tractor-trailer, The land was flat and the road ruler-straight as they traveled through the Nebraska heartland. Fields of corn, wheat, and soybeans extended out as far as they could see on both sides of the superhighway. Toronto had been driving the big rig non-stop for nearly four hours and, riding shotgun on this leg, the Road Ranger was on the phone with his chief engineer, Tom Swift.

"I can't wait to try out the prototype!" the Road Ranger said excitedly. "We're coming up on Kearney now. We'll head straight for the FedEx office and pick up the package." He clicked off and stared through the windshield at the road ahead, looking forward to trying out his new invention.

They passed a sign for Kearney, Nebraska. Soon after, Toronto eased off on the throttle and allowed the huge momentum of the semi to bleed off, its speed barely dipping at first and then falling at an increasing rate until it just matched the ramp speed required for the exit.

Toronto stopped at the traffic light at the end of the ramp and turned right onto the cross—road that led straight as an arrow through the center of Kearney, a square checkerboard of city blocks, all streets crisscrossing at right angles. Overhead, at the threshold of the city, an enormous banner announced Kearney's annual celebration:

FALL FARM FESTIVAL
Saturday, October 10
Hooray for our Farmers!

Toronto piloted the rig carefully forward, block by block, until he reached the exact center of town. He then turned right onto the Lincoln Highway and headed east in the direction of the local airport. After about a mile both sides of the highway changed abruptly back from cityscape to farmland, with row upon row of crops in the fields leading all the way to the horizon.

Toronto broke the silence. "Looks like we just hit it right. Let's stay here for the Fall Festival."

"Good idea. These country celebrations are very special. They connect you to the whole community."

Two miles later, Toronto turned left onto the airport access road and braked to a stop near the FedEx office. The Road Ranger got down from the cab and went inside to ask for his package. While waiting at the counter for the attendant to retrieve the box from the back, he couldn't help noticing the local newspaper that lay on the counter. The *Kearney Hub* screamed the headline in seventy-two point type:

ARRESTED FOR MURDER
Boyfriend Insists He's Innocent

He was halfway through the article when the attendant returned, carrying a large FedEx box. She lifted it up to the height of the counter and pushed it forward toward the Road Ranger. "This box sure is heavy! Here, Mister. It's yours now. Just sign the pad."

"It's a prototype of my new invention," the Road Ranger said as he scribbled on the electronic tablet. "I had somebody make it for me and send it here."

"You new to these parts? Haven't seen you before and pretty much everyone comes in here one time or 'nother to send or pick somethi'n up."

"We're just passing through, Ma'am. But my friend and I are thinking of staying around for the festival."

"You should! Best darn shindig you'll ever see. Happens every year 'bout this time."

356

"That's quite convincing," the Road Ranger replied with a warm smile. "By the way, these headlines caught my eye."

"Take the paper with you, mister. I pretty much know everything that's goin' down around here."

"This murder? You know about that?"

"Sure. The whole town's riled about it. First killin' we had in Kearney in some ten years. Real tragic it was, such a nice young girl. Choked to death in her own home. Her father's got a small farm over yonder and works real hard. He out tendin' his fields, gets home after dark and finds her layin' there dead. Almost killed him too, it did. The town's on the verge of lynchin' that boy for it."

"The boyfriend?"

"Who else could o' done it? Warn't a robbery or nothin'. Nothin' missin' from her house 'cept a cheap ol' table lamp. Couldn't be the father. God knows he loved her. Mother passed away from cancer couple o' years ago. Poor man's lost everything now. Breaks all our hearts, it does."

"The boy has no alibi?"

"Says he was home with his mom, and she vouches for him, of course."

"Can they prove he's lying?"

"Sort of. His prints are all over the place where she was killed. One thing though . . ."

"What's that?"

"The p'lice looked everwhere. Plum tore his mother's house apart too, and there's no sign o' the lamp."

"They have no other suspects?"

"Nope. They figure Bobby, that's the boyfriend, musta done it. They got him in the city jail. By the way, you need a place to stay while you're hangin' 'round here?"

"Actually, we have a place, thanks."

"Well, here's your package. Glad to get rid of this heavy thing."

The Road Ranger placed the newspaper on top of the box, grabbed hold of it and turned to go, but not before thanking her politely. "Thank you, Ma'am. Hope to see you at the Festival."

"I'll be there!" she called after him as he walked out the door.

The Road Ranger returned to the tractor-trailer with his FedEx package and the newspaper. His thoughts were no longer on his invention inside the box but on the newspaper article about the murder. He climbed up to his seat in the cab.

"Let's find a parking spot for this rig right here at the airport and ride Silver and Scout," he said to Toronto, referring to their motorcycles. "There's a young man in jail in this city who just might need our help."

TO BE CONTINUED

Would you like to write a story about the Road Ranger?
Visit my website **www.milde.com** and see how you can!